MISSING

MISSING

A Novel

E. A. JACKSON

EMILY BESTLER BOOKS

ATRIA

New York   Amsterdam/Antwerp   London
Toronto   Sydney/Melbourne   New Delhi

EMILY BESTLER BOOKS

ATRIA

An Imprint of Simon & Schuster, LLC
1230 Avenue of the Americas
New York, NY 10020

For more than 100 years, Simon & Schuster has championed authors and the stories they create. By respecting the copyright of an author's intellectual property, you enable Simon & Schuster and the author to continue publishing exceptional books for years to come. We thank you for supporting the author's copyright by purchasing an authorized edition of this book.

No amount of this book may be reproduced or stored in any format, nor may it be uploaded to any website, database, language-learning model, or other repository, retrieval, or artificial intelligence system without express permission. All rights reserved. Inquiries may be directed to Simon & Schuster, 1230 Avenue of the Americas, New York, NY 10020 or permissions@simonandschuster.com.

This book is a work of fiction. Any references to historical events, real people, or real places are used fictitiously. Other names, characters, places, and events are products of the author's imagination, and any resemblance to actual events or places or persons, living or dead, is entirely coincidental.

Copyright © 2025 by Emily Bernhard Jackson

Originally published in Great Britain in 2025 by Faber & Faber Limited

All rights reserved, including the right to reproduce this book or portions thereof in any form whatsoever. For information, address Atria Books Subsidiary Rights Department, 1230 Avenue of the Americas, New York, NY 10020.

First Emily Bestler Books/Atria Books hardcover edition March 2026

EMILY BESTLER BOOKS/ATRIA BOOKS and colophon are registered trademarks of Simon & Schuster, LLC

Simon & Schuster strongly believes in freedom of expression and stands against censorship in all its forms. For more information, visit BooksBelong.com.

For information about special discounts for bulk purchases, please contact Simon & Schuster Special Sales at 1-866-506-1949 or business@simonandschuster.com.

The Simon & Schuster Speakers Bureau can bring authors to your live event. For more information or to book an event, contact the Simon & Schuster Speakers Bureau at 1-866-248-3049 or visit our website at www.simonspeakers.com.

Interior design by Janet Evans-Scanlon

Manufactured in the United States of America

1 3 5 7 9 10 8 6 4 2

Library of Congress Control Number: 2025949005

ISBN 978-1-6680-7980-5
ISBN 978-1-6680-7982-9 (ebook)

Let's stay in touch! Scan here to get book recommendations, exclusive offers, and more delivered to your inbox.

To Lydia Burton

FEBRUARY 6, 2020

For twenty-nine years, Martha Allen had thought she would recognize Nell Beatty anywhere.

Of course, she realizes as she looks at the photograph on her computer screen, that's because she's been thinking of Nell Beatty as she was in the lobby of Victoria Police Station thirty years before: the thick dark hair, the mouth like a ripe berry, the body with its curves that were almost a parody of feminine perfection. That Nell Beatty has lived in Allen's mind for three decades, waiting to be spotted walking down the road, coming out of a pub, stepping off a bus in the same crop top and tight jeans she wore the first and only time Allen saw her.

Allen would never have recognized the woman in this photograph as Nell Beatty, no matter where she'd seen her. This woman's coarse, dyed-black hair dangles over the bench's slatted back, and her loose body stretches the fabric of her black tights so that her skin, bleached by cold and death, gleams through. There are crumbs of scarlet lipstick at the corners of the sagging mouth.

"Where is this?"

"Dale Park. East Bristol, about half an hour's walk from the city center. Found at five thirty this morning. I'm the senior investigating officer." Detective Chief Inspector Manley Desbury's voice echoes a bit as it comes through the desk-phone speaker, but it's still as smooth as it was three decades before.

"It's her," he says.

"How do you know?"

"Look at photo two."

She clicks on the second JPEG attached to his email. It shows a sheet of paper in a clear plastic evidence bag. Once Allen puts on her reading glasses, she sees that it's a letter from the Department for Work and Pensions, inviting Miss Nell Beatty, 36 Walpole Road, Bristol, BS5, to an interview regarding her Universal Credit.

"Found in her bag," says Desbury.

Forgetting that he can't see her, Allen shakes her head. "It's some other Nell Beatty. It must be. It's a common enough name." *As I well know*, she doesn't say.

"I thought that too. But look at the next picture."

She clicks. It's a photo of another bit of paper, in another evidence bag. This time it's a yellowed newspaper clipping, softened by age and nearly worn through at creases made by repeated foldings and unfoldings. "Scene of Crime found it in the inside zip pocket."

Allen has no trouble recognizing the clipping. The article is thirty years old, but she remembers it as vividly as if it had been published the previous day. BABY BELLA HAPPY AND HEALTHY AFTER MIRACLE RETURN, the headline screams. Underneath is a black-and-white photo of a smiling man with dark hair, his head pressed close to that of a beaming woman with lighter hair. Between them is a grinning baby with hair as dark as the man's. The picture's caption reads, "Baby Bella back with her parents."

A cold finger swipes down Allen's spine. "Hold on."

She goes back to the first photo. When the body appears on the screen again, she looks closely. The woman is wearing a black miniskirt, cheap vinyl knee-high boots, and a grubby lilac puffer jacket. Burst capillaries thread her nose and cheeks; her skin is roughened by years of substance abuse and neglect. But, yes, when Allen squints, there is something in the line of the nose, the curve of the high cheekbone under the pallid skin, that could be the remains of the young Nell Beatty.

"Sorry to start your day like this, but I thought you'd want to know." She imagines Desbury frowning and pursing his lips, the way he used to when he had to deliver unsatisfactory information.

"I do want to know."

Of course she does. She sighs. When Desbury's email arrived in her inbox a few minutes before, she was taken aback, but anyone would feel that way when faced with a message from someone they hadn't spoken to for decades. When she opened the message and read the single sentence asking her to call him on the number below as soon as possible so he could "speak with you about the attached," she felt uneasy—uneasy enough to wait to open the attachments until she had him on the phone. Even as she'd punched in his number, though, she'd refused to think that this might connect to the Baby Bella case. She'd been given an order to let that case go, and she's been trying to obey it ever since. But one glimpse of Nell Beatty, even in this state, and she feels the old itch once more.

She tries to distract herself by focusing on the photo again. The woman's thrown-back head reveals a band of purple bruises around her throat. Allen knows that when the coroner rolls her over in the morgue later, they'll find finger-shaped marks where the neck meets the spine, just as she knows that when they open her eyes, they'll find the red dots that indicate death by strangulation, and when they strip her, they'll find bruises covering other parts of the body too—upper arms, shoulders and back, maybe even inner thighs. She knows this because she's dealt with countless deaths like this as she's climbed the police ladder from constable to detective inspector to detective superintendent. In her head there lives—or rather doesn't live—an endless line of women whose bodies show that they've been first abused and then disposed of by some man more concerned about where he can dump the weight than the fact that he's just killed another human being. What path has Nell Beatty's life taken that it's ended in this banal, sordid way?

"Is there any indication of what she was doing in the park?"

"It's close to Stapleton Road, one of our areas that's popular with working girls, but until I hear from Scene of Crime and the coroner I'm not drawing any conclusions."

She hears a door open. Desbury says, "Thanks," and there's the sound of a guzzling sip. Then silence. What else do the two of them have to talk about? Casual small talk would be ridiculous in the face of these photos, and in the face of the memories they call up.

Finally she says, "It's Parker's memorial today. Service with reception to follow."

"Oh yes, I saw it in this week's national bulletin." Desbury snorts softly. "I don't envy you, having to go to that."

"Yeah. They're all going to be there, all the old boys. Beck's coming out of retirement to give the eulogy."

"Course he is. Never one to miss an opportunity to step into the spotlight, our Beck. Well, as my mum would've said, try to enjoy it."

"Oh, I'm sure we'll share stories and have lots of laughs. After all, those blokes and I are such good mates."

But they both know that if she doesn't show up, it'll be held against her. Thirty-five years on the force, one of only five female detective supers, and she's still being scrutinized and judged.

She sighs again. "Listen, could you send me whatever you've collected for this murder? I'd like to have a closer look when I get back. Just to see if there's anything . . ."

"Absolutely. And contact me if you see anything you want to discuss. I'll send you my mobile number."

His voice sounds heavy when he says goodbye. As she puts on her coat and sets off for the memorial, she wonders why. Weariness? Tension? Then the corpse's face appears in her mind's eye, followed by Nell's face as it was in the summer of 1990, and she thinks she understands. The heaviness in Desbury's tone had been sadness. After all, he'd seen Nell Beatty then. He must remember her too.

AUGUST 1990

1

Thursday, August 2, 1990, was the hottest day London had known for half a century. Detective Inspector Martha Allen could feel the sun even through her bedroom curtains, bright and hot and relentless. She glanced at her watch as she buttoned her shirt. It was only 7 a.m., and already a drop of sweat was inching its way from her bra band down her back. She looked at the suit jacket on the chair next to her, imagined leaving it behind, then thought better of it. Woman, recently promoted, in charge of a missing-child investigation any of those on its own required all the authority she could muster. Taken together, they called for a full suit, even on a morning that felt like the inside of an oven.

The call had come twenty minutes earlier. A child missing from the Bellevue Hotel in Pimlico. A five-month-old baby girl, the control room said. Apparently taken through an open window while the parents slept. Disappearance reported by the hotel owner at 6:22 a.m. Allen was the first available DI. A team had been sent, and they and her sergeant would meet her there.

She gathered her hair off her neck and made a bun. She knew why she'd been assigned to the case, and it had nothing to do with availability. A child's disappearance meant distraught parents who required sympathy, probably a mother who needed the gentle touch. The situation would require tact and emotional skill. Almost certainly someone would have to make tea. In the minds of her superiors, all of that meant a woman.

Not that she could blame them. Who would they send instead? She'd seen the eyes of the male probationers glaze over when they'd covered domestic crime during training, been on the receiving end of their blunt questions when they'd practiced interview techniques. On that evidence, she really was the right choice for the job. But in the six months since she'd been made a detective inspector, she'd encountered nothing like this incident. She'd handled three murders and a number of robberies, large as well as petty, but never anything involving children since her brief stint in Youth Crime. She couldn't even remember the last time the Met had dealt with something similar.

If she wanted to get out of it, she reminded herself . . . In her mind, she saw the shelf in the bathroom cabinet, the plastic stick with two thick lines across its little windows. She and Phil had known for two weeks that she was pregnant, but she hadn't said a word to anyone else. She'd planned to keep it secret for as long as possible, until it was too late to transfer her to something dull like economic crime, or to stick her behind a desk for months. But she knew that if she wanted to be taken off this investigation, all she had to do was reveal that she was going to have a baby. Detective Chief Inspector Beck would never let a mother-to-be run a child-kidnapping case—and, yes, she told the critic in her head, she was aware of the irony of one kind of sexism relieving her of the burden imposed by another. Still, if she told Beck she was pregnant, she wouldn't have to listen to raw pain with carefully calibrated earnestness, or offer well-intentioned comfort to two terrified people. As if there could possibly be any comfort when your child is missing!

Nausea overwhelmed her. She rushed to the bathroom.

Afterward she sat on the edge of the bath, rested her head against the sink's cool side, and tried to breathe evenly. She knew perfectly well that she wasn't going to pass on this investigation. She thought again of the stifled yawns and ham-fisted questions of the male probies in the practice interviews—*Didn't it occur to you, Miss Allen, that that kind of outfit would be seen as an invitation?* She didn't trust any of them to deal with these bereft parents the way she would. And, well, even though she hated thinking this way, a child abduction was an important case. Handled successfully, it could make the men respect her—the ones above her as well as the ones she worked with.

Returning to the bedroom, she shrugged into her suit jacket and sat on the bed next to Phil's sleeping body. He murmured and shifted but didn't wake, so she bent to kiss his cheek and, when he didn't react to that, buried her face in his hair. Strands tickled her cheek; his scalp smelled like warm bread. Oh, she remembered, they were out of bread.

The door buzzer sounded. Control had said they were sending a car.

As she entered the front room, she stopped for a second, pulled herself up, closed her eyes, and took a deep breath. She imagined the investigation as a dot in the distance, then concentrated on that dot until personal concerns, stray thoughts, even ambition, were all pushed out by complete focus. Good detection, the first sergeant who had supervised her used to say, was 90 percent details. *Slow and careful wins our race. That's why they call us the plod.*

She opened her eyes, picked up her bag, and left the flat.

2

As Allen climbed out of the car in front of the Bellevue Hotel, she checked her watch: seven forty-five. The baby had been missing for more than an hour. She pushed the door shut and took in the hotel.

The Bellevue was one of countless identical hotels that lined Pimlico's Belgrave Road. All had neoclassical facades, and all had seen better days. The off-white paint on the columns that held up the Bellevue's portico was grimy and chipped in places; the letters that spelled out its name in blue above the door were faded.

But Allen was too busy making other observations to notice much more than that about the hotel itself. By her estimate, Belgrave Road was a half mile southeast of Victoria station, with its Tube stop and trains to Gatwick. It was roughly the same distance southeast to the Vauxhall Bridge, with its easy access to the A2 motorway and via that to the port at Dover. Closer to hand, she could see two small private gardens a short way up the road, each one filled with potential hiding places and—grimmer to contemplate—easily accessible rubbish bins.

Three steps up, and a dark blue door with a polished brass handle took her into the lobby. This was an open space about twenty-four feet square, with a stairway on her left leading to the upper floors and on the right a wooden reception counter with a narrow space behind it and a door in its back wall. On the far side of the lobby was a closed door, its top half divided into square panels of reeded glass, through which came the clinking of cutlery. The dining room. Next to that, a corridor ran back into some unknown depth of the building, hidden by a wall that boxed off the far side of the reception area. Thinly carpeted and furnished with a chrome-and-vinyl three-piece suite of the type in vogue two decades before, the lobby smelled of furniture polish and disinfectant. It was spotlessly clean.

Behind the reception counter, a worried-looking Indian man clawed his beard, scraping the hair up and down. When he saw her, he snatched his hand back down to his side.

"You are the police inspector?"

She nodded and took a step forward, flashing her warrant card. "Detective Inspector Martha Allen. And you are?"

He began to smile, then realized what he was doing and stopped. "I am Amrish Patel. I own—"

At that moment, a tall blond man emerged from the corridor on the other side of the lobby. Allen recognized her sergeant, Ray Norton.

Occasionally Allen wondered if the Met had assigned Norton to her out of a perverse sense of humor. More often, she was sure they had. Before she'd been promoted six months earlier, Norton's attitude toward her had been a mixture of condescension and scorn. Since then he had added barely veiled contempt. Allen imagined whoever determined assignments at Victoria Police Station laughing at the thought of her trying to command loyalty from someone who so obviously thought he was her superior in all but rank. To add to the fun, Norton was an unashamed clotheshorse, somehow managing to stretch his sergeant's salary to support a wardrobe of elegant, perfectly cut suits. Allen, on the other hand, shopped at Marks & Spencer and John Lewis, and she'd never visited a tailor in her life. On the few cases they'd worked together so far, the civilians had automatically assumed that he was the senior officer. She warmed a little toward Mr. Patel for not making that mistake.

Seeing her, Norton stopped short. He had the gift of being able to say and do what was expected while at the same time making his real opinion silently but perfectly clear. Now he raised his eyebrows as if he'd been wondering why she was taking so long to arrive but was too polite to say so.

"Guv." His tone dismissed the title even as he used it.

"Norton." She walked the few steps it took to reach him, lowering her voice so Mr. Patel wouldn't hear. "Where are we?"

He couldn't tell her much more than she'd heard from the control room. The parents opened the window a few inches before going to sleep then woke to find the baby missing and the window fully up. That had been at 6:15 a.m. His only further information was that he'd contacted the Scene of Crime technicians, who should be arriving any moment, and that he'd announced to all the guests currently in the hotel that they needed to be interviewed before they could leave.

"All right." She nodded, one quick jerk of her chin. "Send officers to every platform at Victoria, and alert Dover to be on the lookout. Search those gardens across the road, including the bins. Especially the bins."

"Already thought of it, guv." A smirk twitched his lips, and it took all of Allen's self-control not to say, *Yes, but you didn't do it, did you?* Instead she asked, "Where are the parents?"

"I put them in the lounge to wait for you."

"How are they?"

Norton heaved the heavy sigh of someone forced to answer a ridiculous question. "As you might expect. She was hysterical. The hotel called a doctor, who gave her some sort of injection. He's holding up, but he's got his hands full comforting her."

He turned and walked back the way he'd come, leaving her scurrying to catch up. The corridor was shorter than it had seemed, six or seven feet long with a door at the far end. Opening onto the lounge, presumably.

When she stepped through the door after Norton, it was as if she had entered another world. Perhaps to fulfill the expectations of tourists who thought of London as the city of Dickens and Jack the Ripper, or perhaps because furniture from the period was so ugly that it could be bought cheaply, the hotel lounge was a monument to Victoriana: everything wooden was dark; everything upholstered was burgundy velvet. The bookshelves were crowded with porcelain knickknacks variously pierced, painted, molded, and gilded. The carpet was deep maroon, patterned in an extravagant design of golden foliage but thin under her feet. Someone had drawn the red velvet curtains across the windows, and as a result the room was not only as hot as an oven but also oppressively dim.

On an elaborately carved sofa set against the far wall sat a dark-haired man and woman. The man was fully dressed, but the woman wore a lightweight blue dressing gown with a few inches of matching nightdress visible below the hem. Her feet were bare. The two of them huddled together, knees touching, one of his hands over hers, his free arm around her shoulders. She rocked back and forth slightly. He rested his lips on the crown of her head, his eyes closed. Although they looked to be a few years older than she was, Allen thought they seemed like two lost children.

She sat in an armchair that faced the sofa and waited for them to notice her. When the man finally lifted his head, she leaned forward. "Mr. and Mrs. Carpenter, I'm Detective Inspector Martha Allen. I'm going to be leading the investigation into your daughter's disappearance." The woman didn't move, but the man nodded. Allen clasped her hands in her lap. "I know I can't begin to imagine how you feel, but I want to tell you how terribly sorry I am about what you're going through. We'll do everything we can to find your daughter."

She paused. She could feel sweat itching its way down the nape of her neck. Over her shoulder she snapped, "Could you open a window, please? And pull back the curtains."

A clash of metal rings and the room was abruptly illuminated, dust motes filling the slanting light. She heard Norton exhale, then exhale again, and when she turned to look he was wrenching the bottom sash of a window upward, flecks of white paint landing on the sleeve of his navy jacket. He flicked them off, pursing his lips, then turned back to the window, opening it about ten inches.

It turned out that this was exactly what Mr. and Mrs. Carpenter had done the previous evening.

"It was so hot." When Mrs. Carpenter at last raised her head and spoke, the words poured out. "The room was so hot, we didn't think

Bella could sleep in such a hot room, and we wanted to cool it off. We opened the window to cool the room off. That's all. We opened the window to let in some cooler air, so Bella could sleep, because it was so hot."

She was a thin woman, and Allen could see that she might be pretty in better circumstances. Now, though, her eyes were red and swollen, her hair hanging in lank rats' tails around her pale face. As Allen watched, her hands escaped from her husband's and began to move, first the left flattening the back of the right, then the right flattening the back of the left. Her husband picked one up and kissed it. Mrs. Carpenter leaned against him, but the fingers of her free hand continued to clench and unclench.

Carpenter looked apologetic. "The doctor gave her something, but it doesn't seem to have started working yet."

Allen took in his expressionless face. He had the kind of Byronic looks suited to tragedy, his red-rimmed brown eyes and high cheekbones giving him an air of stoic nobility. He seemed calmer than his wife, but Allen knew you could never tell. Men might keep their emotions in, but that didn't mean they didn't have them.

She kept her voice even. "Do you think you could tell me what happened last night?"

He lifted his free hand and dug it into the front of his hair, his fingers pushing so hard that she saw their tips turn white and the skin of his hairline bulge outward. Then he dropped it back to his lap.

"Viv's right. The room was very hot. I would say it was even hotter than this." He looked around the lounge as if the heat were a person he was trying to locate. "We opened the window first thing. Then we brought Bella down here for a little while, while we waited for the room to cool down. When we thought it would be cooler, we took her up again."

Why did they both keep harping on about the temperature? But Allen thought she knew why. They wanted to impress upon her that they'd been taking care of their child, thinking of her best interests.

They wanted Allen—and themselves—to know that they really were good parents, despite what had happened. It had been drummed into her over and over again during her time on the force that when a child disappeared the most likely perpetrator was a parent or stepparent, but she found it hard to believe that either of these destroyed people should be considered a suspect.

"We got her settled," Carpenter continued. His voice broke on the final word, but he recovered. "We went to bed. Around ten, I'd say. It was still hot in the room, so I left the window open about five inches. I do the night feeds, one at midnight and one at 3 a.m. After I gave her the three o'clock bottle I went back to bed."

His wife suddenly sat up straight. "And when we woke up again she *wasn't there*! The window was wide open and she was *gone*!" Her voice rose to a scream on the last word and she began to sob, rocking her body so hard that Allen worried she would propel herself off the sofa. Her husband embraced her again, but this time it had no effect. She increased her force so that they both jerked back and forth.

Allen turned in her seat, looking for Norton. He was leaning on the wall behind her, arms crossed.

"Could you call a woman PC for Mrs. Carpenter, please? I'm sure she'd be more comfortable if she could lie down."

The WPC arrived. It took her a few seconds to convince Carpenter that his wife would be all right without him, but eventually she was able to lead Mrs. Carpenter, now becoming woozy, out of the room. As they left, they crossed paths with an Indian girl carrying a tray that held glasses of ice water and a pile of napkins. Her face impassive, she put two of the napkins on the coffee table, then a glass of water on each of them, then a pile of napkins between them. All this she did silently. She made no more noise as she turned to offer Norton the remaining glass and a napkin before she left, closing the door softly behind her.

Carpenter reached for a glass and drained it in three quick gulps. Allen waited until he'd finished wiping his mouth with a napkin before she spoke. "I'll try to make this as quick as I can, so you can join your wife. I know it's hard to focus on anything but Bella right now, but it would increase our chances of finding her if we had as clear a picture as possible of the time leading up to her disappearance. Do you feel able to tell me again what you remember about what happened from the time you arrived until the time you went to bed? In as much detail as you can manage."

Once more he dug his fingertips into his hairline, but this time he removed them quickly, and when he spoke his voice was firm. "I'll do my best."

He repeated the story he had just told, speaking more slowly this time. He added no significant detail or revelation, but the very act of telling calmed him, as Allen had known it would. When he finished, she waited a moment then said, "Thank you." He dipped his head. "Now, you arrived here around seven yesterday evening. Can I ask where you came from?" She smiled. "That's my fancy way of saying where do you live?"

In her experience, people never answered such simple questions simply. Something in them felt the need to elaborate. Mr. Carpenter was no different. "We have a house in Wells. We moved there three years ago when we decided to start trying for a baby. I work for an estate agent in the town center, and Viv's a painter. Well, now she's a full-time mum."

Allen could hear the scratch of Norton's pen behind her as he took notes. "And what brought you to London?"

"It was meant to be a sort of summer holiday." He stopped looking stricken and looked embarrassed instead. "I don't . . . I'm not high enough up the food chain at work for us to have a real holiday—you know, abroad—but we hadn't even been out since Bella was born. I thought it would be nice to go somewhere. So we decided on London. Viv wanted to visit the museums, and we thought of going to the theater if the hotel could arrange a sitter." At this sudden reminder of his daughter, he swallowed hard. The rims of his eyes reddened.

"Do you like Wells?" Allen asked.

The distraction worked. He calmed down as he described a place caught between a village and a city, a little dull after the years they'd spent in London but a good place to raise a child.

When he paused, she asked, "What time did you leave to drive here?"

"About two in the afternoon."

She was taken aback. "Five hours from Somerset to London? That seems a long time."

"We stopped a couple of times to take Bella inside a motorway service station." Again he looked apologetic. "My car's an old-model BMW, and it doesn't have air-conditioning. We wanted to cool her down."

"I see. And did you notice anything odd either time you stopped? Did anyone take particular interest in Bella, or ask where you were going? Did you see any cars following you as you left the service area?" These were all long shots, but still they needed to be ruled out.

Carpenter shook his head. "No, nothing like that. The first time we only went in for five minutes. We stayed longer at the second place. We had some sandwiches and Viv changed Bella, but no one came near us. The place was pretty much deserted."

"And this was . . . ?"

"Just after we turned onto the M4. About an hour from here. And the first one was just outside Salisbury."

She heard Norton's pen again and knew he would have someone locate the service areas and see if they had security tapes.

"Now, bear with me. Could I ask you to close your eyes and tell me everything you remember about last night, starting from when you arrived?" She had read about this method, encouraging the witness to envision incidents rather than just recite them, in a manual the previous year, and she'd used it ever since.

He shut his eyes obligingly. "We drove past Victoria Coach Station, and I turned onto Hugh Street, then this street. I'd looked the route up in the *A–Z* beforehand. There was nowhere to park, so I drove around until a place opened up. I carried the bags in, and Viv carried Bella in her basket. The man at reception explained to us about breakfast and so on, handed over the room key, and we went up. God, the room was like an oven! So I opened the window, and we brought Bella down here in the basket while we waited for it to cool down."

"Did you lock the door of your room behind you when you left?"

"Yes, yes, absolutely, because Viv left her bag in there."

"And you didn't use the time while the room was cooling down to go out for a meal or anything like that?"

"No, as I said, we had some sandwiches the second time we stopped. And it was too hot to be hungry, if you know what I mean. No, we just sat down here talking for an hour or so then took Bella back up. The room was cooler—well, less hot—so we settled in. We put her basket on the folding luggage rack. It fit perfectly." Again his voice cracked; again he recovered. "We watched a little television with the volume turned down, then Viv gave Bella a feed. Then we went to bed."

"You're absolutely sure you didn't go out once she was asleep? Not even for a minute, maybe to get a breath of fresh air or check on the car?"

Carpenter showed his first sign of any emotion other than terror, saying snappishly, "I've said no. We were with Bella every second."

"All right." Allen held up a placating hand. "You stayed in the room. You went to sleep around ten, and at midnight and 3 a.m. you woke up and fed her? You, not your wife?"

"Yes. My wife takes a sleeping pill. She developed terrible insomnia after Bella was born, and our GP prescribed lorazepam. He said it wouldn't harm Bella. Viv uses a breast pump"—he colored slightly, although whether at the revelation or the mention of breasts Allen couldn't tell—"and I give her bottles for the night feeds. After I finished the 3 a.m. feed, I reset the alarm for six fifteen. And when it rang, she wasn't there anymore. She wasn't there!"

His voice rose, but unlike his wife he didn't cry. Instead he put his head in his hands and sat unmoving.

Again she gave him a moment's space. Then she said, "Thank you very much, Mr. Carpenter. You've been very helpful. I have only one more question. Do you have a photo of your daughter? We'll put out appeals for further sightings right away, and the chances of someone spotting Bella will be considerably improved if the media can show a picture of her."

He nodded and dug his wallet out of a back pocket. Opening it, he handed her a snapshot.

It was a close-up. Mrs. Carpenter sat facing the camera, holding a baby on her lap, Mr. Carpenter next to her with his arm around her. The baby's lips curved into a gummy grin, her dark hair standing up in tufts. The parents both gazed down on their child. The looks on their faces said they had never seen anything so wonderful.

"She's ten weeks there. She'd just started really smiling." Carpenter turned his face away and swallowed hard.

The baby in the photo wore a romper with alternating blue and red stripes. "Was this what Bella was wearing last night?"

He looked, then shook his head. "She's grown out of that."

"Do you remember what she was wearing?"

"A pink sleep suit. A summer one with short sleeves and no legs. And her nappy, of course."

He looked completely drained. It was time to let him go. In any case, after three repetitions of his story, she'd almost certainly got everything useful she could get from him.

"Thank you very much, Mr. Carpenter. I can only imagine how difficult this was for you, and it's been enormously helpful." She rose. "DS Norton, could you see to it that someone takes Mr. Carpenter to Mrs. Carpenter? I'll meet you in the room they used last night."

She headed back to the lobby and made for the reception desk. Up close, she could see that the man behind it was older than she'd thought. There were gray hairs in his beard and sideburns, and faint crow's-feet radiated from the corners of his eyes. They nodded at each other again. The day would be full of nods, she thought, awkward substitutes for the usual smiles.

"Were you on duty yesterday evening?"

"Yes. I worked the front desk from six thirty."

"And did you check Mr. and Mrs. Carpenter in?"

"Yes. I put them in room 201."

That meant they would need to interview him, but for now it just made her job a little easier. "Could you take me there, please?" Nothing down here was going to show her how the abduction might have been committed.

3

Scene of Crime were already in the corridor outside the room, unpacking tweezers, bags, slides, and strips, all the tools of their grim trade. One of them thrust a pair of white latex gloves at her, then at Norton as he hustled up behind. They snapped them on before stepping across the threshold.

At first glance, there was nothing to suggest the room was anything more than a place where two adults and an infant had spent a night. The furniture was a little shabby and the carpet had seen better days, but there was nothing obviously out of place. As Carpenter had said, the Moses basket was on the luggage stand. It was made of woven raffia, its sides bent slightly inward from use, a fabric canopy folded down against the back edge. A blanket lay crumpled at its bottom end. Because it used up all the rack space, the Carpenters had put their suitcase on the narrow desk that stood across from the end of the bed, where it crowded the small television to the far end of the desktop. The case was shut, but its locks were open and the top was slightly off center: it had been opened and closed in a hurry. Probably in those desperate moments while the Carpenters were irrationally hoping that baby Bella might be somewhere, anywhere, Allen thought. Then a voice in her head said, *Parent or stepparent.* She tapped a finger on the case's top.

"Make sure the SOCOs go through that, and make sure they send us a photo inventory ASAP."

A changing bag rested on the floor next to the basket, its top unzipped. She pulled it open and peered inside. A row of folded disposable nappies took up most of the space, with a gap the size of three or four. Carpenter had mentioned his wife changing the baby the second time they stopped. Had they used another after arriving? If not, the kidnapper must have taken them. That suggested a plan to hold on to the baby for, what . . . twelve hours? Twenty-four?

The bag showed nothing else of interest, just a box of wet wipes and a tube of what looked like nappy cream, squashed about halfway up. She turned to take in the rest of the room. The bed was unmade, and each of the side tables had a used cup and saucer, one with the tea bag still in it. Allen knew that the SOCOs would pick all this over and bag up the cups and saucers, so she didn't look further. Instead she crossed the five steps to the window, where the bottom sash stood open about a foot. Outside was the rickety iron landing of a fire escape, with equally precarious steps leading up and down from it. She moved closer and peered down. All she could see was a section of concrete courtyard and what looked like the corner of a skip.

"Careful. They'll want to dust that."

Allen was sure she wasn't imagining the sliver of satisfaction in Norton's voice at the idea that she might smear any lingering prints. "I'm not touching anything." Then she winced. She shouldn't defend herself to an inferior officer.

"Climb out, stay steady, escape down without losing your footing or making any noise," she said. "Tough to manage all that when you've got a baby in your arms."

"If you're determined enough, you can do anything."

But you can't do it silently, Allen thought. Especially if it required as much dexterity as the sequence she'd just outlined. Was it possible that someone with a key entered the room by the door instead, opened the window wider to throw off suspicion, picked up the baby, and closed the door behind them, all without being heard by the sleeping Carpenters? And was it possible that, having done so, that person could then make it out of the hotel without drawing any attention? That would mean the kidnapper was someone who wouldn't be noticed, whose presence—and presence carrying a bundle—wouldn't be remarked on. An employee? A member of the housekeeping staff?

"Detective Inspector?" She turned. A young DC stood in the doorway. "Scene of Crime would like to get started."

"Right." Shuffling by him into the corridor, she asked one of the white-clad men, "Do we need to give you time before we go into the yard?"

He shook his head.

Access to the yard was through the kitchen. This branched off the dining room, which itself extended down the length of the corridor that led to the lounge and was a good twenty feet across. Allen began to see that the hotel was much larger than it appeared. The room was filled with square wooden tables of the type that all budget hotels seemed to buy for their dining rooms, either occupied by people eating breakfast or neatly set with white crockery, a napkin folded into a fan shape resting on each plate. The three windows in the far wall were half-open, oscillating fans resting on their ledges trying to cool the air. The floor was uncarpeted, and Allen heard her heels clack against the linoleum as she walked. Diners stopped talking when she and Norton passed then started muttering to one another again behind them.

The temperature in the yard hit her like a hammer. The sun was blazing, the sky a hard bright blue. Exhaust fumes from cars passing on the road behind were magnified by the heat. She tried not to gag.

The yard was empty except for an overturned bucket next to the kitchen door, a few cigarette butts ground out next to it, and a skip, standing against a weather-beaten fence on the right. She crossed to it, fished a plastic glove out of her shoulder bag, and slipped it on before lifting the lid. Empty.

"Rubbish pickup between six and seven this morning," Norton called from the doorway.

Damn. Damn, damn, damn. That meant any evidence the kidnapper might have left in the bin was gone. A small chance, but still a lost one. Unless . . .

"That's Park Royal transfer station. Send a couple of uniforms over there to see if they can head off the lorry. And get someone to take these into evidence." She gestured at the discarded cigarette ends. "In fact, make sure the techs check over this whole area."

She crossed to the fire escape and stood with her back to it, looking around. The increasing heat was a reminder that time was passing, but she fought against her instinct to hurry. Looking mattered, she reminded herself. Seeing mattered. Something you noticed because you were observing calmly, carefully, could end up making all the difference. *That's why they call us the plod.* And that's why she needed to put it out of her mind that the first twenty-four hours in a missing-person case were the most important, and that every moment in which she wasn't moving might be a moment in which the case was moving too slowly.

The back of another building overlooked the yard, separated by a wall and a few low trees. The only easy way out of here other than via the hotel was through the black-painted gates opposite the bin. Were they locked? How many people had a key? The cement walls that bounded the yard on all sides were the height of her head, and she was six feet in heels. No ladder that she could see, but that didn't mean there wasn't one. Its location might be well-known to every employee. The same people who had passkeys to the rooms.

With an effort of will she ignored the scent of sausages that seeped out the kitchen door and made her mouth water. She shaded her eyes and looked up. The fire escape was dilapidated all the way to the ground, a rusting structure of skinny ladders and skeletal grated landings. Surely no one could get down that without making noise? As she watched, a crime-scene tech climbed through the Carpenters' window. Proving her point, the landing on the next floor down swayed. The metal clanked a little. The tech braced his feet and bent over. He scraped lightly at the railing with some sort of implement then dropped the scrapings into a plastic bag. Then he bent closer, peering. He straightened up and addressed someone inside the room. There was a sudden bustle inside. A hand emerged, holding an evidence bag.

"They've found something."

By the time she reached the room, the techs were back at work, all except the one nearest the window. He was writing on an evidence bag he held flattened against his palm.

"What is it?" She crossed the room, Norton at her heels once again. "What did you find out there?"

Rather than answering, the tech held up the bag by its top. "Ma'am."

Inside was a tiny scrap of pink cotton, a few threads hanging loose where it had snagged on the railing of the fire escape.

4

The fabric made it clear by which route the baby had been taken, but it also drove home to Allen how long Bella had been gone, and how far behind they were. Suddenly her tour of the yard seemed leisurely, her interview with the Carpenters unnecessarily long. Turning back down the corridor, she began issuing orders to Norton over her shoulder. Immediately increase the fingertip search to cover a mile-wide radius from the hotel, including every park and garden in the area. Post officers with copies of the baby's photo at all London train stations, at Heathrow and Gatwick, and at all ports. Copy the photo to make up "Have you seen this child?" flyers and put them on every lamppost and through every letterbox in the area, then hand it over to the media liaison with instructions to send it to all television and radio outlets and to every national newspaper. Interview all the residents of the neighboring buildings to determine if anyone saw anything between nine last night and six thirty this morning. Locate a blueprint of the hotel and bring it to her. Ask the hotel owner if they could use the dining room for guest interviews, then organize a team of DCs to question those guests who were still in the hotel. Check the register to find out which guests were out for the day or had checked out that morning. Locate and interview them.

Once the blueprint was found and couriered over, she and Norton searched the building from top to bottom. Allen had never realized how many cupboards and storage areas a hotel required. Early on, the linen cupboard between the Carpenters' room and the hotel staircase seemed promising—a lump of badly folded blankets had briefly appeared to hide something. Two hours later, a dark storage room in the cellar, which was supposed to be empty, instead had a box on one shelf, but when Norton opened it, it turned out just to contain some towels. Nothing else yielded anything that could even be mistaken for a clue. Still, Allen tried to comfort herself as she climbed the cellar stairs, at least now she knew where the baby certainly wasn't. That was something.

Once they'd finished, Norton headed back to the station to organize the incident room. Allen sat down in the lounge again and interviewed the hotel's owner, drafting in a passing DC to take notes. She had gratefully accepted the offer of a sandwich a little while earlier, managing to eat half before the hotel search, and throughout the interview she was aware of a rich, yeasty scent as the bread of the remaining half slowly baked in the heat on a side table. It took almost all her self-control not to reach out and finish it as they talked.

Amrish Patel seemed unaware of the smell. He sat across from her on the sofa, his face creased with concern, the dark shadows under his eyes making him look exhausted by events. As no doubt he was, thought Allen. She gave him the smile substitute, a nod. "Thank you for agreeing to talk to me again."

"Of course." His voice was firm. "I will do anything I can to help."

"Could you start by telling me what you remember about last night? Mr. Carpenter has told us what he recalls, but it helps to have as many points of view as possible."

He thought for a long moment before he began. "Mr. and Mrs. Carpenter arrived around seven in the evening. Mrs. Carpenter was carrying the baby in—one of those baskets with a . . ." He sketched a semicircle in the air.

"A canopy? To protect the baby's face from the sun."

"Yes, a canopy. Mr. Carpenter told me who they were, and I checked them in. I explained our arrangement for guests who return late at night, told them our breakfast hours, and gave him the key. He carried the baby upstairs."

"He left his wife with the bags?" This wasn't what Carpenter had said. Why lie about that?

"No, my son carried the bags. Mr. Carpenter took the baby's basket from Mrs. Carpenter and carried it up. She followed him."

"All right. And did you see them again after that? Maybe they went out for a meal? Or for a walk once it was cooler?" Anything that might have given someone time to slip into the room and look around, to formulate a plan for how to take the baby later.

"They didn't go out. But I did see them again, yes. After a few minutes, they came down with the baby in its basket. He said the room was too hot. He had opened the window, and he asked if there was somewhere they could sit until it cooled down a bit. I directed them to the lounge. They sat there for perhaps an hour, maybe a little more. I arranged for my daughter to bring them some water."

"And after that?"

"After that they went back to their room. I didn't see either of them again until Mr. Carpenter came running down this morning and told me to ring the police, that the baby was missing. I telephoned the moment he told me. I didn't waste any time." At last his composure broke. His words came in a rush. "This is a very safe hotel. We have never had a robbery, never anything. Not even a tramp outside."

"I'm sure that's the case, Mr. Patel. Please don't worry. No one is suggesting anything about your hotel." She guided him back on track. "Did anything happen after your son took the Carpenters to their room last night? Or while they were in the lounge? Did you notice anything unusual? Anyone coming in from outside? Maybe someone without a booking who asked for a room?" Carpenter had said no one had followed them from the rest areas, but he could have been distracted by the fussing baby.

But Patel shook his head. There had been nothing. A few guests had gone out and returned, but none very late. The last had been a couple down from Yorkshire for a wedding, who had returned just after eleven. "I'm afraid I don't remember their name, but I can check the register."

"Thank you. You said there were arrangements for guests who return late? Is that a night porter? Someone who would have seen if anyone left the hotel during the night, or in the early morning?"

Another headshake. He and his son took it in turns to act as night manager. Whichever was on duty at reception at midnight locked the hotel's doors and checked that the padlock on the back gates was locked. The hotel doors were unlocked again every morning at five. Employees who needed to come in before 5 a.m.—"our housekeepers and laundresses, our dining-room help"—were issued a front-door key for the week that they were on—"I don't ask anyone to work those hours for more than a week at a time"—and they returned it when that week ended. From midnight to five, he or his son slept on a camp bed in the room behind the reception area. Guests who thought they might be out after midnight could request a key to the front door, and there was an intercom for admission in case of emergency.

"And last night you worked the overnight shift?"

"Yes."

"And you were asleep in the office from midnight to five?"

Patel shook his head. "I stayed up doing paperwork until half past midnight. Then I tried to sleep, but it was too hot. I dozed off at about two for a couple of hours, but I never really slept."

Hence the shadows under his eyes. Still, if he'd only dozed, that meant that short of a plan involving one person who made no noise handing a sleeping infant over a six-foot wall to another person who made no noise, or a kidnapper who could teleport, there seemed no way for the abduction to have occurred.

"Does the hotel have a ladder?"

"A ladder?" Patel looked confused by the change of subject. "Yes, for changing light bulbs and so on. We keep it in the cellar. I don't know exactly where. I could ask my son. But only the people who work here would know—and none of them . . . They are all good people. I know they are."

"Sometimes we don't know people as well as we think. Do you run any kind of background checks on the people you hire?"

"The agency we use takes care of that. They work with immigrant aid organizations to find recent arrivals who need work. My family were Kashmiri refugees, so I like to hire immigrants." He looked embarrassed, like a man realizing he'd made a foolish mistake. "I can give you their telephone number."

"Also a list of your employees, please." She foresaw a long day for some poor DC, waiting on the phone with Immigration and Interpol. "And now I'd like to speak to your daughter and son. Individually, please." Mindful of the rules, she added, "If either is under sixteen, you're welcome to sit in on the interview."

5

Kalpen Patel's lightly pimpled face, spotted on the upper lip with wisps of mustache, wore an expression that mingled wariness and excitement at the situation in which he found himself. He could offer no new information beyond the fact that both Carpenters had seemed tense, and that Mr. Carpenter had given him a pound as a tip. When she asked about the ladder, his expression switched to confusion. Yes, it was in the cellar. In a cupboard next to the laundry room. He had used it a couple of hours ago to change a bulb in one of the corridors. No, he didn't remember it looking any different from the last time he used it. Yes, it had been in its usual spot when he fetched it.

Nisha Patel was the daughter who had brought water to the lounge that morning. Whereas Kalpen had looked half adult and half child, Nisha, released from acting as water-bearer, was all teenager. As she sat down in the chair across from Allen, she looked simultaneously bored and resentful. Her sigh was the heavy exhalation of someone with many better things to do.

Yes, she had brought the Carpenters water at quarter past seven. Yes, she'd carried the glasses on a tray. Her father made her use a tray when she was serving the customers.

"And how did the Carpenters seem to you when you brought the water?"

A long pause, then, "Worried."

"Worried about what?"

"About the baby." Another pause. "Like, really worried."

"Can you give me an example?"

She heaved another sigh, but as she thought back, her voice lost its truculence. "I was in the room for maybe five minutes, and while I was there she asked him twice if he thought their room would cool down enough for them to use it. She said maybe they should book into another hotel, one with air-conditioning."

"And what did Mr. Carpenter say to that?"

"He said they couldn't afford to."

"And did he seem as worried as she was about the situation?"

"He seemed worried, but not really about the situation. More about her. He made sure she drank the water, and when he answered her he was very gentle. Both times. I would've been annoyed the second time, at least, but he wasn't."

"Can you remember what he said to her?"

"The first time he said, 'I really think it will, Viv. But we'll need to give it at least an hour.' Or something like that. The second time he said, 'Yes, I do.' I remember that because he sounded so sure. You know, firm. She was calmer after that."

"And that was all they said? They didn't talk between themselves about seeing someone they knew on the street, or anything odd that had happened to them on their way from the car?"

The girl looked at her as if she were mad. Allen couldn't blame her. It was ridiculous to imagine the two people she'd just described, the mother worried about the baby and the father worried about her, stopping to discuss anything so trivial. She went in another direction.

"How about the baby? Was she crying? Making any noise?" Had the heat made Bella restive, or had it exhausted her? How much of a fuss would she have made when picked up by a stranger?

"She wasn't doing anything. Some of them don't, you know." Nisha spoke with adolescent superiority. "My little sister's a baby, and all she does is eat and sleep and poo."

"And after Mr. Carpenter reassured his wife? What happened then?"

"I don't know. I left."

"And you didn't have any other interactions with them?"

She shook her head.

And that was that. "Thank you. You've been very helpful."

After the girl had gone, Allen sat with her hand over her mouth, thinking. Her own niece, Emma, was a placid toddler who had slept easily and heavily almost from her first weeks. It seemed Bella was a similarly "good" baby. But was any baby really good enough, quiet enough, to be taken from her basket, out a window, and down that unsteady fire escape without making a cry?

She became aware that her blouse was sticking to her back. Despite the open window, the room remained stifling hot. Was this what it had been like in the Carpenters' room last night? Had it exhausted them so thoroughly that, although Bella had cried, they had slept right through the noise? She remembered her mother telling her that once you had a baby you never really slept soundly again. But Mr. Carpenter wasn't a mother, and Mrs. Carpenter had taken a sleeping tablet.

A drop of sweat crept down the side of her neck. She swiped at it, then thought of the air-conditioned station house, the endless glasses of cold water she could drink there. She was hungry again. She eyed the half sandwich. The bread curled upward, showing the dried edge of a slice of ham. She found herself yearning for the chips the station canteen served, brown and crisp with fat. She checked her watch: ten fifteen. There wasn't anything more she could learn here. She would let the men interviewing in the dining room know she was leaving and commandeer one of them to drive her back.

Ten minutes later, she ducked under the cordon strung between the hotel's front pillars. To her astonishment, a crowd of reporters were waiting, outstretched arms holding handheld tape recorders and microphones. One man held a huge fuzzy mic over her head.

The crowd yelled questions: "Why've they sent you out, love?" "Any developments?" "When will we hear from the senior investigating officer?"

She could see the unmarked car rounding the corner, but the last question drew her up short. "I am the senior investigating officer. And there's nothing to report at this time."

As she passed through the scrum, they turned to follow her. She kept her head down, focusing on making her way across the pavement without being tripped up.

But a pair of patent-leather court shoes with brass buckles stepped in front of her, and she had to look up. Black skirt, black jacket over a white T-shirt, glossy pink lipstick, eyes rimmed in blue eyeliner, blond hair in a Princess Diana cut.

"Just a moment of your time. Just one question."

She sidestepped, but the woman sidestepped, too, then stuck a recorder in her face. "D'you think being a woman is a disadvantage for leading a case like this?"

Allen was so surprised that she stopped. "What?"

"It's a baby-napping. Don't you think there's a risk that your natural maternal instincts might undermine your effectiveness?" The woman pushed the recorder a little closer. "Do you think the Met are taking a risk by appointing you senior investigating officer?"

As she asked the question, she took a step back, and Allen saw a clear path to the car. She jumped in, slamming the door behind her. The air-conditioning made her shiver as if someone had walked over her grave.

6

As much as Allen disliked Ray Norton, she had to admit he was good at his job. He'd organized a humming incident room with clusters of officers working at the front, those at the telephones huddled at the back, where the noise would be less. She saw that he'd placed the action book on his own desk. This meant that he'd made himself the de facto incident-room manager, responsible for ensuring that the information gathered was recorded, organized, and made available to those who needed it. Again, fine with her: She knew he'd be good at it.

She walked to the front of the room and cleared her throat. No one paid any attention. She cleared it again. "Everyone!"

Slowly the hubbub died down and the room turned toward her, until even the men working the phones fell silent. Looking out, Allen saw familiar faces, but also plenty of strangers. Seconded in from West End Central for the duration, she supposed.

"Some of you I know. Some of you I don't, and I hope you'll take it the right way when I say I'm hoping you won't be around long enough for me to get to know you." A few understanding nods. "You can call me 'guv,' or 'guv'nor,' or best of all, 'ma'am'—I like being mistaken for the queen." Some chuckles. She cleared her throat again. "Now. You don't need me to tell you that this is a case where time is of the essence, so let's try to make this briefing as quick as possible." She picked up a "Have you seen . . . ?" flyer that lay on the table and held it up, Bella's photo facing the room. "This is Bella Carpenter. She's five months old, and she was taken from the Bellevue Hotel in Pimlico sometime between three and six fifteen this morning. That means she's been missing for somewhere in the region of six and a half to ten hours. And that means that at best we have only seventeen of our first twenty-four left. So let's hear your updates, and if I don't know your name, tell me at the start."

Daniel Martin, a DC on her usual team, put his hand up. "DC Claridge and I went to Park Royal transfer station. They couldn't find the lorry that took the Bellevue's rubbish, and no one knew where it might have been dumped." He ran a hand through his curly brown hair and looked apologetic. "We walked the place just in case, guv, but, well, it turns out all rubbish looks pretty much the same."

A big laugh followed this weak joke. It showed how tired and frustrated everyone was, Allen thought. Still, the transfer station had been a long shot, so nothing had really been lost.

"What about the rubbish we do have? The cigarette ends?" In the back of the room, one of the strangers held up a hand. "Yes?"

"Carter, guv." His light voice was surprisingly at odds with the meaty hand he now let fall. "DC Roy Carter."

"You're dealing with the tab ends?"

He shook his head. "Employee interviews. I spoke to Arvind Patel, the owner's cousin. He's been helping with the cooking. He told me that the ends were his. Apparently during his breaks he sits on the bucket and smokes."

Another general laugh, but Allen sighed. "Someone still took the ends to Forensics, though, yes?"

A man with a handlebar mustache raised his hand. "That's me. DC Henry King."

"Did they give any sort of time frame for processing the scene?"

"Around a week to process. Another to get any kind of results to us."

"Two weeks! Do they know what crime we're dealing with?"

He held up both hands, palms out. "That's *because* of the crime we're dealing with. They told me it normally takes at least three weeks. Serology, fibers, hair . . . According to the tar—girl I spoke to at the lab"—he put on a high-pitched, babyish voice—"'these things take time.'"

The room laughed again.

"Okay, okay, that's enough of that." If Forensics hadn't been in touch with any results by the next morning, she'd pay them a visit.

The head of the lab, Kate McMullan, was one of the few other women she knew in a supervisory role. They'd gone to the pub together a couple of times; Allen would almost call her a friend. Kate wouldn't object to a little fact-finding visit.

She turned back to Carter. "Did you get anything useful from any of the other employees?"

A shake of the head. "Not so far, but we're less than halfway through. A lot of them have second jobs or aren't on the phone, so we're having trouble reaching them."

"Well, let's hurry it up. Go to their homes if you need to. Talk to Norton about getting more DCs." She saw Norton make a notation in the action book. "Who's checking out the guests?" A blond man at the front raised his hand. "What's going on there?"

"DC Gary Lancaster, guv. Nothing from most of them. There was a couple who'd been to a wedding, got back just after eleven, but apparently everyone else was tucked up in bed by ten—nobody heard a thing after that." Seeing her face, he added, "There was something from one couple. Not sure how much use it's going to be, though. They're staying on the same floor as the Carpenters, and they passed their room at about nine thirty last night, on their way back from a meal out. They heard a woman say, 'She's asleep now,' and then something about taking a tablet."

That sounded like some sort of exchange before Vivien Carpenter took her lorazepam. "How can they be sure it came from the Carpenters' room?"

"They didn't know it was the Carpenters' room, but they said it was the room nearest the stairs. And that's the Carpenters.'"

"All right." It wasn't much, but it was something. "Tell them not to check out until we say they can." He nodded. "Which reminds me: Who's tracking down guests who've checked out?"

A young man to her left held up a hand. "PC Peter Graves. I was told to do that, but no one had checked out before DS Norton told everyone to stay."

He looked concerned, as if someone might blame him for not doing what he couldn't have done, but Allen just nodded. "Right. Now, who's handling the surrounding buildings?"

That was two young PCs at the back. But here, it seemed, there was a problem. While the buildings on either side of the Bellevue were also hotels and happy to share their guest lists, the building that backed onto it was a block of flats. With the exception of the harried mother of a teething baby, the tenants whose windows overlooked the back of the hotel and the yard had all left for work by the time the detectives arrived to question them. They'd slipped leaflets asking for information under their doors and would check back later, but for now there was nothing to report.

No point in complaining. Allen moved on. "And who's doing background on the Carpenters?"

A woman with her dark hair yanked back into a bun raised her hand halfway then snatched it back down. "Wanda. WPC Wanda Greenhill. Desbury and I are doing that."

"Desbury's just gone for a piss," an unidentifiable voice called from the middle of the crowd. Allen saw a knot of men behind Carter snicker.

"You're surprisingly knowledgeable about his toilet habits. Did you want to go and shake it for him?"

Silence. The men stopped snickering.

She turned back to Greenhill, whose eyes were wide. "What've you found out?"

She opened her folder. "Thomas Carpenter, thirty-two years old, born February 3, 1958, in Manchester. Went to the University of Leeds, graduated with a degree in journalism. That's where he met his wife. They moved to London after university. He worked in the Marks & Spencer complaints department for a year, then as some sort of office assistant at LSE before becoming a journalist. No problems at any job. In 1987, he and Mrs. Carpenter moved to Wells, and last year he started working at Glaister Properties." She turned a page. "According to his boss, he's a nice bloke although not a great seller. Since the baby came, he leaves bang on time every day. For the first couple of months he talked nonstop about her, had new photos he showed round the place every week, although that's tailed off recently."

Even doting fathers got used to their children, it seemed. "Any especially persistent clients? Ones who seemed more interested in him than in property? Any women dropping by, or long lunches where he comes back with a smile?" Could Carpenter have had a stalker, or a mistress who'd thought that if he and his wife no longer shared a child he might leave her?

But Greenhill shook her head. "Nothing like that. He's crazy about his wife. Those were his boss's exact words. When the other blokes sound off about theirs, he never joins in, just says he must be lucky."

Someone in the crowd groaned. Allen ignored it. "And what about her?"

"We found less there. Born in Birmingham on December 24, 1957—"

A wolf whistle from the back of the room. "An older woman!" a voice called out.

Greenhill blushed, but she kept going. "She has a degree in fine arts, also from Leeds. Obviously. When they moved to London, she worked as a receptionist at an art gallery. A place called Rilston Fine Arts. It closed down last year, so no joy finding anything out there. She quit when they moved to Wells, and she's not had a proper job since. She's had a couple of exhibits in a place down there, the Bors— Brorsson Gallery. She's a modern figurative painter." Her eyes flicked upward. "I don't know what that means. The woman I spoke to at the gallery told me that her paintings sold reasonably well, but she's gone quiet since the baby. She said Mrs. Carpenter brought her in once or twice."

"Did she say how she acted with her?"

Greenhill nodded. She glanced back down at the folder. "She said she adores her. Although, in her opinion, she seemed a bit overworried. She constantly had her eye out for hazards and potential dangers, but the baby wasn't even at the sitting stage yet."

"Did the woman see anything that warranted concern?"

"She didn't mention anything. Desbury's waiting to hear back from the pediatrician. He's also trying to contact the grandparents, but no luck so far. And we're waiting for their bank to sign off on releasing their account information."

The door to the corridor swung open, and a young Black man walked into the room. He stopped abruptly when he saw the crowd.

"Your girl did your job for you, Desbury," Carter called out. "She's been presenting what you found as if she did the work herself."

Greenhill joined in the laughter, but Allen saw something twitching under her smile. "Enough!" The laughing stopped. "Detective Constable Desbury, I presume?" The man looked at the floor and nodded. "You might want to plan your relief breaks a bit better from now on. Although, as it happens, Greenhill did very well on her own." She dipped her head in the girl's direction. Greenhill glowed. "Now, who's liaising with Immigration and Interpol?"

A slight man in the front lifted his chin. "Viner, guv. Me and Novak are handling that." The red-haired man sitting next to him nodded. "But we've only just started, and so far most of Immigration seems to be on a tea break."

As if prompted by the words "tea break," Allen's stomach growled. It came to her that it was nearly one in the afternoon and she hadn't eaten anything that day except the half sandwich at the hotel. She wasn't going to give these men a chance to say she'd parceled out orders and then swanned off to lunch while they did the hard work, but she worried that if she didn't put something in her stomach soon she might faint. And that would be even worse.

"Okay. If that's what we have so far, it'll have to do." She turned toward the door then hesitated. She wanted to leave with a show of strength. "I'll be back in ten minutes. While I'm gone, someone needs to check with the morgues."

7

She was walking back from the canteen with the chips in a bowl, eating as she went, when Norton came up to her. "DCI Beck's asked for you, guv."

"Now?"

"He did say as soon as, but I can tell him you're eating and'll be along once you've finished." His voice and face were bland.

"No, no. Here." She handed him the bowl. Immaculate even without his suit jacket, he took it with distaste. "Could you put this with the canteen's dirty crockery, please?" She wiped her fingers on a paper napkin and dropped it in the greasy bowl then smoothed her hair as she turned down the corridor that led to Beck's office.

He was standing behind his desk, his back to her. On the desktop a newspaper lay open. When he turned around, he wore the same expression he wore at the start of all their encounters, confusion tinged with uncertainty, as if he were face-to-face with an animal he'd never seen before and couldn't really comprehend.

It wasn't that Beck was against women in the force. He wasn't even against women rising through the ranks. He just didn't see why they couldn't be happy rising through the ranks in areas that suited them: child welfare, juvenile and domestic crime, sex offenses. He couldn't fathom why a woman would want to immerse herself—why she should be *allowed* to immerse herself—in the brutality of the murder squad. But Allen knew he was also determined to climb the greasy pole, and he must have been aware that recent accusations of sexism meant the higher-ups were clamoring to showcase women in investigative roles. It was just his good fortune that a case had appeared that allowed him to square his ideas about female officers with his ambitions. A missing baby was, after all, both a child-welfare issue and a domestic crime.

"Allen." He didn't gesture for her to sit.

"Sir."

"Where are you on this disappearance?"

She summarized the investigation. When she was done, he asked, "No contact from whoever took the missing child?"

"No, sir."

"No note at the scene? No phone call to the hotel, or contact with us once we arrived?"

"None, sir."

"So it's an abduction, not a kidnapping." They both knew what that meant. Since the abductor had no motivation to return the baby, the police had a requirement to assume the baby was in imminent danger.

"This is highest urgency, Allen. Highest urgency." The afternoon sun slanting through his window spotlit his face. Allen had always thought that he looked like a stereotypical English schoolboy, all ruddy cheeks and smooth brow, but now she saw bags starting to form under the bright blue eyes and two vertical lines lightly marking the skin above his nose. She realized she knew nothing about his private life. Did he have small children he was suddenly seeing differently, a baby he wanted to hurry home to, just to check?

If he did, he wasn't going to mention it. Instead he closed the newspaper and turned it to face her. It was the midday edition of the *Evening Standard*. She saw the photo of Bella Carpenter, enlarged so it took up most of the top of the page. A headline above screamed in huge capitals, BABY SNATCHED AT PIMLICO HOTEL. The article underneath took up the two left-hand columns. Next to them was the picture Martha had had taken for her first police identity card. She remembered that they'd all had them done at the end of the graduate-scheme induction day. The face in the photo wore the awkward half simper of someone trying to look simultaneously stern and approachable. Beneath it, a caption asked, *The best face for the case?* Beck rested a finger on it.

"I gave you this case because I believed you had what it took to lead it. I hope you're not going to prove me wrong."

You gave me the case because you knew it would look good for you. But Allen's shoulder muscles tightened. He might be a self-focused careerist, but he was still her superior officer. He had the power to make her life miserable if she made him look bad.

"I'm doing my very best, sir."

"This investigation is an opportunity for you, Allen. A satisfactory result could be a"—he lingered on the word—"career-maker. From what you've told me, so far you've made firm decisions, taken decisive action. That's the sort of thing Command likes to see. Now what we need is a swift conclusion. They'll like that even more."

"My men are working full out, sir. I've got the incident-room team running background on all the hotel employees and guests, and a team at the site doing a fingertip search out to one mile. And I searched the hotel myself, top to bottom."

Beck looked pleased, but before he could say anything, someone knocked on the office door.

"Come!"

Norton appeared. "Sorry to interrupt, sir, but we've had a call from the hotel. The Scene of Crime principal officer would like DI Allen to come right away. They've found something in the yard."

8

DC Desbury drove her back to the hotel, making the trip as smoothly as if the clogged roads were empty. Allen used the time to put on some lipstick. Foolish, maybe, but it made her feel more capable.

At half past one in the afternoon, the Bellevue had long since ended breakfast service. The dining room was empty, its windows still open but the fans switched off. Not for the first time, Allen thought how much more lifeless an empty room felt if it had been designed to hold many people. There was a special hollowness to a busy room laid bare.

"There you are." Out in the yard, the Scene of Crime PO stood waiting. "I thought you'd want to see this in situ before I bag it."

Someone had rolled the skip against the back wall of the yard. He stood where it had been. "The rubbish collectors put the bin back in a different spot after they emptied it. We only found this when we knocked into it while taking photos."

He pointed down. On the ground lay a brownish cigarette butt, about an inch long.

Allen squatted down. "Is it the same brand as the ones by the kitchen door? Maybe the cousin who smokes stubbed it out while he was throwing away some rubbish."

The PO crouched next to her, shaking his head. He produced a pair of needle-nose tweezers from one of his pockets. "This is completely different." He picked up the butt and brought it closer. Now Allen could see that the outer wrapping was not paper but some sort of leaf. "Kretek," the PO said. He held the stub near her nose. She smelled a sweet spiciness, nothing like the stink of burnt tobacco. "Also known as clove cigarettes. A mixture of tobacco, cloves, and other unregulated additives. Very bad for the lungs, and readily available at your more exotic tobacconists." From his other pocket he drew out an evidence bag and dropped the butt into it. "It's not discolored or dried out, and although we had drizzle yesterday and last night, it's dry—although it could have been under the bin for some or all of that time. Still, I feel reasonably safe saying that someone stood in this spot within roughly the past twenty-four hours and smoked this cigarette. And look what their view would have been." He held up his arm and pointed at the hotel.

As she had that morning, Allen shaded her eyes and looked up. She had a clear view of the fire escape outside the Carpenters' room and of the window that looked out onto it.

She looked back at the PO. "Could've been one of the housekeeping staff taking a break. Or maybe even one of the guests."

"It could've been, certainly. But come see." He stood up, waving her to follow him. Her knees popped as she rose.

A small table had been set near the back wall of the kitchen. On it lay a series of evidence bags. The PO reached for one that contained a padlock, opened it, and slipped the lock into his gloved left palm.

"This is from those doors." He nodded at the gates that led from the yard to the street. "But look."

As she watched, he lifted the metal loop of the shackle out of the padlock's body with his tweezers. Then he inserted the points into the hole where the end of the shackle had been, squeezed, and drew out a piece of what looked like gray wax.

"Chewing gum." He sniffed. "Spearmint, if I'm not mistaken. Someone dropped it in the hole, then pressed the shackle in. The padlock would have looked locked, but when reasonable pressure was exerted, it would slip open."

Allen thought of Patel's remark that whoever was on night duty checked the padlock when they locked up at midnight. "What's reasonable pressure? Would it have held in place if someone flipped it up and then let it fall? If they gave it a pull?"

"Certainly if they flipped it up and let it fall. In this heat, the gum would have melted enough to grip tightly. If they gave it a pull, also yes, provided they didn't yank it. Reasonable pressure would be if someone pulled it hard, or pushed hard against the gates from the outside. Then the lock would pop, and with a bit of back and forth or up and down they could shake the hasp open enough to reach through and get in." He slipped the lump back into the lock and the lock back into the bag. "Ingenious, really."

Allen had no time to admire the ingenuity. "So what you're saying is that someone who works here rigged this lock so the gate was unlocked last night, and you think that connects to the cigarette."

"I'm not saying anything happened last night, or was connected to anything else, or was done by someone who worked here." Allen remembered that Forensics was careful when it came to building stories out of evidence. "But, yes, the elasticity of the gum and its scent suggest that it was inserted relatively recently, and that could only have been done by someone who was inside the yard at the time. And at some time in the past day or so, judging from the state of it, someone also left that kretek end."

Allen stared at the table, but she wasn't seeing it. She was imagining someone spotting Bella Carpenter, wanting her, making a plan to get her. Putting the gum in the lock, then smoking the cigarette while they watched the Carpenters' room and built up the courage to climb the fire escape, slip into the room, and take her. If it hadn't been someone in the hotel, they must have been helped by someone there.

In the absence of Norton, she turned to Desbury. "Get hold of everyone in the building except the Carpenters. I want to see them all."

She would interview them one by one until she found out who was involved.

She saw them in the lounge, DC O'Leary sitting in to take notes, Desbury outside the door to make sure the interviews weren't disturbed. She gave each person the same information and asked them all the same questions. An unusual cigarette of a type called a kretek, also known as a clove cigarette, had been found in the yard. Did they know where it might have come from? Did they themselves smoke such cigarettes, or know anyone who did? It also seemed that the padlock on the back gates had been tampered with at some time in the recent past. Did they know anything about that? Had they been in the yard recently? Had they noticed anything unusual about the lock?

One after another, guests and employees explained that they didn't smoke or that, yes, they smoked, but they smoked Silk Cut, or Rothmans, or some other common brand. The guests said they'd never been in the yard; most of them didn't know there was a yard. The employees explained that they never had anything to do with the padlock: the gates were always locked and unlocked by Mr. Patel or another member of his family. All of them consented to have their bags and cases searched.

Meanwhile, the lounge became hotter as the afternoon wore on. Even after one of her men wrenched open a second window, there was no hint of a breeze. When Kalpen Patel entered the room after the first hour of interviews, she felt a sneaking relief to see that his forehead was beaded with sweat too. At least she wasn't the only one suffering.

Immediately feeling guilty for the thought, she smiled at him as he sat. "We found the ladder where you said we would. Thank you."

"That's okay." He clasped his hands in his lap.

"And now here we are hoping for your help with something else." She explained about the padlock once again, ending with, "And I know you check that lock when you're on night shift, so I wondered if you'd noticed anything unusual in that area?" She gave a little laugh. "You're very much our go-to man in all areas, it seems."

It was a poor attempt at humor, but she would have expected at least a polite smile in response. Instead he just shook his head. The gesture loosened a bead of sweat on his forehead, and as it made its way down toward his nose, he lifted a hand to wipe it. She saw that the hand was shaking.

She looked at him more carefully. He was biting his lip, his eyes fixed on his lap. But he'd been shy in his first interview, and these could just be signs of shyness.

She thought again of the sergeant who'd made the remark about going slowly. Sergeant Pebworth, that was it. He'd also once given her some advice about interrogation. "Guilt is a burden," he'd said to her after she'd failed to force a confession during a mock interview. "Nine times out of ten, people want to lay it down. Be gentle. Make it easy for them." Gentleness would work equally well now whether Kalpen was a shy boy or a man with something to hide.

"You know, Kalpen"—she made her voice reflective—"it strikes me that after your father, you probably know this hotel better than anyone. You've lived here all your life, and, according to him, these days you take quite a lot of the responsibility for running it. Is that right?"

A nod.

"So you must have seen all sorts of things, been asked all sorts of things by guests, am I right?"

Another nod.

"And I don't think you'd ever deliberately do anything to put your family or your guests in danger. But in my experience dangerous things don't always look dangerous at first. And I can see how, to be helpful, you might have done something, or might have let somebody else do something, if you didn't think it was going to be dangerous."

He still didn't speak, but a tear rolled down his nose and fell onto the clasped hands.

That was all the evidence she needed. He wasn't just a shy boy: He was a guilty one. "Is there something you'd like to tell me, Kalpen?"

He shook his head.

"Are you sure?"

He hesitated, then shook it again.

Apparently this was going to take something more than gentling.

"All right." She stood up. "We obviously need to move this conversation to a more formal setting. One of my men will take you to the station. I'll let your parents know what's—"

"No!" If the boy hadn't been so frightened, he might have yelled the word, but as it was it came out a squeak.

Allen sat back down.

"I . . . I did . . . I don't . . ." At last he looked at her. "Don't tell my parents." He took a deep breath. "I didn't do anything to the lock. I really didn't. But it's like you said, I didn't think it was dangerous. She just asked me . . ." He broke off.

She. So now they had a gender. Not that Allen was surprised to learn they were dealing with a woman—she would have been surprised to learn the opposite—but it was still something to have that assumption confirmed. She felt her shoulders relax a little.

"She? Who is 'she'?"

The boy didn't move. Allen hardened her heart and her voice. "Kalpen, you need to tell me what happened. A baby could be in danger because of your actions. If you don't tell me, whatever happens to her will be partly your fault."

He sat silent for another moment then straightened in the chair and met her eyes. He had come to a decision. "All right. You're right. I'll tell you. Yesterday afternoon, while I was at reception—"

There was a sharp rap at the door. Without waiting for a reply, Desbury poked his head in. "Mr. Patel and his daughter would like to see you, ma'am."

"Not now, Detective Constable."

"He says it's urgent, ma'am."

"Not *now*, Detective Constable."

Desbury had no chance to respond because an unseen hand pushed the door wider. Amrish Patel hustled into the room, followed by Nisha. He was holding her by the wrist.

He stopped beside Kalpen's chair, facing Allen. "My daughter has something to tell you."

This was a very different Nisha from the one Allen had spoken to earlier. Gone was the surly, bored teenager. In her place was a young girl who stared at the carpet with a tearstained face.

"Go on." Patel was also transformed, no longer a kindly hotelier but a stern judge. "Tell them."

Nisha kept her eyes down. Her father tugged her hand. "Tell them!"

The girl's lower lip trembled. At last she muttered, "It was me." She looked up and burst into tears. "I did it! I put the gum in the lock!"

In future years, Allen would be able to see that this episode had all the elements of farce: mistaken identity, outraged father, confused representative of authority. But she would never be able to laugh at it. In the moment, she considered it a miracle that she stayed calm as the truth came trickling out.

Nisha kept talking. "Yesterday afternoon when Kalpen was on reception, I asked if I could have the keys to take some rubbish out to the skip. But when he gave them to me, I used them to unlock the padlock instead. Then I chewed some gum I'd brought with me and stuck it in the hole before I put the loop thing back. I know Baba checks it by pushing it together and then tugging it to be sure it's really locked, so I pressed the pieces together, then tugged, and it held. But when I shook it hard, it opened." She started to cry again. "I saw it on *Murder, She Wrote*!"

Allen ignored that. She turned to Kalpen. "This is the 'she' you meant." He nodded miserably. "And when you were interrupted just now, you were going to tell me that she came to reception and asked if she could have the keys." He nodded again. She turned back to Nisha. "But why did you want the lock unlocked? Did someone ask you to unlock it?" Had she been wrong about which Patel child the kidnapper had approached?

"No." Nisha shook her head. "I . . . I . . ."

"You what?" Her father's voice rose as he continued. "I'll tell you what. You fixed that lock and then someone came in here and took that baby, that's what!"

"No one came in here! We just stayed out back and talk—" Nisha realized what she'd said. She snapped her mouth shut.

"We? Who is 'we'?" Now Patel was nearly yelling.

"Yes, who is 'we'?" Allen felt the interrogation slipping out of her grasp. "Someone asked you to let them in? Or paid you to? Do you remember what they looked like? Did they give you their name?" Could it be that someone who knew where the Carpenters would stay had traveled to London earlier in the week to set a plan in motion? Hadn't Greenhill said Vivien Carpenter sold her paintings at a gallery run by a woman? Had she told the woman where they were going? What was the woman's maternal history? Had she lost a baby? She went cold. Could the woman and Vivien Carpenter be working together?

"It was someone from school, okay?" Nisha directed this at her father. She turned to Allen and said slightly less sullenly, "It was someone from school."

"Someone from school?" Patel spoke before Allen could. "You were standing outside in the yard at midnight talking to someone from school? And who is this person who was worth putting a baby in danger for?"

Allen stood. "Mr. Patel, please. I am investigating a serious crime. Let me ask the questions."

He held up an apologetic hand. Allen turned to his daughter. "I'm going to need the name of the person you were meeting."

Nisha studied the carpet. Finally she lifted her head. "His name is Aanish. Aanish Upreti."

Patel couldn't contain himself. "Aanish Upreti? The boy you told us about, the one who looks like the singer from that pop group who eat people?"

Nisha might have stalled a police investigation, she might be facing a punishment worse than any she'd faced before, but she was still a teenager. Her voice dripped with contempt as she said, "They're called the Fine Young Cannibals."

Allen controlled her irritation. Someday she would have a child this age, maybe a daughter exactly like this. This moment could be good practice. She kept her tone level. "Never mind what they're called. Tell me what happened."

"He's in the form above me, and we talk sometimes. Then on Saturday I saw him at the community-center disco, and he said he wished we had more time away from other people. You know, alone. I had seen *Murder, She Wrote*, so I said that if he didn't mind waiting until late one night I could arrange it so we could meet here. I didn't tell him about the trick with the lock. I just said that if he waited until after midnight then pressed hard on one of the gates, he could make enough room to stick his hand through and take the lock off, and I'd be watching from my room and come down. He said he'd come on Wednesday night—last night." Perhaps hoping to buy mercy, she added, "The cigarette end is his. He was smoking a cigarette when I came out last night. He put it out when he saw me."

"And the two of you were out in the yard together the entire time? Did you come inside at any point, or go anywhere?" The girl shook her head. "And you didn't see anyone else in the yard when you went out there?" Another shake. "And how long would you say you were out there?"

"I came down around twelve forty-five, after my mother went back to sleep after feeding my sister. And when I went back to bed, my alarm clock said two fifteen."

Forty-five minutes before Carpenter had done the final feed. Even fifteen minutes later and she might have seen someone else coming through the gates!

She looked at the girl. "Because I can't accept your story without corroboration, I'll be sending two of my officers to your school to talk to this Aanish Upreti." The horror on Nisha's face told Allen she had been right to think that this was an effective penalty. Still . . . "Be aware that you have wasted police time, a serious offense for which I could have arrested you. As it is, I'm sure your father has some ideas about appropriate punishment."

Mr. Patel glowered at his daughter. "For a start, you will be spending the rest of the summer with your Auntie Razia in Dudley."

The last thing Allen heard as she closed the lounge door was Nisha's outraged "But that's not f—"

O'Leary had followed her out. "Make sure no one tells the parents," she said over her shoulder. The last thing the Carpenters needed was to feel even one second of hope that would be snatched away from them. "Desbury, we're heading back."

In the back seat, she squirmed with irritation. Had she ever been so angry? Had she ever had to deal with such a load of time-wasting nonsense? Maybe she should have charged the girl.

Realizing Desbury could see her in the rearview mirror, she forced herself to sit still.

They pulled into one of the bays in the car park, then Desbury slid out and opened her door for her. Once she was standing, he hesitated to close it behind her.

"Is there a problem, Detective Constable?"

"No, ma'am. But may I say something?"

She nodded.

"When I was a probie, one of my sergeants once said to me that everyone thinks investigation is about opening doors, but just as often it's about closing them." He ducked his head. "Not that I need to tell you anything, ma'am."

As she walked toward the station door, he fell into step behind her.

9

"This whole case makes me think of the Lindbergh baby," Phil said. They had met for sandwiches in a new place on Victoria Street, all done out in maroon and white. The level of her anger and frustration in the car back to the station had shown Allen how tightly wound she was. If she wanted to continue working effectively, she needed some kind of break. She could spare fifteen minutes. She'd rung him up and asked him to meet her.

If someone had told her two years before that she would shortly find herself dating, then moving in with, the new area Crown prosecutor, she would have laughed in their face. At that time, like all the police at Victoria Police Station, she had a vague dislike of the Crown Prosecution Service and its rigid requirements for what constituted sufficient evidence. But twenty-four months later, here she and Crown Prosecutor Phil Barnard were sharing a flat in West Hampstead and about to be parents. And she loved him—sometimes she was surprised by how much she loved him. Her family were a collection of careful people, her whole professional life had been an exercise in learning rationality, suppression, and coolness, but Phil was exuberant, full of unexpected ideas and actions, bold enough to cross the room at a police Christmas ball and ask a complete stranger to dance.

Now his dark hair shone against the white-painted walls. Someone had propped the shop door open, and she could hear the sound of a busker playing acoustic guitar outside. Although she felt guilty for stealing time away from the incident room, she did feel herself relax.

"The man whose child was kidnapped?" She spoke through a mouthful of egg and cress. "The one who flew solo across the Atlantic?" They'd learned about the case during her training, but time had made the details hazy.

Not for Phil, though. "The kidnapping happened after the flight. Lindbergh had become a huge celebrity. Someone took his baby son from his country house. Climbed up a collapsible ladder and through the nursery window one night. They left a ransom note on the windowsill. Police found the baby's blanket on the ground outside. It took a while, but they tracked the kidnapper down."

"How long is 'a while'?"

He looked downcast. "Two years." Then, brightening, "But they got him in the end."

"Well, our kidnapper didn't leave any ransom note. So we don't even have that to go on."

"There are people who say Lindbergh himself had a hand in it. I suppose you've—"

She cut him off. "We ran background on the parents, and nothing jumped out. I'm also having Scene of Crime document and check everything they find in the luggage they brought with them. I'm not taking any chances. But, Phil, you should have seen them. She's a wreck, and he's only holding on because he thinks he needs to support her. Watching them is . . ." She felt her good mood vanishing. "Could we talk about something else, please?"

"Sure." He swallowed. "How about the cricket? I can't believe Gooch got his triple century."

She gave him a look. She knew he was teasing: He knew she was bored by all sports except the World Cup.

"Samuel Beckett played cricket! He's in *Wisden*!"

"You say that every time you want to talk about cricket." But she was smiling. "And I'm going to say what I always say. No matter how much I love Beckett's plays, he will never make me like cricket."

"Oh yeah, you do always say that. Fine. How about those two German blokes who were caught lip-synching? Milla Vanilla, or whatever it is?"

She sighed and shook her head again. It wasn't working.

"Never mind. Finish telling me about the Lindberghs. Did they find the baby?"

"Two months later."

"Where?"

He became very interested in his plate. "Hidden in some trees nearby. They found his body. Dead from a blow to the head." He looked up, miserable. "I'm sorry. I shouldn't have mentioned the case."

"No, no, I asked." She looked at her watch and stood up. "I'd better head back."

Out on the pavement, she suddenly felt sick. She wasn't sure if it was from guilt at having stepped away from the investigation or because of the baby. Was there such a thing as afternoon sickness?

As she started to walk, she put a hand on her stomach. It was flat. Of course it was: It had been flat that morning, and no doubt it would be flat tomorrow. She couldn't be more than six weeks along.

When would she start to show? So far she hadn't really felt pregnant. Even when the morning sickness had arrived, it hadn't brought any instinctive awareness of the body growing inside her. She was just sick in the mornings, that was all. The books she'd bought told her that the baby was still only about the size of a pea, but she'd expected to be more aware of it by now, to feel it and to feel some connection to it. Would that happen when she could literally see the evidence in front of her?

Out of nowhere, the reporter from in front of the Bellevue Hotel popped into her head. What had the woman meant, "your natural maternal instincts"? Was she supposed to have maternal instincts all the time? Because she'd just established that she didn't have them now, even though she was about to be a mother. She stopped. Did that mean she was going to be a bad mother? Did good mothers feel their impending motherhood from the moment they were pregnant?

She frowned at herself. That wasn't what "maternal instincts" meant, and it wasn't what the reporter had meant. The woman had been asking if she was too emotional to handle a missing-baby case. If women in general were too emotional to handle those kinds of cases. She got that sort of thing all the time at the station, but she hadn't expected to encounter it from another woman. Another working woman at that.

But then she remembered Vivien Carpenter's face, and she did feel a stab, a wince of empathy. Would that empathy keep her from dealing with the case effectively? As a soon-to-be mother, would she find herself overwhelmed by her desire to end the pain of another mother?

She knew what Phil would say. *That woman asked the question she thought was most likely to create drama. The more drama there is, the more papers they sell.* Well, maybe that was true.

She checked her watch. God, it was 3 p.m.! Nine hours of the first twenty-four gone, and here she was wasting time thinking about herself. She should be ashamed. She *was* ashamed. She picked up her pace as she headed toward the station.

When she arrived back at the incident room, someone had set a combination television/VCR on one of the desks. It was broadcasting the end of the ITV news bulletin, and as she paused in front of it, the presenter looked out at her gravely, Bella's photographed face behind him. "Police are continuing their search for a baby who disappeared from a London hotel early this morning. A thorough search has been made of the local area, and inquiries are ongoing. We will bring you more as the story develops."

She reached out and switched the set off. Without its noise, the room was quiet, even though it was busy. Officers were reading over notes or transcribing them, pecking out the letters on one of the typewriters dotted around. She could hear the photocopier whirring in the next room as someone made a contribution to the growing collection of papers. Three officers stood around a table trying to outline an area they could manage to search again before the sun set.

In the back of the room, she could see Viner on the telephone. The seat next to him was empty. She made her way over and waited until he put the receiver down.

"Where's Novak?"

"Gone to the break room for a bit of kip." He turned back toward the phone. "But no rest for the wicked, eh?"

"Never." She sat down next to him. "Tell you what: Give me half the list, and I'll get started."

If these men were there all day and night, she would be too.

10

At six thirty the next morning, after she'd spent the night trying to gather immigration records and combing through witness statements with no result, a DC slid an envelope onto her desk. *MPS Scene of Crime Office* was stamped on one corner, and it bowed slightly from having been stuffed too full. When she opened it, she found it filled with a stack of eight-by-ten photos, a list on the top.

"Contents of Bags, Room 201, Bellevue Hotel, Case Number: 357209PAS" was typed across the top. Then, two lines below, "Bag 1: large soft bag, label reading mothercare (photo 1a)."

She ran her eyes down the list of the nappy-bag contents. All as she'd seen, plus two or three mysterious items she imagined she'd be familiar with in a few months' time. She moved on to "Bag 2: medium soft case, branded St. Michael on interior top (photo 2a)." Here the list was much longer, and she had to go more slowly. She sifted through the photos as she went, matching them up with the list: enough baby clothes to clothe an army of infants in all but the coldest weather; three pairs of men's socks and three of pants; one pair of jeans; two T-shirts. Two loose dresses ("linen. See photo 2j"); two nursing bras; three pairs of cotton knickers; two pairs of "low-cut foot socks" (she'd thought they were just called "footies"); one breast pump with accompanying bottles; one copy of *A Prayer for Owen Meany* ("author, John Irving"), one copy of *Possession* ("author, A. S. Byatt"). Allen, who had been wanting to read the Byatt book herself, lingered over the photo of its Pre-Raphaelite cover before flipping to the next, a picture of the book's flyleaf. Someone had written a name on the top right corner, but this had been scored out. In the center of the page, someone had written in looped handwriting, *For My Beloved Viv, Your Tom*. On the list this was identified as "interior inscription."

She couldn't have asked for better or more. At the same time, though, it offered her nothing. No evidence possibly hidden by an abductor—a pry bar? An extra room key? She didn't know, but something—and nothing to suggest the Carpenters had intended anything more than a hopefully relaxing few days. She moved on to the contents list for the two toiletry bags also found in the room, but that only showed a collection of common toiletries, all own-brand, and a Remington electric shaver ("rechargeable, charge lead separate").

She tossed the list and photos on her desk. Whoever had brought the envelope had also brought a stack of the morning papers. She saw the *Sun*'s headline screaming up at her: NIGHT STALKER SNATCHES BABY FROM HER BASKET. She rubbed her gritty eyes and checked her watch. It was seven. The first twenty-four hours were over.

She closed her eyes. She wanted to push everything off her desk and prop her elbows there, weary head in her hands, but she couldn't risk one of the men coming in and thinking he'd caught her crying. She opened her eyes again. Kate McMullan would be at the lab by now. She would go there and see what she could get from her. Then she'd visit the Carpenters and update them. Somehow she'd put a positive spin on things. And maybe by the time she made it back from the hotel, the team would've found out something. Or she would have thought of some way out of this dead end.

She put a piece of spearmint gum in her mouth to make up for not brushing her teeth, thought of Nisha Patel, and spat it into the bin. She pulled at the front of her blouse a few times, trying to air it. She cursed herself for not following the example of some of the men she worked with by keeping a clean shirt in her office—she'd been worried about being labeled as obsessed with her appearance for the rest of her career.

Ignoring her yearning for a shower, she shrugged into her suit jacket and went out through the incident room. It was even quieter than it had been the previous evening, although a few stalwarts lingered. She saw that Viner was still on the phone, and as he felt her eyes on him, he turned and made an exasperated face. Their work had been slow and mostly fruitless, but her willingness to stay through the night meant that he, at least, was in her corner now.

If she took the Tube from Victoria, she thought as she passed through reception, she could get off at Vauxhall. Walking might wake her up. It might even help to suppress her raging hunger.

Once she'd passed through the morning traffic on the Albert Embankment, the walk was almost pleasant, made more so when she admitted defeat and veered into a McDonald's for a breakfast sandwich to eat on the way. The heat forestalled any real enjoyment of anything, though. It was, if possible, even hotter than the previous morning. She took off her jacket, but it didn't make any obvious difference. Once again she felt the sweat pricking her hairline, and by the time she reached the building that housed the forensics lab, her shirt was stuck to her back. When the frigid air-conditioning of the lobby hit her, it felt like a light breeze.

The lift took her up five floors, opening directly onto the lab. The huge space was early-morning quiet, its white countertops bleached even further by the fluorescent light. There was something eerie about the silent sterility, and she shivered for a second.

Before she reached Kate's office, she stumbled across Kate herself. Sheathed in lab coat, surgical mask, gloves, and goggles, her auburn hair held back in a ponytail, she was bent over one of the lab's counters, using a pair of tweezers to lift a single fiber onto a slide. As Allen watched, she opened the tweezers and let the fiber fall, dipped them in some fluid in a petri dish next to her, then sealed a square of plastic over the fiber with the drop that fell from their tip.

"Keep back. I don't want any risk of transfer," she said as she observed her handiwork. She looked at Allen. "I know why you're here. In fact, this is some of yours."

"Oh yes?" Allen saw that the fiber had a faint blush to it. Part of the scrap from Bella Carpenter's sleep suit. "Please tell me that this is the last item left after your extraordinary rush to work through everything as fast as possible."

"I would if I could, but I can't, so I won't." Kate's quick grin and light Dundee accent softened the childhood taunt. She stripped off her latex gloves and stuffed them in the pedal bin at the end of the counter. "Come away into my office, though, and I'll tell you what we've done so far."

Kate was a scrupulous scientist, but her personal space was a different story. Papers of various shades crowded her desk, some clipped together, some single, some lolling out of the tops and sides of manila file folders. The plastic frame of her computer monitor sprouted Post-its covered in reminders and notes scrawled in her illegible handwriting. One long wall was lined with rows of shelves crammed with reference books and journals. The other featured an enlargement of a remarkably detailed—and remarkably inaccurate, she'd once told Allen—medieval woodcut showing a man laid open, his exposed viscera neatly labeled. The whole room was infused with a damp vegetable scent, the legacy of countless mugs of tea.

Now Kate switched on the kettle behind her desk. "Tea?"

"It's nearly eighty-six degrees outside!"

"Auch, a hot drink's the best thing for a hot day. It's a scientific fact." She held a tea bag over a mug.

Allen shook her head. Kate waited until the kettle boiled then made a mug for herself, leaving the bag in when she added the milk. She'd once told Allen that she liked her tea so strong the spoon stood up in it.

Setting the mug on the desktop, she sat down. "Right, so, the Bellevue Hotel scene." She reached for a folder. "As it happens, I have been working on it, in as much of a rush as accuracy will allow."

"And what do you have?"

"Not a great deal. Accuracy doesn't allow for much rush." She flipped the folder open. "I can tell you that we found an impressive number of fingerprints, and we've been matching them to the elimination prints we took. So far we've identified some that belong to the young man I gather showed the parents to the room and two very clear palm prints and two full sets of fingerprints belonging to the baby's father on the window frame." Those would be from opening the window, Allen thought. "The mother's and the father's prints are all over the Moses basket, along with some smears that are probably from the baby. The dermal ridges are so faint at her age that you really only get oily residue. There were prints all over the room that we couldn't link to anyone we printed, but they also didn't match any known villains."

"Terrific." Allen tilted her head back and closed her eyes. "Anything else?"

"Well, there's the fabric you saw me working on. It's possible there might be some transfer on that. There was some soil on the carpet under the window. And almost as many hairs as fingerprints. Several from the bed—probably the parents', but you never know. More from the carpet. One in the basket. But I have to wait until Siân comes in to know anything about them: She's our hair and fiber man."

"How long will it take to get results on them once she starts?"

"I'll have to ask. But look. It's a two-star hotel in central London. There's heavy foot traffic; there's been God knows what kinds of activity in the room over the years. Even in the best hotels, cleaning doesn't leave the rooms sterile. Trying to find evidence that we can be certain is relevant is the equivalent of trying to find a six-year-old in the Live Aid audience." She flicked to a new page. "Of course, as soon as I say that . . ."

Allen sat forward. "What?"

"They found a drop of blood. A quarter of an inch in diameter, on the lower edge of the window frame."

"Do they know how old?"

"No. It was dry, but yesterday's temperature means virtually any liquid would have dried almost right away. Bhanji's written here that he's going to run a rate-of-dissolution test." She glanced up. "In other words, he's going to see how long it takes a sample of that blood to dissolve in water, which should give us some idea of its age."

"Can you get DNA from it?"

"Ah, Dr. Jeffreys's magic bullet." Kate sighed. "Sure, you can get DNA from it, and if there's a root on any of the hairs, we could extract DNA from that too. But DNA testing takes minimum six weeks at either of our two reliable labs, and it'll take a two-thousand-pound bite out of your budget. Plus it's exactly the same as those tab ends you sent me. You can only match a suspect to it, not use it to find one."

"So the takeaway here is that you haven't really turned up anything."

"Hey!"

"Sorry, sorry. I didn't mean it that way. But I need to go and see the parents"—Allen checked her watch: 8:40—"well, now, and I want to say something that would give them at least a little hope."

"Tell them the Forensics team collected a great deal of evidence at the scene and are working through it as quickly as they can."

It was Allen's turn to sigh.

"Okay, okay. Tell you what. Ask the parents if they'd be willing to give blood samples. Just a drop or two. Tell them I'll send a tech over to do it. Pity we don't have any of the baby's—it'd be a forensics utopia if they typed at birth, but they don't. Still, I'll find out what the parents' blood types are, and once Bhanji's found the blood type of the drop on the frame, we can see if they're a match. It's not much, but it might at least eliminate them and help us start the process of finding out who did leave that blood." Seeing Allen's face, she said, "I know, I know. But you don't have to make it sound that vague to them. Say . . . say that we'd like samples in order to identify a drop of blood we found on the window frame. That sounds more promising, doesn't it?"

"It sounds that way." Allen stood.

Kate gave her a sympathetic smile. "Chin up. Remember the baby snatched from St. Thomas's Hospital in January? They found her alive and well after two weeks."

11

In the lobby of the Bellevue Hotel, Amrish Patel was once more at reception; once more he called his wife to take over while he led Allen to the Carpenters. This time, though, they continued up the stairs past the second floor. He and his son had created a suite for the Carpenters on a new floor, he explained, out of two rooms with connecting doors. "I thought they might be more comfortable there. Especially since the grandparents arrived last night."

The sitting room of the makeshift suite didn't seem terribly comfortable. A sofa had been pushed against one wall, nightstands doing duty as occasional tables on either side and a square coffee table centered in front. On the other side of the coffee table, two armchairs angled inward, a bureau with a television on it behind them. While this might have worked in a larger room, the sitting room was scarcely ten feet on any side. It was also, once again, oppressively hot. Someone had opened the small window set into the far wall, but that only let in the occasional exhaust-filled breeze and the sound of cars. The result was a sense of cramped closeness, the three people grouped together on the sofa hemmed in by the temperature, the walls, and the noise.

Carpenter sat in the middle, his head in his hands. A gray-haired woman sat next to him, an arm around his shoulders, murmuring to him. She lifted her head as Allen entered. On Carpenter's other side, a man of around sixty sat on the very edge of the sofa, his knees almost touching the coffee table. He clasped Carpenter's shoulder with a suntanned hand, the rolled-up sleeve of his white button-down shirt revealing an equally tanned forearm.

Silent and deferential as a Victorian servant, Patel retreated. Allen waited until the latch clicked before she spoke. "Good morning, Mr. Carpenter."

There was no response. Not sure what else to do, she showed her warrant card to the two others. "Detective Inspector Martha Allen. I'm the lead investigator on this case."

The woman rose and held out her hand. "Evelyn Cook." She had a singsong Midlands accent and a strong, intelligent face. Her hand was cool and firm. "And this is my husband, Leonard."

The man rose a fraction then sank back down. "Good to meet you." He had the same accent as his wife. "We've been hoping to talk to the police since we arrived last night."

"It was very good of you to come so quickly."

"How could we not?" Mrs. Cook shook her head. "We were in the car as soon as we heard."

"My parents are flying back from Corfu on Monday, when their holiday ends." Carpenter spoke without lifting his head.

"Well, it's easy to get here from Birmingham. Not so much from Corfu." Leonard Cook's tone was soothing but also faintly embarrassed.

Mrs. Cook gestured to the free chair. Allen sat.

"Mr. Carpenter, I wanted to pay a visit to see how you and your wife are doing." No response. "I also wanted to bring you up to date on the progress of the investigation."

Now he raised his head. He looked like a man recently returned from a trip to hell. "Fine. Go ahead."

"Do you think your wife would like to join us?"

"My wife." He spoke with a kind of bitter amusement. "My wife is currently next door in bed. I'm sure she'd love to hear a progress report, if only the doctor hadn't decided that the best way to keep her from harming herself—by which I assume he meant killing herself, although he was too polite to say so—was to fill her with tranquilizers." He lifted a hand toward his hairline, but Evelyn Cook intercepted it, lowered it to her lap, and held it between her own.

"I know it's difficult." Mrs. Cook spoke to Carpenter as if he were a child. "It's always difficult to watch someone you love suffer, and even more so when you're suffering yourself. But the police are doing everything possible to bring Bella back. We should—"

"No!" Carpenter yanked his hand back. "Let's not pretend. It's been over twenty-four hours. I used to be a journalist. I covered the Lee Boxell disappearance two years ago. I know what it means when the first twenty-four hours pass with no developments." Covering his face again, he began to sob.

Allen moved forward in her chair. "With respect, Mr. Carpenter, the two incidents are totally different. Lee Boxell was a teenager, out on the high street on a Saturday afternoon. Your daughter is an infant, taken in the middle of the night. That's much more likely to draw notice, much more likely to be remembered. My team is working as hard as they can to find Bella. Officers are talking to any and all possible witnesses, gathering all the information available. We're hoping someone saw something, but we're also trying to piece together possible scenarios for the abduction so we can explore those to find her. We're also speaking to everyone who lives in the surrounding properties, and I myself spent last night on the phone as part of an effort to gather background on everyone staying at or employed by this hotel. Moreover—"

But she broke off as she looked at his bowed head. There was no way she could interrupt such pain with something as matter-of-fact as a request for a blood test. Besides, she wasn't sure he was even listening.

She looked at the Cooks. "If you don't mind, I'd like to ask you some questions. In the corridor."

They nodded and rose. Allen followed. Carpenter didn't move.

When Allen reached the door, she stopped, looking at the top of his head. Glimpses of white scalp showed through greasy curls. "Mr. Carpenter, you don't need to stay here. The Met would be happy to put you up somewhere more"—she stopped herself before she said "pleasant"—"comfortable. Your in-laws, as well."

He looked up. His eyes were red and swollen. "Thank you, but that's not possible. Vivien won't move. Her parents already offered.

She thinks that whoever took Bella might bring her back, and she wants to be here when that happens." He snorted then raised a hand to his forehead again. Free from his mother-in-law's interference, he once more pushed his fingers into his hairline until the flesh of his scalp strained between them. This time, when he pulled the hand back down, Allen saw four scarlet crescents where his nails had been. "This is all my fault. I made a terrible mistake."

As a fellow human being, Allen longed to reach out and comfort him. As a police detective, she wasn't allowed to. She tried to put all her compassion into her voice instead.

"Sir, you are not responsible for what happened to your daughter. You opened a window on a hot night; anyone would have done the same. Only the person who took Bella is to blame here."

But he turned his face to the wall.

Out in the corridor, the Cooks stood a couple of yards from the door. As soon as Allen approached, Evelyn Cook began talking.

"I'm so sorry. Tom has never been . . . He's always been a pessimist. Vivien is the one who . . ." She ran a hand over her mouth. "This is terrible. Terrible. A horrible thing for them to have to bear. We were supposed to go to Wells next weekend to see them." With this sentence, all her brisk composure fled. Her chest began heaving. "It would have been our first time seeing Bella in three months!" She buried her face in her husband's shirtfront and sobbed.

Allen had seen collapses like this before. In her experience, they always happened to those who were strongest in the aftermath of a crime. Some people could hold themselves together as long as action needed to be taken or others needed comforting, but as soon as they had space to concentrate on themselves, they crumbled.

Mr. Cook put his arms around his wife. "That's right. Let it out. You've done enough for one day. I'll take it from here." He looked at Allen over his wife's head. "We've not seen Bella since May because we've been in Abu Dhabi for my work. I'm a petroleum engineer with BP. We only got back last week."

She nodded. "Mr. Cook, my men and I have been trying to figure out who might have wanted to take Bella. Usually infant abductions happen in hospital, and—forgive me for the painful image—soon after birth. Obviously Bella wasn't taken in those circumstances, but we're wondering if it might have been done by someone who saw her then and who was determined enough to keep track of your daughter and son-in-law until they saw their chance. Were you at the hospital for the birth?"

It was Cook's turn to nod.

"And did you notice anyone taking a particular interest in Bella? A nurse or nurse's aide who seemed a little too eager?"

He thought. "No, nothing like that."

"Or maybe you didn't see it yourself, but your daughter mentioned something to you? A health visitor who seemed unusually interested, who visited more than was strictly necessary?"

Mrs. Cook had stopped crying. She lifted her head. "Before we left, I spoke to Vivien almost every day. She never mentioned anything like that. I would have remembered."

Allen knew that abductions of children by strangers were vanishingly rare, abduction of infants by them even rarer. Yet the evidence, and the lack of evidence, was telling her that this was exactly what had happened. A stranger had taken the baby, and taken her from a room in a crowded hotel in a city the parents didn't live in, and while the parents were asleep in that room. Almost the first police acronym she'd learned as a probationer was "ABC": Accept nothing. Believe nothing. Challenge everything. It seemed that the Carpenter baby's disappearance was doing the challenging here. Bella had apparently been taken by an abductor with no previous contact, with no ransom demand or clue of any kind except the scrap from her sleep suit, and in an unbelievably risky way.

She remembered her original reason for bringing the Cooks out of the room.

"I'd like to ask for your assistance, if I could. Our Scene of Crime officers collected a piece of evidence from the scene."

"What kind of evidence?" Leonard Cook leaned forward.

"A drop of dried blood." At Evelyn Cook's gasp, she made her voice soothing. "Only one drop, on the window frame. Our Forensics team isn't even sure yet if it's connected to what happened. But the head of Forensics would like to have blood samples from your daughter and son-in-law, for elimination. It would help to begin the process of determining if the blood belongs to the person who took Bella. The technician would come here to take the samples."

"Will they check the DNA? The way they did to find the man who killed those two girls in Narborough?"

She swallowed. "As I understand it, at the moment they're testing blood type. That's a very quick process, whereas it can take a long time to get results back from DNA testing."

"I know people at the University of Leicester. I might be able to talk to Alec Jeffreys directly."

"Leonard, please." Evelyn Cook's voice was steady again. She straightened up and wiped her cheeks. To Allen she said, "We'll speak to Tom, and try to persuade Vivien. Of course we will. Should I ring you once they've agreed?"

Allen was writing Kate's name and the lab's telephone number on the back of one of her business cards when Patel's head appeared at the top of the stairs. Seeing her with the Cooks, he stopped. "Detective Inspector, there is a telephone call for you. He told me to tell you he's ringing from the station."

As she reached the bottom of the staircase, the lobby's clean scent greeted her. She breathed it in. Anything to clear her nostrils of the tiny sitting room's smell of unwashed skin and rancid fear.

She picked up the receiver from the reception desk. "Allen."

"Norton. You need to get back here."

No "ma'am," no "guv," not a request but an order. She made her voice cold. "I'm updating the parents. What's so important that it can't wait?"

He didn't change his tone. "One of the neighbors saw something. We've got a suspect."

12

Margaret Derryman was an A&E nurse at St. Thomas's Hospital in Westminster, and the previous day her shift had begun at 6 a.m. The heat had brought a tidal wave of cases to Casualty: dehydration, heatstroke, injuries from arguments that might have resolved themselves in cooler times but turned violent at ninety degrees. Because of this she had been drafted in to work back-to-back shifts, and it wasn't until early that morning that she'd arrived back at her flat to discover a photocopied sheet shoved under her door, asking anyone who might have information related to a kidnapping from the Bellevue Hotel the previous day to call the number below. Of course she'd heard about the kidnapping. The television was on all the time in the ward's break room. She'd rung the number right away.

"Carter spoke to her." Norton handed Allen the report. "She lives on the top floor of Egerton House, on the corner across from the Bellevue. Front flat. It seems that while she was getting ready for work yesterday, around 5 a.m., she looked out her window and saw a woman come out the hotel's front door. She said the woman was carrying a bundle and moving quickly."

Allen felt relief course through her. A lead at last. Then good sense took its place. Not much of a lead without more. "Was she able to see this woman's face?"

"She wasn't. According to Carter, she said it was too dark, and she was too high up. But she said the woman was, and I quote, 'of African descent.'" He rolled his eyes. "And she was wearing one of those draped scarf things some of them wear around their heads. So I had Carter check with Viner to see how many of the women who work at the Bellevue are Black Muslims, and how many of those were working Wednesday night."

The answer turned out to be two: Faduma Isaaq and Abeba Bayu. Norton had sent Carter to Bayu's home and another officer to Isaaq's.

Out at her flat on the Mozart Estate in Kensal Green, Abeba Bayu wasn't in, but her son was. He worked as a night porter at the Chelsea Barracks. If his mother had an overnight shift, he picked her up on his way home from work, and they rode the 6A bus home together. The previous day he'd collected her from outside the Bellevue Hotel at 4:20 in the morning. When they arrived home, his grandmother made them breakfast. The grandmother backed up the young man's story. When Carter pressed for a more reliable alibi, the son rummaged around in his pockets and managed to find two bus tickets, date-stamped and numbered. Although, Norton added, they could have taken the baby on the bus with them.

"The Mozart Estate is a good forty-five minutes away from the hotel," Allen pointed out. "That's a hell of a long way on a bus with a scared and hungry baby."

Norton kept on as if she hadn't spoken. No one had answered the door at Faduma Isaaq's flat, but just as the officer was leaving, the woman who lived opposite appeared and stopped him. "Fair knocked him over she was so excited to see him," Norton said. "One of those old ones who likes nothing better than spying on her neighbors. Probably she was thrilled to have someone to report to at last. According to her, she saw Mrs. Isaaq come home at dawn yesterday morning."

"She was looking out her window at dawn?"

He consulted a sheet headed "Witness Statement." "She told Carter she woke up to go to the bathroom then couldn't get back to sleep. So she decided to make a cup of tea and watch the sun rise. And while she was drinking her tea, she saw Isaaq coming along the breezeway, and, I quote, 'haring along and carrying something in her arms.'"

In her arms. Now, that was promising. "All right. And where did all this take place? Where does Isaaq live?" If it was as far away as the Mozart Estate, there was no point in pursuing it.

"Churchill Gardens."

Only ten minutes from Belgrave Road by bus or foot. It was more plausible. But still . . .

"Well, it's hardly conclusive, is it? Leaving work late and a bundle seen by a nosy neighbor don't make a kidnapping."

Norton raised an eyebrow.

"Well, then perhaps you'll be interested in what Viner discovered when I had him cross-check Faduma Isaaq with Immigration."

Viner had been standing next to Norton the whole time. Now he flipped open his pad. "According to Immigration, Faduma Isaaq emigrated from Somalia last summer, fleeing a massacre. Government soldiers executed her husband, but she, her daughter, and her mother-in-law managed to escape. They applied for refugee status when they arrived at the port of Dover. The application was approved last September. In October, they were moved out of temporary housing and into a council flat in Churchill Gardens, and in March Isaaq started working at the Bellevue. The local immigrant aid society got her the job."

"So she's an immigrant with a terrible past. Are immigrants automatically baby-nappers? Or are Black immigrants?"

Viner's face said he would very much answer yes to one or both of those questions, but Allen didn't give him a chance. "I'm hearing a sad story, but I'm not hearing anything that says she must be our kidnapper. Is there more?"

"You could say." Viner snapped the pad shut. "The reason Isaaq, the daughter, and the mother-in-law are all that's left of the family is because when the soldiers shot her husband, he was holding their baby, and the bullet killed the baby too." He closed his folder. "She was five months old."

Both he and Norton watched her.

Allen closed her eyes and focused on the dot in the distance. The revelation was shocking and seemed significant, but her time living with a Crown prosecutor had taught her more than just how to share a wardrobe. As evidence, Viner's discovery was hardly definitive.

"That's certainly interesting. But not much more. We bring her in on that and it turns out we're wrong, any solicitor will make sure we don't get a second chance."

"Due respect, guv"—Viner's voice was tight. Allen could feel whatever goodwill she'd built up with him vanishing—"but the old lady's statement and the background are enough to get her here, and that's all we need now. The interview is where we get the rest."

"'Suggestive,' I think the university criminology courses call this kind of information," Norton said. "Then the right kind of interview brings out the confession."

It was the *right kind of interview* that worried Allen. She had in fact done a unit on coerced confessions at university, and now the Guildford Four and Derek Bentley danced waltzes in her head. What's more, the memory of what had happened with the Patels the previous day was fresh in her mind. She made her voice crisp. "I'm reluctant to bring in a witness on fragile evidence and then exert pressure that could cause problems on appeal. Not to mention that bringing this woman in pulls manpower away from the search for the baby."

"Yes, guv." Norton nodded. "I can see how you wouldn't want to risk it."

He put a whisper of emphasis on "you." Was he suggesting that because she was a woman she would prize finding the baby over capturing the abductor? Or was he taking a dig at her overall courage? It didn't really matter. He'd made his point.

She looked at her watch. 11:30 a.m. Bella Carpenter had been missing for more than twenty-nine hours. She glanced at Viner's irritated face; she heard Beck talking about highest urgency and swift clear-up; she thought of the fiasco in the Bellevue lounge and what it would mean to have a career-maker right now. How it would set up her future.

"All right. Viner, bring her in." He started to turn, but she put out a hand. "If she still isn't home, sit on the flat until she is. And once you have her, make it clear that we're just asking her in for chat. Don't give her the idea that she needs a solicitor. Radio in when you're on your way back." She lifted her chin at Norton. "My office in ten minutes for interview prep."

13

It was clear both that Faduma Isaaq was terrified and that she was determined not to show it. Below the dark purple hijab that encircled her face, her eyes were huge with fear, and she bit hard into her lower lip. But she sat very tall, with her hands folded on the table in front of her.

"Look," Allen had said to Norton half an hour earlier. She'd had time only for an awkward wash in the ladies' room sink and a quick check to make sure that none of her clothing was obviously sweat-stained before Irene from reception had rung through to let her know that Viner was on his way. Now she stood in front of a hand mirror she'd propped on her office shelves, trying to smooth her hair back into a bun while they talked. "We need to use a soft touch here."

"I don't see why." Leaning against a wall, Norton watched her the way she imagined a cat observed the clumsy humans around it. "Viner said the baby wasn't on the premises. We want to know where she's stashed it, and a softly-softly approach will cost us time. It's already been almost thirty hours."

Allen looked at him in the little mirror. If he'd been a different sort of man—a different sort of person—she might have told him about Sergeant Pebworth's advice. But Norton didn't seem like someone who had much time for words of wisdom unless they lined up with the way he liked to do things. So she just said, "*If* she took the baby, a light touch might persuade her to tell us where she is. And if she didn't take the baby and we go in guns blazing, we're likely to forfeit our chance to learn anything useful she knows about other possible suspects."

"There isn't anyone else. There's this crazy girl who went mad when her kid got shot in front of her and who snatched the Carpenter baby to make up the difference. If we lean on her hard enough she'll crack and tell us what she's done with the kiddie. The briefs can sort it out from there." Norton pushed himself off the wall. "Guv."

The door rattled on its hinges as he shut it behind him.

Allen thrust in the last hairpin then crossed to her desk and picked up the telephone. "Send a DC to Interview Room 3 to take notes, please. Sergeant Norton is unable to assist." She thought of the smooth rides in the car the previous day. "Send DC Desbury, if you can."

Now Faduma Isaaq sat at the table in front of an untouched cup of tea, the interpreter she'd been provided with next to her. Across the table sat Allen, Desbury next to her with pad and pen.

Under the fluorescent light, Isaaq's round eyes and apple cheeks made her look very young. Allen felt even more certain that she needed to be gentle.

"Thank you for coming in." She smiled.

The other woman's expression didn't change. On the Formica tabletop, the nails of her folded hands were white where her fingertips pressed into her skin.

"As you know, we've asked you to help us with our inquiries regarding the disappearance of Bella Carpenter from the Bellevue Hotel yesterday morning. You're aware of that disappearance?"

Isaaq nodded. For a moment, fabric hid her face.

"Now, this is what we call an investigative interview. That means there's no tape on, no camera, nothing more than DC Desbury here taking notes. You don't need to worry."

"I understand." Isaaq's voice was soft, her accent heavy, but she spoke clearly.

"You work at the Bellevue Hotel, isn't that right?"

Another nod.

"And how long have you worked there?"

A pause, then, "I have started in March. I have been there for five months."

"Tell me how you got the job. Did you apply at the hotel, or go through an agency, or did you find it some other way?"

"Through the . . . Through my . . ." She turned and spoke to the interpreter. The woman bobbed her head up and down as she listened then turned to Allen. "The refugee assistance center in her area listed the job. She interviewed with an agency, and they recommended her."

So far, everything matched the information they had. Allen proceeded through a series of questions designed to relax Isaaq. How did she find working at the Bellevue? How were the Patels as employers? Were the guests generally polite? None of these appeared to have the desired effect. Isaaq's teeth continued to bore into her bottom lip, and the skin beneath her nails grew whiter and whiter. But her answers were straightforward and her body language didn't suggest deception. She was terrified, certainly, but Allen didn't see any signs of guilt.

Perhaps that would change as Allen approached her goal. She cleared her throat. "Now, the hotel timetable shows that you were working there from 8 p.m. on Wednesday to 4 a.m. on Thursday. Could you tell me what you did during that time? Let's say from when you left for work on Wednesday to when you came home on Thursday."

Isaaq frowned for a second, then began haltingly. "I take the number 11 bus from where I live. Always early, because I want to be on time. Then, at the hotel, Mr. Patel ask me to . . ." She made a motion with her hand as if placing something on the table then said something to the interpreter.

"She laid the tables for breakfast."

"Yes, I laid the tables for breakfast." Isaaq lingered over the words, memorizing them for future use. "Then I clean empty rooms that will be used tomorrow. Then I make the trolleys for the morning ladies. Soaps, tea, and coffee in the top. Towels and sheets in the bottom."

"At any time while you were working, did you see this couple with this baby?" Allen laid on the table an enlargement of the photo Carpenter had given her, facing Isaaq.

The woman flinched and turned her head away. She muttered to the interpreter.

"She doesn't like to look at babies."

Allen made her tone kind. "I'm sorry. But I need you to look at this one."

Isaaq turned her head back for a second, looked down, then turned away again. "No." Then, clearly, "No, I never see those people."

"You didn't see them in the lounge?" A shake of the head. "Or later, when you were tidying the rooms?" Another shake.

"All right. Thank you." Allen turned the enlargement over. "Now, please tell me what you did when your shift ended."

The air in the room changed. Isaaq's hands began to quiver. Seeing Allen glance at them, she slipped them into her lap and looked down. Now only the purple top of her headscarf showed. Finally she said stiffly, "When it is time to go, I use the key Mr. Patel gives us to leave. Then I catch the number 11 bus home."

She was a bad liar. But most people who were bad liars were bad liars because they didn't lie very often. They only did it when they truly needed to—when they had something important to hide. Allen felt her skin prickle, but she kept her voice soothing. "You're certain, Mrs. Isaaq? You're certain that right after your shift you left the hotel, and you went directly home on the number 11 bus?"

"It is not 'missus.'" Isaaq sat up straight and frowned. "Isaaq is my name. It was my father's name. In Somalia, this is how we do."

But Allen recognized redirection when she heard it, and she refused to be distracted. "Thank you for explaining that. In that case, *Ms.* Isaaq. Ms. Isaaq, you're sure you left the hotel right after your shift, and you went directly home on the bus?"

Isaaq licked her lips, bit the lower one again, then released it. "Yes. That is what I did."

"Then can you explain why a woman who lives across the street from the Bellevue Hotel says she saw you leaving there at 5 a.m., an hour after your shift ended?"

Isaaq looked down then back up. Allen saw a drop of blood on her lower lip. "She must be wrong if she says this. I am not the only one who worked this shift. Mrs. Bayu did also. Perhaps this lady saw her."

Allen shook her head, took three typed sheets from the folder in front of her, and laid them in front of Isaaq. "Mrs. Abeba Bayu was picked up by her son outside the hotel at 4:20 a.m. That's his statement on the top. He said there was no one with his mother when he arrived, and no one came out before they left. A witness who lives across the road from the hotel saw what she describes as a woman of African descent leaving by the front door at 5 a.m. She says the woman was carrying a bundle, although it was too dark for her to see any more. Her statement is under Mr. Bayu's. Another witness saw you arrive at your flat at Keats House just as the sun was rising yesterday morning. That was around 5:45 a.m. She also says you were carrying a bundle. 'Cradling it in your arms,' in her words. Her statement is at the bottom. You can read them all." She looked at the interpreter. "Could you help her with all that, please?"

The woman spoke to Isaaq, pointing at the statements. Isaaq shook her head, then shook it again. She turned to Allen. "No. This is not me." Lifting her hands from her lap, she thrust the pile back at Allen. Turning back to the interpreter, she spoke intently. Eventually she stopped to draw breath.

The interpreter turned to Allen. "She says the neighbors on her landing are always spying on her. They gossip about her and make up stories that aren't true. And she says she's never even seen anyone who lives across from the hotel. She wants to know how someone can identify her if they've never met?"

Isaaq stared at Allen, her chin jutting.

Allen began to consider that maybe Norton was right, after all, and gentleness wasn't the answer. She gave a frosty smile. "Ms. Isaaq would have made an excellent barrister. She's done a fine job of discrediting our witnesses. But I notice that she still hasn't been able to do the simple thing I asked and explain how Ms. Derryman could have seen her at 5 a.m. If these witnesses are wrong, it will help you much more, Ms. Isaaq, if you just tell me where you were at five o'clock yesterday morning."

Again the interpreter whispered to her, but this time the response came immediately, and in English. "I was on my bus."

"I see. The number 11 bus stops on Belgrave Road at 4:23 a.m. and again at 5:03 a.m. You were on the 4:23?"

Isaaq began to nod, then stopped. She said something to the interpreter.

"The bus was late. Perhaps this woman at the hotel saw her while she was waiting for it to arrive and confused the time. Once it arrived, she stayed on it all the way to her stop."

Allen shook her head. "I don't think so. Because while we were waiting for Ms. Isaaq to arrive here, I had one of my men check with London Buses. Both the 4:23 bus and the one at 5:03 ran perfectly to timetable yesterday." She had no idea if this was true, but she had run out of patience. The woman was hiding something, and it seemed increasingly likely that it was something about Bella Carpenter's disappearance. Norton had been right: They were losing precious time.

She leaned forward and tried to make her voice sympathetic. "Ms. Isaaq, I'll be honest with you. I think you aren't telling me the truth. I know about what happened to you in Somalia. I know the way our pasts can make us do things. If there's anything you'd like to say to me, I promise I'll understand."

Another translation. Then Isaaq said something that sounded like "Garyakan."

Allen looked at the interpreter, who turned to her. "That means 'solicitor.'"

Norton was waiting in the corridor. A muttered exchange with Desbury and he strode toward her. "I told you! I told you it would be this Bl—"—he remembered Desbury—"this foreign bitch."

"It isn't anyone, yet." But Allen could feel her own heart knocking against her breastbone. In her experience, innocent interviewees didn't ask for solicitors. "Go ring the duty solicitor's office and tell them to get someone up here." As he set off down the corridor, she switched her attention to Desbury. "Ten minutes. Make the most of it. I'll be in my office if you need me."

Back at her desk, she noticed that the phone's message light was blinking. She hit speaker and punched in her voicemail code.

There was a message from Kate, left at 12:22 that afternoon. "Just to let you know that the father's agreed to a blood test. The woman who rang said we might be able to do the mother, too, but apparently she's very fragile. I'm sending the tech over now."

14

The duty solicitor, Isaaq, and the interpreter huddled together. Allen had turned off the microphone so the three could confer, and the silently moving lips, the background of gray carpet and white walls, and the colors bleached by the fluorescent light made her feel like she was watching a silent movie. She half expected a title card to appear: *The Suspect Confides in Her Lawyer.*

She popped the last square of Cadbury Fruit & Nut in her mouth and checked her watch: 1:10 p.m. "Right. That's the time the brief asked for done. Let's get cracking."

When she opened the door, the three people at the table sprang apart. The solicitor ran a hand over his smooth brown hair, settled his face into impersonal passivity, and nodded acknowledgment. Allen nodded back and sat.

"Ms. Isaaq, at this point I'm going to give you the standard police caution, and I'm going to begin taping this interview. This is to protect everyone in this room, including you." She recited the caution, and as the interpreter murmured it to Isaaq, Allen snapped the tape on then listed those present. When she looked across the table, Isaaq was almost vibrating with fear.

The solicitor held up a forestalling hand. "Before my client says anything, she wants your assurance that she won't be sent back to Somalia."

Isaaq let out a keening wail. "They will kill me there! They are waiting to kill me!"

Allen groped in her brain for the rules of deportation. "The Metropolitan Police Service doesn't make deals for information. But I can assure you that Ms. Isaaq's previous experiences in Somalia will be taken into account in any court." She looked directly at the woman across the table and spoke slowly. "And such a court will also look positively on anything you tell us that will help us find Bella Carpenter."

Isaaq shook her head. "You do not understand! I said I never saw that child. I have . . . I do . . ." She began speaking rapidly to the interpreter, her voice rising. The woman put a hand on her arm and whispered something. Isaaq put her head in her hands.

The interpreter turned to Allen. "I told her that without a complete explanation there's no way she can leave here. But, as you can see, she's terrified. She doesn't understand that—"

But Isaaq had somehow gathered herself together. Now she put a hand on the interpreter's arm. She raised her head and looked at Allen, then leaned forward.

"My mother-in-law is ill. Ill here." She touched her temple. "She does not talk. She will not wash herself or eat for herself. I must have someone to watch her when I am at work. And she cannot watch my daughter, so someone must also look after her." She shook her head. "I do not complain. I am very grateful to Mr. Patel. He pays me good. But it is not enough."

What did any of this have to do with Bella Carpenter? Had Isaaq taken her for money? If so, why hadn't there been a ransom demand? Or had someone given her money to take Bella for them? "Your circumstances don't interest us at the moment," Allen said. If Isaaq was trying to build a defense that she'd taken Bella while under some kind of duress, now was not the time. A court would rule on that once she entered her plea. All that mattered now was recovering the baby. "We just want to find Bella."

The solicitor said, "My client isn't talking about the Carpenter abduction."

Tired, confused, and flooded with a rush of energy from the chocolate, Allen lost the temper she'd held on to so far. "Then what is she talking about? Because if she can't explain right now what she was doing inside the hotel for an hour after her shift finished, and what was in the bundle two witnesses saw her carrying, I'm going to arrest her!"

"She's talking about washing."

Allen thought she must have misheard. "Pardon me?"

"Washing. She was using the hotel laundry to do washing that she takes in to make extra money. She didn't want to tell you because she didn't ask permission of the hotel owner, and because the job is off the books. She's convinced she'll be sent back to Somalia because she's committing a crime."

"Oh, for God's sake." Allen pushed back from the table and stood. "We're not Immigration. We're not going to deport her for a fiddle on the side. If she'd told us this right at the start we could have used the time we've wasted here to find Bella Carpenter." She grabbed Desbury's pad and slid it across the table toward the solicitor. "Have your client write down the names and whatever contact information she has for her washing-service customers. My detective constable here will check them out while my sergeant goes through her story with her again."

Once again, Norton was in the corridor. "She wasn't carrying a baby," she snarled at him. "She was carrying washing. So much for your bright idea to bring her in."

He raised his eyebrows. "With respect, guv, I wasn't the one who gave the order. I made a suggestion and offered plausible evidence, but final decisions are the responsibility of the SIO."

He was right. As far as command was concerned, this fiasco was all down to her. My God, first the padlock and now this! Two failures in twenty-four hours, the baby still missing, and nothing to show for any of their digging. She barely made it to the sinks in the ladies' before she began to vomit, grinding retches that continued even after there was nothing left to bring up.

Once the nausea subsided, she rested her head against the cold metal of the taps. Why, why, had she allowed herself to get caught up in this desperate witch hunt? She groped for a rationalization, then admitted the truth. She'd given in to insecurity, to Beck, to the challenge of that stupid, stupid newspaper caption. No, right at this moment she was *not* the face for the case.

An hour later, Desbury slipped a stack of neat notes onto her desk. He'd managed to track down seven of the names Isaaq had given, all fellow Somalis who lived on the Churchill Gardens estate, and they'd all confirmed that they paid her to do some of their washing. "More out of pity than need, one said, ma'am." He'd passed the information on to Norton, and that, along with the fact that her explanation never wavered no matter how many times she repeated it, had been enough to send Isaaq home.

Allen supposed she could be thankful for that, just as she was both grateful for and impressed by the speed of Desbury's investigative work. But neither of those could change the fact that she knew the grapevine had been working since she'd left the interrogation room. By now, everyone knew the girl had fucked it up.

15

"No one is blaming you." Commander Parker brushed invisible dust off the blotter. Beck had asked him to sit in on the meeting, and he'd taken the chair behind the desk as a matter of course. Apparently he was even more fastidious than its usual occupant. Now, satisfied with his ministrations, he folded his hands on the immaculate surface and continued. "You remain the SIO. But the current approach isn't yielding results as quickly as we'd like, so we've decided to add another one. A public appeal. They can have great impact."

You mean they can have a great impact on public perception, Allen thought. Whether they were actually effective was another question. In her first weeks as a WPC, she had been assigned to assist on a murder investigation. After a month with no result, the station's chief super had authorized a public appeal and tip line. When the squad room heard, a collective groan went up. Her assigned mentor there had been Sergeant Tom Bateman, a thirty-year veteran of Vice and Murder. He'd never hidden his contempt for her—she supposed she had to give him credit for his honesty, at least. She'd dealt with the problem by asking him the fewest number of questions possible, writing them down and instead slipping into the police library at the end of her shifts to look up the answers. But no book was going to tell her why a room full of officers moaned at the idea of appealing to the public for information. So she risked Bateman's sneer to ask.

"Because most people who respond to an appeal are vindictive, mistaken, or nutters. Some slut wants to get her ex-boyfriend into trouble; a man saw your missing blond teenager in Brighton, and when you go down there it turns out she's a forty-year-old brunette; some old biddy reckons Queen Victoria appeared to her and told her we need to search Loch Ness." He shook his head. "The higher ranks love an appeal because it makes the public think we're doing something, but the men who answer the phones know they'd be better off using the time to follow up real leads." He shuffled some papers and held them out to her. "Archiving."

Now Beck was saying, "We've arranged it for tonight, just after the six o'clock news. We'd like the parents to make the appeal live on camera, with a member of the force giving a statement after with the tip-line number and reward information. We've been working out a reward amount with the CPS, and Carpenter's employers have generously offered to make a contribution. Print and other media will be present, so it'll get full coverage in tomorrow's papers. Maximum reach, maximum results." His eyes shone.

Allen frowned. "I don't think Mrs. Carpenter is in any condition to appear in front of cameras, sir. According to what her husband told me earlier, she's nearly catatonic."

"Oh, you'd be surprised how mothers perk up when it comes to their children." Beck shrugged. "Or she can just sit next to him. Loving father pleading for information about his baby daughter with the mother clinging to his side? The public will be falling all over themselves to help."

Please don't let him move any further up the ranks. But she looked at his immaculate uniform and generically handsome face, the way he managed to sit loosely enough to suggest he was comfortable with the commander but not so loosely as to suggest they were equals, and she knew he would rise. He had what it took.

She resigned herself to the inevitable. "Very good, sir. And I assume the media liaison will draft my statement?"

"DCI Beck will lead the appeal." Parker leaned back in his chair. "As you know, the Metropolitan Police Survey shows that ninety percent of the public prefer to see a male officer as the face of an important investigation. We think his presence will improve response levels. But not to worry." He offered a smile. "Sergeant Norton mentioned you've been liaising with the family, so we thought you'd be the logical choice to speak to them about appearing. Impress on them how much the appeal will help. Get a firm commitment. And after you do that, you can nip home for a bit." He made it sound like a birthday treat. "You've been working since the call came in yesterday morning, isn't that right? That's almost thirty-six hours straight. Take a couple of hours to freshen up, watch the appeal from the comfort of your own home, then come back to follow up."

When Mr. Patel ushered Allen into the suite's cramped sitting room half an hour later, she was surprised to find Vivien Carpenter next to her husband on the sofa, her mother on the other side of her. She sat ramrod straight, wearing an obviously new Laura Ashley dress and with her still-damp hair pulled back from her face in a tortoiseshell clip. She was almost unrecognizable as the woman Allen had encountered the previous day.

She barely let Allen finish making Beck's request before she responded.

"Yes. Yes, we'll do it." She seemed to rise from the sofa cushions, as if she thought a film crew was waiting outside the door. "You said it'll go out on national television?"

Allen nodded.

"Then of course we'll do it. Everyone watches television these days. Doesn't everyone watch television these days, Mum?" She didn't wait for an answer. She began making the same gesture she had the previous morning, her left hand scraping down the back of her right, her right hand grinding down on the back of her left. "I remember reading somewhere that even people who can't afford to eat properly have a television. So we'll reach everyone. Or even if the person who took Bella doesn't have a television, they could still watch it in a pub, or at a friend's, or maybe in a shop window, and they'd see us that way. Or maybe they'll see a photograph in a newspaper. You did say it would be in the papers, too, didn't you?" Allen opened her mouth, but again Mrs. Carpenter didn't pause. "So they'd see it there. Even if they don't buy a paper they'd see the front page if they go in a shop. Or maybe if someone left a paper on a bus, or a bench, they'd pick it up. And they'll see Tom and me, and see how much we love Bella and how much we want her back, and that could be just the thing. The thing that makes them bring her back to me. Don't you think so, Tom? Don't you think that could be just the thing?" At last she stopped. Two burning circles stood out in her cheeks. Her brown eyes were open so wide that the whites showed all around the irises.

"Yes." Carpenter sighed. "Yes, that could be just the thing." He glanced at Allen. "So of course we'll do it."

She rose. "DCI Beck will be very pleased to hear that. He has high hopes that an appeal will draw out more witnesses."

She'd promised herself not to get involved. If Beck and Parker wanted her to do their work for them, she'd do that and nothing more. But listening to Vivien Carpenter's fevered voice and watching her hands made her feel she needed to do something. It didn't matter how much people pitied the Carpenters or sympathized with their pain. On television, Vivien Carpenter would come across as a madwoman, and people's first instinct with the mad was to flinch away. She caught Carpenter's eye and tilted her head toward the corridor.

Once outside, he shut the door behind him. "The doctor was afraid to keep her under sedation any longer. She's been like this since she woke up. At lunch, she started talking about how we should put posters on every lamppost in London asking if people had seen Bella. She wanted to go to the planning office to find out how many lampposts there are so we could run off photocopies and start right away."

"If you want her to make the appeal with you, get the doctor back here. Or get another doctor. She can't go on television like that. She needs something that will calm her down in the next"—she checked her watch: 4 p.m.—"two hours. Something that will make her more"—she hated even saying the word—"accessible."

"Accessible." For a second Carpenter looked as if he were going to burst out laughing, and Allen thought she'd have two hysterical parents on her hands. But he just shook his head. "What a fucking mess. She'll never recover from this."

Giving in to instinct for a moment, Allen put a hand on his shoulder. "She will if she gets Bella back. But that won't happen unless you can calm her down."

He looked dubious, but he nodded. "All right. I'll ask for the doctor to come back."

16

On the television screen in Allen and Phil's living room, the buttons on Beck's uniform gleamed. When he turned to murmur to Carpenter, his profile was firm, his gaze attentive and sympathetic. He looked every inch the capable, compassionate authority figure, determined to do whatever was necessary to return Bella Carpenter to her parents.

Allen had managed an hour's nap. Then Phil, just home from work, had offered to run out for fish and chips while she was in the shower. By the time he'd returned, she'd managed to dry herself off and slip on the huge black T-shirt that she liked to wear around the flat; she felt almost human again. Now they sat side by side on the sofa, Allen crossing her legs under her and holding bits of battered fish with her fingernails to avoid making her shower-clean fingers greasy. She saw the televised Beck raise a hand, appealing for silence in the face of a barrage of popping camera flashes. His expression was patient but expectant, his hand relaxed but ready to turn firm. As much as she hated to admit it, even she felt reassured by his presence.

But the Carpenters seemed beyond reassurance. Tom Carpenter looked as if he were heading to his own execution. His face was gray and drawn, his eyes bloodshot; he rolled his lips in and out between his teeth. He wore the same clothes he'd been wearing for the past thirty-six hours, and sweat stood out on a forehead shiny with grease. Next to him, his wife hunched in her chair. It seemed the doctor had been willing to sedate her again, because she sat silent and unmoving. The only remaining traces of the woman Allen had seen were the floral dress and the pulled-back hair, and even the hair was deteriorating, strands beginning to make a frizzy halo around her face. Carpenter held one of her hands as she pressed her lips with the other. While he spoke, she gazed ahead at nothing.

"We love our daughter, Bella, and we miss her. Bella is a good baby. She's brought so much happiness to her mother and to me. If you have Bella, or if you think you've seen Bella or might know who has our daughter, please let us know. We're desperate. Having our daughter, Bella, back would mean everything to us."

Phil frowned. "Why does he keep saying her name like that? And calling her 'our daughter'?"

"He's trying to personalize her. The media liaison will have coached him. The idea is to make the abductor realize that they've taken a human being, and taken her from two other human beings who love her. It might prompt them to return her out of guilt, or pity."

On the screen, Carpenter had begun to cry, crushing a tissue against his eyes. After a moment, he wiped them, then swiped at his nose before squeezing the tissue in his fist. "Bella is our daughter. Please bring her back to us. We love our daughter, Bella."

Vivien Carpenter gave a sudden start. She began to make a noise that was at first only a keen but then resolved itself into words—or one word, endlessly repeated: "Bella-Bella-Bella-Bella." Even the cameraman must have found it unbearable to watch because the picture gave a sickening lurch and then Beck was on-screen, looking stricken. He quickly collected himself, pulling his microphone toward him and beginning to read from a sheet of paper.

"A photograph of Bella Carpenter will shortly appear on your television screen. She was wearing a pink knit sleep suit when she disappeared from the Bellevue Hotel on Belgrave Road in Pimlico sometime between 3 a.m. and 6:15 a.m. yesterday, Thursday, the second of August. She is five months old and has dark hair and brown eyes. If you have any information that might lead to her return, please call . . ." As he recited the number, it flashed up on the screen next to the familiar photograph of Bella's face. "The Metropolitan Police are offering a reward of five thousand pounds for any information that leads to Bella's return and the capture of her abductor. Mr. Carpenter's employer, Glaister Properties, has contributed another five thousand pounds.

This makes a total of ten thousand pounds' reward for any information leading to the return of Bella Carpenter and the apprehension of her abductor. Please contact us if you believe you have any useful information. Thank you."

After a second, the ITV logo appeared.

"They consulted me on that." Phil ate the last of his chips. "The reward."

"They did?"

He nodded and swallowed. "As a CPS representative. This morning. They've never had an infant abduction, and they weren't sure what they should offer."

"I don't think they'll need to worry about paying it out."

He looked confused. Then his face cleared. "The Sergeant Bateman principle? You think the appeal won't help?"

"Partly that. But also . . . it's an abduction, not a kidnapping. There's been no ransom demand. If someone didn't take her for money, I don't think they're going to return her for money. And even if a reward would make a difference, it seems too soon for a public appeal to me."

"What do you mean?"

"I mean, all right, we made a mistake with . . ." She couldn't bring herself to finish. "We made a mistake earlier. But we still haven't completed background checks on all the other hotel employees, or finished going over the notes from our first interviews with the guests." She frowned, considering. "Or maybe it seems too *late* for an appeal. We're up to around thirty-six hours since disappearance now, and there's been so much publicity that I think if someone had seen Bella or wanted to report the person who took her, they'd have done it." Another frown, another reconsideration. "Or maybe you're right, and I just never think it's the right time for a public appeal."

Phil stole a chip from her heap. "I didn't say that. But also, I'm not sure it's too early, or too late. You can keep a baby out of sight for a day pretty easily. After that, though, it gets harder. Babies make noise, and they need a lot of things that are specifically for babies. And they make *a lot* of rubbish. One nosy neighbor at the supermarket, one split bin bag showing an unexpected nappy or baby-food container . . . People are going to notice. Your friends are going to notice. Your *family* is going to notice. A public appeal might make them think, then call in."

It was a fair point, so Allen nodded. But she didn't agree with him. She thought Bella Carpenter was already dead, she realized. She didn't know whether it was a result of her pregnancy or of her involvement with the case, but something in her had changed over the past two days. For the first time, she understood how fragile babies were, how easily and even accidentally they could be harmed. It wasn't an intellectual awareness; it came as a sudden knife thrust into her gut. She *felt* the knowledge. The kidnapper might not have meant to kill Bella, but they didn't need to. All it would take was one slip on the fire escape that knocked the baby's head into the railings, one silencing hand accidentally placed over her mouth and nose, even a too-tight squeeze that pressed her face into a shirtfront for a fraction too long. There were too many ways to kill her for her to still be alive. All they could do now was try to find her murderer and bring her parents some peace. But this seemed too awful, too defeatist, and above all too emotional for a detective inspector to say to a Crown prosecutor.

The ringing of the telephone saved her.

It was her mother. "Sweet pea, Daddy and I just saw the press conference. Yesterday's *Evening Standard* made it sound as if you were in charge. Who's this man they had up there?"

"That's DCI Beck. I told you about him, remember? The powers-that-be felt people would be more likely to respond if they saw a man in charge. Apparently it's more reassuring."

"Oh. Well, that's just silly." Her mother's voice implied that no one could be more reassuring to the public than her daughter. Then Allen heard her put her hand over the receiver, and her voice became muffled. "Les, it was a superior officer. She says the Met thinks people respond better if a man's in charge." A rumbling in the background, then her mother took away her hand. "Daddy wants to know if you want him to write a letter."

Some fathers watched football in their free time; some tinkered with cars. Allen's father wrote letters to the newspapers. He used them to share reminiscences, or to correct something in an article, or to express outrage. The corrective ones and the outraged ones had never brought about any change. As far as Allen knew, they'd never even brought a response. But her father maintained a firm belief in the power of a letter to the paper.

"No, that's all right. Tell him thanks, but I don't think it'll do any good."

More rumbling. "Or should he write to the Met, he says?"

"No!" That was the last thing she needed in her file: an angry letter from her father. "No, thanks but no. I'm fine about it, truly."

"All right." Her mother sounded relieved. "How are you, otherwise? We didn't want to phone because we thought you'd be too busy."

"You were right. I've hardly been home in the past thirty-six or so hours, and I don't anticipate being home much in the next twenty-four. But otherwise I'm fine." She and Phil had decided not to tell their families about the pregnancy until the end of the first trimester. They'd read that after that, miscarriage was much less likely.

"Yes, there's nothing much to report here either. Except that Caroline has a second interview for that job I told you about."

Caroline was Allen's younger sister, for the past three years locked in a losing battle with her mother to be called Carrie. She'd interviewed for a job as a copywriter the previous week. Allen listened while her mother explained that Caroline had been required to come up with taglines for a new type of detergent to present at the interview, then while she brought her up to date on the activities of her brother Greg, Greg's wife Mary, and their daughter Sasha. Allen loved her mother and her siblings, but as the minutes passed she began to feel the tug of the incident room. Time was slipping away. When she turned around, she saw that *Wogan* had started. It was seven o'clock, and she'd been home since four thirty.

"Mum, I need to go."

"Oh, of course! Sorry, what am I doing? Those poor parents! Good luck. Love to Phil."

"My mum sends her love." She put the phone down. "I should go back."

"Already?" Phil's face fell.

"I'm sorry. I wish I could stay all night. But Parker told me to come back in after the appeal to follow up on any results. So I have to go sort through the angry girlfriends and the nutters and the old biddies." She smiled at him, sharing the reference.

He returned the smile but said, "A male DI wouldn't go back."

She felt her face tighten. "A male DI wouldn't have been told to."

17

It was dark outside the Bellevue Hotel, and the street was silent. As Allen walked down the hotel steps, she noticed for the first time how close the building was to Warwick Square. Warwick Square had a garden, one of those small areas of enclosed greenery that dotted London and were accessible only by keys handed out to residents. Had the team been able to borrow a key and search it? She couldn't remember, but if they hadn't, it was an enormous oversight. God knows what they might have missed.

She crossed the road and put her hand on the gate. It swung open. She stepped through.

The garden was overgrown. Stray ferns and softly leaved branches stretched into the unlit paths like long fingers. She put out her hand, felt something grab it. Yanking it back, she found it covered in sticky spiderweb. She wiped her arm on her hip and walked on.

Suddenly she became aware of a lamppost ahead of her, throwing light onto the wooden bench next to it. There was a heap of fabric on the bench. No, not a heap—as she drew closer, she saw that it was an abandoned blanket. Some rough sleeper had left it behind, or some resident had forgotten it after a day sitting in the sun. Although maybe not, because she now saw that it had been folded into a tidy square. Giving in to instinct, she reached out and pulled back the top layer.

There lay Bella Carpenter. She wore the pink onesie Mr. Carpenter had described, and her silky hair lay smooth against her scalp. Her face was black with putrefaction.

Allen jerked awake. She was in her office at Victoria Police Station, not in the Warwick Square garden. She shook her head to clear it, but the bloated baby face still swam in front of her.

Again she barely made it to the toilets in time.

As her stomach subsided, she looked at her reflection. Her face was greenish white, her eyes as deeply shadowed as Mr. Patel's. "We have to stop meeting like this," she said to the creature in the mirror. Every part of her seemed to hurt: her lower back from spending most of the night hunched over her desk reading, her neck from sleeping slumped over the same desk, even her legs from being bent in her chair for so long. The hours after her arrival in the incident room had been filled with ringing phones and men with their ears pressed into receivers, nodding, muttering, cajoling, and then sighing as they put the phone down. At regular intervals, Greenhill came round with a tray full of teas and biscuits. It had been a night of reviewing interview transcripts and plausible open lead sheets generated by the appeal. The last thing Allen could remember was going over Amrish Patel's statement once again around three in the morning. She turned her wrist to look at her watch: 6:05 a.m.

She filled her cupped hands and rinsed her face, cursing as she felt water trickle down her blouse and soak the waistband of her trousers. She grabbed a fistful of paper towels and used them to dry her face then turned on the hand dryer and bent awkwardly, trying to make the blast hit the front of her shirt. The small of her back twinged in protest. Rinsing the sour taste out of her mouth and then smoothing back her hair, she deliberately avoided checking the mirror before she opened the door. However she looked now, it would have to do.

She nearly ran into Desbury.

"Oh, ma'am." He stopped short. "I was just trying to find you."

"Sure, yeah. Why?" She tried to focus.

"I know I should speak to DS Norton first, but I've looked all over, and I can't find him, so I thought . . ." He shifted from foot to foot awkwardly.

"It's all right, Desbury. We've shared an interview and two car journeys. You can talk to me directly."

He didn't smile. "Well, you see, I've been watching the tape of the appeal, and I think I've noticed something. I could be wrong, because the telly in the incident room isn't very big, but I think I've spotted . . . well, that is, I saw something . . ." Then, at last, "I'm almost certain Carpenter wasn't actually crying."

She didn't understand. "You mean while he was speaking? I'm sure you're right. He wouldn't have been. The media liaison would've told him it was important to speak clearly."

"No, not while he was speaking. I don't think he was crying when he was . . . well, when he was crying."

She resisted her sleep-frustrated instinct to snap at him. "None of our heads are as clear as they might be at the minute, Detective Constable. What exactly do you mean, you 'don't think he was crying when he was crying'?"

He met her eyes. "I'm pretty sure he was faking it."

Now she was awake.

"I watched the tissue." He must have realized how unclear that still sounded because he took a breath and backed up. "A couple of hours ago, the tip calls began to taper off. They sent me to photocopy the open lead reports for you and Norton, and when I finished they sent me to work on the tape of the appeal. They told me one team member always has to memorize taped events, in case the tape gets damaged later." Allen started to say that this was nonsense, but then Desbury raised his eyebrows. He'd known he was being hazed. "After you see something three or four times, you start to notice things you normally wouldn't, and I noticed the tissue. It was something about the way he held it. So I let the tape rewind and watched the whole thing again. As far as I could see, the tissue was never wet. Not when he held it to his eyes or when he held it to his nose."

"Are you sure?"

"I . . ."—he became all policeman—"I couldn't swear to it in court, but . . ."—the inferior officer reappeared—"Could I show you the tape, ma'am?"

He rolled the television trolley into her office. Then, she on the edge of her desk and he standing next to the set, they watched the appeal.

Again Mrs. Carpenter sat like a store mannequin until the final seconds. Again Carpenter pled for his daughter's safe return. Again he wiped his eyes and nose.

"There!" Desbury stopped the tape. He pointed at the screen.

"I don't see anything."

"Wait." He lifted his finger from the pause button, and she heard the cassette rewind. "Let me turn the volume down. That way the noise won't distract you."

Now Carpenter mouthed a sentence, then another. Then he lifted the tissue to his eyes and wiped.

"There!" Desbury jabbed the pause button and pointed to the tissue frozen below Carpenter's left eye.

Allen leaned in, squinted. He was right. The tissue did seem to be dry. "Well, it's not as if he's been crying for fifteen minutes. He's just broken down."

"No, it isn't that." Remembering who he was talking to, Desbury hastily added, "Ma'am." Then he continued. "Look at his eyes after he takes the tissue away." He let the tape rewind again then put it on frame by frame. The Carpenter on the screen jerked through his motions. As they watched, the tissue covered his eyes. His lips frowned; his Adam's apple moved up and down in what at a faster speed would have been a convulsive swallow. But when he moved the tissue from his eyes to his nose, his eyes weren't bloodshot or swollen, and there was no shine of tears.

"Can you run it again, at normal speed?"

Now that Allen was watching for it, she saw it. Neither Carpenter's cheeks nor his eyes were ever wet. And the tissue balled up in his hand seemed to be just that: balled up, but not damp.

But she remembered the ABCs she'd lost sight of with Faduma Isaaq: Assume nothing. Believe nothing. Check everything. "It could be down to conditioning. You know, an Englishman doesn't cry in public and so on."

"With respect, ma'am, I'm an Englishman, and if my daughter went missing, I'd be crying till my eyes swelled shut, in public and everywhere else."

"You have a daughter?"

"Two. Amy and Jemmelia. Jemmelia's ten months; Amy's four."

She watched his face come alive as he said the names. On the screen, Carpenter now had his arm around his wife. Into Allen's head came the memory of him looking up from the sofa in the tiny sitting room and laughing with disbelief at the idea that his daughter might be returned. But that and a tissue weren't much to go on. Perhaps Carpenter was one of those people who turned practical rather than emotional under stress. Her own father was like that. Perhaps Carpenter really did believe in the stiff upper lip.

Then more memories came. Carpenter's rueful voice in the corridor when he said, "What a fucking mess." The look on his face in front of the cameras, as if he were about to be punished for some terrible crime. And, most damning, the vision of him the previous morning, crying out that his daughter was never coming back, that he'd made a terrible mistake, that it was all his fault. There'd been real tears then. At the time, she'd thought he was blaming himself for bringing his family to London in the first place, or for leaving the window open overnight. Now the words took on a different meaning.

"All right." She bit a thumbnail. "We need to review everything we have about Thomas Carpenter. Bring me all the information you and Greenhill collected. But, Desbury"—he turned back to her, his hand on the door handle—"don't mention this to anyone. Just bring what you have."

She didn't need to say more. After all, they'd shared two car rides and an interview.

As it turned out, they didn't have much more than Greenhill had laid out two days earlier. The Carpenters had been easy for her to dismiss then: two terrified parents from impeccable middle-class backgrounds who'd spent the entire night of their child's disappearance asleep in the same bed, thereby alibiing each other. Besides, "This isn't the kind of thing we're looking for." Allen shook her head, shoving Carpenter's file away from her. "If anything about him rang alarm bells, we'd've flagged it at the start. Whatever kinds of clues there might have been aren't going to be as obvious as what his boss thinks of him. Maybe . . . Did you talk to the baby's doctor?"

"They faxed us her records." Desbury pushed a sheet of thermal paper toward her. "Nothing sticks out."

"You didn't talk to him?"

Desbury shook his head. "Besides, there's confidentiality."

There was. Allen sighed. "How about Mrs. Carpenter's friends?"

"We talked to the woman who owned the gallery. Nothing memorable there either." He began rooting through the folder. "And aside from that she didn't really have any friends. Neighbors who were friendly, but they just said they seemed like a loving couple and she kept to herself after the baby came."

Which could be significant. Or it could mean nothing except that a new baby took up a great deal of its mother's time. She supposed she'd have a better idea of which of these was true in about eight months' time, but that was no use to her now. She sighed through her teeth. This information wasn't going to turn up the kinds of hints she was looking for: The questions had been designed to get a general overview, not to help with deep analysis. To find what she wanted, they needed a different approach.

"Who's in charge over in Wells?"

"I'm not sure, ma'am. But I can find out."

"Do. And tell him to expect us. We'll leave in twenty minutes."

18

The drive from London to Wells was mostly on roads bounded by green spaces. Allen, who had been born in London, lived all her life in London, and would be happy to die in London, thought she had never seen so many fields. On the whole, she preferred Hampstead Heath, with its reassuring sense that a city was only minutes away, but she did find the scent of drying hay intoxicating. She rolled down her window to let it fill the car. For the first time in a week, the air felt fresh on her face, not close and clammy but cool and pleasant.

Desbury sniffed appreciatively. "Smells like home."

"Home?"

"I grew up in Axminster. My dad was a pharmacist there."

Allen, who had assumed he was a child of somewhere like Brixton or Tottenham, looked hard out of her window to hide her blush.

She'd spent the first minutes of the journey briefing him, but there hadn't been much to say. They were going to interview those who seemed as if they'd know the Carpenters best; the goal was to elicit information that suggested what Tom Carpenter was like with his wife and baby when he wasn't trying to make an impression. First stop was the Wells nick, to acknowledge they were on the Wells DCI's patch and to get what help they could from him. Once that was done, she'd lapsed into silence. She spent the remainder of the journey repeatedly going over every move she'd made since seven forty-five on Thursday morning, trying to find something that would either definitively confirm or definitively refute her suspicions about Tom Carpenter.

Desbury nodded at a sign at the side of the motorway that read "Wells 26, Weston-super-Mare 45."

She grunted. He drove silently for a second, then said, "Forgive me, ma'am, and I know it's a bit late to ask this, but should we perhaps have waited and spoken to Vivien Carpenter's parents again before we left? Surely they could tell us all about Carpenter's relationship with their daughter."

She shook her head. "They adore him. And it's pretty clear that he and his parents aren't close, so I don't think it'd be any use talking to them either. Much better to at least start with people who've seen the family recently, who know them with some intimacy. But still," she said, for herself as much as for him, "we need to remember that we might not learn anything significant, that back at home they might be finding a better suspect while we're out here in the weeds. We're really just trying to see if there's any reason to bring him in for an interview." She shifted in her seat. "Keep an eye out for a petrol station or a pub or something like that, would you? I need to stop before we get to the nick."

Wells was a town made for postcards. All the buildings looked freshly painted, the shopfronts decorated with red and pink begonias in frilly bloom. It was all very charming. But as a place to live? To her eyes, there didn't appear to be much to occupy you once you'd visited the shops and the cathedral that somehow managed to appear at the end of every road. Certainly it didn't seem like a good town in which to be an estate agent. It felt more like a place where people lived in the same house for lifetimes, if not generations. Was this a strike against Carpenter—man finds questionable job just so he can move his wife to a town small enough for him to know where she is every second? Or was it a point in his favor—man with bad job nonetheless spends money to take his family on a holiday, however humble? Or had it been Mrs. Carpenter's idea to move to Wells, and Carpenter had taken the job he could find? Well, that was the kind of thing they were here to find out.

When they turned into the car park in front of a double-fronted Georgian building of honey-colored brick, Allen thought Desbury was just turning the car around. Then she saw the man lingering on the step. Wearing a rumpled gray suit that had seen better days and with a midsection padded by fast food and slow pints, he could have been transplanted to Victoria Police Station without anyone noticing. Policemen, it seemed, were policemen everywhere.

As they opened their doors, the man began to make his way across the tarmac, his thinning hair lifting slightly in a breeze. Once in front of them, he looked from one to the other, then back again, then frowned. At last he offered his hand to Desbury. "Detective Chief Inspector Ian Salloe."

Desbury's face remained neutral. Allen took Salloe's hand. "Detective Inspector Martha Allen. And this is Detective Constable Desbury."

Salloe looked abashed. Allen felt for him. Apparently it was a day for making embarrassing assumptions about people. "Well. Well." He cleared his throat. "Let me take you inside."

The conference room at the front of the station was large and airy enough to be gracious, but the bureaucratic need for ugliness had been fulfilled by someone's decision to paint the walls industrial green and furnish the room with a cheap MDF table and cushionless plastic chairs. A disposable aluminum ashtray, well used and half-cleaned, sat on the tabletop.

Once they were seated, Salloe took a folded sheet of paper out of his breast pocket and passed it across the table to Desbury. "There are the names and numbers you asked for. They're expecting you. But I'm afraid I don't have anything else. I looked over my notes, and there isn't anything I didn't already tell you. The Carpenters never came to our attention before this unless you count applying for a resident's parking permit, and it's really the council that handled that. After you rang, I ran their names again, but all I found was a parking ticket in Chelsea five years ago. Which I don't suppose is the sort of thing you're after, and which you probably found yourselves."

"We did," Allen said. Desbury nodded.

Salloe took a packet of Silk Cut from his breast pocket and held it out. They shook their heads. He fished one out, patted his pockets for a lighter, then lit the cigarette, inhaling deeply. "Look, I understand that you've come down here because you want to find out more about the Carpenters, but I don't understand why you've done that. Has something changed since Thursday morning?"

Allen explained what Desbury had seen, and what Carpenter had said. "And with the appeal currently about as useful as public appeals generally are"—Salloe rolled his eyes—"we thought we'd come have a recce and do some follow-up."

He made a doubting face. "As I said, I never heard about any troubles with him. We have our share of domestics—there was a couple used to live out by Keward, and my men must've been round there every Friday until they moved away—but I never heard a word about the Carpenters that way. Wells is a small place, and they're incomers. Word would've got round. We'd've heard about it via trickle-down."

"Sometimes people don't know what they've seen until they think back on it."

Salloe made the doubting face again. "Sometimes." He pulled on the cigarette. "If that's the sort of thing you're after, I suppose it makes sense to start with the doctor. Palmer. All the new mothers go to him." He pointed at the sheet of paper. "The surgery address is on the bottom of that. It's open on Saturday mornings, so he'll be there now. I'll let him know you're on your way." He ground out the cigarette and stood up. "Then I'm going to watch that appeal again."

Given the chocolate-box charm of the town, it made sense that the surgery waiting room looked like something out of a book. Three of its pale blue walls were decorated with fluffy clouds that had been painted to look as if they were moving. On the fourth wall, a huge painted rainbow extended from one top corner to the opposite bottom one, with children's drawings in cheerful primary colors pinned to it. A heap of toys was being scavenged by toddlers, and the chairs for waiting clients were so comfortable that the woman across from Allen had fallen asleep, her lightly snoring baby in a sling around her neck.

When Dr. Palmer came out to the reception desk, he, too, seemed have stepped out of a 1950s children's book. A bald pate and fringe of white hair set off a face in which twinkling blue eyes creased into reassuring wrinkles when he smiled. He was lean but not skinny, tall but not looming, and his white coat was crisp and clean. Three brightly colored lollipops peeked out of the top pocket.

Once he spotted Allen and Desbury, though, the illusion of warmth vanished. He pursed his lips and flapped a hand, indicating that they should come through. As they swerved through the roaming toddlers, he checked his watch, then checked it again. The implication was plain: they were wasting his valuable time.

"You know I can't tell you anything about Tom and Vivien Carpenter or their daughter." He let them lean against the counter in a narrow examining room while he took the chair. "My duty of confidentiality doesn't permit me to reveal anything that might have passed between us. Indeed, if you'll allow me to anticipate what the circumstances suggest might be your next question, confidentiality wouldn't permit me to tell you anything even if Bella Carpenter is deceased."

But Allen had done some checking before they set off.

"I understand your concern, Dr. Palmer, and I admire your ethics. I'm sure you know, however, that BMA guidelines allow for disclosure where that disclosure would assist in the prevention, detection, or prosecution of a serious crime. That's the case here." He looked taken aback. Allen could tell that he wasn't used to being challenged, let alone contradicted. "Doctor, Bella Carpenter has now been missing for more than two full days, and none of the information we currently have has been enough to find her. As you know, police guidelines require that we consider her to be in imminent danger." There was no reason to think he did know that, but flattering him couldn't hurt. "I wouldn't have come here if I didn't feel your knowledge was material to the investigation, and you have my word that I'll only ask you questions that can assist us."

She knew Palmer would try to reassert his power by staying silent for as long as he could, and she wasn't disappointed. She waited.

At last he sighed heavily, a man reluctantly giving in to forces beyond his control. He nodded at her to continue.

"Thank you." Out of the corner of her eye, she saw Desbury take out his pad. "You've been Bella Carpenter's doctor since she was born?"

"Since they brought her home from the hospital, yes. The obstetrician was Pithian, at Bridgwater. A good man."

"I see. And when did you last see Bella?"

"About two months ago. I can have our receptionist check the date. I know I was due to see her for her six-month checkup in the next couple of weeks. Again, Sharon can check the exact date."

"Two months without seeing her? Isn't that rare with a newborn? Especially with first-time parents. I thought they'd be in here for every little thing."

"Bella was a very healthy baby. A little cradle cap when she first came home, and once she coughed up a tiny spot of blood after finishing on the breast, but that was nothing to worry about. And there was nothing else. She didn't even cry when she had her jabs. A good baby, healthy and good."

The questions were insubstantial, the answers simple. Allen could see him relaxing. She said smoothly, "And when you saw her for her jabs—or for the cradle cap or the concern over the blood—did you notice anything out of the ordinary?"

"How do you mean, 'out of the ordinary'? She didn't seem deficient in any way, if that's what you're asking." Then he reared back in the chair. "Are you asking about injuries? Certainly not! I would have reported those immediately."

"I didn't mean to imply those things at all, sir." Although she had, and now she had her answer. "I apologize if I expressed myself poorly. I meant more in terms of the baby's responses, her personality—her affect, if you'll allow the term."

"Ah, well." He smoothed his tie and smiled indulgently. "I'm not sure I'd say a three-month-old has an 'affect,' Detective Inspector, but no, I saw nothing concerning there. As I said, she didn't seem deficient in any way. She was a happy, healthy, alert little girl."

"Thank you. And what about Mrs. Carpenter? When you saw Bella, how did she seem?"

A moment's hesitation. "Yes, well, Vivien Carpenter had some difficulties . . ."

Allen could tell that he was struggling with the question of whether Mrs. Carpenter should count as a separate instance of confidentiality. She decided to help him out. "Her husband told us she'd had the baby blues, and that you'd prescribed tablets to help her sleep."

He relaxed. "Yes, that's right. When you've been a doctor as long as I have, you've seen a lot of crying spells and mood swings after a birth. Of course, you've also seen them resolve themselves, which is why I'm reluctant to prescribe anything. But she was also having trouble sleeping, and I felt that a mild soporific would not only alleviate that but would also go some way toward helping with the moodiness. In my experience, most of these baby-blues cases are really just down to old-fashioned exhaustion. A couple of weeks of good solid sleep and Mum is back to normal."

"Did you ever make a house call? Perhaps after the incident with the spot of blood, or a home visit to follow up on the prescription? Something where you saw them at their home rather than here in the surgery?"

"I know what a house call is, Detective Inspector. The local health visitor would be the one who saw them at home. Sharon can give you her details, if you want to make contact."

"That would be very helpful, thanks. And when Mrs. Carpenter came to see you about her trouble sleeping, you didn't notice anything unusual aside from the low feelings she described? I know couples with new babies can have trouble. She didn't mention any problems between her and Mr. Carpenter?"

She tried to leave a space in which he could consider, but she needn't have bothered. He answered immediately.

"Look, it's clear to me that these questions are your clumsy way of trying to determine if Tom Carpenter was hurting his wife or daughter. I can tell you that the idea is ridiculous, and I would have told you the same if you'd simply asked me directly. I don't think I've ever come across a more loving husband and father. He came to all the appointments with his wife. Yes, that's right." His tone was triumphant, as if Allen had tried to put something over on him and failed. "He told me he took the time out from work to come. Because he wanted to support her. And he told me he'd take care of filling the prescription, so his wife wouldn't forget because she was feeling low. Vivien told me he'd even taken over the nighttime feeds so she could sleep. To suggest that he was anything other than most attentive or understanding is preposterous." He stood up and opened the door. "Now, I think my patients have waited long enough. You can see Sharon for the information you need."

His steps receded down the hallway as they stood in silence.

"I feel like I've been dismissed by the headmaster," Desbury said.

Allen laughed. "I was just thinking the same thing."

19

The health visitor was a stocky woman in her late fifties named Naomi Frith. She had suggested they come to her house rather than speaking on the phone—"that will give me time to have a rootle around in my notes before you arrive"—and now she was offering them tea in her garden, her rather grandmotherly face puckering with concentration as she poured. She'd switched from nursing to acting as a health visitor five years before, she told them, "after Thatcher's restructures put the rot in the NHS." For a moment, she looked fierce, but then her face relaxed. "Still, never mind about that. You wanted to talk to me about the Carpenter baby?"

Allen nodded. "We're trying to get a sense of the family's life before they visited London. To see if there's anything in the bigger picture that can help us."

Mrs. Frith held out a cup to Desbury. "I'm afraid I don't have much to offer. I only saw the baby once."

"But I thought health visitors made regular checks during the first few months?"

"We're supposed to do that, yes. But in the Carpenters' case I wasn't able to." She sighed. "It happens occasionally. Some mothers see the health visitor as a meddler. Or they just aren't interested in our help. They're not obliged to use our services, so some don't."

"And that's what happened with the Carpenters?"

"To be honest, I don't really know. We had a perfectly routine first visit, as far as I could tell. They answered my questions, seemed interested in what I had to say. But the next time I called round, no one answered the door. I assumed they were out. I rang them two or three times in the evening to try to fix a time that would be convenient for them, but no one picked up. Beyond that, there isn't much we can do. As I say, they're under no obligation to meet with us. I did try once more, in June. Then I gave up. We're allowed to do that, if we feel our time could be better used elsewhere. I can give you the exact dates if you need them."

Allen shook her head. "Thank you, though." She took a sip of tea and instantly started to sweat. "What about that initial visit? Can you remember it?"

"As it happens, I remembered that visit right away when you rang. It was quite an unusual one. Dad was there with Mum and baby."

"That's unusual?" Allen glanced at Desbury the father to check his reaction, but his face was impassive.

"We send families a leaflet about our visits in the final month of the pregnancy, and it does say there that ideally both parents would be present at the visits. In reality, though, they hardly ever are." She looked downcast for a second then brightened. "But at the Carpenters', Dad *was* there. And not just there but *involved*. That was what made it so memorable. He sat beside Mum and held her hand while we chatted, and as often as not he was the one who answered my questions. Made the tea too."

"And Mrs. Carpenter. What was she like?"

"Now, that's harder to remember. I know this sounds odd, since it's really Mum and baby we're there to check on, but she was somehow less *distinct*, if you know what I mean. I do remember that she was . . . well, I'd say subdued. She seemed quite nervous, but you see that with a lot of new mums. At first they're terrified by all the things they think can go wrong. And she looked exhausted. Even more exhausted than the usual mother of a ten-day-old, if you can imagine that." She reached for a battered Black n' Red notebook that lay near her on the wrought-iron table and flipped through its pages. "Yes, here we are. 'Quiet, pale. Not been sleeping well. Doctor's appointment next week.' That was on March 12."

"And the baby? What do your notes say about her?"

Mrs. Frith trailed her finger up the page. "Here it is. 'Eight pounds, twenty inches. Slight rash and scaly skin on forehead. No feeding difficulties, according to mother. OBW.'" She glanced up. "Over birth weight." She returned to her text. "'Beginning to focus eyes. Placid.'"

How could a ten-day-old baby be anything *but* placid? Allen wondered. As if reading her thoughts, Mrs. Frith said, "You'd be surprised how many babies aren't, even at that age. Angry at leaving the comforts of home, I always think." She smiled, then closed the notebook. "That's all there is, I'm afraid. I wish I could tell you more, but I have upward of fifty newborns at any one time, and if all is well with an individual case, my notes tend to be brief. As I say, I only really remember the Carpenters because it was unusual to have Dad at home on the day." She looked hopeful. "Still, perhaps that's something in itself? The fact that there aren't many notes means I didn't see anything to worry about."

"What d'you think?" Back in the car, Allen adjusted her seat belt and turned toward Desbury.

"I think he sounds a lovely bloke. Makes me feel inadequate, anyway. Loving husband, engaged father . . ." He shook his head. "Maybe it's like you say, and he just isn't a man who cries."

"I don't know." Allen caught her lower lip between her teeth then let it go. "Something feels off."

Desbury shook his head. "Women."

"What's that supposed to mean?"

"It means women say they want a caring, supportive New Man, but then when one comes along, you say something feels off." He added, "Ma'am."

Allen didn't care about the possible insubordination, but she was stung at being misunderstood. "That's not what I meant. I meant that he feels almost too supportive. *He* fills the prescription; *he* answers Mrs. Frith's questions . . . and then she never gets through the door again or manages to reach them on the telephone . . ."

"That makes it sound sinister. She just said no one answered the door or the phone."

"And I could accept not answering the door. But the phone? In the evening? Carpenter told me they hadn't been out since the baby was born. And I *really* don't like it that he went with her when the doctor prescribed the sleeping tablets. That he was there while she described how she felt." They'd both done the spousal-abuse training; Desbury knew as well as she did that hovering husbands could be controlling husbands in disguise.

But Desbury thinned his lips. "At best it's inconclusive."

It was. She sighed.

"So where to now?"

She checked her watch. A little past noon. An estate agent would be open by now. "How about someplace where people knew Carpenter in his own right rather than as a supporting player to his wife? We can see what he was like when he was on his own." She dug in her pocket for Ian Salloe's list. "Glaister Properties, 74 High Street."

He started the car and backed out of Mrs. Frith's long drive, heading into the town center with the assurance of a native. He seemed to have a road map of all of England stored in his head. When she remarked on it, he shrugged and said, "I studied the *A–Z* before we set out. My memory for maps is very good."

Lucky you, thought Allen, who got lost going round the block.

20

They weren't offered tea at Glaister Properties. In fact, at first they weren't offered anything except a rather startled young man in a white shirt and a tie with a discreet company logo (*Glaister* in script across the point), clearly flummoxed by the appearance of what he took to be an interracial couple in his reception area. He stood up and came out from behind the slender wooden desk, extending his hand slowly.

"Good afternoon. Decided to move somewhere more sedate to get away from city life? Well, you'll find Wells a very welcoming town, Mr. and Mrs. . . . ?"

Allen flashed her warrant card. "Detective Inspector Allen and Detective Constable Desbury. We're here to see Terrence Glaister."

"Terry! Please, Terry!" Glaister insisted as he shook their hands a few seconds later. "No one but my wife calls me Terrence, and even then only when I'm in trouble." His smile showed off a long pair of canines, and he seemed to have dressed to match them. His suit was dark gray, his tie a thin tongue of red, so that as he bared his teeth in the smile he resembled nothing so much as a wolf trying very hard to ingratiate himself with potential prey.

"Tom's a great bloke, absolutely great." He gestured for them to sit in the bentwood chairs in front of his desk. "A real team player, and showing terrific promise as a salesman. This is such a tragedy for him and Viv. I was happy to help out with the reward." His expression switched to a frown. "But I'm really not sure what I can do for you here and now. Ian Salloe's an old friend—I sold him his house, in fact—and I'd love to help him out, but I can't think of anything I didn't mention to your boys back in London. He loves that baby, adores his wife. As well he should. Viv's a smasher. I've only met her once or twice, but she seemed terrific. An artist, I gather, and quite talented, according to Tom. Really going places, both of them."

Allen felt as if he was about to tell them that the Carpenters were conveniently located and easy to maintain, but she hesitated to cut him off. As an interview technique, free recall usually yielded the most useful results, and this breezy monologue was a form of free recall.

To her surprise, though, Desbury spoke up. "We heard that Mr. Carpenter was quite a doting father. Do you have kids yourself?"

Glaister looked taken aback, but he nodded. "A boy and a girl."

"I have two girls." Desbury's tone was conversational. "When they were born, I couldn't stop showing photos of them round the office. Looking back on it now, I can see that I must have driven the other blokes mad with my stories and the pictures and whatnot. One of my colleagues mentioned that Mr. Carpenter did something similar. Is that right?"

Glaister nodded. "But he wasn't irritating. My boy's six now, and I'd say Tom was just the way I was in the beginning." He smiled at Desbury. "It's natural. For the first couple of months, you can't get over them. Everything they do is magic. But then real life creeps back in, and all that dies down."

"And that's how it was with Mr. Carpenter."

"Over the past few months, yes. For the first two, it was photos and stories all the time. Then less and less, and for the last little while it's just been a catch-up if you ask him. Back to normal." He gave a little laugh. "Tom's version of normal, anyway."

"Tom's version of normal?"

Carpenter smiled his long-toothed smile. "Don't get me wrong. Tom's a good mate, a class bloke." In Allen's experience, this construction only ever preceded a "but," and, sure enough: "But, my God, does he love to talk about his wife. Before the baby, after the baby . . . Sometimes I think the only time he wasn't talking about his wife was during the few months he was talking about the baby."

"And what does he say?"

"How wonderful she is. So clever, so talented, so good at unpacking the moving boxes . . ." He put up a hand. "I know, I know. I shouldn't.

And as I say, she seemed like a lovely girl the couple of times I met her. But . . . it gets annoying. It's great that you love your wife, but talking about it all the time isn't a good way to make friends. You know, you're out with the lads, you let off some steam about the wife. Even if you don't really have anything to complain about, you might make something up just to grease the wheels. But not Tom." He shook his head ruefully. "After the baby was born, I thought it might change." He leaned in toward Desbury. "You know how it goes. She's more interested in the kid than you; she's got these great"—he raised cupped hands—"but they're all for the nipper. I thought maybe we'd have a bit of fellow feeling then, but . . ." As he trailed off, he glanced at Allen. "Sorry. Men, eh?"

Allen raised a forgiving hand, silently vowing never to buy a home from Glaister Properties.

Desbury prodded. "But there was none of that with Mr. Carpenter?"

"Just the reverse. He left early to get home and help her out. He did all the shopping for her, took time off to go to doctor's appointments with her, made sure to be there when the health visitor stopped round." He sighed. "Let's just say I didn't tell my wife what he was like, in case it gave her ideas."

"And did all that die down, like the baby photos did?" Desbury leaned forward, all mates together.

"Not at all." Glaister sat back. "If anything, I'd say it increased. He was never one for going out with the lads after work for a quick one, but over the past couple of months he was gone on the dot of six. Asked not to work weekends so he could be at home . . . I hate to say it now, but when he came back from this holiday, I was planning to have a short, sharp talk with him about where his focus needed to be." A momentary look of determination, but then his expression became sorrowful. "Does any of that help at all?"

"It could." Allen stood. Desbury followed suit.

"How close are you to a breakthrough? I watched the appeal, and my heart just bled for them. I don't know what I'd do if someone took one of mine."

"We're doing our best. The investigation is ongoing, obviously, and we still have hope."

"Good." Glaister held out his hand to Desbury and smiled at Allen. "If you think raising the reward will help, let me know. I'll see what I can do."

21

Back in the car, Desbury turned to face her. "Ma'am, I want you to know that I've never complained about my wife to the other lads."

"Glad to hear it. And that breast thing!" Her lip curled as she cupped her hands in front of her and parodied Glaister's tone. "'She's got these great . . . but they're all for the nipper.'"

But Desbury was suddenly preoccupied adjusting his seat belt. When he'd sorted it out, he turned the key in the ignition. "Where to next?"

"We're not really managing to get a clear picture of Carpenter, are we? He could be a New Man, as you put it, or he could be a control freak. He could adore his wife, or he could be suffocating her. Well"—she unfolded Salloe's list—"we've heard from the professionals, we've heard from his work, now let's hear from her work. Brorsson Gallery. Priory Road."

By now the temperature outside was well into the mid-eighties. Even the two-minute walk from their parking spot to the Brorsson Gallery was unpleasant. The gallery, however, seemed to have been designed precisely to combat such weather, its clean space cool and soothing after the light and heat outside. On the white walls of the empty expanse hung a series of oversized, brightly painted canvases onto which bent and torn black-and-white photos had been glued, seemingly at random. Allen cocked her head and considered them.

"They're meant to contrast daily life with the more vivid world of fantasy," a woman's voice said behind her.

She turned. The woman was very tall, over six feet, with pale blond hair pulled into a bun at the nape of her neck and fair skin lightly tanned over the nose and cheeks. She wore a shapeless black dress that tied at the neck and hem with white drawstrings. It was sleeveless, and the arms that emerged from its sack shape were lightly but strongly muscled. Her red lipstick looked as if it had been painted on with a fine brush. Allen was suddenly very aware that she was wearing the same clothes she'd slept in, and that her bath that morning had consisted of a couple of splashes in a sink.

The woman held out a hand to Allen. "Alison Brorsson. Ian Salloe rang to let me know I'd be having visitors, so I assume you are Detective Inspector Allen and Detective Constable Desbury."

She led them into her office and offered coffee. They declined.

"I can't say I know Tom Carpenter at all well." She sat down behind a smoked-glass desktop balanced on two white-painted trestles. "It's Vivien I know, and even then she and I aren't intimate."

"More like business connections?" Allen crossed her legs in the rather narrow chair she'd chosen. Its back and arms were made of a single sheet of leather strung on a curved metal rod, and the effect was uncomfortably claustrophobic. Next to her, Desbury had almost vanished into his.

"No, more than that. I represent her, yes, but she'd also stop by to chat every now and again. She came in with the baby once or twice, to show her off." She winced. "God, that poor baby. God, poor Viv. I saw her on the television. Poor thing. I hope this can still end well for her."

"We're here trying to make that happen, Ms. Brorsson. How long have you represented Mrs. Carpenter?"

True to Allen's rule, this simple question produced a long answer. "About two years now. She came in with some photos of her work. Charles Gaultier had given her my name—he was a teacher of hers, and I know him from when he had a little summer cottage here in the seventies. Her work was very good. Not great, but very good. Nothing that would frighten any unsophisticated buyers, but at the same time not sentimental or run-of-the-mill. We get a lot of people from Bristol and London here, looking for pieces to display in their weekend places, and her canvases were ideal for that. Interesting, sometimes bold, but as I said not overly challenging."

"And they sold?"

"Yes. Well, I mean, she wasn't going to live a life of luxury from them, but both her exhibitions did very well."

"And in the course of your time working with her, how often would you say you came into contact with Mr. Carpenter?"

"Not often. As I say, I hardly knew him. He was at both of Viv's openings, of course, so I saw him there, and he picked her up once when she came to see me with the baby. Oh, and he dropped by once while we were hanging."

Allen knew that she meant hanging the pictures for the exhibition, but still she had a brief vision of Brorsson in her black dress and Vivien Carpenter in her Laura Ashley frock dangling from the ceiling, Tom Carpenter looking up at them.

"What was your impression of him?"

The other woman put her fingers to her lips. They were long and thin, with square nails cut short. Up close, her strong-boned face, an inheritance from some Scandinavian forebear, also had a raw look at odds with the sophistication of her surroundings and her cool, precise voice. Now she said carefully, "I'd say tense. He always struck me as being tense."

"About anything specific?"

"About Viv!" She tried to lighten the statement by smiling, but her face wouldn't cooperate. What appeared was more of an uncomfortable twitch. "I don't think I've ever met a man more concerned with his wife's happiness and well-being. And that's good—of course it is. It's what one wants. But his focus seemed to keep him . . . 'vigilant' is the word I'd use. He was always watching out for her comfort, making little adjustments or anticipating her demands, in a way that ended up feeling more . . . well . . . tense than anything else."

"Tense for him, or for her?"

"Both, really. He always seemed ready to spring to attention. And Viv . . ." But then she frowned silently for a second. "The difficulty is, Viv was very different before and after the baby, and she seemed to feel differently about his behavior before and after, as well."

Allen planted her feet and sat up on the slippery leather. "Let's start with before."

"Well, at her openings, she seemed to revel in it. Showing off by sending him to get her another drink or track down a canapé she'd liked the taste of. Nothing unpleasant, just a little bit of showing people what she had, if you see what I mean. She was a bit drunk at the openings," she added apologetically. "And, honestly, I also thought she might've been doing it to get a bit of time away from him. He scarcely left her side either night."

"And after the baby was born?"

"Well, I only saw her twice, so really I can't judge, but both times her life just seemed . . . much narrower than before. She watched Bella obsessively." She lifted a preempting hand. "Please don't misunderstand me. She absolutely adored her. But it was also obvious she was depressed—I mentioned this to the person who rang me from your team. Part of the way that depression expressed itself was that her focus narrowed. She wasn't really interested in producing new work—I offered her another show, and she said no—she came into town less often, and she was very, very nervous. Not nervous like a regular new mother. I've been a new mother myself, so I know how nerve-racking that is."

Allen would have liked to ask exactly how and why being a new mother was nerve-racking, but she controlled herself. Instead she said, "How was this different?"

"She was fixated on the baby's comfort. On every aspect of her well-being, really. The first time she brought Bella to see me, she was only about two weeks old. She spent the whole visit asleep. But Viv tucked the blanket round her in case she caught a chill, then took it off in case she was too hot, checked to be sure she'd brought enough clean nappies, kept hold of a toy just in case Bella woke up and needed to be distracted . . ."

"And was it the same the second time?"

"If anything it was worse. Bella must have been about three months old. She was awake, and very engaged, looking all around." She smiled at the memory. "I told Viv she was an art critic in the making. But then she sneezed, and all of a sudden Viv was completely taken over by the idea that she'd caught some kind of bug. She started looking for the antiseptic wipes, checking her forehead. She couldn't focus on anything else."

"And how does this connect to Mr. Carpenter's behavior?"

"She asked to use the telephone and rang him to come pick them up."

"Which he did?"

"Which he did."

"And what was her reaction to his arrival?"

Brorsson gave a little disbelieving laugh. "I can honestly say she collapsed into his arms. I never thought that description could be real, but in this case it was. She almost fell onto his chest when she saw him. As if something terrible was happening and she couldn't get through it without him. She told him the baby had sneezed, could she be getting a cold? What if it was pneumonia, or some sort of undiagnosed allergy? They needed to leave right away, she said, to see the doctor before the surgery closed. She was nearly hysterical. And Tom . . . all of a sudden his focus on her was just the right thing. Instead of being embarrassing, he seemed capable. He said, yes, it certainly sounded worrying, but the first thing to do was to get Bella home and safe, where they could see if any more symptoms had developed and where he could take care of her. Viv, I mean. And then he just"—she made a scooping gesture—"swept them up and took them off."

"Did you see Mrs. Carpenter again after that?"

"I rang about a week later, but she said she didn't want to risk bringing Bella again. I didn't say anything. I thought of suggesting I go to her, but, as I said, we weren't friends in that way. I felt awkward. At the second visit, she'd been talking about starting to paint again, and I . . . I know it's awful, but I told myself I was giving her space to do that, that she'd be in touch with me when she was ready to show me something." She sighed. "And if I'm being honest, I thought it would be easier to be with her when Bella was older, once Viv had seen she wasn't so fragile." She scraped at an invisible stain on the desktop, biting her lower lip.

"You've been very helpful, Ms. Brorsson." Allen tried to sound comforting.

The other woman looked up. "Have I?"

"Yes. People act in accordance with their characters, and you've given a great deal of insight into the Carpenters' characters. It helps to flesh out our investigation."

She smiled. "I'm so glad. As I say, I like Viv. Very much. I can't help feeling I should have done more."

Was a further revelation coming? "More how?"

"I don't know. Just . . . somehow."

22

Out in the street, the sunlight bounced off the cream-painted facades, doubling its force. Allen shaded her eyes as she looked at Desbury. "You were very quiet in there, compared to the estate agent's."

"I was too busy fighting off my chair to say anything." He grinned, then shook his head. "No, I just didn't see what I could add."

For a moment she thought of Norton, of his pushiness and his disdain, and she fought not to smile back. Instead she looked at her watch. It was just past one.

"So." She moved under the awning of a nearby newsagent. "We—"

A shout interrupted her. "Excuse me! Excuse me!" Shading her eyes, Allen saw a woman waving outside a shop on the other side of the road. The long sleeve of her woven dress fell back as she did so, its rainbow stripes reminding Allen of the lollipops in Dr. Palmer's pocket.

The woman crossed the road and stopped in front of them. "I think you're the police officers from London?"

Were they that obvious? But when Allen considered their suits against the liveliness of the woman's dress—against the flowered background of Wells in general—she had to admit that they were. Still, out of habit, she flashed her warrant card.

"Detective Inspector Allen, Detective Constable Desbury."

"I'm Marjorie Wallingford. Ms. Marjorie Wallingford. I'm a friend of Vivien Carpenter's. Could I speak with you a moment? In my shop?" She gestured back across the road to a glossy green shopfront with *Wallingford Books* written across the front window in gold paint.

Inside, the light from the window filled the room, winking off a polished floor and shelves crammed with books of every height and thickness. As they made their way in, Allen spotted Hanif Kureishi's

The Buddha of Suburbia and Amy Tan's *The Joy Luck Club*, their glossy covers turned outward to tempt browsers, but also shabbier copies of *The Prophet, The Electric Kool-Aid Acid Test,* and two or three of Germaine Greer's *The Female Eunuch.*

"New *and* used books." The woman twisted her long graying hair into a rope, held it up, and fanned the back of her neck with her free hand. "With an emphasis on counterculture in the used stock."

"I see." Allen's fingers itched to browse, but she forced herself to focus. "How can we help you, Ms. Wallingford?"

"Well, really, it's more if I can help you. I think I might be able to. As I said, I'm a friend of Vivien Carpenter. I've been following what's going on since I saw the news on Thursday. I tried to call the hotel to speak to her, but her husband said she wasn't able to come to the phone." She pursed her lips in a way that suggested that this was what she would have expected. "After the appeal last night, I thought perhaps I should ring in, but then I thought I really ought to leave the line free for people who had information about what happened in London. What I have is really more, well, background, I suppose." She fanned her neck again. "But then I saw you go into the gallery, and I thought since you were here I'd just stop you."

"Well, whatever prompted you, Ms. Wallingford, thank you. We're happy to listen. In fact, we're here because we're trying to get background."

"Oh, well, then . . . But do please call me Marjorie." By this time she had moved behind the shop counter. She gestured at a chair that stood nearby. "Sit, sit."

Desbury brought the chair over, nodding at Allen. He leaned against a nearby display table and took out his pad and pencil.

"I met Viv about two years ago, when she first started showing her paintings at Alison Brorsson's gallery. In fact, that's how we met. She came out of the gallery and saw my window then came in to browse. We started chatting. I'm from London originally, and I did my degree at Leeds, although about ten years before her, so we had connections.

After that, she'd come in whenever she happened to be in the town center, to have a catch-up."

"And you grew close?"

"Very. Wells is a village, really. And like most villages it doesn't much take to incomers. I've been here since 1973, and they're only now beginning to accept *me*." She gave a little laugh. "It was hard for Viv, and I think she partially liked me because I'd been in the same boat as her. And then, we'd both been Londoners. I think she'd thought, or maybe just hoped, that Wells would be a bit more stimulating than it is. Have a bit more to offer. And she knew I'd understand that."

"Did she say what brought them here from London?"

"Oh, that was her husband's idea. He was a journalist, and between the two of them they could hardly keep their heads above water in London. They wanted to have children, and he thought it would be cheaper in the country. He sold some newspaper on the idea of a series about it. You know, London man muddles along in the countryside amusingly, that sort of thing. Only once they'd scraped together the deposit and bought somewhere, the newspaper pulled the plug after a couple of columns. He did other bits of work, freelance stuff, for a while. He was always popping up to London for this interview or to cover that event. But it was hardly enough to live on, really, so he decided he'd better cut his losses and find a real job. Which is how he ended up as an estate agent and Vivien ended up stuck in Wells."

She pursed her lips again and raised her eyebrows.

Allen prompted her. "And you dislike Mr. Carpenter because of that?"

"No." One brisk snap of her head. "I dislike him because of the way he treats her."

Allen heard Desbury's pencil stop. She took a breath. "How does he treat her?"

"He was always pushing at her, or pushing in front of her. I don't mean physically. I mean he was always taking over for her, answering for her, or checking up on her. I had them round for a meal once, and he kept supposedly smoothing the way for her in that way that's actually dominating: 'Viv, you don't want more wine, do you?' 'Viv, you seem tired; do you want to go?' 'Viv doesn't really care for Ken Loach's films, do you, Viv?'" She gave a little shudder at the memory. "And that was before the baby!"

"What happened after the baby?"

"Look. Vivien's an artist, for God's sake, and she couldn't get the kind of stimulation an artist needs in Wells. So it wasn't as if she was happy in the first place. But after the baby came she had serious postpartum depression. I'm sure Alison mentioned it; we talked about it once. And Tom Carpenter used that depression." Her eyes found Allen's. "You know, a man doesn't have to hit a woman to abuse her. Tom batters Vivien with kindness. He's always getting things for her before she's even had time to decide what she wants, hovering over her to support her." Allen could hear the speech marks around "support." Marjorie crossed her arms. "She came to visit with Bella a couple of times. Tom delivered her and picked her up. He wouldn't even let her drive! And he stayed here the whole time, at least on her first visit. The next time I suggested he go for a coffee, but he was back after less than an hour, hustling her out of here so fast she hardly had time to say goodbye. 'Oh, Viv, you look tired! Let's get you home.' 'Oh, Viv, the baby's fine! Don't worry; I'll handle her.' He took the stroller from her, carried the baby so he could be certain she'd follow him."

Allen glanced over at Desbury, saw him scribbling frantically. "How recently would you say you saw him act this way?"

"Well, the last time I saw her was more than two months ago, and he did it then."

"You haven't seen Mrs. Carpenter for two months?" From her descriptions, Allen assumed they'd been in regular contact.

Marjorie looked uncomfortable. "I only saw her those two times after Bella was born. She last came in the middle of May, but it wasn't until the beginning of last month that I realized I hadn't heard from her since. I did ring, but when she picked up she said she couldn't speak for long because it was the time when Bella usually woke up from her sleep. We hardly had time to make a little small talk before she said she could hear her and rang off. I did go out there one evening a couple of weeks later. I stopped by after I'd shut up the shop. But he answered the door and told me Viv was having a lie-down. The baby'd been ill the previous night, and Viv had been up with her." A shrug. "I sent my love and left."

Carpenter had made no mention of this illness. Neither had Dr. Palmer. Was that significant? Allen looked at Desbury again. This time he was looking back. He raised his eyebrows. So he'd noticed too.

"And there was no contact after that? She never rang to thank you for dropping by, for example?"

Marjorie bowed her head and shook it. Allen realized she had started to cry. "There was nothing else before they went to London. And I don't even know if what I told you is significant, really. Maybe he's a protective husband and I'm an old feminist who reads male domination into everything. And what does all of it have to do with Bella, anyway? I never saw him do anything to *her*." She wiped her eyes, then looked up at Allen. "It's just that he wasn't even really crying during that appeal."

23

They stopped at a Little Chef off the M4. Desbury had an egg salad and black coffee. Allen ordered a cup of tea—"with milk and leave the bag in, please"—and the full Early Starter breakfast. She waited until the waitress was out of earshot, then asked, "What do you think?"

Desbury rested his arms on the table. "I think . . . I think everything we heard paints a picture of a loving husband. But in the Wallingford woman's version, it also paints a picture of a man who tries to control his wife. Maybe he seems a little too loving, but maybe you can put that down to him trying to be supportive about her depression. Maybe he's trying to reduce her anxiety by helping and has gone a bit overboard, or maybe he's jealous and domineering." He smiled at the waitress as she put their plates in front of them, waiting until she left before he said, "So I think we don't have enough to decide either way."

"What about the illness Ms. Wallingford mentioned? Why d'you think he didn't mention it to the doctor?"

"Maybe he didn't want his wife to look bad, if he's as devoted as Terry Glaister suggested. Or maybe the baby was overheated and the mother exaggerated it into illness, if she's as obsessive about the baby's well-being as the two women suggested. Again, I'd say not enough to decide either way."

Allen grunted agreement as she put a bit of fried egg and rasher in her mouth. Some of the luster had certainly come off Carpenter, but, just as when she'd decided to interview Isaaq, what they'd learned was far from conclusive—and she wasn't eager to repeat that experience. She wasn't going to go back and suggest to Beck that Carpenter had harmed his daughter because he was jealous of her, or that he'd done it to relieve his wife's postpartum anxiety by getting rid of its source. The first would make him a monster, while the second would make him insane. It was a long jump from hypercontrolling to either of those.

"But"—Desbury cut into her thoughts—"that does bring up the question, what about the mother? The depression? Mothers with severe baby blues have been known to kill their kids."

"Oh, surely n—" She stopped herself. Whatever she wanted to believe, whatever gender stereotypes asserted, he was right. Mothers did kill their children, even if by accident. Vivien Carpenter could have caused Bella's death without meaning to. After all, hadn't Allen imagined several ways that could happen the previous evening? Horrified and distraught, she could've hidden the body or somehow got rid of it. Allen thought of the skip at the Bellevue, emptied at six on Thursday morning and easy to reach for anyone who climbed down the fire escape. It would've been an easy and accessible place to hide a . . . She stopped thinking.

She wiped her toast around the edge of the plate, pressing so hard that it tore in half. She'd hoped the trip would bring her closer to resolving the case, but all it had done was muddy the waters. For one wishful second, she closed her eyes. If only the baby could somehow magically reappear and be reunited with her parents! The Carpenters would be overjoyed; there could be a celebratory press conference to announce that the police had succeeded; everyone would be happy. She wouldn't even mind if they didn't catch the perpetrator. Bella could be found like Moses in the bulrushes for all she cared.

She shoved the bread in her mouth.

"You're really enjoying that breakfast, huh, ma'am?" Desbury grinned at her.

She swallowed. "Sorry. Not very ladylike, I know. But there's something about a full English on an empty stomach that hits the spot."

He nodded. "My wife was the same in the first couple of months. Didn't want to eat anything but fat and grease."

"What?" She tried to lift her teacup, but when she saw the liquid vibrating, she put it back.

"Oh." He looked confused. "I thought . . . You're not . . ." He leaned in and lowered his voice. "I thought you were pregnant."

Allen's face burned. Of course she could deny it. But in six months he'd know she'd lied, and what would that do to her ability to command his respect?

She spoke so quietly that he had to lean in even farther. "How did you know?"

"You've gone to the toilet at least five times today already. You were sick this morning before we left and the other morning after the interview. I haven't seen you eat anything that wasn't packed with fat, and, like I said, my wife was the same. I have two kids. I know the signs."

"Does everyone know?"

Desbury snorted. "I don't know if you've noticed, but 'everyone' and me aren't such good mates. Why d'you think I got partnered with a WPC? But, no, I don't think they know. They're not the sort who give these things much thought. They probably think you're being sick because you don't have the stomach for the case."

"Whereas as a New Man you know different."

"That's right."

"That's right, ma'am."

For a second he looked worried. Then he saw she was smiling. "That's right, *ma'am*."

She took a swallow of her tea then said, "I don't know your Christian name."

"It's Manley. Manley Desbury. My parents named me for Norman Manley, the first premier of Jamaica." From the way he said it, she could tell he'd been explaining it his whole life.

She swallowed. "All right, Detective Constable Manley Desbury. This stays between us. And that's an order. Are we clear?"

He sketched the ghost of a salute. "We're clear, guv'nor."

"Then let's get the bill and be on our way."

The vinyl car seat burned to the touch when she tested it. They ran the air-conditioning for a few minutes before getting in. Once inside, the heat, the lack of sleep, and the heavy meal all combined to make her brain feel thick. She wanted a shower, she wanted to sleep in a bed rather than a chair, and she wanted some time to let what she'd heard during the day settle in her mind.

She gazed out at the fields as they drove through them again, hypnotized by their repetition. As they entered London and made their way down Buckingham Palace Road, she automatically performed the ridiculous action that had become a habit in childhood and checked to see if the queen was in any of the passing cars.

When they pulled into the car park next to the nick, she said to Desbury, "How long have you been on?"

"Since Thursday morning, same as you."

"Type up the interviews, then go home."

"But you're—"

"No 'buts,' Detective Constable. You've done a full week's hours in three days. I'll probably already get a bollocking about your overtime." She grinned to soften the words. "Go home. You can start fresh tomorrow. If anything happens in the next sixteen hours, I'll let you know."

"Can I at least make tea before I type the interviews? Bag in, with milk?"

She kept her face stern. "Fine. But then you do the forms and go."

In her office, she shut the door, then bent over and tried to touch her toes. Her lower back protested. She sat on the floor and stretched her legs in front of her, tried to fold herself in half, but again her back wouldn't let her. This was what all day in a car did to you, she thought. Well, that and all night in a desk chair. She lay on her back and closed her eyes, trying to align all her vertebrae into one straight line. It was a move her GP had taught her to combat what he called "desk back."

When she opened her eyes, the office was filled with golden light. She checked her watch: 7:45 p.m. She'd been asleep for almost two hours! She scrambled up. On the desk next to her mug of cold tea she saw a stack of typed interview report forms. On top was a handwritten note: *Go home. Ma'am.*

24

When she came out of the West Hampstead Tube station, the sun was low in the sky, but it was still hot. She realized that she had no idea if Phil had eaten dinner without her, or even if there was anything in the flat to eat. They hadn't spoken since the previous evening. At 8:30 p.m. on a Saturday, the corner shop by the station still had its door open, so she stopped and picked up some eggs and bacon. Breakfast for lunch had been delicious, so why not have breakfast for dinner too?

At home, Phil was in the second bedroom. He'd been using it as a makeshift study since they'd moved in, although they kept reminding each other that they should be turning it into a nursery. As she closed the door he came out, smiling.

"This is a nice surprise. I wasn't sure you'd be home tonight."

"I'm a little surprised myself. I've just spent the day in Wells, and I didn't know when we'd be back." She kissed him. "Sorry I didn't ring, but there wasn't time to even look for a phone. And then when we came back to the station I fell asleep. Which is why I decided to come home." She left out the note from Desbury. The story sounded better without it.

"Wells? What were you doing there? And who's we?"

She told him everything, from Desbury's discovery on the videotape to Marjorie Wallingford's convictions to her own growing suspicion of Carpenter. When she finished, she said, "And now that you're up to date, I desperately want to take a shower and brush my teeth. Can we talk more when I've finished?"

Phil nodded, glancing at the eggs and bacon on the counter. "I haven't eaten. Why don't I make us bacon omelettes while I wait?"

But Allen's day had made her sensitive about helpful partners. She shook her head. "I'll do it when I get out."

She thought she'd never enjoyed a shower so much. She dug her fingers into her scalp, washed her hair until it squeaked, and scrubbed herself twice with the loofah while she waited for her conditioner to work. She made the water as hot as she could bear, a trick she'd learned from her father to combat the heat, and when she stepped out she actually did feel cool for a few seconds.

In the kitchenette, she beat the eggs until they foamed so the omelettes came out light and fluffy. The sliced bacon inside them added just the right amount of salty savor. She made a modest pile of buttered toast to go on the side. By the time they sat down, the twilight was deepening, and through the open window she could see a few stars in the sky. She almost—almost—felt that all was right with the world.

"My mother rang." Phil reached for the pepper. "She and my father are coming up in October for some work thing of his. She asked if they could stay with us for a couple of nights."

"Of course."

He cut a mouthful of omelette and chewed it as he looked around the room. "I've been thinking over the past few days. We should move."

"We have plenty of room for visitors. That's what the second bedroom is for until we redo it. Anyway, we could never sell and buy somewhere else by October."

"No, I didn't mean move before my parents' visit. I meant in the longer run. I think it's a good time to buy around here. Maybe in the spring, after the baby comes."

It was her turn to look around. "But we took a flat with two bedrooms *because* we wanted a baby."

"I know. But it turns out I really like using the other bedroom for my study. And this place doesn't feel right for a family. I walked to Hampstead today, and there was a house standing derelict, a huge old thing with all its windows boarded . . ."

"Hampstead? I think even a derelict house in Hampstead would be beyond our reach. And think about how much it'd cost to do it up. And with a new baby at the same time?"

"No, I didn't mean that house. It was much too big. Like a mansion. I just meant we should buy somewhere bigger."

Allen carried the plates to the sink, then brought back a pair of shriveled nectarines from the bowl on the counter. The bowl was made of white porcelain, and in the summer she liked to pile it with red and orange fruit then admire the contrast. The nectarines were all that was left of her last haul from the greengrocer.

"Why did you go to Hampstead?"

"Oh, I needed to look up a case, and the book wasn't here. I walked over to the library to see if they had it."

"Did they?"

He shook his head. "So I bought the new le Carré at Waterstones and read it in the Coffee Cup for a bit."

"Oh." Allen wrinkled her nose. Phil loved John le Carré's novels, but she found them slow. As if prompted by just the idea of one, she yawned. "Sorry, sorry."

Phil laughed. "I know you've had a long two days, so I won't take that as criticism of my reading choices."

"I really have. It really isn't." She looked at her wrist then remembered that she'd left her watch on the edge of the sink. She twisted round to see the clock on the kitchen wall. How could it be only nine thirty? "D'you mind if I go to bed? I'll shut the door so you can watch television if you want to."

"That's all right. I've got work to do."

In the bedroom, she looked at her suit pooled on the floor, crumpled white shirt on top. She ought to put the shirt in the hamper, fold the sweaty suit ready to take to the dry cleaner, but she found she couldn't be bothered. She stripped off her T-shirt, bra, and knickers, dropped them on the little pile of clothes, and slipped under the sheet.

She didn't know how much later it was when she was woken by the mattress shifting as Phil lay down next to her. She turned over and pressed her chest against his back. In one of those convoluted thoughts that sometimes come to the half-awake, she thought how interesting it was that no matter how hot the night, the warm body of your bed companion was always welcome. But she had no time to meditate on this profound truth because she immediately fell back to sleep.

25

When she left the flat the next morning, the weather had broken. Although the heat wave had only lasted four days, it felt odd to walk up West End Lane without breaking into a sweat. Once on the platform, she saw the few people waiting with her settling back into the summer they were used to, squinting at the sky to assess the likelihood of future rain and folding their arms to clutch at skin revealed by sleeveless tops.

Walking from Victoria Station to the nick, she felt renewed. Amid the locked shops, a newsagent's door stood open, and she stopped to buy a copy of every Sunday paper. She would read whatever they had to say, whatever interviews they had done. She'd reexamine everything her team had collected over the past three days, every interview report they'd written up after talking to a hotel guest, her own interviews with the Carpenters, the Patels, and the Cooks, and every open lead form from the tip line. Then she'd read Desbury's interview forms from the previous day. After all, evidence review was where most new leads turned up. *That's why they call us the plod.*

She stopped at Norton's desk to pick up the action book. She could tell from the uncluttered desktop that he hadn't come in yet. Well, it was—she looked at her watch—8 a.m. on a Sunday. He had a wife and children he deserved to spend time with. And it was a relief to know that for the moment, at least, he wasn't going to be asking her why she'd gone to Wells and subtly suggesting that the trip had been a waste of time. She took the book back to her office and settled in.

Two hours later, the reexamination hadn't advanced very far. She tried to look at the evidence objectively, but she couldn't tell when she was being objective and when she wasn't. She tried to read the collection of documents with fresh eyes, but those eyes saw nothing that offered any leads, except the descriptions of Carpenter as an overbearing husband.

Maybe the answer wasn't to review the evidence but to try to get more. She could start by interviewing the drivers of all the buses that had departed from Belgrave Road early Thursday morning. Had they only interviewed those who'd arrived at the end of the 8 p.m. to 4 a.m. shift? That's what the forms suggested. Should they go back even earlier? Were there any earlier buses? She should get one of the team to find out.

Or maybe Vivien Carpenter had been on to something, and she should start by posting another round of flyers asking for information. Blanket the whole of central London with them. Or perhaps the whole of London. Or an even wider radius. If the baby had been abducted, it could be anywhere in the country by now. The baby who'd been taken from St. Thomas's Hospital in London in January had turned up in the Cotswolds.

Or maybe she should start by bringing in the other woman from the hotel—what was her name? She found Carter's interview form: Abeba Bayu, that was it. Should she bring in Abeba Bayu, after all? Two bus tickets didn't prove that she and her son hadn't had a baby with them. And as for the alibi provided by Bayu's mother, if your mother wouldn't lie for you, who would?

Or should she just admit the most likely possibility and have someone contact the city morgues again?

At ten fifteen, her telephone rang. She reached for the receiver. "Allen."

Kate didn't bother with a greeting. "I might have something for you."

Allen straightened up. Her neck muscles sang like guitar strings. "What?"

"Bhanji finished the dissolution test. It shows that the blood was deposited on the window frame sometime in the past week. When you interviewed him, did the father mention cutting himself after they arrived at the hotel?"

"No."

"Did he mention finding any blood on his clothes? A spot on his cuff, or anything like that? Something that could have been left by a cut he didn't notice?"

"No. Why?"

"Because the blood on the window frame is B positive. Normally that would be a good thing. Only eight percent of people are B positive. But in this case one of those eight percent is the baby's father. So we can't eliminate him."

Allen's heart thumped, a single hard knock against her ribs. The evidence from the interviews in Wells hadn't been definitive, but that evidence plus blood evidence . . .

She pulled herself back. "What about the mother?"

"No. She's O positive. Most common blood type in the world. It's just the father I need to be concerned about here. I need to know the blood on the window isn't his before I can say for certain that it could have been left by your kidnapper. Are the parents still in London?"

"Yes." Allen's throat was dry. She swallowed and tried again. "Yes."

"Good. Find out if Carpenter remembers cutting himself. Ask both of them about it, if you can, to be sure. You know what men are like. She may remember where he doesn't. And get someone to bring what both parents were wearing on Wednesday over here."

"Right. Okay. Right."

She hung up the phone and sat back. Just for a second, she gave in. She let her heart race, her cheeks burn, her adrenaline pump. Kate needed someone to check the Carpenters' clothes; she needed someone to question them further. The simplest and quickest solution was for her, Allen, to talk to them at the station while the lab examined the clothes.

She shuffled through the papers that covered her desk, plucked out Desbury's reports, then found her own transcription of her earlier interviews with the Carpenters. She tidied them all into one stack. Then she crossed to the little mirror propped on her shelf and looked at herself. Not as bad as the previous couple of days. She smoothed her hair then opened her office door.

More men had trickled in. She could see Norton at his desk, the top of his golden head shining as he leafed through some forms. One immaculate shirt cuff grazed his cheek as he leaned on a hand to read them.

"Detective Sergeant Norton?" She pitched her voice loudly enough that everyone in the room looked up. "Get one of the men over to the hotel." She took in the room. "Bryant, you don't look busy. Forensics needs the clothes the parents were wearing when they arrived at the hotel, and they want us to ask them some follow-up questions. Go over there, pick up the clothes, and bring the Carpenters here. Then you can take the clothes to the lab." She found Desbury at a desk on the right side of the room, jacket off and tie loosened. She caught his eye. "I'll see the Carpenters in Interview 1, and I'll need someone to take notes."

She shut the door and began rereading the stack of documents.

26

Twenty-five minutes later, there was a soft knock. Greenhill's voice said, "Guv? Irene wants you in reception."

That was quick. She'd expected it to take a while for Bryant to find and pack up the clothes, for the Carpenters to prepare themselves. But then again, it was a Sunday morning. Traffic would be light.

"Be right there."

Reception was surprisingly crowded. Normally populated by one or two people slumped in the spoon-shaped plastic chairs or pacing the thinning carpet, today it was almost full. A small group of men she vaguely recognized from the drugs squad upstairs were chatting in a corner. Jimmy Farrell, the probie just assigned to supervised patrol, leaned on the reception counter, worrying over some paperwork. The two young constables who assisted Irene in the back office had come out front and were busying themselves tidying up the leaflets that hung in a rack on the wall. Irene herself was trying to help a young woman who stood at the counter next to Farrell.

"You asked for me, Irene?"

The young woman at the counter turned around, and Allen understood why the lobby was so crowded. She could have been a 1960s pinup, Diana Dors before she bleached her hair. She wasn't more than eighteen, and her pillowy mouth was the shape and color of a strawberry. Her unblemished skin was pink and white, her heavy-lidded blue eyes set off by black lashes and arched black brows. Thick dark hair fell over her shoulders. Her stonewashed jeans were cinched with a wide white belt that drew attention to the smallness of her waist and the curve of her hips, and a crop top exposed an inch or so of velvet-skinned midriff.

All of this Allen registered in an instant, because no sooner had she said Irene's name than the older woman stepped out from behind the reception counter. In her arms she held a baby. It wore a grubby onesie turned sludgy green by too many washings, and its dark hair stood up in spikes as it solemnly surveyed the room with its dark eyes.

Unbelievably, at that moment, the door to the street swung open, and the Carpenters walked in. Bryant, holding an armful of evidence bags, followed a few steps behind. Afterward, Allen thought her mind might be embellishing things, but in her memory the Carpenters paused on the threshold like film stars displaying themselves before the public. Then Vivien Carpenter let out a piercing scream. Running across the lobby, she snatched the baby from Irene's arms.

"Bella!" She buried her face in the baby's hair. "Bella-Bella-Bella-Bella."

Behind Allen, people poured into the room, brought by the scream, then froze at the sight that greeted them. Carter, Norton, even Desbury, watched transfixed as Vivien Carpenter covered the baby's face in kisses, smoothed the hair from its forehead, examined it, then kissed it some more as she began to cry.

But Allen watched Tom Carpenter. He stood stone-still, his face paper-white and his eyes huge. She'd never seen someone look more shocked.

Then he shook himself and ran across the space. He threw his arms around his wife and child, burying his face in his wife's hair as he clutched them. "Oh, Bella." His voice was a sob. "Oh, my Bella."

As if everyone had been waiting for his cue, the room sprang alive. Norton rushed to the parents' side. The three men from the drugs squad galloped back up the stairs, competing to be the first to tell their division what was happening in the lobby. The men who'd come out of the incident room rushed to get back, heading for the telephones that would allow them to tell their wives, their mothers, that Bella Carpenter had been found—alive.

Like Moses in the bulrushes.

Allen walked to the counter and touched the young woman's arm. "Excuse me. You brought the baby in?"

She nodded.

"Please come with me."

She guided her into Interview Room 1, catching Desbury's eye on the way.

"Bring this young lady a cup of tea."

Once in the room, she gestured for the girl to sit. But she stayed standing.

"I only—"

"Please. Someone is bringing you your tea, and then we can get started."

"Started?" Her eyes darted around. "I thought . . . I need to get to work."

"We'd like to ask you a few questions first. It won't take long." She nodded at the chair across the table from her.

The girl sat reluctantly, perching on the edge of the chair with her bag on her lap. After a second, she glanced around at the blank walls, the high window made of frosted wired glass. "There's no mirror."

"Excuse me?"

"Like on telly. The rooms where the police talk to people on telly have mirrors. There's no mirror here." She sounded personally injured by this failure on reality's part.

Allen smiled. "Our interview rooms don't have mirrors. In fact, a lot of what they show on television isn't anything like actual policing."

"Oh." Losing interest, the woman began to root around in her bag.

She was no less stunning up close. Her skin, the color of the cream on top of a bottle of milk, glowed as if lit from inside. As she hunched over, the soft shape of her breasts pushed at the crop top, and her full lower lip thrust out into a pout, made even more provocative by the fact that it seemed unconscious. A flowery scent emanated from her, as if she were perfumed by her own beauty. While Allen watched, she drew a short tube covered in red silk out of her bag, snapped it open, and peered at a tiny mirror set into its lid. Taking a lipstick out of the container's compartment, she started to apply it.

There was the sound of the door opening, and Desbury appeared, a pad under one arm, a teacup and saucer in the opposite hand. Allen noticed that he had tightened his tie and put on his jacket. He put the tea in front of the girl and drew from his pocket three little tubs of milk, three packets of brown sugar, and three packets of white sugar. "I didn't know how you take it, so I thought I'd cover all possibilities."

The girl gave him a dazzling smile but paid no attention to the tea. "I need to be at work," she said to him.

Allen coughed. "This will only take a few minutes. What's your name?"

"Nell. Nell Beatty."

"Thank you. I'm DI Martha Allen, and this is DC Desbury. Now, Ms. Beatty, you believe the baby in reception is Bella Carpenter?"

The girl stared. "I guess so. Her parents recognized her. What more proof do you need?"

Allen couldn't know that this question, in different forms, would become a refrain over the next few days. For now, she only said, "Please tell us how you found her." Good old free recall.

"I saw her on a bench. When I was leaving my flat to go to work. Maybe half an hour ago. Now can I go?"

"Not quite." Someone had left Bella Carpenter on a bench like a forgotten bag of shopping? Allen didn't believe that for a second. "Where is your flat?"

"Lillington Gardens. Flat 14, Parkinson House, Lillington Gardens."

Despite herself, Allen gave a jerk. She had been expecting somewhere that would put the supposed discovery as far from the Bellevue Hotel as possible, but the Lillington Gardens estate was just off Belgrave Road. Could Bella Carpenter really have been that close all along? To buy a few seconds to recover, she asked, "What's your telephone number there?"

"I'm not on the phone, but I'll give you the number where I work." She recited the digits, including an inner London area code. Desbury diligently wrote them down.

"And where is that? Your work?"

"The Rose & Crown in Chelsea."

Allen knew the Rose & Crown. It was on Lower Sloane Street, about twenty minutes by foot from Lillington Gardens. A perfectly reasonable distance to walk on a warm day. But the story still felt wrong. It was so improbable!

"And it's your assertion that you found the baby as you left Lillington Gardens heading for the Rose & Crown?"

The girl's strawberry lips tightened slightly. "I don't know about assertion, but I found her on a bench on the green. I walk that way to get to work."

"The pub is open on a Sunday morning?"

"They have Sunday hours, don't they?"

"I've been in the Rose & Crown. I've never seen you there."

"I only help out sometimes." She straightened up. "I'm a model, really." Now, that Allen *could* believe. "Well, I'm starting out. I help behind the bar at the Rose when I need money." She gathered her bag under her arm. "Now that I've told you what happened, can I go?" She lifted her wrist and looked at her watch, a round gold face circled in dark green and red and mounted on a thin gold bangle. "They're just about to open, so I'm already late. They don't like that." Again she looked at Desbury. "I might get fired."

Allen didn't move. "We can arrange for someone to drive you, and to explain the reason for your lateness."

"No, I don't need a ride. I'd just like to go." But she must have seen from their faces that it was no use. A sigh, then she slumped back in the chair. "Okay."

They kept her for another forty-five minutes, asking her to repeat her story again and again, but it never changed. She'd been walking from her flat in Lillington Gardens to the pub in Chelsea when she saw the baby on a bench. No, it hadn't been crying. Yes, it had been wearing what it was wearing now. At first she'd thought its mother might have left for a second while she ran to fetch something, but after waiting five minutes and seeing no one, she concluded that it must be abandoned. Only once she had it in her arms did she notice how much it looked like the photo of Baby Bella and think . . .

"But anyway, you can't see a baby alone on a bench and ignore it, can you? What kind of person would do that? I had to bring it in. And I remember the man on the telly gave this station name"—she imitated a male voice—"'DCI John Beck at Victoria Police Station'—so I decided to bring it here."

The whole tale was ludicrously improbable, like some nineteenth-century mother's explanation for where babies came from. Yet the details were entirely plausible. Beck *had* given the station name at the appeal. Lillington Gardens was walking distance from both the Rose & Crown and the nick, and it was both large enough and probably quiet enough on a Sunday morning that someone might be able to leave something on a bench without attracting notice. But a baby?

"Ms. Beatty, I think you can see how unlikely all this sounds."

The girl shrugged. "I can't help that. It's what happened."

Her face had taken on a mulish look. Allen recognized it as the expression of a witness about to stop cooperating.

"All right, I'll tell you what. I'd like you to drive back to Lillington Gardens with DC Desbury here and show him the route you took from your house to where you found the baby. While you do that, I'll call the Rose & Crown and explain everything, and DC Desbury will drop you there when you're finished at Lillington Gardens."

"It wasn't a route." She sounded remarkably like Nisha Patel. "It was a few steps."

Neither Allen nor Desbury responded. The girl wrapped her arms around her bag and slumped down. She looked at her watch again, then sighed. "Well, I guess I don't have a choice, do I? But can I at least use the ladies' before I go? I really need the loo."

"Of course. I'll take you there myself." Allen nodded at Desbury to stay where he was.

From her vantage point next to the toilet door, she could just see through the square of glass set into the conference-room door. She made out Beck's head and chest. If she stood on her toes, she could glimpse the top of the Anglepoise lamp that stood on the conference table. A few steps closer, and she saw the tops of the Carpenters' heads. Two more, and she saw that they were bending over the baby, who was smiling up at Vivien Carpenter, reaching out to her with a starfish hand.

She checked her watch. The girl had been in the toilet for five minutes. That was long enough. She opened the door. "Ms. Beatty? Let's get going. We don't want to make you later than you need to be."

There was no reply. She went in, rapped on each cubicle door, then pushed them open. They were empty.

She ran the few steps back to the interview room. Desbury sat at the table, writing something on the pad. He was alone.

"Have you seen the girl?"

"The girl?"

"Yes, Nell Beatty. Did she come back in here?"

He stood up so fast that the pad shot across the table. "She hasn't been in here since she left with you."

They ran to reception, looked at the empty space, the tramp sitting in one of the chairs, and raced out to the street. There were only oblivious pedestrians on their way to other places. Allen ran to the right, Desbury to the left, checking doorways and open doors. But there was nothing to find. The girl was gone.

27

Later, she learned that after the Carpenters were visited by Beck they'd been seen by Commander Parker, and eventually by the commissioner himself. Kate came over from the lab, made a tiny pinprick in the baby's foot, then squeezed out a drop of blood and typed it right there on the conference-room table.

"It was B positive," she said to Allen many times afterward. "The same as Tom Carpenter's."

In the afternoon, there was a press conference. Beck and his polished buttons stood at the podium with the Carpenters and announced the recovery of Baby Bella, who was clutched in her mother's arms. The air filled with the glare of flashbulbs as photographers surged forward to get the best shot of Bella sandwiched between her smiling parents, Bella grabbing her mother's hair, even Bella crying from the noise and confusion. Mr. Carpenter thanked the police for all their hard work and for producing the resolution he'd prayed for. Then Beck took over again. There would be no questions at this time. The Carpenters understandably wanted to get home as soon as possible. The police would release a full statement shortly.

The front pages of Monday's papers were taken over by inch-high headlines: BABY BELLA BACK IN MOTHER'S ARMS; BABY BELLA HAPPY AND HEALTHY AFTER MIRACLE RETURN; MOTHER'S SMILE SAYS WHAT WORDS CAN'T, a photo of the grinning parents and baby underneath. "DCI Beck of the Metropolitan Police today announced the safe return of five-month-old Bella Carpenter," all the articles seemed to begin. In later years, Allen would reflect that Beck had probably done her a service by taking over the public appeal and the press conference. The return of Bella Carpenter became a feather in his cap, but it would almost certainly have been an albatross around her neck. He had presided over a determined investigation and a successful outcome. A woman would have been seen as running a search that failed to find a culprit and was salvaged only by a miraculous piece of good fortune. Because of his eagerness to rise, she was also able to keep climbing.

At the time, though, she wasn't thinking about any of that. Instead she was in the dim and sticky interior of the Rose & Crown pub in Chelsea, where no one had ever heard of Nell Beatty. Just as they hadn't heard of her in the Rose & Crown in Mayfair, or Southwark, or Hammersmith. Just as when she rang the number the girl had given them, a recorded voice told her the number didn't exist.

After that, she went to Lillington Gardens. There was a bench in a green area a few yards from Parkinson House, but when she climbed the stairs to flat 14, the door was opened by a fat, red-faced man who told her no one named Nell Beatty lived there. He'd moved into the place four years earlier, and in that time he'd never heard of anyone with that name or encountered a girl like the one Allen described. He'd remember if he had, he added with a deep laugh. Allen knocked on the door of every other flat on that floor, but no one had seen or heard of Nell.

The next day, Allen sent her team on a house-to-house to see if Nell Beatty lived in any flat in Lillington Gardens, or if anyone who lived there knew of her at all. The estate had more than 1,500 flats, and after eight hours all the men came back empty-handed.

"I knew she was lying," Allen said triumphantly to Phil at dinner that evening. "She made the whole thing up."

Phil picked a shred of meat off the chicken carcass. "I can't imagine your lads were best pleased."

"What's that supposed to mean?"

"Well, the investigation's been wound up, hasn't it? The parents have identified the baby; she's been matched to them by blood type. Jesus, she looks exactly like them, and like the picture Carpenter gave you! I imagine the lads were looking forward to a bit of rest, not banging up and down tower-block stairs trying to find someone you knew didn't exist."

It was the first time he hadn't been on her side. "She exists. I just haven't found her yet."

"I don't understand why you're even looking." He leaned back as she picked up his empty plate. "Nobody's asking for any follow-up."

"*You* don't understand?" She clattered the crockery in the sink. "You're a solicitor, for God's sake. We have rules. We have laws. We catch and punish offenders so other people don't commit crimes, so justice can even the scales."

"Okay, okay." He held up a hand to calm her. She hated it when he did that. "That's not what I meant. I meant, why is she so important to you?"

Allen gripped the edge of the sink, gathering her thoughts before she turned to face him.

"Child kidnappers don't leave the children they've kidnapped somewhere for someone to find. You and I both know that if a child kidnapper wants to get rid of the child they've taken, they kill it. Like the Lindbergh baby all those years ago. Like that Walsh boy in Florida."

"And in Australia the year before last, a ten-year-old was abducted and released after eighteen hours."

"*One* case. One case among hundreds."

"Fine, that's an anomaly. But this baby is here, alive. How do you account for that?"

"That's the part I can't figure out. At first, I thought maybe the girl took her then regretted it. A real baby is a lot harder to handle than one you create in your fantasies." She felt a stab of worry as she said that but pushed it down. "I thought maybe this was her way of returning Bella when she found she didn't really want her."

"From what you told me, she doesn't sound the type to climb in and out of a window and down a fire escape."

"Which is why I gave up on that idea. Now I wonder if she and Carpenter . . . Maybe they were lovers, and the baby she brought in was theirs."

"You think she and Carpenter, who everyone says was devoted to his wife, even obsessed with her, had an affair and a baby exactly the same age as Carpenter's daughter with his wife, and when she heard theirs was missing she thought she'd substitute hers instead? Even if that weren't implausible, it's a hell of a risk to take. What if you had found the real Bella?"

"You didn't meet this girl. She didn't give the impression of being a long-range thinker. Or maybe they connived together in it somehow so she was sure we'd never find Bella." She saw the look on his face. "I know, I know. It's awful. And it's ridiculous. But there's something there. And I have to work to get to it."

"Assuming that there is something there, I don't see how you can get to it. False address, false work information, not even a photo. I don't see how you can even trace her."

"We can find her by looking up her birth certificate, then contacting her parents," she said to Desbury the next day.

"How old is she?" He looked up from the box he was filling with open lead reports.

"You were in the room with her. What would you say? Eighteen? Maybe younger? Call it between eighteen and sixteen."

"So you want to work through the birth certificates of all girls born in the UK between 1972 and 1974 named Nell Beatty, or Ellen Beatty, or Eleanor Beatty, Helen Beatty, or anything else that could be shortened to Nell? If that's even her real name. She gave a false address and employer. Why should we believe she gave her real name?"

How could Allen explain that there was something in the way the girl had said the name, snapping it out automatically, that made her think it was real? Anyway, it didn't matter. He was right. Any attempt to search for her by birth certificate would be hopeless. And Phil was right too. Continuing to try to find the girl was an exercise in futility.

"No, forget about her. Instead I want you to ring up Terry Glaister and talk to him again. He liked you. You were mates. Try and poke at his description of Carpenter's devotion to his wife. You heard what he said. Men tell tales when they're together, and there's an unspoken understanding that they won't be repeated. Maybe all his descriptions of Carpenter's adoration were a smoke screen to put us off. See what you can get out of him."

"Why?"

"I told you why. To see what he really knows about Carpenter's private life. Specifically, to see if he can tell us that Carpenter was seeing the girl."

"But why go to all that bother?" Desbury gestured around the incident room, at the officers moving packed boxes, the techies unplugging the bank of telephones. "The case has been closed. The Carpenters identified Bella, and now they're all back home, overjoyed. Why keep investigating where there's no need?"

Because I'm your superior officer, and I tell you to, Allen wanted to say, but after their time together it was too late to pull rank. *Because what happened doesn't feel right.* But how could she say that to a fellow officer, as trained as she was to prize logic and rationality? *Because I am senior investigating officer on this case, and I still have questions.* But as he had just pointed out, there was no case anymore. Therefore, she was no longer senior investigating officer. Therefore, any questions she might have no longer mattered.

Behind him, she saw Viner smirking as he eavesdropped. He elbowed the man next to him and whispered something. They both laughed. Her face burned. Like a sulky child, she shrugged at Desbury then turned and walked back into her office.

"I sent all the evidence to storage this morning. Why?" Kate swept files off the chair in front of her desk. "Sit down."

Allen sat. "No real reason. It's just that . . . it feels wrong. The idea that someone would take a baby, then abandon her, and then she would be found and brought in by a completely unconnected individual, seems improbable. It's too much of a coincidence."

"Once you spend some time in a forensics lab, you learn that improbable has no relation to impossible. Impossible depends on the physical evidence, not the human mind. Mothers do abandon their babies, which seems improbable given the strength of the maternal bond. But it happens. And abducted babies have been found unharmed before. Like the one taken earlier this year."

"Yes, you said that before. But that baby was found by the police with the woman who took her, not stumbled on by a stranger. And mothers who abandon their babies usually do that at a hospital, or a church, not in the middle of a council estate." She'd had time by now to come up with some evidence to support her feelings. She began to list all the oddities of the case: not just the discovery but the abduction, apparently performed in silence, and the lack of any apparent motive.

When she finished, Kate stayed silent for a long time. Then she said, "Without the girl, there's no real hope of proving any genetic connection between her and the baby. But if you could get a larger blood sample, or a cheek swab, from the baby, I could have a DNA test run on it, and on the parents' samples. That could tell you if one or both of the parents isn't the baby's biological parent. Though you'd have to find a way to pay for it, and it would take a while for the results to come through."

Allen thought of her house deposit savings account. "I'll pay for it. And at this stage I'm fine with a while. It's better than never knowing, which is the other option." She started to stand, ready to set out immediately.

Kate put out a hand. "Maybe wait for the weekend. If nothing else, it'll give you time to think of an explanation."

"I don't need time to think of one. I'll tell them . . . I'll tell them . . ." But nothing came into her mind. She slumped back against the chair.

In the end, she waited until Saturday, and by then she'd realized she didn't need to come up with an explanation. She would tell them the truth. Surely the intelligent, well-educated Carpenters must have wondered if this miracle baby was really their daughter. Surely they'd want to know if she wasn't.

Only once she was inside the Carpenters' home did she realize how little she understood about parenthood.

28

"It wouldn't hurt her at all," Allen explained. "Just a little needle prick, then a little squeeze. Or a swab from her cheek, if you'd prefer."

She could see how the deposit on the Carpenters' house would have stretched a freelance journalist and a painter to the limit. It was a huge Victorian with a back garden that extended at least forty feet. Remembering her conversation with Phil the previous weekend, though, she could also see how it would have appealed to two future parents. It would be a wonderful space to bring up children—were it not for the fact that everything was run-down. The long garden was a mass of bracken, the floorboards of the house were worn almost raw, and in the front room, one wall had been half painted pale green, then abandoned.

"But you don't need another test." Vivien Carpenter was a completely different person. Gone was the zombie clinging to her husband, the hysteric manically planning impossible campaigns. In her place was a cheerful woman with a warm smile, spooning homemade puree into the mouth of the baby on her lap. This Vivien Carpenter wiped her baby's mouth with one expert flick of a napkin, frowning slightly. "This is Bella. Tom and I told you that. Why do you need to do another test if you know who she is?"

"They don't need to." Tom Carpenter, who had been staring out the French windows at the garden, turned around. "They don't, and they won't." He locked eyes with Allen. "We have no intention of causing our daughter even one more moment of discomfort, just so that you can prove something we already know."

"I understand your concern. But with all respect, you don't *really* know . . ."

"We do." Carpenter had changed too. No longer a man at his wit's end, he had become a lofty patriarch, speaking in pronouncements. "This is our daughter. We know that."

"But—"

"We'd like you to leave now." He laid a hand on his wife's shoulder. She smiled up at him while the baby stared at them both.

Outside Beck's office window the next day, the afternoon sky was heavy with impending rain. Beck sat back in his chair, observing her over steepled fingers.

"Thomas Carpenter says you came to see him and his wife. He said you asked for a blood test for their daughter that you then admitted was unnecessary."

"That's not exactly right, sir. I asked if they'd let me take a small sample of blood or saliva from the baby so we could test to be certain she's Bella."

"Of course she's Bella!" The spring under his seat groaned as he leaned forward. "They identified her, and we did a blood test! What more proof do you need?"

"I wanted to run a DNA test just to be absolutely certain, sir."

"A two-thousand-pound test to tell us what we already know?" He tutted. "How d'you think Command would react to my ordering that? Our budget is scarcely enough to run our investigations as it is! And Norton tells me you've had men running all sorts of inquiries to find out if Carpenter ever had a mistress, or arranged to take a baby from another woman to replace the one that went missing, or some other mad theory."

"Again, that's not quite correct, sir. I've been—"

"I don't care what you've been doing. I just want you to stop. Carpenter is threatening to file a harassment complaint." He inhaled, then spoke more calmly. "We've come out golden here, Allen. The baby was found; the parents identified her. Baby back, parents happy. *You've* come out golden. All right, the little bombshell that found her told you a bunch of porkies and vanished into nowhere, but since that means we don't have to pay out the reward, that's one for us too."

"Sir, I—"

"No." Beck slapped his hands flat on the desktop, fingers splayed. "The investigation is closed. You did stellar work, Detective Inspector Allen. Now it's time to move on. Stay away from this case, and from the Carpenters. That's an order."

For a second, the office was so silent that Allen could hear a car starting in the street below. Then Beck said, "You can go."

29

Two weeks later, she had a miscarriage. She woke up in the middle of the night with cramps and bleeding, and when she was finally seen at A&E, they told her she had lost the baby. They kept her in overnight and had her come back ten days later for a follow-up. The kind doctors assured her there was no reason to worry. First-trimester miscarriages weren't uncommon, and they had no bearing on future pregnancies.

"Plenty of time," Phil said as he rocked her back and forth at night when she cried. "We have plenty of time."

She didn't take any sick leave, and she didn't tell anyone at work except Desbury. Even him she told weeks after it happened. Things had been different since he'd challenged her about the case. The two of them were awkward where a couple of weeks before they'd been loose; she avoided working closely with him because she didn't know how to explain how he'd offended her. When she told him about the miscarriage, he looked stricken, but the closest they came to their former intimacy was his responding that his wife had had one, too, before becoming pregnant with their first daughter. Not knowing how to reply, Allen stood mute in front of him until he reached out to pat her shoulder, then walked away.

Still, it seemed Phil and the doctors were right, because in the spring of 1991, she fell pregnant again, and, although that resulted in a second miscarriage, she was pregnant once more in the autumn of 1993. She and Phil bought a large flat on the border of West Hampstead and slowly did it up.

In the meantime, new cases came and went. There was a burglary at a jewelry store on the King's Road, a long and careful operation that resulted in the breakup of a major vice ring, a few murder investigations that Allen brought to a successful close. As the years stretched out, she rose through the ranks. She was made a DCI in 2002, a superintendent some years later. She had her picture in the papers a few more times, and now none of the articles suggested her emotions might interfere with her work. She knew these promotions helped the women coming up behind her, but for her they just seemed to mean a life of more paperwork and less activity. If anyone ever made a realistic show about a policewoman, she sometimes thought, it would have to consist mostly of scenes of her rereading documents alone in a room. It was ironic that being good at something she loved meant she was promoted farther and farther away from it. Still, the promotions also meant that when New Scotland Yard opened at Victoria Embankment in 2016, she was moved into one of its large, clean spaces. There was a picture window overlooking the Thames, and she moved her desk so that she could watch the London Eye rotating while she signed her stacks of forms.

Desbury moved up the ranks too. They still ran into each other occasionally as he became a DS and then a DI, but then he transferred divisions, and she lost sight of him. She heard that he'd moved to Bristol. His parents lived there, and his mother was ill, DI Wanda Greenhill told her when they met up for one of their semiregular lunches. He'd taken a job with Avon and Somerset Police so he could be near her and help out. After that, Allen saw his name from time to time in the national crime bulletin, linked to an arrest or initiative in the Bristol area. She was always proud when she read about these, even though the two of them hadn't spoken in ten, twenty, twenty-five years.

Throughout all this, she stayed away from the Carpenters. A well-trained police officer learns to suppress a great deal: fear, adrenaline, and hysteria that might lead to mistakes, the natural instinct to run away from life-threatening danger rather than toward it. They also learn to suppress their own wishes in the face of a direct order. Like the army, the police force can only work if every member agrees to the sacrifice of independence that makes up the chain of command. When Allen joined the force, she made that sacrifice. She did what Beck had ordered and never even ran the Carpenters' names through a database. After a while, it got easier.

But once a month, for years, she locked her office door, sat down at her computer, and checked to see if a Nell, or an Ellen, Eleanor, Helen, Helena, or even Nella Beatty had been arrested. None of those names ever appeared. Finally, after 124 fruitless months, she decided to greet the new millennium by abandoning old hopes. She stopped looking in December of 2000.

She still thinks about the Baby Bella case. As time goes on, though, it would be more accurate to say that thoughts of it come to her. Sometimes when she sees a dark-haired baby on television, once when she read a poem about Wells Cathedral, every time she thinks she might've caught sight of Nell Beatty on the street. Life grows over her itch to know, covering it with schedules and timetables, welcome drinks and leaving dos, restructurings and removals and remembering to pick up milk on the way home. In the back of her mind, she often thinks there'll be time to do a thorough search for Nell once she finishes this memo to all DCIs, this presentation at a colloquium, this service on the subcommittee in charge of determining equitable hiring methods. Once that's taken care of, she'll find the beautiful Nell Beatty somehow, and she'll get it all out of her. She'll make her tell her who she really is, and she'll figure out how that connects to what she's certain was the murder of Bella Carpenter.

FEBRUARY 2020

1

By three in the afternoon, the sun is low in the February sky, and the reception after Parker's memorial is nearly over. Allen stands by the arch that leads into the funeral home's function room and watches those few of her contemporaries and superiors who remain.

In a corner, Retired Commander Beck talks quietly to Parker's widow. He's redder in the face and thicker around the middle than he once was, but his uniform is still immaculate, and the creases in his trousers are sharp as a knife edge. His eyes, focused on the widow, are full of caring. As Allen foresaw, he's made his way up the chain of command by just the right combination of looking good and acting appropriately.

A short distance away, the other lingerers have formed a cluster next to a table holding a collection of half-empty bottles of wine. Commander Peter Thune, plain DS Thune when Allen worked with him in Child Abuse as a newly minted sergeant in the eighties, has also worn his dress uniform. During Allen's first week on the CA team, Thune had come up to her in the break room and told her the best way to climb the ladder was on her knees. Next to him is Detective Superintendent Henry King, DC King all those years ago when Allen was a DS, who still refers to every woman he encounters as a tart unless she's over fifty, in which case she's an old biddy. King's talking to Retired Deputy Assistant Commissioner Adam Fraite, who'd been Superintendent Fraite when he recommended Allen for DCI after she'd closed down a major smuggling ring in her late thirties, then, over a celebratory drink, earnestly asked her if she felt that being past the menopause made her better at the job. Retired Chief Superintendent David Marrogate laughs at a comment one of them makes. Marrogate would've been the deciding vote against her promotion to super five years before if he hadn't retired early on a full pension after someone leaked his remark that the force was trying to attract more Black PCs because "they blend in better with villains."

On the far side of the huddle, she can see Norton, a good thirty pounds heavier than he was when they worked together but his blond hair still shiny and plentiful. He made it to DCI then left to work in private security—which is probably why his jacket and trousers fit like a glove and gleam discreetly among the aging baggy suits that the others wear. He catches her looking and raises his glass with a smirk.

Allen remembers these men when they were young pups, and now here they are as old dogs, stiffening, paunchy, and denying their deterioration as powerful men do. She watches Fraite reach for a ham sandwich, then another.

If they're old dogs, what is she? Like them, she's done her thirty and more. Like them, she's nostalgic for a past that was far more exciting than her present. Maybe the only difference is that they're in a group while she's off to the side. Of course, they're the ones who put her there. There's another burst of laughter from the cluster. Christ, she hates male camaraderie.

"A fine turnout." Beck has materialized next to her. "And thoughtful of the ones who really knew him to stay behind. I'm sure it means a great deal to Annabel." As they watch, Norton walks up to Mrs. Parker and begins murmuring. Mrs. Parker nods her head as if keeping time.

"I saw you as I was giving my eulogy," Beck says. "It was good of you to come. He would have been pleased at the show of respect."

Does he have a psychic hotline to the dead Parker's opinions about respect? But this isn't the first time she's been patronized by a superior—it isn't even the first time this year—so she just says, "I liked him."

It's true. Parker had been one of the few senior male officers who'd never made reference to her gender. All right, for the most part he'd achieved that by appearing not to notice that she had any gender at all, but it was still a welcome relief. And relief had made her like him.

"Didn't we all." Beck's sigh interrupts her thoughts. "Didn't we all."

Over the years, Allen has sometimes wondered if Beck has forgotten the order he gave her all that time ago, to stay away from the Carpenters and the Carpenter case. After all, many investigations have come and gone since then, numerous and important enough to block out a random order given in a moment of irritation. But those same investigations have also pushed aside her thoughts of testing his memory. There was always something more important to attend to. Now she decides to see.

She treads gently. "I happened to speak to Detective Chief Inspector Desbury this morning, sir. He sends his regrets."

"Desbury? Do I know him?"

"You might remember him as Detective Constable Desbury? He worked at Victoria nick. He's in Bristol now."

"And he called about Commander Parker? Thoughtful. Of course, Ned Parker touched many lives."

She needs to pull him away from the clichés he finds so comfortable.

"No, sir, his call wasn't about Commander Parker. Not specifically. He called in connection with a case. A murder in Bristol. The victim was a woman named Nell Beatty."

"Oh?" Beck's voice is bored. He's looking yearningly at the little knot of men near the refreshment table.

"Yes. She was connected with a case Desbury and I once worked." She swallows to wet her dry throat. "The Carpenter case."

"The Carpenter case!" Suddenly she has all his attention. "The case with the couple who got their baby back?"

"Yes, sir." She says hopefully, "It was a long time ago now."

"It may have been a long time ago, but you don't forget a case like that." As if to prove it, he rattles out, "Tourists. In town for a few days and someone snatched their baby from the hotel. You brought in the wrong suspect for questioning. As I recall, three days later the baby was found and returned to her parents."

"You have a very good memory, sir," Allen says miserably.

"As I say, you don't forget a case like that. Every parent's worst nightmare. But happily resolved. And a sterling success for us." He frowns at her, the vertical creases above his nose deepening. "I also remember that once the case was resolved, the parents complained of harassment, and I ordered you to have nothing more to do with it. I trust that the reappearance of DC Desbury won't change that."

"No, sir."

"Good." As if the curtain has just dropped on a particularly distasteful evening at the theater, Beck straightens up and turns away. His buttons catch the light. "Good to see you here, Allen. I'm sure it means a great deal to Annabel." He drifts over to the group by the table.

Allen has already offered her condolences to the widow. Since this leaves her with nothing more to do, she turns to go. Behind her, she hears a burst of laughter. The back of her neck burns. Maybe it hadn't been the result of some comment about her, but maybe it had. Years of experience tell her to assume that it had.

Years of experience have also taught her to let such moments roll off her back, and by the time she reaches the Tube station, her thoughts have moved on. Moved back, really. Nell's colorless face against the wooden bench swims up in front of her, followed by a vision of her as she was in her glory on that August day. And then, inevitably, the questions that have nagged at her ever since: *Who was Nell Beatty, really? Who was the baby she'd brought to the police station? What really happened to Bella Carpenter?*

She leaves the Piccadilly line at Green Park. From there, the Jubilee line will take her north to her stop at Finchley Road. If she goes in the opposite direction, it'll also take her south to Westminster, and from there a short walk will take her to the Yard. She stands in front of the maps for the diverging platforms. The warm air shifts as a train approaches.

Of course she goes south. An old dog following her nose.

2

When she moved to New Scotland Yard four years ago, she brought her parents for a visit. She knew they'd be pleased, but she hadn't anticipated how pleased. Her mother kept touching the nameplate that said Superintendent Martha Allen, while her father insisted on taking her picture next to it. "Allen of the Yard," he'd said. "Remember that program from the BBC, Daphne? *Fabian of the Yard.* And now here we are, Allen of the Yard." He'd had the photo framed later, and that framed version now stands on her desk. He'd died a year after he'd taken it; in his honor, Allen wrote to every newspaper she could think of to announce his death. Her mother died a year after that. Allen likes to look at the photo on days when the Yard just feels like the place she works.

Recently, the photo's been joined by a very new, very fast computer. The sleek and shiny result of the police service's latest upgrade, the monitor arches up from her desk on a silver stem, its chips and circuits housing a collection of databases that would have taken up whole buildings thirty years before. Like every police officer of a certain age, she remembers learning that the Yorkshire Ripper investigation amassed so many files that the floor of the incident room had to be specially reinforced. Now they could have it all stored in one ten pound box with a twenty-four-inch screen.

Sitting down behind her desk she takes off her shoes, wiggles her toes, and types "Nell Beatty" into the Police National Computer.

When she'd stopped checking for Nell in the PNC in 2000, she'd congratulated herself for finally making the break. Looking at the screen now, though, she wishes she'd held on for just one more year. The record that opens up shows that in 2001 Nell Beatty was arrested and entered into the database for possession of a Class A drug.

Nell's mug shot from that arrest fills one corner of the screen. In it she looks like the young Diana Dors Allen remembers, only reduced.

She's still lovely, but her skin is duller, her hair thinner and lanker. Now you can see her future in her face. Next to the photo, there is, at last, a birth date: May 17, 1972. So she was eighteen when Allen first saw her and not quite forty-eight when she died.

Below the picture, the screen is tight with entries. After the first arrest, there's a steady trickle of minor cautions stretching from 2001 through 2003. Then in 2004, there's another one for possession of a Class A drug, and another, and after that the trickle becomes a stream, then a river.

In 2006, a third Class A possession, then a fourth.

In 2007, two for solicitation.

In 2008, an arrest for possession with intent to supply. That's a serious charge, and, sure enough, on the next line there's a court date then a notation that she received a one-year prison sentence.

2009, she was cautioned for possession again. She could only have been out for a couple of months. There's a note added there too: this time she was sentenced to a government Drug Rehabilitation Requirement program, part of a new initiative to stop addiction-related crime via treatment rather than prison.

After that there's a gap. When the cautions start up again, they're all in Bristol.

2011, two for shoplifting.

2012, cautioned twice for being drunk and disorderly and once for soliciting.

2013, three D&Ds and one caution for soliciting.

2014, two more for soliciting.

Just before Christmas 2014, arrested for assaulting an officer. Another rehab sentence, this time to an Alcohol RRP.

Not even a year later, a caution for shoplifting, then a month later another drunk and disorderly.

2016, one caution for aggressive begging and one for vagrancy after being found sleeping rough.

2017, two for soliciting, once in January and once in November.

2018, soliciting again.

2019, three D&Ds, one caution for shoplifting.

January 2020—a month ago!—another caution for soliciting.

Allen sits in front of this wreck of a life. She can't count the number of people like this that she's seen in her career, people whose lives never righted themselves after their first arrest, first prison sentence, first stint in rehab. As a constable, a sergeant, even still sometimes as an inspector, she would put her finger on the first whatever-it-was and think, *There. That's the moment it all went wrong.* But the longer she was in the force, the more she realized that there was no single moment. People's lives were formed from thousands of decisions that felt right at the time and led to places they never could have pictured. You had to deal with what was in front of you.

For years, Nell Beatty hasn't been in front of her, and she's dealt with other things. But even though Nell and the Carpenter case have receded from the forefront of her mind, they haven't vanished. Far from it. Not a week has gone by without her thinking of them. And, as often happens over a span of years, the more she's thought about the case, the more her belief has hardened: Something about it wasn't right, and if she could just put the pieces together correctly, she could find out what. It's just that she's never been able to figure out exactly what the pieces are, or how they might fit.

For a while, she'd considered the scenario she'd outlined to Phil, the one in which Nell was the kidnapper. Nell had glimpsed Bella somehow, somewhere. Perhaps while the Carpenters were carrying the basket from their parking spot to the hotel, she'd passed by, looked into it, and seen her. That glimpse had triggered something in her, and she'd watched to see what hotel they went into, waited or returned later, then crept up and down the fire escape to take the baby. Only, having taken her, she'd discovered the reality of having a frightened, hungry baby on her hands. Overwhelmed, she'd concocted the discovery story and brought Bella to the station to get rid of her.

But that idea was ridiculous. Aside from anything else, to be true, it would have required a level of obsession that Nell couldn't have hidden behind casual conversation about interview-room decor. So, as the years passed, Allen devised in its place two solutions that centered on her original, and more plausible, suspect: Tom Carpenter.

In the first years after the case, she'd sometimes wondered if Vivien Carpenter had been involved—but then she'd remember her behavior at the hotel, the sound of her voice when the baby had appeared in the lobby of the nick. In the face of those, it was impossible to believe she'd disposed of Bella. Whereas Carpenter's own words—"This is all my fault. I made a terrible mistake"—made him a plausible suspect. And so, in both her scenarios, Carpenter was his daughter's killer. He'd murdered Bella and, Allen reasoned, disposed of her body in the skip that was emptied before he reported her disappearance.

In her first scenario, Carpenter killed Bella on purpose. He and Nell were lovers—or, more plausibly, had been lovers but weren't anymore. Hadn't Marjorie Wallingford said that Carpenter continued to visit London on freelance assignments for a time after he and his wife moved to Wells? He and Nell would meet on those visits, and the baby Nell brought to the station was the result. That baby and Bella looked too much alike for there to be any other explanation. In this scenario, Nell didn't want her baby, and she threatened to expose the affair if Carpenter didn't take it off her hands. Carpenter saw a way to keep his secret and save his family by slotting his illegitimate daughter into his legitimate daughter's place. He did what he needed to do to make that happen.

When she was feeling more kindly toward Carpenter, Allen acknowledged that she hadn't seen or heard anything to suggest he was a psychopath. At these times, she thought he'd probably killed Bella in a moment of rage or exasperation. On a night already hot enough to fray tempers, she imagined, Bella had done something that lit his short fuse. He'd lost control, then concocted the kidnapping story to cover that up. In this version, he and Nell had also been lovers, and Nell also didn't want their baby, but this time he'd asked her to bring their daughter to the station to disguise what he'd done. Maybe he'd slipped out to a phone box and contacted Nell while his in-laws were watching over his tranquilized wife; maybe he'd rung her after he'd disposed of the baby's body. She'd been happy to let him make the substitution because it took the baby off her hands. Allen preferred this version of events. It fit better with what she knew of the participants.

As the years have gone by, and she's worried at these scenarios again and again, she's also started to wonder about the source of her own certainty that one of them must be true. Sometimes, brushing her teeth or putting her washing into the machine, she's reminded herself that she's a police officer, for God's sake. What about "Accept nothing, Believe nothing, Challenge everything"? In some of these moments, she reminds herself of something her university psychology lecturer once said: *Humans are rational animals, and that means that no matter how rational we are, we are also animals, with animal instincts.* When it comes to this case, she tells herself, her instincts are alive: it smells wrong. At other moments, she reminds herself of what she told Phil and Kate all those years ago: that the abduction down a rickety metal fire escape had supposedly been performed in silence; that there had been no note; that against all precedent and logic the kidnapper had simply abandoned the suddenly unwanted baby in a public area in the middle of one of the country's most crowded cities. In the face of all that, she reassures her police brain, she didn't even need instinct.

As for why she continued to devise and refine these hypotheses over the years, poking at them like an aching tooth, she knows that at least part of it was because a solution to the case was both impossible and tantalizingly close. She wouldn't—*couldn't*—contact Tom Carpenter, but Nell was still out there, waiting to be found to help solve the puzzle.

Only now that she has been found, it's too late for her to help solve anything. Allen looks at the diminished face on the screen and curses under her breath.

The sound of her own voice breaks her concentration. She looks up. Outside the window, the lights on the London Eye have come on, and the sky behind them is black. She checks her watch. It's seven fifteen. She's been there for three and a half hours. She shakes her head to clear it, then moves the cursor and highlights Nell's name in the search box. For just a second, her hands hover over the keys, her left middle finger, pinkie, and index finger extended to type C, A, R. Just one quick search, just to see if anything comes up when she replaces Nell's name with Carpenter's.

Then she remembers that use of the PNC is regularly monitored and reported on to make sure it matches the police records management code of practice. Her reason for looking up Carpenter fits none of the categories listed in that code. As she drops her hands, she doesn't ask herself which of the two stops her—ethical qualms or the fear that the monitoring might somehow reach Beck and alert him that she'd defied his order. She just reaches for the mouse to close the screen. Time to go home.

Except that instead of clicking the red Exit button, the cursor travels a little farther and clicks Print. She doesn't try to stop it. All right, strictly speaking she shouldn't print Nell's file. Taking home a copy of a PNC file doesn't breach the Met's Code of Ethics, but it teeters on the edge of it. If Nell were alive, it would be flatly against the rules to remove her record from the building. In those circumstances, Superintendent Martha Allen would give someone who did so a terrifying reprimand. But Nell isn't alive. *Let me keep a copy of this record as her memorial*, Allen thinks. It's probably the only one the poor girl will ever get.

As she puts her coat on, she feels a weight in one pocket. Her mobile. She put it on silent and slipped it in there just before the memorial service began. Pulling it out, she wakes the screen. Seven missed calls, all from London numbers, none in her contacts. Well, she knows what that's about. She drops the phone in her bag, folds the printout into quarters and slips it in after, then switches off the light, closes her office door, and leaves the building. Outside, it's as dark as midnight.

3

The flat's cold when she gets in. It usually is these days. Phil was the one who was good at setting timers and checking alarms, and now that they're no longer together, she forgets as often as she remembers. Meanwhile, over there in West London, he and Scarlett probably come home to a toasty house every night.

She's surprised by this moment of spite. After two years apart, she isn't angry anymore. Truthfully, she hadn't really been angry after the first few weeks, and even then the anger had mostly been the result of shock and hurt.

She closes the door and turns on the thermostat. In the little kitchenette, she switches on the kettle and reaches for the *It's A Fair Cup, Guv* mug her brother, Greg, bought her when she made DCI. She opens the cupboard for a tea bag.

In the time before everybody who mattered knew that she and Phil had separated, the time when she had to explain over and over, Allen told people who asked that after thirty years together they'd agreed that they'd given each other everything they could. The relationship had run its course. It was an easy explanation, and in a way it was true. Phil hadn't cheated on her, or treated her badly, or said he didn't love her anymore. He hadn't left her for Scarlett. He hadn't even met Scarlett until six months after the separation. And he hadn't left Allen because they couldn't have children. He'd never cared about that; he'd told her so many times. Instead he'd left her for a reason hard for others to understand but easy for her. He wanted to leave, he'd told her, because he was tired.

She understood what he meant because she was tired too. It was exhausting, trying to have a baby instead of just having one. The final miscarriage in 1993 had been wrenching, awful, devastating, but as time went on and they tried again and again with no luck, the process stopped being simply unhappy and became wearying. As they planned their sex life around a calendar and a thermometer, trying to become aroused on command and for a specific purpose, the notion of sex for pleasure, or even relief, became more and more distant. And once they started IVF, the efforts became grueling: injections and extractions, donations and implantations, all run to a schedule that seemed designed to produce stress and insecurity. If she hadn't wanted a child so much, she would have said they should stop after a couple of rounds. But she had wanted one, desperately, so she never did. They kept on until they'd spent all their money and all their energy. All for nothing in the end.

Well, all for nothing at any point. Which is how they'd discovered the tiredness of hope. How wearying it was to try again and then again, to think it might work—sometimes to think it was working—only to discover that it hadn't. And then to hope all over again despite yourself, to have a trail of failed attempts that should have taught you not to hope but hadn't, because hope was a feeling that couldn't be educated. It kept springing up long after it served any purpose so that you grew tired not just of the inevitable disappointment that followed it but of the hope itself.

Of course, those were Allen's feelings, articulated to herself long afterward. Phil had said nothing so precise, or so brutal, when he'd told her he was leaving. He'd only said that he was exhausted, and that although he loved her, his feelings for her couldn't be separated from that exhaustion. He loved her, but he wanted a life in which he didn't always feel that he was carrying a heavy load.

"People feel what they feel," Allen had said to Kate McMullan over a glass of wine in Kate's kitchen. "What can you do?"

It turned out, though, that there were many things you could do. You could go out—or stay in—and get sobbing drunk. You could scream, and yell, and say very, very cruel things, not because you didn't understand why what was happening was happening but because you were shocked and hurt, and anger was your immediate response to that. After that, all you could do was apologize.

She hadn't thought there could be worse to come, but there was. It was selling the flat that did it. The loss of the home she'd shared with her partner for a quarter of a century had forced her stubborn subconscious to understand what even the menopause hadn't fully brought home: There weren't going to be any babies. Selling the family home, the home they'd bought for a family, made her give up hope at last. And that was the worst.

So when the time had come to find a new place to live, she'd only wanted somewhere that offered her peace. And when she imagined peace, she imagined blankness. The flat she'd chosen was the newest of new builds, so neutral that it might have been designed by someone who had neither good taste nor bad taste but no taste at all. The kitchen was all brushed steel and white granite worktops, the bathroom gray tile and chrome, the living area and bedroom so whitewalled and white-carpeted that being in them was like standing in a vortex. It was exactly what she wanted. She put her things from the old flat into storage and moved in.

She'd known she was healed from the separation on the day she realized she disliked the place. She'd even started considering getting a cat: something to come home to, a repository for the love she'd begun to think she might feel again. Now she looks around at the walls on which she's hung some art in an unsuccessful effort to make it look homely, at the big vase in the shape of a strawberry that made her smile in the shop but against the white countertop looks like a giant human heart.

For the past couple of months, she's been looking for somewhere to buy. But it turns out that while the selling price of a flat you bought in West Hampstead in 1993 feels like ridiculous wealth, half of that feels like nothing when you want to buy something similar. She puts her phone on speaker, listening to the messages as she finishes making her tea. As she expected, all from estate agents. Over the past weeks, she's widened her search to anywhere north of the river, then to anywhere reasonably central, then to anywhere less than an hour away from the

Yard. Still there's been nothing. But the estate agents remain hopeful, and each of these has something he wants to show her—"only a little outside the price range you gave . . . ," "slightly farther out than we discussed, but . . ."

She'll follow up with them tomorrow. For now, she pulls her laptop toward her. Like a child prolonging the pleasure of anticipation before eating a sweet, she takes a sip of tea, swallowing slowly and feeling it stretch out from her stomach to warm her lungs. The flat's almost a normal temperature now, so she takes off her coat and hangs it on the hook by the door. Then she opens the laptop, types in her password. Once a browser is open, she types "Thomas Carpenter" into the search bar then clicks on Images. None of the pictures are of him, and when she hits All, none of the hundreds of hits seem to have anything to do with him. Finally, at the bottom of the third page, there's a link to a newspaper article rehashing the abduction, but that's dated one year after it happened. She stops at the bottom of the sixth page of useless results and types "Vivien Carpenter" into the search bar. That turns up only the private Instagram account of a young woman with very large breasts in a very small tube top.

She decides to work with what's in front of her. She reaches into her bag and pulls out Nell's record. Then she finds her reading glasses, puts them on, smooths the sheets of paper open on the counter, and starts to read.

If you leave aside the sheer number of cautions and arrests, there's actually not much out of the ordinary. It's the familiar story of a person with an addiction trying to find ways to support the dependency they can't kick. Even the addresses attached to London entries are in areas she's familiar with from her own days working the drugs squad: Islington, Hackney, a homeless shelter in King's Cross she recognizes from the times she brought people there. She doesn't know anything about the geography of Bristol, but thanks to the Internet she can easily find out if the addresses there lead to the same sort of places. She sits in front of the laptop she keeps on the counter and types the most recent into Google Maps. When the map appears, she picks up the little man in the lower right-hand corner and drops him onto the pin.

It's a house. She looks at the address again. Of course it is: There's no letter after the door number. Some cop she is. She looks back to the screen: 36 Walpole Road is a boxy pebble-dash two-story, right in the middle of a terrace of boxy pebble-dash two-stories. The only thing that sets it apart from its neighbors is a basket of pink geraniums hanging from a hook next to the door.

Bristol isn't London, obviously, but council housing regulations are the same across England. A single woman with no dependents would never be granted a house to live in all by herself. So who was Nell living with? Did she have children? A partner?

Allen's teeth press into her lower lip. People tell secrets to their partners. They tell them things they're ashamed of or want to forget or want absolution for. And once they're dead, those secrets just sit there, waiting for the right interviewer to draw them out.

But of course she needs to ask the SIO's permission to do anything connected to his case. She checks the computer's clock. It's nine o'clock. Her mother always told her the latest you could phone someone was ten.

She opens her email to retrieve the mobile number Desbury sent her.

4

Like many native Londoners, Allen has never felt a need to leave the city for long. Born in Clapham, attending university in central London, then spending most of her adult life on the north side of the city, she not-so-secretly believes that she's seen the best of what Britain has to offer. But police training doesn't confine itself to the capital, and in the early 2000s she spent a few days in Bristol doing a management course. As she boards the train at Paddington on Friday morning, feeling like a skiving schoolgirl because she's called in sick with a migraine, she tries to remember what the city was like. All she can recall are the insides of several university seminar rooms and a train station that looked like a long barn with a miniature Gothic cathedral attached.

When she arrives, she sees that she remembered the station right, at least. She buys a sandwich from the Simply Food in the ticket hall and eats it in the cab that takes her to Bristol Central Police Station. Out the windows, the city she passes doesn't really look that different from London. The streets are wider, and there are fewer people, but there's the same sense of bustle and focus, a place more concerned with life than appearance—maybe even more so than London, given the amount of graffiti she sees.

The taxi passes a Primark then makes a sharp left turn, then another, then comes to a halt in front of a gleaming tower of stacked rectangular windows framed in red and set into pale cement. "Central Police Station," the driver says.

She pulls herself out of the cab, stuffs the sandwich container into a bin outside, then pushes through a door into the lobby. The architect has gone for the same blond wood and white paint that decorate the interior of New Scotland Yard, but whereas there it looks clinical, here the wall of glass keeps the space bright and warm even in early February.

Desbury is waiting for her in one of the pale wooden chairs in reception. He's heavier than he used to be, but he stands up in the same abrupt way he'd entered the incident room for the first time all those years ago, and his face wears the same solemn, slightly worried expression it wore when he came to tell her that Tom Carpenter had faked crying at the public appeal. As he moves toward her, though, he breaks into a smile. She feels something loosen in her chest. She smiles back.

"I had to see you in the lobby for myself to believe you'd really come!" He wrings her hands. Up close, she can see other differences between him and the DC she knew. His eyes have crow's-feet at the corners, and two brackets have carved their way from his nostrils down to his lips. His hair is flecked with gray at the temples and crown. But this morning she was struck by just how silver her own hair has become, how the horizontal lines in her forehead have deepened from threads to grooves. Time creeps up on us all.

In the lift, Desbury makes small talk. "How was the funeral?"

"About what you'd expect. The old gang, the usual 'sad loss,' 'remember the good old days.'"

"Sounds like I was right to give it a miss."

"You were."

They lapse into silence. She stares at their fuzzy reflections, side by side in the chrome control panel.

His office, a square glass box, is set inside a larger room filled with rows of cubicles. A young PC sits in front of it at a glass-topped desk, working at a computer as sleek as her own. Inside, the office has a picture window, and privacy is provided by a vinyl mural of a tower that wraps around the glass walls, opaque on the outside but see-through once you're in. The effect is surprisingly pleasant, like being in the keep of a modern castle.

"This is nice."

"Thanks. Yeah, I've been in this building for about ten years, and I still feel like I'm not cool enough for it." He points at the armchair upholstered in a green nubbly fabric that faces the desk. "Have a seat."

He pokes his head out the door. "Shaha, could you get a tea for the superintendent? With milk, leave the bag in." He closes the door.

Allen laughs. "I can't believe you remember that."

He shrugs as he settles into his desk chair. "You don't forget something as important as that."

They sit in awkward silence. She looks around for something to comment on. On the window ledge is a photo of Desbury shaking hands with a man wearing the insignia of a chief constable. Next to it is a chunky glass triangle. Squinting, she's just able to make out that it's an Officer of the Year award from the Avon and Somerset Black Police Association. More frames line the front of his desk, their faces turned inward. Family photos. The desktop is covered in piles of paperwork in various stages of being attended to. She can see the daily arrest report in the center.

"What's your yearly average?" She tilts her head toward the report.

"Ninety-eight incidents per one thousand people. Not quite the worst in the area, but bad enough."

"Understaffed?"

"Who isn't? And recent events haven't helped with recruitment."

He doesn't need to explain. Policing is a small world, and everyone at the Met—probably every police officer in the country—knows the story of the troubles at Avon and Somerset. A chief constable suspended after accusations of inappropriate behavior toward female staff then resigning in disgrace. His acting replacement resigning after a year in the job, and then *his* replacement resigning after five months. The current man's been there for five years, but the word is that in that time the force has been under further strain. It's stretched thin as crime has increased and come under careful scrutiny as the number of women and minority recruits hasn't.

"I feel your pain. It's the same for us in London, if it's any comfort."

"Except that your new chief's a woman. And one who's been vocal about recruiting more women and minorities."

Allen considers telling him about the knot of men laughing behind her back at the reception the previous day. She wants to point out that, despite the promises of the Met's female chief constable, minority recruitment hasn't improved, and, if anything, a woman in the top post makes the men in the force feel gender equality's no longer a problem. But she's a guest, and she doesn't want to start an argument with someone whose help she needs, so she doesn't say anything.

Another awkward silence descends.

Fortunately there's a light knock at the door. The young man enters, carrying two mugs. He puts them on the desk.

"Thanks." Desbury reaches for one of the mugs. "Shaha, this is the Detective Superintendent Martha Allen that I've told you about. Detective Superintendent Allen, this is PC Aakash Shaha, my assistant and right-hand man."

The young man's huge eyes and long eyelashes give him the look of a worried deer, and when Allen says she's pleased to meet him, his cheeks turn rosy. When he leaves the office, he actually backs out. Allen lifts her mug to hide her smile. She remembers being that young, that in awe. She looks at Desbury. He's smiling too. The awkwardness eases a little.

She leans forward and puts her mug on the desk. "You said Nell did live with someone?"

"A bloke called Peter Rainey. He's the original tenant. Lived there with his sister and niece until 2015, when Nell moved in. Two of my DCs went yesterday to do the death notification."

"Anything interesting?"

"They said he didn't seem particularly upset, but we both know that means nothing." It's true. She's seen a murderer weep inconsolably at a death notification and an adoring wife stay as dry-eyed as a stranger.

"But you think he did it."

Desbury frowns. "It isn't that straightforward. Normally first instinct would be the partner, yes. Especially because records show officers were called out there more than once for fighting and domestic-abuse complaints. But you saw from her record that her most recent arrest was for solicitation?" Allen nods. "Well, the park where she was found is walking distance from one of our curb-crawling hotspots. So she could have been killed by a client. On the other hand, she was strangled. Very common in intimate-partner violence but not unheard of in sex work either. Those girls in Ipswich, for example. So . . ." He raises his eyebrows. "As I said, not straightforward."

"So you're going to Walpole Road for a closer look at this Rainey?"

"I want to get a sense of him. And you? What do you want? Presumably you don't think he was involved all those years ago."

"Obviously not." She sighs. "But as I said on the phone, people tell their partners things. Even things that happened long before they knew them. Maybe that's what she did. Maybe she told him what really happened with the Carpenters. I'm hoping." She holds up a hand. "Sorry. I know you think we already know what really happened."

He drains his mug and shrugs. "I don't know what I think anymore. Thirty years is a long time." A moment's pause, then he meets her eyes and smiles, open and guileless. "I know that I'm happy you're here. Everything else is up for grabs."

After all the time and silence, it's as easy as that. How could she have forgotten that his great gift is to make things easy for other people? She wants to thank him, tell him she's glad to be here, too, but after years of learning to suppress emotion, that doesn't come as easily to her.

He smooths his tie, pushes his chair back, and stands up. "Well, now that we know where we stand, let's get moving. He knows we're coming. It seems his sister sent his niece there to look after him. My lads told her to expect us."

5

It turns out that Nell Beatty lived in one of the worst areas of Bristol. Eastville is famous for its poverty and crime. Like many parts of the city, Desbury explains, it's now being colonized by middle-class buyers tempted by the low housing prices, but in the area where Nell lived, the gentrification is progressing slowly.

On the way to Walpole Road, he drives past the park where her body was found. It's more of a garden, really, a long narrow patch planted with a few trees and with a community noticeboard at the edge. On two sides, it's faced by terraces of neat pebble-dash houses, one or two with freshly painted fronts and one with workmen going in and out carrying what look like ripped-up floorboards. On one of the remaining sides, there's a brick-and-glass primary school, built recently enough that it still has the air of polished cleanliness that new builds lose after a few years. On the fourth side, though, is a lumbering, shabby building that could only be a council block. Its concrete sides are pockmarked and graffitied, its rows of narrow balconies decorated with drying washing.

"It's all like this," Desbury says, "only more spread out. Bits where the houses are done up and the money's sloshing about next to five sinkhole streets with a dealer on the corner and a pub full of drunks—or worse."

Walpole Road is clearly one of those streets. It has the shabby houses and cracked pavements she saw on Google, but the Internet failed to capture its sense of defeat. There's a pervasive aura of weary drabness, somehow increased by the saplings the city has dotted in front of houses here and there in a doomed attempt to alleviate the gray. In the chill of early February, their skeletal winter branches add a final touch of failure.

The bright basket of geraniums she'd seen hanging by the door of number thirty-six on Google Maps had given a suggestion of hopefulness, but now the fabric flowers are a faded parchment color, and someone has upended a divan bed base next to them. It's stained and warped by countless rainfalls, one corner of its covering flapping loose to reveal slats black with rot. The front door of the house might once have been glossy, but years of neglect have bleached and puckered its paint so that now it's shabby and peeling. As she and Desbury stand waiting for someone to answer their knock, Allen sees that the bulb in the overhead light fitting is broken off at the cap, the remaining points of glass furred with old dust.

A young woman opens the door. She nods when Desbury flashes his warrant card and moves back to let them in. She's in her late teens and looks as if she'd like to be somewhere—really, anywhere—else. She leads them two or three steps down the miniature hallway.

The interior of the house has the same sense of lost promise as the outside. In the hallway, someone has hung a rectangular mirror with a gold frame, but the frame is dull and the mirror dusty. Although at some point someone looped fairy lights around the staircase banister in an attempt to add charm to the ugly metal spindles, time has dragged the wire into sagging loops, and the top end dangles down toward the floor, twitching forlornly in the draft from the closing door.

The girl pauses briefly in front of a doorway on the right, jerking her thumb. "He's in there." She pokes her head through the open door of the front room. "It's the police again." Then she continues another two or three steps, stepping into the postage-stamp-sized kitchen at the back.

Someone's tried to cheer up the front room, too, decorating the poky space with a square of bright red shag rug spread over the beige carpet and a framed print of two scarlet poppies propped on the small mantel. But the furniture works against this. A dark brown sofa jammed against the far wall, an MDF coffee table in front of it, and a matching easy chair with upholstery worn to an almost satiny texture pulled forward next to the table all contrive to make the room feel cramped and gloomy. It doesn't help that beige curtains are drawn unevenly across the window, the overhead fixture turned on to provide light instead, or that the room reeks of spilled beer and unemptied ashtrays.

A man sits in the easy chair, feet on the floor and knees splayed out, balancing a mug on one of the chair's arms. He stares fixedly ahead. At first Allen thinks he's blind, but then she sees that he's looking at a huge flat-screen television mounted on the wall opposite his chair. It's off, but his gaze is riveted on the blank rectangle of its screen, focused by habit on its unblinking eye.

"Mr. Rainey? Peter Rainey?" Desbury steps forward and holds out his hand. The man looks at it but doesn't take it. He nods.

The length of Rainey's legs suggests he must once have been tall, and he still retains the outline of a lean build. But years of drinking have bent and shrunk him. His shoulders hunch so that his chest curls inward, and the muscles on his bony arms poke out under the loose skin his pushed-up sweatshirt sleeves reveal. His cheeks and prominent nose are covered in broken capillaries, making it look as if he has a permanent flush. The hand that holds the mug is a claw. In fact, Allen thinks, he resembles nothing so much an elderly vulture.

This impression is increased by his thick Bristol burr. As he answers Desbury's first question, the flat *As* make his sentences sound like harsh caws. "No, I didn't think nothing of it when she didn't come home. They was plenty nights she didn't come home till after I was asleep."

"When that was the case, did she stay out for any particular reason?" Rainey stares at him, so Desbury prompts, "With friends? Or to care for a parent?"

"Nell didn't have no parents. She told me she left home when she was sixteen an' never looked back. An' I never heard about no friends. No, she stayed out to pick up a bit of money the old-fashioned way." When Desbury doesn't respond, Rainey rolls his eyes. "She was down Stapleton Road looking for trade, wasn't she?"

It takes Desbury a moment to understand what Rainey's remark means. "You're saying you knew Ms. Beatty was a sex worker?"

Rainey laughs, a high whine. "I wouldn't call it 'work,' lying on your back. But, yeah, I knew she was on the game." He looks at Desbury pityingly. "What, you didn't?" Another snicker. "I knew the filth was useless, but now you got me doing your bloody job for you!"

Desbury doesn't rise to the bait. "You and Ms. Beatty seem to have been very open with each other."

Rainey preens a little. "We didn't have no secrets."

"When did you learn about her work?"

"Long time ago. When we first got together. She didn't do it regular like. Just every now and again, for the money." He glances at Allen and juts his chin. "An' don't give me none of that feminazi talk. She was at it long before she met me. Then it was to pay for the smack."

"How long had you been together?" Desbury sounds barely interested. He's recognized that Rainey is one of those who tells most when he fears being ignored, and he's playing into that.

Rainey shrugs. "Eight, nine years. Keeley!"

His sudden yell makes them jump. After a few seconds, the girl who answered the door appears again.

"What?"

"How long me and your Aunt Nell been together?"

She picks idly at the collar of her shirt, head to one side, then says, "I met her that Christmas we ate at the Welsh Lion. So, six years?"

"There you are." Rainey sits back as if she's proved him right. "Six years." He holds out his mug to the girl. "This tea is cold."

She takes the mug with the tips of her fingers and leaves the room. Rainey turns back to Desbury, a sly look crossing his face. "The ones that come earlier told me you found her on a bench in that park next to Smith Street. That right?"

Desbury nods.

"Yeah, that's where she took them. Close to the road, for speed. Dark too. She needed the dark, did Nell. You saw her." A grin splits his face.

Just for a second, Allen tries to imagine what it must be like to live with this person, to wake up next to him and eat with him and sit in this room watching that giant television with him. Then she tries not to imagine that.

She clears her throat and says, "Mr. Rainey, you say Ms. Beatty told you she left home when she was sixteen."

Rainey seems surprised that she can speak. He keeps his eyes on Desbury as he answers. "Yeah. So what?"

"Did she ever say where home was?"

He shakes his head. "All she said was her parents was too strict for her, so once she left school she went to London and never looked back. Told me she squatted and did a bit of modeling." He rolls his eyes at the idea. "Han't we all, love?"

"That's all she told you about her background?"

"She wan't one for dwelling on the past, Nell."

Allen smiles. "I thought you said you had no secrets?"

His glance is pure hate. "I din't say she never said *nothing*. I said she din't like to dwell. She mentioned this and that when it come up."

"In that case, I don't suppose she ever mentioned the Bella Carpenter case? Maybe she said the Baby Bella case?"

He looks blank. "What's that?"

"Bella Carpenter was a baby abducted and then returned to her parents in the summer of 1990."

"In 1990, I was in the Merchant Navy." He pushes up his right sleeve to reveal a fuzzy anchor tattoo. "I didn't even know who the prime minister was, never mind some missing kiddie." He looks at Desbury again. "What's this in aid of?"

"Another case we're working on. Superintendent Allen is consulting in an attempt to determine if Ms. Beatty was involved with it."

"Not if they was kids involved. Nell hated kids. Said they was noisy and took up too much time. Complained all summer when the ones here played outside. Said she couldn't hear the TV over them. Keeley!"

Allen winces. "I'll go find her." It's obvious she's not going to get anything useful out of him, so she might as well try the girl.

She's sitting at the kitchen table. A textbook lies open in front of her, and she's writing notes in a pale blue exercise book.

"Your uncle's calling you." Allen steps down into the small space. Here, too, there have been attempts to give the place character—a tea towel with a map of Italy pushpinned to one wall, a pink toaster and matching kettle on the countertop—but the hob is covered in a thin film of grease and the air smells sour. The bin overflows with takeaway containers.

"I heard him." The girl doesn't stop writing. "He can wait." She frowns at something in the textbook.

"I'm sorry about your aunt."

Now she looks up. She's pale, mousy, but her eyes are shrewd. "She wasn't my aunt. They weren't married."

"Well, I'm still sorry. I know it can be hard when a relative dies. Were you close?"

She wrinkles her nose. She has an engagingly mobile face, one that registers every change of emotion with a change of expression. Now she cocks her head to one side, considering before she says, "Not really." A shrug. "She was okay. When she first moved in, anyway."

"Did you all live here together?"

A shake of the head. "We lived here until he finished the program. My mum read that you shouldn't leave someone in rehab on their own, so she didn't want to leave until he finished. Nell used to come over sometimes then. Once he finished, we moved out. Then she moved in."

"Your Au—uh, Nell moved in with your uncle immediately after the alcohol treatment program?"

"Are you kidding?" The face molds itself into an expression of surpassing scorn. "She met him there. Can you believe it? She actually *moved in* with someone she met in rehab."

Allen can believe it—after a lifetime on the force, she can believe nearly anything—but she's still surprised. Rehabilitation programs encourage participants not to get involved in romantic relationships in the first year of sobriety, never mind while they're in the program—never mind with someone else in the same program. Nell's counselor must have gone over what a mistake such a move would be.

But she keeps her face neutral. "Did they seem happy?"

The girl raises her eyebrows. "What's happy? They weren't yelling at each other then, anyway."

"They yelled at each other later?"

"Pretty much every time they had a drink, which was pretty much all the time once they'd been out of rehab a few months. Not lately, though. Nell was trying to stay sober."

"But before that she drank all the time they were together? Even right after they'd gone through the program?"

She shakes her head. "She was sober for a while after that. And then on and off. She kept trying."

"What was she like when she was sober?"

"She was always trying to put makeup on me, telling me it would change my life. 'If you're beautiful, you can have the world.'" She flicks her eyes around the grimy kitchen. "I said I'd rather revise, thanks."

"Did she talk about her past?"

"Not unless you count telling me she'd been a model when she first moved to London from Cambridge. She mentioned the modeling *all* the time."

Allen swallows. "Your uncle didn't say she said she was from Cambridge."

"Does he seem like someone who remembers details?"

She dips her head in acknowledgment. "But you do. And you're sure she said Cambridge?"

"I'm sure." The girl straightens up and juts her chin, for a moment looking distressingly like the old vulture in the next room. "I remember because it was the first time I'd ever heard of the place. I went and looked it up afterward, saw the university, and knew I wanted to go there. And now I've got an offer. I'm going to do engineering."

"Congratulations."

She nods a thank-you, then her face grows fierce. "My mum got out by marrying my stepdad, but I'm going to do it on my own. You should never depend on anyone else."

Allen wants to tell her that this is a terrible credo, wants to say that as far as she can see, this is the belief her not-aunt lived by, and look where it got her. But this girl isn't her child, isn't anything more than someone she's engaging with on the chance that they are a potential source. Besides, looking at her press her pen into the page as she takes neat, determined notes, Allen doesn't think she'd listen.

Even though the hallway is short, it muffles conversation, so it isn't until Allen's taken a couple of steps back toward the other room that she hears Desbury saying, ". . . and you believe that Ms. Beatty was injured by a customer, or customers?"

When she enters the front room, Rainey's hands are lifted, palms up, his eyes wide and his lips pursed. He lets them fall. *Isn't it obvious?* this pantomime says.

Desbury reaches into his breast pocket and draws out a pad. He appears to consult it. "According to our database, you and Ms. Beatty had a number of disagreements, loud enough for the neighbors to feel the need to call the police. Three in the past year alone."

"Domestics. Like every couple. We'd have a bit too much to drink, I'd say something she took the wrong way . . . You know what women are like."

Desbury frowns at the pad again. "According to our information, both you and Ms. Beatty had completed Alcohol Treatment Requirement programs. Yet the two of you were still drinking alcohol?"

"Well . . ." Rainey licks his lips. His eyes dart around the room, two frightened beetles. Then, dredged up from some corner of his brain, "It's one day at a time, innit? Nell was always starting up then stopping again, and once she stopped she'd go on at me about it. We'd have a bit of a ding-dong, but nothing serious."

"So the police report from last November that says Ms. Beatty had a split lip when the officers arrived here, that's inaccurate?"

"I don't know about inaccurate, but if she had one it wan't nothing to do with me."

"And the one that says she refused medical attention for a black eye and cut forehead last August?"

Rainey crosses his arms. "Look at the report. Did she say I done it? I bet she didn't. I bet she didn't even mention my name."

Desbury is impassive. "So it's your contention that all Ms. Beatty's injuries, both in the past and when she was found, have nothing to do with you?"

"I never touched a hair on Nell's head." Rainey stabs the air with his index finger as punctuation. "Not a hair. On. Her. Head. You want to go down Stapleton Road and ask some of the men she went with. She told me they wanted all sorts of filthy stuff. Disgusting things. One of them probably beat her black and blue and then done for her when she asked for more money." He's hitting his stride now. His voice rises. "Ent you got nothing better to do than harass a grieving man? A widower? I should report you. Keeley? Keeley!"

After a few seconds, the girl appears again. She's holding a can of Carlsberg. She gives it to him, and he yanks at the tab, takes two long swallows, then wipes his mouth with the back of his hand. In a voice full of outraged dignity, he says, "These officers is just leaving. Make sure you close the door behind them."

6

Outside, the light has gone, and it's started to rain, the kind of fine drizzle that feels inconsequential but quickly soaks through even the thickest coat. Allen waits until they're back in the car, heater on, before she speaks.

"What do you think?"

"I think he beat her anytime he fancied, and I think he killed her." Desbury sighs as he turns the key in the ignition. "But I also think he's no fool. He knows we can't make it stick unless we rule everything else out. That's why he said what he did about her taking customers to the park. If a client could have attacked her, that means potential reasonable doubt. And at the moment there's nothing to say a client didn't attack her."

"He certainly seems to have spotted Nell as an easy mark. The girl told me that he met her in the RRP and they moved in together just after it was over. She hates him, by the way. She didn't use his name once. Just 'he,' 'he,' 'he.' Oh, and this is interesting. She told me that Nell had tried to stay off the drink in the past and failed, but that lately she was managing to stay sober."

He raises his eyebrows as he turns the key in the ignition. "That *is* interesting. Well, I'll send a couple of DCs to talk to the neighbors. See if Nell said anything to any of them about the situation with Rainey, or if anyone saw anything the night before last. And I'll get a female officer to talk to the other women on Stapleton Road. Maybe there is some sick punter they know about. Or maybe she confided in them about what was going on at home. I'll drive us back that way so you can see what it's like."

Stapleton Road is easy walking distance from Walpole Road. The portion that Desbury turns onto is lined with empty shopfronts, their windows scrawled in illegible graffiti. There's a piri-piri chicken takeaway spilling gray fluorescent light onto the pavement, and next to it something called inMoney—"bill payments, MoneyGram, short-term loans." Next to it, the Three Blackbirds pub has a To Let sign in its window. She tries to picture Nell lingering in front of these places, hands stuffed in her pockets, waiting for a car to stop. It's easier with the older Nell than it is with the young one.

"It's farther down," Desbury says. He clarifies. "The stretch they work is farther down. Not that it's any more pleasant there." Then, after a pause, "Did she tell you anything you can use? The girl?"

"She told me that Nell came to London from Cambridge. She remembers her saying Cambridge specifically."

"Cambridge is a big place."

"It's a lot smaller than all of Britain, which was going to be our search area in 1990. Besides"—she presses a fingertip against her foggy window and squints out through the clear oval—"she's not my only possible source. I thought I'd visit the Alcohol RRP facilitator while I'm here, see if Nell ever said anything about the Carpenter case during the sessions. If you can tell me which one she went to, I could pay a visit and still manage to catch a train that gets me home at a reasonable hour."

For a second, the interior of the car is silent. Then, "It was the Lenford Garrison Centre in St. Paul's. But I have a couple of bodies going over there tomorrow."

Allen understands. He's got an investigation to run; she's just looking for information to satisfy her curiosity. She can always get the facilitator's name from him and ring up later. Or make another trip. It's not as if Bristol is hundreds of miles from London.

They drive on in silence. The drizzle turns the headlights of the oncoming cars into stars.

"I tell you what I think," Desbury says at last. "I think that since I'm SIO on the case, Nell's death and anything that led to it are my patch. Nell's life, and any part of it that isn't connected to her death, any part that might connect to something else—that could be anyone's patch. Two of my people are going to the Lenford Garrison Centre tomorrow morning, but beyond that I'm not concerned. And if you stayed in Bristol until tomorrow afternoon, you could stay on a little longer and have dinner with me and Elvina. And I'd drive you to the station after."

She isn't sure. She didn't go to Desbury's home or meet his family when they were working together. And now . . . ? She can practically feel the awkwardness, hear the stilted conversation. But then a vision of her white flat pops into her head. What's waiting for her back in London tomorrow? A Saturday spent looking at flats too expensive or too far out for her.

"All right." She corrects for a little more graciousness. "I'd like that. Thank you."

"Great." Desbury signals to turn off the roundabout. "I know exactly the place."

The hotel he takes her to is one of a budget chain she's used before, basic but comfortable and with a huge breakfast in the morning that will probably see her through to Desbury's dinner. Once she's checked in and used the bathroom, it's stopped raining. She heads out to the shopping precinct the receptionist circled on a map.

Bristol at night is like London at night but also totally different. There's the same glittering cast when the light from the streetlamps hits the wet pavements, the same parade of chain stores: Cards Galore, H&M, a Lush that she identifies from a hundred yards away by its distinctive smell. But even though it's not yet 7 p.m., all the shops are closed, even the Pret A Manger that in London would be putting food on its shelves until at least nine. Fortunately, she sees, the doors of the Marks & Spencer are still open. She'll need a clean shirt and knickers for tomorrow and something to eat tonight, and if there's a beauty section she can pick up some face wash and skin cream, maybe some mascara. Between that and the lipstick in her bag, she can show a business face to Nell's counselor. She always carries a toothbrush and paste with her, so she's all right there.

To get back to the hotel, she has to pass through an open-air sunken area that the receptionist told her was called the Bear Pit. She walked through it on her way to the shopping precinct too. Then there were groups of other people walking through it, too, but now there are only a few. There's a group of homeless people sitting on one of the wooden benches that flank the paved central area, sharing a bottle of wine. One of them suddenly laughs raucously, and Allen's London police instincts kick in. She grips the room card in her coat pocket, angling it so a corner juts through her index and middle fingers. It's strong enough for a quick jab to the throat.

But nothing happens. The little group continue to talk quietly, and although the unmistakable smell of marijuana drifts on the air, no one seems to mind. Bristol might share London's life force, but it doesn't share the air of pressure that underpins London life. That absence is an odd sensation, but it's not unpleasant.

Back in her room, she puts the Marks & Spencer bag on her desk then rummages in her shoulder bag until she finds her mobile. She forgot to ask Desbury the name of Nell's counselor in Bristol, so, as she eats her dinner, she uses the Crown Court database to search for Nell's record. On her phone, the website's letters and fill-in boxes are so small that she has to squint even though she's wearing her glasses, but by cross-referencing Nell's records and number, after a few mistypes she finds what she needs. The program facilitator's name is Ellie Cottington.

Once she's finished, she puts the box from her M&S salad neatly in the bin then goes round the bed untucking the duvet from under the mattress. She takes off her shoes, socks, and trousers and slips between the clean sheets. She picks up her phone again and uses a property website to look at house prices in Eastville. Desbury is right. Half of the places listed are going for a song, and the interior photographs show that they should be. The other half are sometimes as much as twice the price of those, and they're so obviously recently renovated that the paint could still be wet—though she can't help but notice that even these more expensive ones cost less than the flats she's being steered toward in London.

She switches the search to the area around the Lenford Garrison Centre. What was it, St. Paul's? Pricier, but not enormously so. Does Bristol have a posh area? She just types "Bristol" into the search bar. She discovers that if she wants to live in a place called Clifton, or one called Redland, she'll pay a pretty penny. Aside from that, though, there's nothing to match the prices of the places she's been looking at in London, not even for some flats that, as far as she can tell, look nicer than the ones she's been seeing. She's reminded how different the capital is from the rest of the country.

The combination of real estate and Nell Beatty somehow leads her to a memory of Terry Glaister, the estate agent in Wells all those years ago, and from him to the boy with the Glaister-branded tie. None of the estate agents she's currently dealing with wear items of clothing branded with the company name. Do people even do that anymore? The only ones she can think of are Boots employees and bank tellers. Pretty soon it'll probably only be Boots, the way banks are herding people to do everything online.

She realizes she sounds like some sort of pruny dowager, shaking her head at the way the world is going. When she gets to that stage, it's time for bed. She slips off the mattress and heads for the bathroom to clean her teeth. There's nothing like a good night's sleep to make you feel young again.

7

It turns out that on a Saturday afternoon, the Lenford Garrison Centre is a hive of activity. Small girls in pink leotards run past Allen into a studio at the back; in the makeshift café on her left, two middle-aged men sit across from each other with open Bibles in front of them, engaging in whispered dispute; at the table next to them, three teenage boys share a piece of cake while watching something on a phone. "Aw, mate!" one of them yells to the screen as Allen stops at reception.

"The counseling office?" The man at the desk peers at her warrant card then points behind him with a thumb. "It's just on the right down there."

Ellie Cottington is a small, intense woman in her late thirties. Her hair, dark with threads of gray, is cut brutally short, and her arms and hands are festooned with tattoos. Amid the thicket of designs, Allen can make out a serpent writhing its way down her left arm, a complex Celtic-pattern bracelet encircling her right wrist, and the hilt of a sword decorating the back of one hand, its point on the back of the other. But Cottington's face is sweet, and worried, and weary, and her voice is a soft Welsh singsong. Allen can see how this combination of toughness and kindness would be just right to inspire trust from the addicts she works with.

As Allen watches, Cottington moves some files from the desk chair to one of the stacks on the desktop then drops into the chair. The office they're in seems to be shared by several people—there are photos of two or three different families propped up on the metal shelves bolted to the one wall, and on the radiator cover behind the desk, a statuette of Ganesh rubs shoulders with one of the Madonna and Child. Like every social services office Allen has ever visited, this one has an aura of too much work and too little funding. Ellie Cottington has a similar aura, but in her case it's mingled with stubbornness.

"Yes," she says now, leaning back in the chair and crossing her arms, "Nell Beatty was a participant in one of my therapy groups in 2015. But, as I told the officers who visited me this morning, I can't say more than that. I understand that you're here because you're trying to track Nell's connection to this older case, thank you for explaining that, but I still have a duty of confidence."

"Ms. Cottington, unless I'm mistaken, your treatment program is funded by the Ministry of Justice? And you share treatment information with the ministry?"

"Ellie, please. And we share attendance and completion records. Nothing else."

"Well, as I'm sure my colleagues this morning told you, the Data Protection Act 2018 states that where any reporting occurs with the knowledge of a patient or program member, confidentiality doesn't apply. In fact, given the required training for Alcohol RRP counselors, I'm guessing you already knew that."

A brief silence, then the other woman shrugs. "Fine, there's no confidentiality. But I have to warn you, I don't think I can offer you any useful information."

"You don't remember Ms. Beatty?"

"No, I remember her. As I also told your colleagues, she came to see me again about a month ago. The reason I don't think I'll be of much help to you is because I don't enter many notes into the system. I disagree with the DPA regulations, and that's my way of giving my patients the privacy they deserve." She looks as fierce as Peter Rainey's niece the day before.

"I'd still like to try, thank you. As my mother used to say, you never know."

Ellie's face says she thinks sometimes you do, but she bangs a rapid series of letters into the computer and watches the screen. "Okay, here she is. Eleanor Margaret Beatty. Second court-ordered rehab, first rehab for alcohol. Outpatient group therapy here from March to September 2015. Her group met on Wednesdays at four. It says that she didn't speak much in the group. But she came every week, and she kept her journal regularly." She looks up. "I ask them to keep a journal of what they're feeling when they want to drink. It can help them spot triggers. I don't read them," she adds. "But it says here that she brought hers with her every week. And that she stayed sober for the whole six months. That's a real sign of commitment in our population." She leans back again, but now she seems rueful instead of defiant. "I gather from . . . the officers I spoke to that she didn't stay sober. It's too bad. Everything here suggests she had a good chance."

"Well, she moved in with another program participant immediately after completion. That can't have helped."

"Yes." Ellie sighs. "I would have advised her against that."

Allen longs to ask her to read out her notes on Peter Rainey but holds back. That's not her concern.

"Do the notes show that she ever mentioned the Bella Carpenter kidnapping? The Baby Bella case?" Like Rainey, the girl looks blank. It's a sharp lesson in how little your preoccupations matter outside your own mind. "Bella Carpenter was a five-month-old baby who was kidnapped from a hotel in Pimlico in the summer of 1990. Four days later, she was found and returned. Nell Beatty was the person who returned her."

"Nell did that? No, she never said anything about it. I would have remembered."

"Did she ever mention any children of her own? Maybe a baby she had when she was young then gave up?"

Ellie squints at the screen. "I'm not seeing anything in the notes. That kind of trauma is directly linked to future ongoing addiction issues, so I certainly would have noted if she'd mentioned it."

"Maybe she mentioned an affair with an older man?" Allen's getting desperate now. "Or maybe being raped as a young woman?"

"My God, no! Look, I can read you everything I have in less than two minutes. Name, Eleanor Margaret Beatty. DOB, May 17, 1972. Sex, female. Mother's Christian name, Margaret. Place of—"

"Wait. I'm sorry, could you repeat that?"

"Place—"

"No, before that. You have her mother's first name?"

"We ask for it for recordkeeping purposes. You might get two Eleanor Beattys, but you won't get two whose mothers have the same Christian name."

Nell wouldn't tell her partner her mother's name, but she handed it over to the government because a form asked for it. Allen marvels at the power bureaucracy holds over people. As Ellie repeats the name, Allen writes MARGARET BEATTY in careful block letters on her pad. Although God knows how many Margaret Beattys there are in Cambridge.

"Bristol."

"Sorry?" She looks up.

"You said in Cambridge. But it's Bristol."

"Sorry, I didn't realize I'd said that out loud. Another one of my interviewees told me Nell was born in Cambridge. I was just thinking about how many women named Margaret Beatty there could be in Cambridge—or anywhere, really."

"But Nell wasn't born in Cambridge. That's what I was saying when you stopped me." Ellie points at the computer screen and reads aloud. "'Place of Birth: Bristol.'" Then, as if Allen might not have grasped what that meant, "She was born here in Bristol."

8

"I can understand it." Desbury nods. "Your life's in a terrible state. You want to start over. You go home. It's instinct."

"But she never *went* home." They're in the Desburys' small dining room, and Allen has to squint slightly to differentiate the actual Desbury from the one reflected in the window behind him. The dining room itself, with its terra-cotta walls decorated with bright woven grass baskets and its small sideboard covered with family photos, feels too cozy to hold even a mild disagreement. Still, she continues. "And that suggests she didn't actually want to go home, which in turn suggests she didn't want to see the people who lived there. So it's pretty risky to move back to somewhere where she's likely to run into them."

Desbury snorts. "You people from London. You think everywhere else is a village. Elvina! Elvina!"

His wife opens the swing door from the kitchen. "You don't need to shout. I can hear you just fine in this room that's six feet away from where you're sitting."

"Sorry." Desbury smiles apologetically. "But now that you're here, how often do you see your sister? Sarah."

"Sarah? We saw her at Christmas. Why? Do you need me to ask her something?"

"No, how often do you see her? Run into her when you're out, bump into her at a bus stop?"

Elvina Desbury is one of those people who radiate warmth. When she'd opened the front door an hour before, she'd ignored Allen's outstretched hand and enveloped her in a hug, ushering her in as if she were a long-lost relative. Now, though, she raises her eyebrows, and her Jamaican accent gives her words an edge of exasperation. "This is to prove some point, I'm guessing. Well, as you know, I never run into my sister when I'm out. We see her at Christmas, and again in July at the family barbecue." The door flaps behind her.

"Sarah lives in Totterdown. Three miles that way." Desbury points to his left. "All cities are big cities. You could live in Bristol for twenty years and never run into anyone you know."

Allen is properly chastened. "As Nell did."

"As Nell did."

Elvina comes through the door again, holding a casserole dish in oven-gloved hands. When she puts it on the table and lifts the lid, a cloud of garlic-scented steam rises up. Allen inhales appreciatively.

"Gnocchi with squash and spinach." Elvina hands her a serving spoon. "Please, help yourself."

For long minutes, there is only the sound of three people enjoying their meal. Then Elvina puts down her fork. "So, Martha, Manley tells me you're here to help him with his latest murder."

It takes Allen a second to remember that Manley is Desbury's first name. Then she says, "Not exactly. It's more that I encountered the victim in connection with another case."

"The Baby Bella case. I remember."

Allen smiles. "Well, apparently you're one of the few who do. Both of the people I've mentioned it to since I've been here had no idea what I was talking about."

"This Beatty girl who's just been murdered brought the baby back to the station. Manley told me at the time."

Desbury swallows his mouthful. "We were talking about it before you arrived. Elvina wondered if you'd been sent here because of the link between the two cases."

His wife cuts in. "I was saying how glad I was that they were bringing in some women after that trouble with Chief Constable Grabby Hands."

"Elvina." Desbury's tone is a warning.

"What? You've told me more than once that if something bad happens in one police force it goes around all the other forces like wildfire.

So I'm guessing Martha knows that whole story. And I'm guessing she feels the way I do about making the police force of the present look and act a lot less like the police force of the past."

Desbury looks at his plate; Elvina looks at Allen. This is precisely as awkward as Allen had feared.

She clears her throat. "I'm not here in any official capacity. It's a personal trip. Des—er, Manley agreed to help me while I see if I can find out anything that might help satisfy my curiosity about the Carpenter case."

She picks up her fork again. For a minute, they eat in a heavy silence. Then Allen says desperately, "I heard you moved back here to be closer to your mother, ah, Manley. Is that right?"

Desbury looks up. "It was my father, actually. He had a stroke. My mother died when I was in my twenties, and he didn't have anyone to look after him."

"Oh, I'm sorry."

"Thank you. He had another good fifteen years after that, though, with all of us around him. We moved in here, if you can believe it." He looks around as if he means they moved into that very room then shakes his head. "It was a squeeze, but it meant I was with him right to the end. And it made it easier to manage when the time came to put the girls through uni. No loans because we'd managed to save so much on housing."

"Through uni!" Allen couldn't believe that the little girls he'd talked about in the Little Chef were now university graduates. Well, she calculated quickly, university graduates and then some. "What do they do, your daughters?"

"Amy is head at a sixth-form college in Exeter, and Jemmelia works for a charity that finds housing for homeless teenagers who've aged out of foster care. I have two grandsons too."

"Barrett is Amy's son, and Amari is Jemmelia's." Elvina stands and takes a framed photo from the sideboard. It shows two boys, one tall and slender and one a round little ball, with their arms around each other. "Amari is the older one. He's only seven, but he's big for his age." Her voice is proud.

After that, they fall easily into stories of the Desbury children and grandchildren, their education and talents and achievements. Elvina explains that after the girls reached school age, she went back to university and earned a doctorate in education. She thinks that watching her do that may have inspired them to end up in the jobs they have—"although they saw their father working hard all that time, too, which is probably why they climbed so high." Desbury smiles and says all he ever wanted was for his girls to be happy, and now that they are, that's enough for him. All of this takes them through the coconut cake that Elvina serves for dessert and the coffee Desbury makes afterward, so it isn't until their cups are nearly empty that he finally says, "So, are you going to talk to Nell's mother?"

His face says he already knows her answer.

"I'm going to try. That's assuming she still lives in Bristol. It's too good a lead to miss out on. Nell was eighteen when she showed up at our nick, and we have no proof she was actually living in London at that time, or had been living there for any length of time. She could've recently left home, or been kicked out when they found out she was pregnant. Her mother or some other family member might know all sorts of things about the baby, the father . . ." *And Wells is less than an hour from Bristol*, she thinks. It would have been even easier for Tom Carpenter to reach than London. "I checked on my phone last night, though, and the Bristol electoral rolls aren't online. If I want to find the addresses of Margaret Beattys who live here, I'm going to need to make a trip to the Central Library."

"So you'll be staying another night?" Elvina's face lights up.

"I wish I could. But I've a Recruitment Committee meeting at eight thirty on Monday. All the documents for it are on the computer at my flat, and I only have tomorrow to read them. I was thinking I'd come back next weekend."

"That's Barrett's birthday. We'll be in Exeter." They both look disappointed.

"Well"—she addresses Desbury—"I promise I'll catch you up if I learn anything worthwhile." She puts her napkin on the table and smiles at Elvina. "Thank you for making me feel so welcome. And for letting me lure your husband back into my old, cold case."

"Oh, please! Manley's been talking about you for thirty years. I'm glad I finally got to meet you in person."

"I hope he said good things." Allen tries to make it sound as if she's joking.

"This man?" Elvina puts a hand over one of Desbury's where it lies on the tablecloth. "Never anything but good things. He was born sweet-natured." She smiles at him and stands. "Now, I'm going to wrap up some cake for you. It's a long trip back to London."

9

The Recruitment Committee meeting is as long and tedious as she expected. When did her job become so dull? Of course she's known for years that it offers her less than she originally signed up for, less than she wants, but like the frog in the gradually boiling water, the fact that her exposure is constant means she's become used to it. Now that she's had a couple of days of the adrenaline rush of investigation, though, her boredom with her real job suddenly feels almost exquisite, a knife slicing slowly through the layers of her brain.

"Right," says the head of recruitment. "If you could all turn to item 24a in the CSEW subfolder, we can discuss the proposed new role of the PDU."

By the time she meets Kate McMullan for dinner on Wednesday, the excitement of the previous weekend has almost completely ebbed away. They've grown into close friends, she and Kate. It's not just that they both work for the Met—although God knows it's hard for people who work in policing to find friends outside. They also make each other laugh, make good cheering sections for each other's successes and good sounding boards for each other's troubles. Kate let Allen stay in her spare room for two weeks while she and Phil were separating; Allen is godmother to Kate's daughter, Danielle, and she's always thought Kate asked her in the hope that it might go some way toward making up for what she was missing. She likes to think that for an atheist she's a pretty damn good godmother. She's put in seventeen years of giant ice-cream sundaes and visits to the Christmas pantomime, and, although Danielle doesn't know it yet, she's cleared it with Kate to pay her first year's university fees.

She and Kate meet every couple of weeks in the Jolly Gardeners, a pub close to the climbing center Kate uses. It's been renovated into a light, open space with a bar in the center and green plants everywhere, the kind of place that invites you to linger and has food that makes you want to. Usually Kate's there first, since the climbing wall is a short walk away, but tonight Allen's been seated at the table scrolling through her phone for a good ten minutes before she opens the door. She has the rosy and slightly damp look of someone who's recently showered.

"A pint of Guinness, please," she says to the server who appears to take their drinks order. She looks at Allen. "Full of iron and antioxidants."

"So you've said before. A glass of cabernet, please." Allen smiles at the server. "Good for the heart," she says to Kate as the girl leaves.

"Well, then, here we are: two women having a healthy snack after one of them has finished exercising." Kate raises her eyes to the ceiling. "I feel like a saint."

"Even a saint would envy your arms." Revealed by the sleeves of her T-shirt, Kate's biceps are impressively sinewy.

"Aye." The years had softened her accent, but they'd never make her English enough to say "yes." "That's true. But, honestly, that place is a workout for the whole body. And the mind, trying to figure out where to put your hands and feet next." She nods her thanks as the server puts her pint in front of her then takes a long sip. "You should join me sometime."

"No, thanks." Allen breathes in the spicy scent of the Cabernet. "I'm happy with my swimming. If I did climbing, I'd always be worrying I was going to fall."

"You wear a harness."

"Which suggests falling is inevitable. Again, no, thank you."

Kate shrugs. The conversation moves on. She and her husband, Ron, watched the first episode of the new Agatha Christie adaptation on television on Sunday night. Allen, finally caught up on her paperwork, switched on just in time to see it too. They discuss what they thought of it, its fidelity to the original, the other Christie adaptations by the same screenwriter, and by this meandering route they arrive at Danielle's decision to study film at university the next year.

"It doesn't seem a very *safe* degree to me." Kate frowns over the monkfish she's ordered. "But what do I know? I did biology. What did you do?"

"Criminology. You know that."

"That's right. And would you say it's taken you far?"

Kate's tone is joking, but Allen's answer is at least semiserious. "I'd say it's taken me about as far as I can go." For some reason, that makes her remember the brief, awkward exchange in Desbury's office when she first arrived. Without thinking, she says, "I saw Manley Desbury last week."

Kate's face is a blank.

"Detective Constable Desbury. From Victoria Police Station? Only he's Detective Chief Inspector Desbury now, up in Bristol."

"What were you doing in Bristol?"

"They found Nell Beatty's body there. She's the victim in a murder case."

As soon as she says Nell's name, she regrets it. Years ago, after listening to Allen run through her theories yet one more time, Kate had told her point-blank that she was too fixated on the Carpenters. "You're wasting your time and headspace on something there's no evidence for. I don't want to hear about it anymore." Allen has avoided the subject ever since. Of course, that avoidance hasn't been perfect. Sometimes she slips up and mentions it, but at those times she's aware of Kate's twitch of irritation. The twitch says that Allen is tedious, that she's fixated. She'll do a lot to avoid seeing that twitch.

"Sorry." She concentrates on her mock-chicken burger.

"No, no, it's okay. So, the girl's dead. Well, it's an ending. Maybe not the ending you wanted, but an ending."

Allen chews, then chews again. When the fake chicken is paste in her mouth and she can't hold back any longer, she says, "Her mother still lives up there, apparently. In Bristol." She hears her voice speed up with excitement. She can't stop it. "At least she used to live there, and I've searched the death certificates for Bristol and not found any the right age with her name."

There it is, the slight flare of the nostrils and narrowing of the eyes. Then, deliberately, "Have you told this to Phil?"

"No."

"Why not? He would be interested." A ghost of emphasis on "he."

"And you're fine about what happened between you by now, right?"

"I am. It's just. I don't want to do that. He's not part of my life. Why would I want to talk to him?"

"Fine. It's your choice." But that doesn't mean Kate's willing to listen in Phil's place. She turns the conversation. "How was Desbury? What's he like after all these years?"

Allen takes the hint. She tells her about the dinner, about the clever mural that wraps around Desbury's office, about the now-grown daughters and their children. They talk about time, how it telescopes—"The days are long, but the years are short," Kate says, then adds, "I read that somewhere"—and by the time dessert arrives, they're onto the subject of retirement.

"I've been thinking about it recently," Kate confides. "It's not because I feel like I'm less able. It's because of the machines. They make everything easier and much more accurate, they're much more precise than we ever were, but I miss doing it myself. I miss being involved in the process the way I used to be. And since that's not going to change, maybe . . ." She shrugs. "What about you?"

"I don't know. I have been thinking about it, since Parker's memorial. God, it made me see how old we all are! And the job feels . . . not more mechanized, not on my side, but certainly less interesting." She thinks of the admin-filled days just past. "It's probably the paperwork."

"Well, they do say that when you feel out of place in the new world, it's time to leave."

"Really? I never heard that. Who says that?"

Kate stops and thinks, frowning. "You know what? I think it was me."

They decide to have a liqueur. Because, as Allen points out, it's good for the digestion.

10

Three days later, Saturday, she hires a car and drives to Bristol, heading for the Central Library and the electoral register it holds. The satnav tells her the library is slightly to the west of the town center, near the university, but with her unerring ability to get lost, she somehow overshoots it and finds herself only narrowly avoiding crossing into Wales. At last she works her way back to where she should be.

The library is on the opposite side of the city from Desbury's neighborhood. Here the buildings are all massive edifices of cream-colored stone with gracious Georgian and Edwardian fronts. She finds a car park, and after two minutes and a consultation with Google Maps, she's crossing a grassy square, stopping on the far side in front of a statue of a man with a turban and an impressive mustache. *Raja Ram Mohan Roy*, the bronze plaque on the pedestal beneath him says. She files the name away to google later.

The Bristol Central Library is a hulking, Gothic building, its mullioned windows topped by stone reliefs depicting something Allen can't make out. Inside, brass chandeliers dimly illuminate a lobby made up of arches that lead to other arches in some kind of surreal maze.

The drama ends at the door to the main room, though. Like most public libraries these days, this one seems to be given over to every imaginable non-book-related activity. On bright carpet cut into interlocking circles, a toddler playgroup is banging tambourines and shaking sticks of bells while their mothers mime astonishment; a group of pensioners at a computer cluster are being given instruction on how to navigate the Internet; just to the left of the door, a chalkboard has a bright pink arrow drawn below the word "Café" in red and, underneath, "Goulash, £3.50 with a slice of granary bread."

At the information desk, a young man wearing a laminated staff badge clearly has no idea what she's talking about when she asks to see the electoral register. He excuses himself and comes back with a woman around her own age, who points her toward the reading room. In its silent, balcony-lined space, a similar woman seats her at one of the long wooden tables then brings her a stack of binders. Bristol has a non-student population of around half a million—Allen looked it up yesterday—but she's only interested in those in the first binder, *A* to *E*.

Given the ordinariness of the name Margaret Beatty, she expects to find more than one listed in the electoral register. She isn't disappointed: there are eleven Margaret Beattys on the rolls. She notes down their addresses, closes the binder, and brings the whole stack up to the issuing desk, nodding her thanks.

The early days of any police career involve a lot of walking, and Allen had always enjoyed it. She still loved walking cities, watching the hundreds of small occurrences and interactions that made up their ongoing life. But it turns out that driving through an unfamiliar city is a much more taxing experience. Staring at Google Maps risks not seeing oncoming traffic; roads have no identifying signs until it's just too late to turn around easily; drivers beep at her when she corrects her route abruptly. By the time she's crossing the sixth Margaret Beatty off her list, she's ready to stop.

But she's only hired the car for the day, and she's promised her sister Carrie she'll come round for a family lunch tomorrow. So she makes her way to Redland, which she at least knows as the home of some of Bristol's most expensive flats. There, the seventh Margaret Beatty turns out to be a brisk academic, none too pleased to be disturbed in the middle of working on an article. The eighth Margaret Beatty is a woman in late middle age coincidentally living a few streets away, hosting what sounds like a street party but what she assures Allen is lunch for her grandchildren. Neither of them knows, or has ever known, a Nell Beatty.

There's no one at home at the ninth address. When she taps on a neighbor's door and flashes her warrant card at the man who answers, he shakes his head and says it's very sad: Mrs. Beatty died two days earlier. Her son's closed up the house until after the funeral. No, he doesn't know where he lives, but he thinks he remembers his name. Garth. Or is it Gareth? Or maybe he's thinking of Geoff. Something like that, anyway. Nice chap. Supports Aston Villa.

People get old, Allen reminds herself glumly over a cup of tea at a nearby café. They become ill and frail, and if they're old enough to have a forty-eight-year-old daughter they could quite reasonably die. It wasn't Margaret Beatty's job to stay alive until Allen found her.

Or maybe that was simply the wrong Margaret Beatty. There are two more on the list, after all: Margaret Joan Beatty at 15 Down Road in somewhere called Bishopsworth, and Margaret Artemis Beatty at 51 Wellington Close in somewhere called Fishponds. She opens Google Maps again. The addresses are on opposite ends of the city. At this rate, she'll know Bristol better than she knows London. She flexes her feet to stretch her calves, drains the dregs in her cup, and heads back to the car.

Down Road is so flat that its name seems like a deliberate joke. Its beige brick house fronts stretch into the distance, their doors painted muted shades—olive, taupe, pale blue. Even the door that might once have been red has faded to bleached pink. There are no front gardens, no huts hiding the bins. The doors open directly onto the pavement with only a single granite step separating outside from inside.

The woman who answers the clay-colored door of number fifteen is unequivocally plain. Her heavy jaw and button nose clash with each other, and between them her mouth is little more than a line marked out in pale pink lipstick. Her white hair is cut into a shape so dowdy that Allen can hardly believe anyone would choose it, fluffed into fullness at the crown and top but narrowing as the sides curve toward the chin. A fringe slices straight across her eyebrows, covering the forehead that might have balanced out her jaw. In addition to the lipstick, she wears a touch of powder and a layer of mascara, a loose beige jersey top, a cream skirt with pale cream low-heeled shoes, and tights of the shade that is called nude but matches no nude leg. The overall impression is of a woman running toward the invisibility of old age with open arms.

When Allen flashes her warrant card, the woman confirms that, yes, she's Margaret Beatty. Allen can't see anything in her that resembles any of the photos of Nell Beatty, but when Allen asks if she knows an Eleanor Beatty, a series of expressions scud across her face like clouds. Confusion, clarity, disbelief, hope. Worry.

"You better come in." She stands back to let Allen step past her then closes the door firmly behind them both.

11

Margaret Beatty is a thorough, even fanatical housekeeper. The front room is spotless; every polishable surface gleams. They stand awkwardly on the thick beige carpet for a moment. Then she says, "Eleanor was my daughter. I haven't seen her since 1988. Seen or spoken to her. So I don't think I can help you." But she gestures toward the porridge-colored sofa. "Let me give you some tea before you go."

As she waits for her to return, Allen glances around the room. It's not unlike her own flat, if the decorator of her flat had been aiming for unimaginative rather than ultramodern. Beige dominates, not just the carpet and sofa but also the two overstuffed chairs and the walls papered in beige stripes that, when she moves her head slightly, shift into a pattern of silvery-beige stalks of wheat. The throw pillows and curtains are pale pink and taupe; beneath the coffee table is a pale pink throw rug. On one wall are framed reproductions of Turner's *The Fighting Temeraire* and Van Gogh's *Sunflowers*. The magnolia-painted mantelpiece between them is crowded with framed photographs. Before she can check if any of them show Nell, Mrs. Beatty comes back into the room with a laden tea tray, speaking as if she never left.

"I have four other children. Robert's a plumber like his father, and Mark and Paul are in the building trade. My Sheila works at the local primary school. Secretary to the head. Well, I say 'secretary'—these days they're called administrative assistants, aren't they? We made sure they all stayed in school until they were sixteen, and then Cal, that's my late husband, found the boys a trade. Sheila went to secretarial college. They've given me eight grandchildren between them. Two of the boys are graduating uni this summer, and Sheila's youngest finished last year. They all come visit me every week for Sunday lunch, if you can believe it. We have a roast with all the trimmings, and the little ones watch a film after. I don't know how many times I've seen *Frozen* by now."

Allen wonders why the woman is telling her all this. But she's never lost her belief in the value of free recall, so as she takes the cup and saucer Mrs. Beatty holds out, she just prompts her gently.

"But Eleanor wasn't like your other children?" The tea tastes like milky hot water.

Mrs. Beatty nods. "You're exactly right. She was always different. I remember when she was doing her O levels. The others, they knew once they'd finished their exams Cal would help them find an apprenticeship—or, as I said, the secretarial course for Sheila. But when Eleanor turned sixteen, she told Cal she'd already decided what she wanted to do after her exams. 'I'm going to be a model.' A model, if you please! She said men were always telling her she was pretty enough to be one, so—"

Allen interrupts. "Did she mention any particular man?"

Another shake of the head. "Cal would never have permitted that sort of thing. The girls weren't allowed to go round with boys until they'd left school." In Allen's experience, such restrictions never stopped anybody, but Mrs. Beatty's faith at least makes it plain that if Nell had been seeing someone her mother knew nothing about it. Allen will need to talk to someone else for that information.

But someone or something had taken Nell to London, and Allen guesses her mother is working her way toward it. "What did you say when she said that about the modeling?"

"Well, Cal tried to set her straight. He told her why men might tell an ordinary girl she was pretty. What men are like, you know. But Eleanor didn't want to listen. She said look at that Samantha Fox, and that Mandy girl who was going round with that one Rolling Stone. They'd been ordinary girls before they were famous models, and she was as pretty as either of them." She leans forward. "And the truth is she was pretty. People were always telling me so. She said that after her exams she was going to move to London—you had to move to

London to be a model, she said. She'd read about that, and she'd asked Gina Macey from over the road what she needed to do to live there. Gina went to London when she finished school. Got a job in an office. Nell said Gina told her London was very expensive, so if she wanted to move there she'd need a lot of money. She had a Saturday job at Boots, and she said she was going to start putting all her wages aside. Cal was *furious*. We went to Mass every Sunday as a family; he said morals were the backbone of life. He asked her if she knew what kinds of girls went round with Rolling Stones. But she just stuck her chin up and said he was old-fashioned."

Allen wants to laugh. Could any girl really be so naive about the brutal realities of modeling? Would any parent really take such a fantasy version of a model's life seriously enough to be enraged by it? But then she remembers that this all happened at the end of the 1980s, when there had been no #TimesUp, no #MeToo, no Internet to inject a note of ugly reality into the world painted by magazines like *Jackie* and *Smash Hits*. And the incident had occurred in this household, where the ideals of the 1960s seemed to have been alive and well—in fact, still seemed to be.

In a flash, she understands the reason behind Mrs. Beatty's list of her family's ordinary achievements, the reason behind this dull room, even behind her choice of hairstyle. It isn't old age Mrs. Beatty is running toward, but respectability. She wants Allen to know that whatever happened to Nell, in all other aspects she, Margaret Beatty, has managed a life of spotless propriety, untouched by the twin embarrassments of public attention and uniqueness. The worry she saw flit across the woman's face wasn't worry about what might have happened to Nell but worry about what Nell might have done.

But Allen admits to herself that she admires the version of Nell her mother is describing. This Nell sounds imaginative and determined, a girl that *Jackie*, which Allen herself once read avidly, might have praised as *v. spiffy*. Even though she knows how the story ends, she finds herself rooting for this Nell.

"Then what happened?" She's surprised to hear that her voice is a little breathless.

"Cal wanted to kick her out. He believed in teaching hard lessons the hard way. He told her she could go live with Gina Macey if she liked her that much. But I reminded him that when our Sheila was fourteen she'd wanted to be a lady newspaper reporter, and two years later she'd forgotten all about it. That seemed to do the trick. He calmed down and let her stay. And, bless him, the next year when Eleanor was finishing up, he sent away for leaflets from colleges that offered courses in hairdressing and doing makeup for weddings, that sort of thing. He even asked the local salons if they did apprenticeships."

"Was Eleanor interested?"

"I thought so. She said thank you and took the leaflets up to her room. I must have been wrong, though, because"—Mrs. Beatty inhales, then exhales raggedly—"I let her have a lie-in the day her results arrived. I had some Cumberland sausages in the deep freeze, and I decided to cook them for her. She loved Cumberland sausages, but usually she wouldn't eat them. She wouldn't eat any sausages. She was always slimming. Still, I thought, *It's a special day, she might make an exception.* I put them in a pan and brought her up a cuppa to have in bed. But when I went in . . ."

Allen waits. After a few seconds, Mrs. Beatty clears her throat. "At first I thought maybe she'd gone on holiday with some friends without telling us. Very naughty, but Eleanor wasn't a thoughtful girl. And she'd left behind some of her clothes, so I thought she might be coming back." She swallows hard. "But when I checked the hall cupboard, I saw she'd taken her winter coat."

Allen waits again then very gently asks, "You didn't hear from her after that?"

Mrs. Beatty shakes her head. "I asked her friends. John and Dora Macey gave us Gina's telephone number, but when I spoke to her she didn't know anything about it. I wanted to go to London to look for her, but Cal wouldn't have it. *She* left *us*, he said, so it wasn't our responsibility to look for *her*. And you didn't want to bother the neighbors by going on about it, or go barreling off to London for no real reason. After all, she hadn't been taken. She'd left of her own free will. That's what he used to say whenever I was low: 'She left of her own free will, Margaret Joan.'"

What's the right response to this? The police officer in Allen wants to tell Margaret Beatty that no matter what she'd done she wouldn't have found her daughter: London is a place people go to be lost as well as discovered. The human being in Allen would like to dig up Cal Beatty and tell him he should be ashamed. But the Allen who sits on Mrs. Beatty's oat-colored sofa stays silent.

"I used to wonder if it was my fault." Mrs. Beatty's voice is small.

"Why would it be your fault?" Was there a revelation here after all?

"I entered her in a bonny baby contest. The local paper ran one when she was nine months old. You paid fifty pence, sent in a photo, and then they published them all in the paper and the readers voted." She tries to laugh. "I know it was silly. Cal said I'd be better off putting the fifty pence in a post office savings account and leaving it there until she was eighteen. But"—her voice rises as if she's defending a shameful truth—"she *was* a beautiful baby. And she won. Ten pounds. She loved that story, but after she left I wondered if it turned her head." She folds her lips together. "When she was ten, she started begging us to let her wear makeup. Cal said no. The rule with the girls was no cosmetics until they were fourteen. And the *day* she turned fourteen she went for that job at Boots then used her wages to buy every kind of makeup you could imagine. And magazines. All the fashion magazines the newsagent sold."

She stares into her teacup for a minute then looks up. "Is she dead?"

Allen isn't prepared for this. "I'm sorry?"

"You haven't said anything about why you're here, and you've let me ramble on about her, so I thought . . ." She meets Allen's eyes. "Is she?"

Legally, it's up to the next of kin to decide who's informed of a death and who isn't. But Allen doesn't know who Nell's next of kin is. She hasn't heard anything that suggests she and Peter Rainey were married, so next of kin could well be Mrs. Beatty. Besides, how much must it cost a mother to ask that question, and to ask it so baldly? For that reason alone, it deserves an honest answer.

"Yes, she is. I'm sorry."

The hand holding the teacup shakes a little. Some liquid slops onto the saucer. "How did it happen?"

But that's too much honesty even for Allen. Let someone else fill this woman's head with the image of her daughter beaten to death on a park bench; let someone else tell her that she'd moved back to Bristol eight years before and never made contact. "I'm sorry, I'm not at liberty to say."

Mrs. Beatty opens her mouth. "Pl—"

Allen thinks she'll just lie to the woman, spin a story of a peaceful death in a sunny hospital. But a long marriage spent bowing to a greater authority and decades spent chasing respectability are too much for Margaret Beatty to overcome. She's not going to challenge a police officer. She stops. "Of course," she says instead. "I see. Of course."

Allen wants to offer her something, something that will let her remember her daughter as more than just a disappointment. "I'm actually here about Eleanor in connection with an old case. I don't know if you remember the Baby Bella kidnapping?"

"The little girl who was taken from the hotel room all those years ago and then found?" The wary look comes back. "What did Eleanor have to do with all that?"

"She was the one who found her."

"Oh my. Eleanor did that? She brought that baby to the police? Well, I suppose Cal was right: What they learn early stays with them."

"At the time, we knew nothing about her but her name, but because of her death we have more information. That's how I was able to find you. And we're using that information to try to tie up all the loose ends in the case." It wasn't exactly a lie.

Mrs. Beatty frowns. "Then I'm sorry to have taken up your time with a wasted visit. That would have been two years after she left, and, as I said, I didn't know anything about her then."

"No, but it's possible you know someone who might be able to give me more information about her. For instance, would you have a current phone number for Gina Macey?" Allen has no idea if Nell contacted this Gina once she arrived in London, but it's worth exploring. Certainly a girl is much more likely to confide in another girl about an illicit boyfriend than she is to confide in her mother. Maybe Gina Macey knows about Nell's involvement with Tom Carpenter.

"Not her phone number, no." The fact that the other woman doesn't hesitate before she answers tells Allen that this isn't the first time she's considered Gina Macey as a contact. But all Mrs. Beatty says aloud is, "I might have an old address. We used to exchange Christmas cards, but not anymore. They tailed off a few years after her parents died."

While she's out of the room, Allen crosses to look at the photos on the mantel. A balding man with his mother's mouth and two children in front of him, posing in front of a lake. A sweet-faced blond woman holding a Christmas present in her lap and smiling at the camera. Neither of them look anything like Nell.

Mrs. Beatty comes back in holding a slip of paper. "Oh, that's my family collection." She joins Allen, picking up a photo of two stocky men squinting against the sun. "That's Mark and Paul on holiday in Corfu." Then a soft-focus portrait of a blond girl in a cap and gown. "Sheila's Lindsay when she finished sixth-form college. And this"— she runs a finger across the silver frame of the largest photo—"is me and Cal on our wedding day." A younger version of Mrs. Beatty, eyes wide at the seriousness of the endeavor, presses against the side of a smiling blue-eyed man with thick black hair. In his face, Allen can see Nell's high cheekbones, her seductive smile in the curve of his lips. She savors the irony for a second.

"No photos of Eleanor?"

"Cal made me throw them away when she left. Gone means forgotten, he said." She contemplates the collection on the mantel before turning to lead Allen to the door.

Then she turns back. Reaching out a thumb and forefinger like someone trying to prevent themselves from being burned or a naughty child stealing a sweet, she plucks a snapshot from behind the frames and thrusts it at Allen. The picture's edges are curling, its colors bleached, but it's still easy to see the toddler sitting forward in her pushchair. A pink bow holds back her dark curls and a wide grin reveals her tiny milk teeth. Her eyes stare straight into the camera, fringed with thick dark lashes, her eyebrows arched like feathery wings above them. A single dimple dents the plump cheek to the left of her mouth. She is indeed a bonny baby.

They stare at the snapshot together. "For years after she left, I checked the magazines in the newsagent's, to see if she was in them." Again Nell's mother tries to laugh at her own foolishness. Again she doesn't quite succeed. "She never was."

12

The advent of mobile phones has made it very difficult to find a phone number. Fewer and fewer people have landlines, and there's almost no way to track down a mobile number associated with a particular name or address without a warrant and pressure on mobile service providers. Besides, Allen's always been in favor of unannounced visits. With no time to prepare and in the curious state of relaxed comfort that being at home brings, people tend to make revelations. So the next day, early enough that she'll still be in plenty of time for Sunday lunch at Carrie's, she takes the Tube out to Wembley Central, the stop closest to the address Mrs. Beatty gave her, and makes her way to the flat that belongs to Gina Macey, or at least belonged to Gina Macey fifteen years before. If Macey does still live there, Allen thinks, she's unlikely to be out on a Sunday morning. Most people aren't.

Russell Court is a squat 1970s block of flats with windows framed in white aluminum and a frosted-glass central door. Miraculously the label next to the bell for flat B says G. Macey. Allen can't believe her luck. She presses the bell. After a few seconds, a man comes into the foyer.

He's short and slim, but a small potbelly swells the front of his faded blue polo shirt. He has a round, pug-nosed face with deep-set brown eyes. Gray streaks his beard and receding hair. In another ten years, neighbors will be asking him to dress up as Father Christmas and restore faith in their doubting children. For now, though, he holds a tea towel in one hand and opens the frosted door with the other. "Can I help you?"

"No, no, I'm sorry." Allen takes her warrant card out of her pocket and flashes it. "Superintendent Martha Allen, Metropolitan Police. I'm looking for a Gina Macey. This is her last known address. When I saw the name next to the bell, I thought . . . It didn't occur to me that it was just an old label. My mistake. I'm sorry to have bothered you."

But instead of making the appropriate noises and receding back inside, the man opens the door wider. "Come in." He doesn't seem at all fazed. He smiles and flaps the towel as if brushing her inside.

The interior of the flat is a riot of joyous chaos. The walls are covered in posters for art exhibitions and events; Arabic tiles and Indian carvings fill any free space. Photos of groups of happy people, framed and unframed, are propped on every surface. Throw cushions of all colors and patterns lie strewn on the two worn sofas that form an L in the far corner, and an oriental rug in shades of red and orange has been spread over the thin navy wall-to-wall carpet. A scuffed coffee table centered between the two sofas bears a half-completed jigsaw puzzle of blowsy peonies and a mug that says *I Woke Up Like This*.

"Sit, sit." The man gestures toward one sofa and sits on the other.

Both he and the room are too welcoming for her to stay standing. She pushes aside a green throw pillow and feels a little air sigh out of the overstuffed sofa cushion as it adjusts to her shape.

"Is Ms. Macey in? Or do you know where I could find her?"

He holds up a delaying hand. "Please. Can I get you a coffee? Tea?"

The coffee comes in a mug covered in painted poppies, a chip missing from the bottom edge. It's delicious. The man smiles while he watches her taste it. "Not too much milk?"

"Perfect. But—"

"But you're here to find Gina Macey, and you want to know if I can help."

"Yes."

He picks up his own mug. "Yes, I can." He takes a sip then swallows. "I'm Gina Macey."

"I'm sorry?" She looks at his thick beard and mustache, his receding hairline.

He shakes his head. "No, I'm sorry. I tried to think of a way to ease into it while I was in the kitchen, but there really isn't a way to ease into *that*. Perhaps I should have said, 'I used to be called Gina Macey; now I'm called George Macey.' Same person, different gender, different name."

She takes a deep swallow from her mug. As if he recognizes that she needs a few seconds to readjust, Macey keeps talking.

"I transitioned in 2002, after my parents died. I know a lot of people want to forget about their pre-transition lives, but I don't. I was born in the wrong body, but I did a lot of things in that body that made me who I am. I owe a lot to Gina."

"I see." Allen leaves a pause, then says, "And when you were Gina, you knew Eleanor Beatty?"

"Nell. No one outside her family called her Eleanor."

"All right, Nell. Her mother said you were friends."

"Oh, that's how you found my address. Mrs. Beatty." He shakes his head. "That poor woman. But I wouldn't say Nell and I were friends. We knew each other, the way you know kids on your road who aren't the right age to be your mates. Or at least that's how we knew each other until she came round on my first visit back to Bristol after I moved, wanting to know all about London."

"When was this?"

"1987. June of 1987. I remember because it was the day after Thatcher was reelected." He wrinkles his upper lip.

"And she just rang the bell and asked to know about London?"

"Almost that." He shakes his head again. "I know how it sounds. I thought it was ridiculous too. She rang the bell, asked to speak to me, and when my mother called me down, she said her mother had told her I'd moved to London, and would I tell her about it because she was going to be a model, so she'd have to move there, and she wanted to be prepared. She said it all in a rush, just like that."

"And what did you do?"

"Like I said, I thought it was a fantasy. She was fifteen! I didn't see any harm in indulging it, though, so I brought her into the kitchen, made her a cuppa, told her a few stories. I remember I exaggerated.

No one had admired me before, and I wanted, well . . . to seem cool. I told her I worked in central London—that was true—and I threw in a few celebrity sightings. And I thought that was that."

"But it wasn't?"

Macey leans back against his multicolored cushions. "She was not an ordinary fifteen-year-old. She was absolutely focused. Like a laser beam. When she came round the second time, she remembered every word I'd said. She treated it like gospel. That's when I told her London was very expensive, and if she was serious she'd need to save a lot of money. I thought it would put her off, break the fantasy. But when I came home for Christmas, she called round and told me she'd started saving her pocket money and the wages from her Saturday job. Told me she always kept the money with her so her father wouldn't find it, or find a bank account passbook." He spreads his hands in a gesture that says, *Look at what kind of person she was.* "That's why I wasn't surprised when she left. Anyone who knew her could've seen she was going to do exactly what she said." He pauses. "Well, apparently anyone but her parents."

Allen sips her coffee. "Nell's mother tells me that after Nell ran away, she asked you if you knew anything about it, and you said no. Were you telling the truth?"

Macey looks at his little paunch.

"So you were in touch with her."

"She lived here for a bit." His voice is a mumble. Allen doesn't say anything. He looks up. "I'm not proud of lying about that. But she needed somewhere to stay. She showed up one day, and I couldn't tell her to go sleep in the street."

"You weren't surprised to see her?"

"I didn't say that. I was very surprised." A strange look crosses his face, a combination of shame, fear, and yet also a kind of nostalgia. Then it's gone. "And I wasn't at all pleased. When you tell someone in passing that you'd be happy to help them if they move, you don't expect to open the door one day and find them on your doorstep. But in that way she was a child. She didn't understand that someone might say something out of politeness."

"So what did you do?"

"I told her she could stay for a couple of nights. She had this mad idea that she was going to walk into a modeling agency—she knew all their names—and they'd sign her on the spot. I thought that as soon as she found out it wasn't that simple she'd head back to Bristol with her tail between her legs." His face says he should have known better.

"But?"

"Well, of course it was a disaster. The first place she went to, the receptionist asked to see her book. Nell thought she was trying to tell her she'd have a long wait! She must have found the one kind modeling agency in London, because the girl actually explained to her what a book was. You know, photos showing how a girl photographs in different lights and poses. Professional shots, with professional makeup and hair. Then she told her how much it would cost." He shakes his head. "I think that was the only time I ever saw Nell look defeated. I asked her how much she'd managed to save. It was nothing for London, never mind for a professional photography session. So I said she could stay here until she found a job and built up enough savings."

"And did she find a job?" Allen wants to get to the part of Nell's life where she might have encountered Tom Carpenter. The part where she gets a job in Chelsea and runs into him in a newsagent's on her lunch, or serves him in a shop.

"I wouldn't say *she* found a job. I found one for her. I used to spend my lunch hour walking in Soho, and I saw a Help Wanted sign in a café. I mentioned it to her, she went down there, and they gave her a job waitressing." Macey raises his eyebrows. "I can't imagine she was good at it, but I can see why they'd hire her. She'd certainly bring in customers. She used to come home with a fortune in tips and tell me about all the men who'd asked for her telephone number or offered to wait for her after work."

"What makes you say she couldn't have been a good waitress?"

He snorts. "Because she was the most self-centered person I've ever known. Even when she used to drop round in Bristol she never showed any interest in me. I was just a way for her to learn about London. I find it hard to imagine her caring much about the customers. Still"—he shrugs—"I couldn't really blame her. All her life people had been oohing and aahing over how lovely she was—except her windbag of a father—so naturally she thought Nell Beatty was the most fascinating thing in the world." He snorts again. "From the moment she got here she spent all her time either in the bathroom or staring at herself in any reflective surface she came across. It was like living with Marilyn Monroe." Allen's face must show her confusion, because he explains, "Apparently MM spent hours in front of the mirror. It was why she was always late—she couldn't tear herself away from herself. Nell would have understood. She couldn't be away from a mirror for more than fifteen minutes. But after six months I'd had it. She hadn't given me one penny since she'd arrived, and I had to wait hours to use my own bathroom. I suggested perhaps she might like to help with the rent. Two days later, she came home and told me she'd found somewhere else to live. A girl at work had told her about a squat."

"A *squat*?"

He grins. "I thought much the same. But I'm guessing economics won out over access to mod cons. That was the thing about Nell: She was naive in some ways, but she was canny in others. Why stay somewhere where someone wanted her to pay rent when she could stay somewhere free? A couple of days later, she was gone. All she left behind were her hair crimpers."

Allen's curiosity is piqued. "If you don't mind my asking, if she was so much trouble, why did you let her stay so long? With the kinds of tips you describe, surely she'd saved up enough to manage on her own long before December."

Macey doesn't answer, but the strange look crosses his face again.

Allen waits.

"You need to understand something," Macey says at last. "When I lived in Bristol, where I lived in Bristol . . . My parents thought gay men should be locked up, for God's sake! They called them 'man women.' And I was a girl who fancied men but also felt like a man? I didn't know what that was, but I knew it must be disgusting. I didn't leave home so I could be myself. I left home because I thought I was sick, and if I moved away maybe I could get the help I needed without my parents ever knowing." He gives a little laugh. "And I was right, although not in the way I thought. You walk around Soho on your lunch hour and you see a lot of things. And some of those things helped me understand who and how I really was. But understanding doesn't make you less ashamed. As my counselor would say, it doesn't undo a lifetime's conditioning. So I thought maybe I could find a happy medium. Be Gina Macey, nice girl, outside, but inside the house be . . ." He rotates his hand as if to say, *You know what comes next*. "And that's what I was doing when Nell arrived. I thought she was a Jehovah's Witness or something. At eight thirty on a Saturday morning? So I opened the door. And—"

And Nell, self-centered, canny Nell . . . "She threatened to tell your parents you were a cross-dresser. She blackmailed you into letting her stay."

"Not at all. She was *uninterested*. Totally indifferent. Like I said, she was completely self-centered. Bandage round my chest, shirt and tie, trousers with suspenders, and for all she cared I could have been wearing a dress and high heels. All that mattered to her was that she'd made it to London." He laughs in disbelief. "But at that stage indifference was a victory to me. That's why I let her stay, and why I never said anything to her mother. Out of gratitude for her indifference. That's where I was then. So grateful not to be attacked that I lied to a grieving mother without even being asked." Now he just looks ashamed. "I'd do it differently today."

And that, Allen thinks, is a feeling anyone can understand.

"Do you remember the name of the café?"

"What?"

"The café where Nell worked. Can you remember what it was called?"

"After all this time?" He pulls a face. "Café something. Okay, wait." He closes his eyes. "Café . . . Café . . . some Italian city." He opens them. "Café Firenze. That's it. In one of those little alleys near Old Compton Street."

She writes it down, though she knows it's a long shot. Still, her luck has been good so far. "And you never saw her again once she left?"

"No." Macey winces. "That is, not exactly." He stands up. "Bear with me."

After two or three minutes in which Allen sits drinking her coffee, he returns. He's holding a magazine. "About a year after she left, I was in the newsagent's, and I saw this." He hands it to her.

It's called *Amateur Lens*, and its layout is a masterpiece of 1980s design, all sharp angles and vivid turquoise and pink. *New Year Cover Contest Winner!* says a jaunty red ribbon across the bottom corner. Above it is, presumably, the winning picture. Taking up the whole cover, it's a soft-focus and hypersaturated color photo of Nell.

The shot is a medium close-up. Nell's body is in profile, but her face is turned toward the camera. Her shoulders are bare, and you can just make out the swelling tops of her breasts. Lip gloss gleams on her slightly parted lips, and her blue eyes, wide and earnest, look out at the viewer. She looks young and fresh and very sexy.

Macey looks at Allen. "You see what I mean when I say 'not exactly.'"

On the walk back to the Tube, the copy of *Amateur Lens* feels heavy in Allen's bag. The moment Macey showed it to her, she recognized the look of it from her days as a constable in Soho. Then, space there had still been cheap to rent, probably because the area had been a warren of sex shops and black-windowed massage parlors, prostitutes' flats crowding the stories above. She can still remember the furtive men ducking into and out of doorways, the hard-faced women forcing themselves to look interested under washed-out white and yellow neon signs promising XXX videos and live shows. It was a dangerous place in broad daylight, never mind what happened after dark.

But that danger and the cheap rents it fostered made Soho home to countless amateur camera clubs. Groups of men could chip in together and afford to rent a space in which they shot and developed photographs, at least some of which were of the kind euphemistically referred to as "glamour." Allen can remember seeing cards pinned up in the windows of Soho camera shops seeking "figure models" or, more boldly, "broad-minded female models." In those pre-Internet days, the same stores would offer a shelf of magazines aimed at the members of those camera clubs, magazines with titles like *Practical Photography* and *Amateur Photographer*. They were packed with articles about lenses and lighting sandwiched between endless advertisements for cameras and film and filters, and the cover of every issue seemed to feature a different tousle-haired, heavy-lidded girl who pouted out at the viewer.

It was easy to imagine Nell spotting the word "model" on one of the pinned-up cards and calling the number. After all, the women who answered those adverts became cover girls. The proof of that was right there only a few feet away! Samantha Fox had been a glamour model—undoubtedly this was why Cal Beatty had been so enraged when his daughter mentioned her. And the rates for glamour models could be quite high, very high when compared to the wages of a waitress. For a girl who wanted to make money fast, the opportunity would have been almost irresistible.

But in the decades since, Soho has remade itself into a bustling urban village of expensive boutiques and open-air cafés. No amateur camera club could afford to rent a studio there now. Not to mention that there isn't even a reason for such a club to exist. Soft porn, like hardcore, has long since moved to the Internet. The men who would have once been thrilled to spend a Saturday snapping "artistic" photos can see all the breasts they want online, and more.

The rents have driven out the cheap little cafés too. Allen suddenly remembers a night in the eighties—1984? '85?—when she and her partner rescued a young male prostitute behind Madame Jojo's, the burlesque club. A dissatisfied customer kicking him to a pulp in the concrete yard, trousers round the man's hips, and the boy's face a mass of blood. "He didn't finish me!" the man yelled at them as they cuffed him. "You should arrest *him*, get me my fucking money back!" There's no more Madame Jojo's now, no more Raymond Revuebar strip club, no more Windmill nude theater. If all the big venues have closed, a hole-in-the-wall restaurant won't have survived.

The blue-and-red roundel of Wembley Central station appears on the pavement a few feet ahead of her and draws her back to the present. Once through the card reader and on a train heading toward central London, she searches "Café Firenze" on her phone. Her luck has run out. The only London restaurant with "Firenze" in its name is an Italian place in Teddington, twelve miles from Old Compton Street. It gets good reviews on Yelp, but it isn't what she needs.

Yet she doesn't mind. Maybe it's the way that each of her discoveries about Nell has led to another; maybe it's the fact that all those discoveries are taking Nell closer to a life in which she could have met Tom Carpenter, even if Allen hasn't yet managed to find the exact moment when she did. Whatever it is, Allen feels certain that this road, however winding, is inexorably bringing her closer to the moment when she'll discover the origin of that baby Nell handed across the counter at Victoria Police Station and to the moment when she learns the truth about what happened to Bella Carpenter. And since she isn't going to stop until she gets there, she doesn't mind if she has to wait a little while to take the next step. She fishes *Amateur Lens* out of her bag, opens it, and starts leafing through.

And suddenly, there's the next step.

13

On Monday morning, she calls Desbury. She sent him a text when she found Margaret Beatty—!!!, he replied—but now she has much more to tell. And she wants to ask a favor. She wants him to come to London.

As the phone rings, though, she feels her courage ebbing away. That had been a very short text—maybe he was just responding out of politeness. Maybe he'd seen her trip to Bristol as one officer working with another on a mutually relevant case; maybe he'd only invited her to dinner out of collegial courtesy, or respect for a former commanding officer. Maybe asking him isn't a good idea, after all.

When he picks up, she buys time. "How's the Beatty case going?"

"Barely moving." His words are a sigh. "I'm trying to cover every possibility while also focusing on Rainey, but so far I'm having no luck anywhere. Rainey's still claiming he stayed home alone after Nell went out, fell asleep in front of the television, and didn't wake up until O'Connell and Mathersmith came round to give the notification. The two of them say he looked as if he'd slept in a chair, which means nothing if you know him, but there's also nothing to prove he didn't. Meanwhile, we pulled photos of punters recently arrested on the Stapleton Road, then went back and showed them to the women we found there. The ones we talked to identified a couple of men who like it rough, or worse, but when we visited them there were no results. All the alibis checked out. A lot of unhappy wives once my lads finished the home visits, I imagine, but no one who was lying about their whereabouts on the night Nell was killed. A lot of the women on Stapleton Road are like Nell, only out there when they need the money, so I'll send some of the team back again this week." Another sigh, this one heavier. "Beyond that, I don't see what else we can do."

She opens her mouth to suggest he try using the media, then remembers he's not a DC anymore. He knows these things as well as she does. Instead senior officer to senior officer, she confirms, "And of course you're taking full advantage of the media's interest in murders."

There's no humor in his laugh. "Media interest in an alcoholic part-time sex worker found dead in a local park? She wasn't young, or pretty. There isn't even a hint of a serial killer. We put up A4 flyers at all the bus stops near the park and all the local shops that would let us. They give the date and approximate time of the murder and ask people to ring in if they think they saw anything. We included Nell's first mug shot. There she's young *and* pretty." He sighs again. "But thanks for asking. Now tell me how Operation Bella's going."

"Check your inbox." She hits send on the email she's created then hears a ping on his end.

Silence. Some clicking. Then he says, "Never mind the mug shot. That's the girl I remember." But he, too, had walked the beat in Soho. "Of course, whatever camera club she posed for will be long gone."

"I know. But look at the second page." She'd scanned it from inside the copy of *Amateur Lens* a few minutes earlier. Now she opens it on her own screen. On the left side is the masthead, the information about the editor and the staff in tiny print. On the right side, purple italics announce *Our 1990 Cover Competition Winner!*, with all the details of the cover photo underneath.

Desbury reads silently at first then in the half whisper people use when they're trying to follow something difficult. ". . . 'was shot indoors using a Minolta 8000i and Fujicolor Reala film. The lensman, Piotr Wyz—Wysh—Wyższej'"—he pronounces it "Vyshedge"—"'tells us he used a white background drape, a diffuser lens, and two Courtenay 1000s with umbrella to light the sitter, a camera club model.'" He tuts. "She couldn't even get her name printed in an amateur photo magazine. Poor girl."

"Hers isn't the name I'm interested in. His is. It's pronounced Visheh, by the way. And how many Piotr Wyższejes do you think there are in London?" Without waiting, she answers the question. "Four. I know because I spent yesterday afternoon going through the district electoral registers. There's one each in Barnes, Forestdale, Hackney, and White City."

"And do they have landlines?"

"Two of them do. Or did. The one in Barnes died in November. The one in Forestdale didn't arrive here until 2001. He's the one who told me how to pronounce the name. Apparently it means 'higher,' as in higher education." She pauses then clears her throat. "I wondered if you'd like to come check out the other two with me."

Deciding the previous evening to interview the two men named Piotr Wyższej, she remembered how good Desbury was with male witnesses. He'd created solidarity with Terry Glaister at the estate agent's all those years ago, and up in Bristol she watched something similar happen with Rainey. Rainey hadn't liked either of them, but at least he'd looked at Desbury when he'd spoken, tried to share jokes with him. If she needed to question men about a woman, she thought, there was an advantage in having someone with her whom men warmed to.

And she could use a friend. That's what she'll never say; that's what made her lose her courage at the start of this call; that's what's making her bite her lip as she waits for an answer.

After a second, Desbury says, "My sheet's pretty full for this week. Can we do it at the weekend?"

He emails her on Wednesday morning to say he'll drive up on Saturday. If she'll send him her address, he'll pick her up and take her wherever they need to go. She starts to smile. After all this time, he still likes to do the driving. But the smile fades as she reads the message's postscript:

PS. *Last night's Stap. Rd. ints. identified one who likes strangling. Bringing him in now.*

One who likes strangling. Her gorge rises. She thinks of Phil, of her father, of Desbury himself. She reminds herself, *Not all men*, but it doesn't help. She still feels the familiar combination of sorrow, rage, and despair, all at once.

Then she closes out of her email and goes to make a cup of tea, because there's nothing else she can do.

14

The Piotr Wyższej in White City is a twentysomething whose English vocabulary seems to be limited to "I call the police." When an exasperated Allen finally barks, "We *are* the police," as she continues to wave her warrant card under his nose, he slams the door in her face.

"Takes all kinds," Desbury says as they make their way down the walk.

The Piotr Wyższej in Hackney might have been handsome once. Under his heavy jowls and hooded eyelids lurks the ghost of a square-jawed, sleepy-eyed young man. His gray hair is still abundant, and he keeps it long on top so that a lock falls into his eyes. Once this must have made him look casually sexy; now that the years have thickened his neck and torso, it makes him look like a slightly rakish bull. A builder, Allen judges from his bulk and from the hand he holds out for her warrant card, calloused and dotted with tiny scars. Or at the very least some sort of manual laborer at one stage.

He inspects the card then hands it back. "Yes?"

"May we come in, Mr. Wyższej?"

He shrugs and lets them past. The house is at the end of a cul-de-sac, red brick with a glossy turquoise door. Inside, the entrance hall looks freshly decorated, papered in a pattern of burgundy and white stripes, the polished white tiles of the floor yet to suffer a single chip or crack. At the far end, a white door opens into a bathroom. Allen knows this because someone has left the door ajar and damp steam drifts out in lazy trails.

Wyższej steps past them to close the bathroom door. "Three daughters," he says, as if this explains everything.

He leads them to a kitchen that's been extended to include an eating area with floor-to-ceiling French windows. Through these, Allen can see a long garden, a path cutting down it to a shed and what looks to be a vegetable plot at the bottom. She can just make out one or two February daffodils blooming outside the shed. Wyższej seats himself so that he can turn his head and look out at this pretty view, leaving them to face the kitchen itself.

She brings out the copy of *Amateur Lens*, laying it on the top of the round table so that it faces him.

"Do you recognize this, Mr. Wyższej?"

He looks at it for a moment then smiles. His teeth are perfect. Allen remembers reading that Poland has some of the best dentistry in the world.

He stretches out his hand and pulls the magazine toward him. "The only thing I ever won in my life." Although time has softened his accent, *th* still comes out as *d*, and the final *g* of "thing" is a *k*.

"Yes, that's how we managed to find you. We're here because we're interested in the girl in the photo. Do you remember her?"

"Remember Nell?" He puts his fingertips on the cover. "You don't forget a girl like that." He looks up. "Why are you interested in Nell?"

Allen moves forward slightly in her seat and clears her throat. She's always hated this part; she doesn't know a police officer who doesn't. "Mr. Wyższej, I'm sorry to have to tell you that Nell Beatty was recently found dead."

Wyższej looks down at the magazine. With the side of his thumb he strokes the black hair of the photographed Nell. "She was the most beautiful girl I ever saw." He swallows. "How did she . . ." He stops, looking quickly out the French windows. "My wife is in the garden."

Desbury steps in smoothly, as if he knows Allen wants him to. Allen recedes into her chair a little. "I understand. No need to say any more about the model. Can you tell us how you came to take the photo?"

Wyższej rests his arms on the edge of the table. "I moved to England in 1987, to work for my uncle. In Poland, I was electrician, and he wrote my mother that he would sponsor a visa for me to come and work for him here. Of course I came: much better pay, much better everything.

But very hard work. Twelve-, sixteen-hour days, work, work, work. No time for friends. Finally, after a year, he hired a second electrician, and I had some time off. In Poland, I belonged to a camera club. I thought the same thing might be a good way to make some friends in England. I found this club"—he taps the magazine cover again—"in the adverts at the back of this magazine. Some weeks we took photos on the streets; sometimes we went to Hampstead Heath, Hyde Park—always with a trip to the pub after. They were friendly. It was nice. Two Wednesday nights a month we did indoor photography. A studio in Soho. Tiny place. Always a pretty girl, never much clothing. Glamour photography, the other fellows told me it was called." A flash of those perfect teeth. "I was twenty-three; I didn't care what it is called! Nell was one of the girls. The prettiest. She showed up a couple of months after I joined."

"What do you mean, 'showed up'?" Allen takes out her pad.

He shrugs. "What I say. One of the blokes, Geoff, he organized the models, and she was one. She answered an advert, I think."

"D'you remember when this was?"

"I joined in March of 1989. So maybe May?"

"And the two of you became close? This is a pretty intimate shot."

He answers her question, but he looks at Desbury. "No, no, that's not how it works. She posed for all of us at once, and no nudity. Here she was wearing swimming costume. I asked her to . . ." He paws lightly at his shoulders.

"You asked her to take the straps down," Desbury says.

He nods. His English falters as he retreats into memory. "I come in very, very tight with the lens, so we don't see straps. I put the front lamp so it hits just above her head. It lights up the whole face, but soft. Makes girl look"—he says something that sounds like *"masichelski,"* then translates—"like a dream. This way it seems . . . intimate . . . without actually being like that. It's good trick. I learned it in club in Poland."

He shrugs again, as if to say, *That's all*. But Allen has heard something in his voice, tight and careful. She leans in. "But you wanted it to be more than a trick."

Wyższej frowns. "I don't understand."

"You fancied her? You wanted the two of you to be really intimate?"

He turns the magazine to face her. "You see this girl? What man wouldn't fancy her?" But as he looks at the photo, a blush blooms on his neck.

Of course Desbury understands before she does. "She turned you down. You asked, and she knocked you back."

Wyższej doesn't look up, but after a pause, he nods.

"Ah, mate, we've all been there. It always still stings. I'm sorry."

The other man raises his head. "Two or three times she said no. Then finally she tells me she has a boyfriend, some man she met at her other work. Rich, owns a big house, he knows people who can help her get started as a model."

This sounds so exactly like the kind of man a girl would invent to keep unwanted attention at bay that Allen almost laughs—except that it also sounds like the kind of story a man would spin to seduce a naive but ambitious girl. Could this man be Tom Carpenter, down from his house in Somerset on an assignment, ducking into Café Firenze for a quick lunch and running across a beautiful waitress, the prettiest girl there?

She focuses back on Wyższej. "Did she say where the house was?"

"Why would I ask?" He looks back at her. "You think she made it up. I thought so too. But a few weeks later, I see her get into a BMW after her session. There was a man in the driver's seat. Then I believe it."

"Did you see the man?"

He shakes his head. "But one of the men at the club, he told me they are all like this, all the models. Only interested in rich men, ones who can give them things and do things for them." He nods. "He is right. Beautiful women are no good for ordinary men. They want too much. This is why when I got married I picked a nice, plain woman. Good cook, three wonderful girls, and always she's pleased to see me when I come home."

They sit in silence.

"Nell let me drive her home once," Wyższej says suddenly. "To Yorke Square."

"Yorke Square?" Allen sits forward in her chair. Yorke Square is a housing cooperative in South London, but in the 1980s and 1990s it was a squat. It was a *famous* squat. Its residents resisted the local authorities to buy the buildings in the square themselves, then renovated them to create the cooperative. They even dug a public garden out of layers of rubble, creating an urban oasis in the square's center. And Yorke Square is only a little way over the Vauxhall Bridge, in an almost perfectly straight line from the Bellevue Hotel and Victoria Police Station.

"Are you sure you took her to Yorke Square?"

"I'm sure. Ten years later, the residents hired my firm to help with the refit after they bought the square, and every morning I parked in front of the building where I dropped Nell. Ivy Lodge. The name was painted on the house."

"When did you give her the lift?" Desbury's tone takes it for granted that he remembers.

He does. "The end of October. She kissed me on the cheek and said, 'There's a Halloween present for you.'" For a moment, Allen thinks he's going to raise his hand and touch the spot.

"And she never asked you for another ride after that? Maybe to another place?"

"I didn't see her again."

Allen cuts in. "What do you mean?"

"What I say. She didn't show up to model again. On her usual day the next month, we waited, but nothing. We went to the pub instead, and for the next session another girl came. I asked Geoff what happened, but he said he didn't know. He rang the number she gave him, but the man who answered said she didn't work there anymore. When the magazine told me I had won, I thought maybe she would spot herself on the cover and get in touch, but . . ." He lifts his hands, palms up.

Out of the corner of her eye, Allen sees a woman emerge from the garden shed. Wyższej must see her, too, because he thrusts the magazine back at them and stands up. His knees hit the underside of the table, and he winces slightly.

"My wife is coming. She is a very curious woman."

A flaw in his perfect average choice, Allen thinks. But she has no interest in seeing the woman Wyższej has settled for. She's found out enough to be getting on with. So she allows him to hustle them down the corridor, makes sure he puts her card in his trouser pocket, and hears the glass door slide open just before the front door clicks shut behind them. Through the wood she hears him shout something in Polish.

15

Desbury drives them from Hackney to Vauxhall, stopping at a Pret A Manger for lunch along the way. While they eat, they watch part of a documentary about Yorke Square on Allen's phone. Like most people, she supposes, she's never really thought about what squatting involves, and she's surprised to see how hard the first residents worked. Committed communists and anarchists, they'd banded together to unbrick windows, rebuild crumbling walls and ceilings, even clear toilets that had been deliberately filled with cement by the London Council. No wonder they fought so hard to keep the houses. The documentary gives the impression that although most of the original inhabitants have moved on, a few stalwarts remain. She crosses her fingers.

What she finds when they arrive is nothing like what she saw on the screen. Yorke Square has become a middle-class, or even upper-middle-class, enclave. Although it's only a few streets away from the busy Lambeth Road, it's almost silent. As they park, a plump tabby cat ambles in front of the car and hops onto a wall, lazily surveying its kingdom. Allen can't see one piece of litter marring the pavement or one weed sprouting at the base of a house front. The paint on the window and door frames is glossy; there's a lot of whitewashed brick. The garden that the squatters brought into being at the center of the square still flourishes, but across the road a café sells five kinds of balsamic vinegar and homemade beeswax candles for ten pounds a pair.

"Not many comrades left here, I'm guessing," Desbury says.

Ivy Lodge faces the garden on the side of the square farthest from the café. Although its ground floor is hidden by billboards promising "A Luxurious and Historical Redevelopment," through the scaffolding wrapping the upper floors Allen can see the stones Wyższej described, one on the far left that says *Ivy* in faded black letters and one on the far right saying *Lodge* in the same script.

The Yorke Square Community Association sits directly across the street from Ivy Lodge. Its reception area is a bright room at the front of the ground floor. A huge corkboard on one wall holds notices advertising everything from a used bicycle (*child seat also available*) to a production of *Twelfth Night* to be held in the garden the following month. There's a reception desk, but no one is behind it. Instead a large hotel bell sits on the desktop, a sign next to it saying, "Ring for service."

Allen smacks the bell. At first there's only more silence. Then a door on the far side of the room swings open, and a dark-haired woman appears. She wears a long cardigan over a T-shirt and jeans and holds a mug in her left hand.

"So sorry. Went to make a quick coffee." She puts the mug down on the desk. "How can I help? Although if it's a flat you want you should check the website. It's quicker."

Desbury flashes his warrant card. "You don't lock the door when you step out?"

She smiles. "The square is still a collective at heart. We choose to believe that none of our residents would steal from us." She leans in confidingly. "And you'll notice we also don't keep anything of value in here."

It's true. There's an elderly multiline telephone on the desk but no computer. The chairs pushed into rows for waiting clients are padded plastic, and, aside from the noticeboard, the room's decoration consists of a carousel stuffed with leaflets.

"So." The woman sits. "How can I help, officers?"

"We're hoping to find someone who knows this woman." Allen shows her the screen of her phone. The previous evening, she'd scanned the *Amateur Lens* cover and cropped it down to just Nell's face. "We think she was a resident here once."

The woman squints at the screen then shakes her head. "No, sorry. Do you know her name? We have tenant and owner records in the back. I could look her up."

"Nell Beatty. Or Eleanor Beatty. She would have been here starting in late 1988 or early 1989."

"Oh. Our records start with our purchase in 1998. Sorry." She thinks. "But you could try Charlie—Charlotte Mortimer—at number fifty-three. She's one of the original squatters. She might know her." She stares at the photo again. "She's very pretty, isn't she? I mean, in an eighties model kind of way."

Allen thinks how much Nell would have relished this compliment. She thanks the woman on her behalf.

The woman who answers the door at number fifty-three has graying hair and a body that seems to be all straight lines. Her shoulders make right angles, her beaky nose stands out sharply in her face, the hand that holds the door is broad and short-nailed, its fingers thin and sinewy. She looks—the words spring instantly into Allen's mind—as if she doesn't take shit from anyone. Like Wyższej, she examines their warrant cards carefully, but unlike him, she doesn't let them in. Instead she holds the door closed behind her and stands on her front step.

"What can I do for the Metropolitan Police?"

"We spoke to the receptionist at the housing association—"

"Rosie. Her name is Rosie."

"Thank you. We spoke to Rosie. She thought you might be able to help us."

At the last two words, the corners of the woman's mouth twitch. But all she says is, "Help you in what way?"

"We're trying to identify a woman who lived here in the late eighties and perhaps early nineties. I understand you were one of the original squatters?"

"That's right. I helped break down doors all up and down this road."

"So you were here in 1989?"

"I was here in every year of the eighties. And every year since then. But I'll tell you right up front, I don't have much time for your lot." She lifts her left arm and pushes up the sleeve, revealing a U of scar tissue on the underside of her forearm. "Brixton riots. Police horse took a chunk out of me." She lets go of the door and crosses her arms over her chest, squaring up. "The association keeps a solicitor on call. I want her here before I answer any questions."

Desbury steps forward. "Would it make you more comfortable, madam, if I told you that the person we're interested in is deceased? And that at this stage we're simply trying to determine if she lived here, and if so, for how long?"

Now the woman's mouth does smile, albeit without humor. "I wasn't aware the police were concerned with the comfort of the people they interrogated. How times have changed! But I tell you what. You show me the person, and I'll decide if I want to say anything."

Everything about her suggests that this is the best they're going to get. Allen holds out the phone.

"That's Nell." The woman looks up, then down at the screen again. "She's dead?"

Allen nods.

Charlotte Mortimer sighs. Then, as if she's doing it against all her better judgment, she says, "I suppose I'll have to let you in."

16

The interior of the house looks as if it hasn't been touched since Charlotte Mortimer broke down the door all those years ago. The floor's planks are unvarnished, the walls bare plaster. On one of them hangs a collage of a tree in full bloom, the trunk made of chips of brown glass, the branches and leaves chips of green. The shards catch the light and throw it back so that the tree seems to be emerging from its background, hanging shining in the air.

"Did you make that?" Allen nods at the collage.

The other woman nods. "Out of broken beer bottles we found when we first cleared the houses. That's what I do. Found-object art."

"It's wonderful."

She dips her head in thanks then gestures toward the trestle table and two benches pushed against one wall. They sit, Allen and Desbury knocking knees on one side, Mortimer centering herself on the other. After a few seconds, she says, "How did it happen?"

"We're not sure yet." Allen tries to make herself more comfortable, but the bench is narrow, and there isn't any padding. "She was found in a public garden."

"Was it . . . was it drugs?"

Allen looks at Desbury. "The autopsy showed no alcohol or drugs of any kind in her system," he says.

Mortimer stares at the table, shaking her head slowly. Eventually she looks up. "It really shouldn't hit me like this. I scarcely knew her. But when you've held someone's newborn in your hands . . ."

Allen goes cold, then hot. She feels Desbury give a twitch. But all she says is, "Why don't you tell us what you remember, Ms. Mortimer?"

Normally at this stage witnesses suggest Allen call them by their first name. But Charlotte Mortimer is made of different stuff. She gazes at Allen through narrowed eyes, not saying a word. Allen knows this look. It's the look of someone weighing up what they'll lose if they cooperate.

Finally Mortimer starts to talk.

"When the collective first occupied the square, it was all breaking down doors and fixing what we found inside. But by the time we'd been here ten years, that was sorted. We'd become more of a stable community." She glares at them. "But we were still committed to our founding principles: self-governance, individual liberty, and the right to live peacefully without interference."

That meant, she explains, there were no official records of who arrived at the square and who left. Residents were used to old faces disappearing and unknown new ones taking their place. Everyone was welcome, unannounced, and no questions asked, provided they were nonviolent and doing nothing illegal. "We had to keep our noses clean so the local authority didn't have any excuse to move us out."

Because of the casual living structure, no one paid much attention when Nell first showed up. It took a while for people to notice that the squat had a new addition. It probably would have taken even longer if she hadn't been beautiful. "The men couldn't stop talking about her."

Allen hates to interrupt, but, "When exactly did she arrive?"

"Sometime after Christmas of 1988, I think? I can't say closer than that. I did say it was a while before we noticed her. I know she wasn't here for that year's Yule festival, but I also know it was winter because I remember her coat. It was a very good coat, but it didn't fit her. It was too short in the arms. Every time I saw her, I wanted to yank the sleeves down."

Could it have been that Nell was still wearing the coat she'd taken from her parents' home? Certainly if she arrived in the winter of 1988 or early 1989 it meant that Yorke Square was the squat she'd told Macey about. The gaps are starting to fill.

Allen looks up from her pad. "Go on."

"At some point, I asked if anyone knew who she was, and someone said she was living with Tattie at number eighty-five."

"Tattie?" Allen returns to the notebook.

"Tattie McDowell. Her real name was Tatiana, although someone less like a Tatiana you'd be hard put to find. She'd joined us about a year before. Fresh out of prison, and with a record, the only job she could find didn't pay her enough to live on." Allen can hear the satisfaction in Mortimer's voice at this demonstration of society's injustice.

Nell lived at number eighty-five all through the spring, summer, and autumn of 1989. She wasn't very outgoing, but a lot of the square's residents weren't outgoing. But Mortimer used to go for a cup of tea in the café every afternoon—"It was a community-run café then, not that elitist bullshit we have now"—and from the window she would see Nell walking down the road. Nell always wore the same thing: a white shirt and a black spandex miniskirt over black tights. "It wasn't a uniform, but it had the look of one. I thought she must be going to whatever her work was. When the weather turned in the autumn, there was the coat again, on top of it. It got so I waited for her. You know how you do when something irritates you? I'd sit in the café waiting for her to walk by just so I could imagine yanking the sleeves down."

And then one day, when she saw her, Nell was pregnant. "I know it sounds ridiculous if I put it like that, but it's really how it was. You couldn't hide anything under that spandex skirt, and she went along day in day out with a flat stomach, until one day . . . It was cold, but she hadn't buttoned the coat. It swung open, and there was a pregnant belly. It wasn't very big, but Joan, my partner in those days, was a midwife, so I knew what I was seeing."

Allen wants to yell out, to bellow that she was right, she was right, all along she'd known it. But she's Detective Superintendent Allen, interviewing a witness, so all she does is clench a hand under the table before she asks, "Did she say anything about it? How it had happened?"

Mortimer snorts. "I imagine it happened in the usual way. But I never asked. I hardly knew her. No one did. I don't think she ever spoke two words to anyone who lived here. Except Tattie, I suppose."

Then her expression softens. "I know it seems strange. But if you'd seen her you'd understand. She just . . . appeared, like some kind of mythical creature. No announcement, no warning, no interest in explaining herself. And so perfect. Like a walking statue. She didn't seem like someone you could chat to, have a cup of tea with. She was untouchable."

Or at least she seemed that way until one night in the spring when Tattie came banging on Charlie and Joan's door, saying Nell was in labor and she didn't know what to do. Could Joan come help? Of course Charlie also went. And there was Nell, lying on a mattress in a room on the first floor, panting and screaming. When Joan went to examine her, Nell grabbed her hand and started to cry. "And I realized she was just a girl. Just a teenager, in pain and scared." There was an electric kettle in the kitchen, so once Nell let her go, Joan boiled some water, washed her hands, and a few hours later there was a baby. A little girl, squashed and angry, with a great big head of black hair and filmy blue eyes.

"But Nell wasn't interested in her. She just fell asleep. Joan went back a few times over the next week or so to check how they were getting on, and she told me it was the same thing every time. Nell acted as if the baby was nothing to do with her. Even when she was feeding her, Joan said, she'd stare out the window until it was over. Not that she did much feeding, I'd imagine, because two or three weeks later, I started to see her going off in her shirt and skirt again."

"Two or three *weeks*?" Allen knows from painful experience that doctors and pregnancy manuals advised new mothers not to start working again for at least six weeks after giving birth.

"We didn't understand it either. The square was a small community. News traveled. Normally we celebrated when babies were born. A naming ceremony, or at least we'd drop off gifts or offer to help the parents. We were a collective. But there was Nell setting off down the street as if nothing had happened, saying nothing about it. We didn't know what to do."

"And the baby?" It was one thing to stare out a window while your child breastfed. It was quite another to abandon it while you went off to work.

"She left the baby with Tattie. I'd see them sometimes sitting in front of the house, the baby in a sling or in a pushchair. She was a lovely little thing. Same head of hair, but her eyes had turned brown. Big smile when she saw you, and she was a great watcher." She darts her eyes back and forth, demonstrating. Then she looks at Allen, and her tone turns defensive. "We *did* wonder, Joan and I. Because sometimes Nell would go off in the morning and not come back until late at night. We wondered what was going on. Tattie obviously didn't have a job anymore, or else she wouldn't be home all day. We thought perhaps Nell was doing sex work, to make money."

"Nell never said anything about it?"

"Like I said, she didn't talk to anyone. After that one night, she didn't even talk to Joan, except to answer her questions about her physical health."

"Did Joan ever ask about the father?" Here would be the connection, the little piece of information that would fill in the most important gap. "Maybe offer to contact him, to let him know he had a daughter?"

The other woman looks as shocked as if Allen had suggested that the midwife was a thief. "Certainly not. If Nell had asked for help in that way, Joan would have done what she could, but otherwise it was exactly the kind of interference we wanted to get away from. People have a right to their private lives, Superintendent." She looks at them with deep disapproval, but the effect is somewhat marred when she adds, "In any case, we never had a chance to ask, because then she and the baby left."

"Left?" Allen is confused. "What do you mean, 'left'?"

"I mean what I said. At some point, I realized I hadn't seen Nell for a while, and when I asked another resident they said the same. And neither of us had seen Tattie out with the baby either."

"D'you remember when you noticed this?"

Mortimer thinks for a long minute, then another. "I know it was after the heat wave, because Tattie and the baby sat outside while that was going on. She and I talked about how it compared to the heat wave of '76. I remember being surprised she was old enough to remember that. But I can't get any more precise. It *has* been thirty years."

Desbury takes over. "It has. And frankly your memory for that time is the best we've encountered so far." Mortimer bridles slightly. She might hate the police, Allen thinks, but she isn't immune to their flattery.

Desbury leans in. "May I ask one more question?" The woman nods. "It's the obvious one. Do you know where she went?"

A headshake. "We tried to find out. Once it was clear that no one had seen the baby or Tattie for some time, we held a meeting and decided we needed to ask." Mortimer looks uncomfortable, as if she's still wrestling with the decision. "There was a baby involved, and a baby isn't an individual the way an adult is, is it? It can't make the choice of autarky. So we sent Joan over with one of the men to ask what was going on."

"And?"

She sighs. "And Tattie was lying on the floor of the toilet with a needle in her arm. Barely breathing, Joan said. They took her to A&E and stayed with her until she was transferred to a ward. They were there all day and night. It wasn't until the next day that we went back to the house. The place was filthy, Tattie's part of it, anyway. Old takeaway containers everywhere, burnt bits of foil. The curtains she used as bedding hadn't been washed in weeks. But upstairs, where Joan and I had seen Nell, it was so clean it was practically sterile. And empty. Not even a stray hair. Only a mattress on the floor."

"No sign of the baby?"

"A few old nappies downstairs in Tattie's part"—she wrinkles her nose—"but nothing else. Joan and I went to see Tattie the next day, but she wasn't in a fit state to tell anyone anything. And when we went back the day after, she'd discharged herself. You can do that, apparently, discharge yourself from hospital at any time. Although it sounded as if Tattie just walked out."

Allen wants to ask if they called the police, if they even considered calling the police. But she knows exactly why this woman, this resident of a community that believed in individual liberty and the right to live peacefully without interference, didn't call the police. And she knows that if she asks, Charlotte Mortimer will just respond with the question dear to every self-serving bystander: *What could the police have done?*

"Did you call the police to alert them that an infant and its mother were missing?" Desbury asks.

"What could the police have done?" Mortimer spreads her hands. "Tattie was gone. Nell was gone. We couldn't give any information that would help find either of them. We didn't even know Nell's surname. Although after that we did start taking them. After that, every new resident had to register by name as soon as they moved in." Her tone suggests she's offering this to show that the squatters learned from what happened, but her face makes it clear that she thinks it's the moment when rot first invaded Utopia.

17

They go to the elitist bullshit café and sit as far away from the other customers as they can. Allen orders an almond croissant, a prize for herself for having been right all along.

Desbury just has a coffee. "It makes you want to ban John Stuart Mill," he says, emptying a straw of demerara sugar into his cup.

Allen squints at him. "What?"

"It's Mill they start with, these libertarian anarchists. He's the one who argues that you shouldn't interfere with other people's lives unless they're affecting the wider society. Whereas a little interference might protect teenage girls from moving in with heroin addicts and then leaving their babies in their care."

"You think this Tattie McDowell did something to Nell and her baby?" *Now that you see that there is a baby.* But she doesn't say that aloud. After all, hadn't he admitted two weeks ago that he was no longer sure she'd been wrong?

"I'm not saying that. But I think if they'd been living somewhere else, people might have been able to keep track of them. Whereas this lot couldn't bring themselves to ask Nell even the most basic questions. As far as I can tell, they only learned her name when the McDowell woman came banging on their door."

"In that case, we should find the McDowell woman. They lived in the same house for more than a year. Even if Nell never spoke a word, McDowell will have information about what her life was like at that time. She'll have noticed where she went, what she did. Maybe she knows who the father of the baby was."

"Tattie McDowell is long dead," Desbury says flatly.

Allen feels her face grow hot. "How do you know?"

"She was a hardcore junkie living in a filthy squat before addicts knew they should be careful about sharing needles. That's not a recipe for a long life."

"So you don't know."

Desbury drinks his coffee.

But Allen can't let go. "We have no idea whether she's alive or dead until we investigate further. And look at everything else we've discovered by investigating. Originally all we knew about Nell was her name, and now we know how and why she came to London, where she came from, where she lived once she got here, and some of her movements during the significant period. And we know from Wyższej that the man she was seeing around the time she fell pregnant had a BMW and a house in the country. Like Carpenter."

"We know he saw her climb into a BMW once. And we only know that she told him she was seeing a man with a house in the country. Whoever this bloke was, he could've been spinning her a line. Or she could have been spinning one for Wyższej to get him to stop bothering her. Anyway, as I recall, Carpenter's BMW was just this side of an old banger. Not exactly the sleek engine of a power broker."

She pushes away her plate, her appetite gone. He rang her up when he found Nell; he drove up to help her with interviews today: he's supposed to be her ally. Why can't he see what she sees?

Desbury stares into his cup. When at last he looks up, he fixes his eyes over her shoulder. "Ma'am—Martha. I worry that you're making all roads lead to Carpenter because you want them to. I admit that it's all but certain that the baby Nell brought to the station was hers. But there's no evidence at all that the father was Carpenter. I saw Carpenter, too, remember? I was at the final press conference. He couldn't take his eyes off his wife and that baby." He puts a hand on the back of his neck, squeezing the muscles. "What I'm saying is, I think we need to be careful not to hear things no one's said."

She softens. He has a point. But it doesn't change her mind. "All the more reason to look for McDowell, then. We're accumulating information, but none of it provides a concrete link back to Carpenter. If we can prove that Nell and Carpenter were involved, that the baby she brought into the nick was his, we've got a reason why he might have killed Bella."

"You're thinking he murdered her so he could pass the other one off as her?"

Again his disbelief stings. But she fights her impulse to turn away and instead tells him the truth.

"I don't know. I don't know why he did it, or how. But I know that if I can confront Carpenter with the fact that that baby wasn't Bella and he knew it, he'll have to explain why he pretended she was Bella. Which means explaining how he knew the real Bella wasn't coming back. This McDowell could tell me if he was the father of Nell's baby! She lived with Nell while she was pregnant; she was there after the birth, took care of the baby. If Nell confided in anyone, it'll be her."

"*If* she's alive, she can tell you. And if she's in any fit state. And even if one or both of those unlikely things turn out to be true, wouldn't we be better off—"

But she doesn't find out what they'd be better off doing because his phone rings. He gropes for it in his overcoat pocket. "It's my sergeant. Back in a sec."

Allen tries to calm down while she waits. She looks up libertarian anarchy on Wikipedia. Then she looks up autarky. *A form of anarchism that upholds the principle of individual liberty, rejects compulsory government, and supports its elimination in favor of ruling oneself.* It sounds like a terrible idea to her. But given her profession, it would.

She circles back to Nell, the Nell she's become familiar with over the past weeks. A girl self-centered enough to turn her back on her family without a word, so determined to succeed that she moves to London and finds a way—however unrealistic—to start a modeling career despite a lack of experience or money. An unexpected pregnancy wouldn't pose any difficulty for that girl, not when there was easy access to abortion on the NHS. So why had she carried the baby to term? Even if she hadn't realized she was pregnant until late—and from Charlotte Mortimer's description, she hadn't started to show until she was (Allen does some quick finger arithmetic) around five months—abortions were provided until the end of the sixth month. So why hadn't Nell had one?

She feels a stab as she forms the question. It suddenly seems to her an enormous good fortune to be in a position to *decide* whether or not to end a pregnancy. She knows this thought is ridiculous, that it borders on the repellent, but she also knows that that's true of many private thoughts. So she gives herself a moment to covet another woman's unwanted pregnancy, even to be angry that it was unwanted. Her envy and her yearning are so strong that for a moment it's as if it's her own child she misses, her daughter that Nell gave birth to and deliberately handed over to someone else.

But the moment passes—she's had plenty of time to train herself not to think about what she'll never have. She turns her mind back to the original puzzle. Why had Nell not ended her pregnancy? Could she have hoped things might work out with the father? (And if the father was Carpenter, what kind of hopes had he given her?) Had the father persuaded her to see the pregnancy through, promising that they'd be together or that he'd take the baby once it was born? (And if the father was Carpenter, which of these promises had he made?) Or had Nell loved the baby, wanted to keep her until it became clear that she would have to give her up? If so, what had made that clear? Maybe she'd hoped to find her again one day. After all, she'd kept that newspaper article. Maybe she'd held on to it as a way of imagining a future like the one that had, in fact, come to pass: a future where grown children and their biological mothers were joyously reunited and the wound of her loss could be healed.

A cold breeze yanks her back to reality. Desbury is coming through the door, grinning.

"My team has made an arrest on another case. A bloke we've been watching for six months just tried to move twenty kilos of cannabis across the Severn into Wales." He takes a final gulp from his cup. "I need to get back. I'm sorry."

"It's all right. But can you drop me at the Yard on your way?"

In the car, she wants to return to the subject of McDowell, to try to convince him it's worthwhile finding her, but then she remembers that he's driven all the way to London and spent his day ferrying her around and getting answers out of people who probably wouldn't have given her the time of day. It's time to ask about his Nell Beatty investigation.

"What happened with your Stapleton Road suspect?"

"Nothing." He keeps his eyes on the road. "Not that he wasn't a shifty little prick, because he was. But according to him, all he'd done was pick up a woman once or twice to try something he knew his wife wouldn't let him do, and now he's got it out of his system. And he had an alibi. Driving home from Plymouth during the relevant time span. A visit to his parents that ran late, he says. We checked the footage on the CCTV at the Clifton Suspension Bridge, and there he is paying the toll at 1:15 a.m. Worse luck."

"I'm sorry."

He shrugs. "I'm sorry that we can't keep an eye on him, because it's only a matter of time until he goes too far with the strangling he's supposedly got out of his system. As far as the Beatty murder goes, though, it confirms for me that it's Rainey."

"What'll you do?"

Another shrug. "I'm thinking if there's no movement in the next couple of weeks, I might try the wonders of the World Wide Web. The higher-ups don't like it, but we've had some success working with on-line community groups, even with tweeting out virtual versions of our posters." He doesn't sound very hopeful.

They drive the rest of the way in silence, but as he pulls up at the curb next to the Yard's rotating silver sign and she opens the passenger-side door, he puts a hand on her arm. "Start by searching for a death certificate. You'll find one."

"I'm not—"

He smiles. "You'll find one."

But she doesn't find a death certificate, because Tattie McDowell isn't dead. She's in Downview Prison, two hours outside London, serving seven years for possession with intent to supply.

18

It takes Allen two minutes to find her in the PNC: Tatiana McDowell, DOB July 19, 1961. Like Nell, she has an impressively long record, but hers is much more serious, including three arrests for possession of heroin with intent to supply. It's the last of these that brought her to HMP Downview, where she's now Prisoner 060482, two years into her sentence.

Allen has noticed before that most English women's prisons seem to be located in the countryside. Why this is she's never discovered, but as the taxi takes her from the Morden Tube station to the prison site in Surrey the next day, she sees that Downview is no exception. The car travels down leafy green roads, passing runners, young couples out for a stroll, and at one point a pair of pensioners wrestling with an excited schnauzer desperate to escape his lead. When at last the cab pulls up in front of the entrance to reception, she can see fields and hedgerows stretching out on the other side of the chain-link fences. To her, it seems cruel to foist this view on women in a closed prison, but maybe it's meant as an incentive rather than a taunt.

The driver looks at her in the rearview mirror. "You work here?"

"I'm visiting someone."

She sees him evaluating her: Maybe her black cashmere coat and expensive haircut aren't what he's used to seeing in prison visitors. But her time on the force has taught her not to care about the opinions of strangers or to explain herself to them. She slides forward on the vinyl seat and puts the fare in the little tray underneath the Plexiglas divider. "Thank you."

"Receipt?"

She shakes her head. He thrusts a card with the phone number of the cab company through the tray slot. "In case you need someone to take you back to the station."

Whatever its setting, inside the prison is like every other one. Its walls are painted industrial green, its receptionist sits behind a metal grate, and Allen's required to fill out a long form, show two forms of ID, and hand over her mobile before she can enter. A bored young man in a poorly fitting uniform watches a screen as briefcases and bags travel down the security conveyor belt. She shows her warrant card and puts her bag on the conveyor then raises her arms so a female guard can swipe her with the metal detector wand. She's given a visitor's badge on a lanyard to hang around her neck.

Once into the body of the prison, she's greeted by a deputy governor. She asks for a private interview with Prisoner 060482, and he leads her to a room at the end of a corridor. It's windowless, its inner wall a one-way mirror. The only furniture is an aluminum table that's bolted to the floor and two aluminum chairs that aren't. She drapes her coat over the back of one of these and sits down, bag in her lap.

After five or so minutes, the door opens. A hard-faced woman in a guard's uniform enters; a woman in tracksuit bottoms and a faded black sweatshirt follows.

Charlotte Mortimer is right: Someone less like a Tatiana it would be hard for Allen to imagine. Instead of the elegant Russian princess the name conjures up, this woman is hunched and scrawny, her cheeks pitted with acne. Her features crowd together in the center of her face, circling a nose that was flat even before a fist mashed the bridge to a pulp. Long-term heroin use has sunk her cheeks and turned her skin yellowish gray. A tattoo of a star reaches its points around her neck.

She sits down. "You can go," she says. Her voice is a Glaswegian rasp. She's speaking to the guard, but she doesn't turn her head.

"Guess again," the guard says. She plants herself more firmly.

But Allen nods permission, closing her eyes to show she'll take responsibility for whatever happens. The guard huffs, but she leaves. They hear her keys rattle as she settles outside the door.

Allen doesn't smile. "Ms. McDowell, I'm here to ask you some questions about a woman you used to know. A girl, really." She puts a copy of the cropped *Amateur Lens* photo on the table. "Named Nell Beatty."

The other woman glances down, then back up. "What makes you think I knew her?"

"I spoke to Charlotte Mortimer, who lives in Yorke Square. She was present the night Nell gave birth in the house where you were squatting."

McDowell looks at her as if she's weighing her up. Finally she says, "D'you have a fag?"

Allen takes an unopened packet of cigarettes from her bag and drops it on the table. The woman's spidery fingers have the cellophane off in a second. She buries her nose in the packet, then looks up. "Light?"

Only once a cigarette is half-smoked does she begin to talk.

"Thirty years and people still want tae ask me about Nell. Used tae be the fellas, now it's the filth." She flicks the photo away with her index and middle fingers, sending it skidding back toward Allen. "What do you want to know?"

"Why don't we start with when and how you met?"

McDowell sucks on the cigarette like it's a lover's mouth. As Allen watches, a half inch of paper and tobacco turns to ash. "I went to university, y'know." Her lips shape themselves into a smile that's half sneer. There's a hole where her left incisor used to be. "I have a degree in sociology from the University of Glasgow. But then I got done for possession with intent, and once you've been inside, nae man wants to hire you. You cannae be trusted, because once upon a time you did something wrong. So I had to take a shit job in a shit caff that paid shit."

Allen is familiar with the self-pity of addicts and criminals. She waits for the woman to get back on track.

"And that's where I met Nell. In the kitchen of that rat hole. Café Firenze. Fancy name for a greasy spoon. They were all like that, there. Trying to be better than they were. Except Nell. She was okay. Looked like Elizabeth Taylor, but wasn't stuck-up. She'd listen to anybody's problems, got on with everyone. So when she told me her roommate had kicked her out and she needed a place to live, I told her she could come to mine. The house where I stayed at Yorke had loads of room, as long as you weren't looking for luxury."

"When was this?"

"Christmas of '88. I remember because fuckin' 'Mistletoe and Wine' was everywhere. Fuckin' Cliff Richard." She drags on the cigarette. "Her moving in was a Christmas gift to me, let me tell you. She should've been the dishwasher. She was a shit waitress, but she could clean. As long as she was there, the place sparkled. I asked her once if her parents had been strict that way, but she told me she didn't have any parents. I said, what, had she been born out of an egg? But she just looked confused and said, didn't I know we all came from eggs?" She raises her eyebrows. "Not much of a sense of humor, our Nell."

"And how soon after she moved in did she fall pregnant?"

"How soon did it happen, or how soon did she know? Because she was such a dafty that she only realized what was going on once she started showing. That was . . . November, I think? It was cold again, anyway." She takes another drag. "I told her to have it out. It's free and it's legal, I said. And what kind of model did she think she was gonnae be if she had to drag a baby around with her everywhere? But she wouldnae do it. Said it would be a sin. I said if you thought that way, wasn't what she'd done to get it a sin too? In for a penny, in for a pound. But she wouldnae. So the baby came at the end of March." Her face softens. "She was a lovely little thing. I called her Chantelle. We used to sit on the step, or in the garden, her and me, watch the world go by together."

Charlotte Mortimer had said much the same, and Allen said aloud what she'd wondered then. "Why were you minding her?"

"Firenze gave me the sack. I'd gone back to a little . . . recreational use. Nothing I couldn't handle. But my man would come round the back of the kitchen to give me the gear, and they didn't care for that.

Said he was an 'undesirable element.' Gave me a week's wages and sent me on my way."

"No, I mean why was it you who minded that baby, not Nell?" In case McDowell misses the point, she adds, "The baby's mother."

The woman snorts. "Nell wasnae what you'd call maternal. She worked at Firenze until the afternoon before the baby came, and once she recovered she wanted to go right back. It was like she pushed it out and then that was that done with. You'd think she'd never been pregnant. She said she needed money for her modeling book. The caff wouldn't have her 'cos she'd missed a week's worth of shifts without warning, but she found somewhere else easily enough. And her tits were huge, so she started with the glamour work again as soon as she could too. Lucky I was around, really. That baby needed someone looking out for her."

"Until Nell took her and disappeared."

McDowell looks confused. "That's not what happened. She gave the baby away before she left."

"Gave the baby away?" Allen's breath catches. "Who to?"

But McDowell's face has gone very still, and her lips have clamped shut. It's obvious she didn't mean to say what she did. At last she says, "Is she deid?"

"Nell? Yes, yes, she is. I'm sorry."

The cigarette is nearly gone. McDowell sucks it down to the filter then lights a second one from the butt. When she looks up again, her expression is wily. She's considering her worth.

She stretches out a hand to cover the cigarette packet. "These are mine?" Allen nods. "Are there more?"

Allen reaches into the waistband of her trousers and pulls out the other two packets she bought at the Tesco Express. The woman sweeps them toward her like a poker player pulling in chips. She might not shoot up anymore, Allen thinks, but she's still a junkie.

As if she hears her, McDowell says, "You can sell them. Thousands, you can make." She tucks the unopened packets into the waist of her tracksuit bottoms and pulls the sweatshirt over them, giving her stomach a little pat. Lifting the lit cigarette to her lips, she inhales, lets the smoke trickle out of her mouth. "It was that couple that were in the news during the heat wave. The ones without a baby. The Carpenters."

Of course, Allen was already certain—she'd said as much to Desbury in the café. But there's a difference between being certain and knowing. She's hit by a powerful wave of satisfaction but simultaneously also a sense of almost overpowering relief. She feels all her muscles relax. If she were standing up, she thinks, her knees would buckle. As it is, she slumps back in the chair. She feels the cold metal crossbar catch her under the shoulder blades.

McDowell tells her story.

Someone left a newspaper in the garden at Yorke Square, and she found it when she was out with the baby. The front page was devoted to an update about the ongoing investigation. There was a large photograph of the Carpenters at the public appeal and a smaller reproduction of the picture of them with Bella. She'd taken it home to show Nell because she couldn't get over how much the baby resembled Nell's. "I said, 'Doesnae that wean look like Chantelle?' I don't think she even knew about the story before that. When I showed her the photo, she looked surprised. But then she said aye, it did." In fact, Nell had done more than that. She'd sat down and read the whole story—the first thing McDowell could remember her reading in the time she'd known her. Nell spent a long while looking at the photos, then going over the article itself.

"I was surprised, but I didnae give it much thought. It wasn't until Monday evening that I noticed Chantelle was gone."

The public appeal had been on the Friday night. All the newspapers had featured it in their Saturday editions. Even allowing for the woman not showing the article to Nell until Saturday evening, that was still a gap of forty-eight hours. "You didn't look for the baby for two days? I thought you said you were the one who took care of her."

McDowell's eyes slide away. She fiddles with the cigarette but doesn't bring it to her mouth. "I was . . . eh . . . otherwise engaged."

"And what did you do when you noticed she was gone?"

"I asked Nell where she was. And she said she'd taken her to the police station and handed her over to the parents of the missing baby."

She says this calmly, even without much interest. Allen doesn't know how to respond. All she can do is catch her breath and fall back on her standard question. "And you didn't go to the police? To say what Nell had done, to tell us a missing child was still missing?"

McDowell looks at her as if she's the stupidest person on the planet. "I wasn't much of a one for the police at the time." She shows her missing incisor again. "Or anytime, really. And if I'm honest, it seemed like a good solution. Nell didnae want a baby; those parents wanted a baby. Now she didnae have one and they did. And if the other baby turned up, well, even I could see Chantelle would be better off in care than living with a junkie and a mother like Nell." She draws fiercely on the cigarette.

"Did she say why she'd done it?"

"Like I say, she wanted to get shot of the baby."

"She didn't say anything about a connection to them, that she knew them, or one of them?" McDowell is staring at her blankly, and Allen's exasperation overwhelms her. "Did she say Carpenter was the baby's father?"

"The baby's father?" McDowell begins to laugh, a loud cackle that turns into a coughing fit. Once it's over, she gasps for breath. She's shaking her head. "Chantelle's father was the bloke Nell was seeing. Harry. Harry Speck. She couldnae shut up about him—his house, his BMW, the fancy jewelry shop he owned, how he was going to help her get started as a model. Once she realized she was up the duff, she told me it must have happened in July. I figured she knew because July was the one time he took her out in public. He was married, so normally they had to meet without anyone knowing, secret like. But this time he told her it was all clear, he was gonnae take her to a party at Gucci. She got all kitted out like she was going to meet the queen, and it turned out the party was for the launch of a new watch!" Again the raucous laugh, but no coughing this time. Then she wrinkles her nose. "She brought him to the house once, before that. Fat stomach, big ugly watch, little piggy blue eyes shifting all over the place." She moves her eyes the same way Charlotte Mortimer did. "But that was Nell. She told me once that she had three rules: don't get distracted by looks, don't drink, and don't give it away. And the first two were to make sure of the third. She said she'd fought off blokes all through school because she didnae want to lose her cherry and get nothing in return."

So much for Cal Beatty's belief in his daughter's innocence. But at the moment it was Nell's actions she was concerned with, not her motives. "And you're sure the father was this Harry Speck? She never mentioned anyone else? Maybe someone she went out with once, or a one-night stand?"

"Nell wouldnae waste her time on that." McDowell leans forward, suddenly intensely serious. "Listen. I cannae remember doing what I got sent down for. I cannae remember how I got this"—she points to the tattoo on her neck—"but I remember how determined Nell was to be a famous model. A junkie always recognizes a junkie, and that was her horse." Then she cocks her head, suddenly reflective. "Mind, after the baby was gone, she was a bit nervy for a couple of days. But I gave her some junk to take the edge off, and it seemed to do the trick."

Allen knows she should attend to this last remark, but her mind is too filled by the effort of comprehending that Tom Carpenter isn't the father of the baby Nell handed over, that he never was the father. She pushes the heels of her hands into her thighs then makes two fists, squeezing them until her nails bite into the fleshy bottoms of her palms.

She can feel Tattie watching her. With immense effort she draws herself back to the present. "So Nell came back after she handed over the baby. What happened after that? When did she leave again?"

McDowell tilts her chin. "Aye, well, that bit's not so clear. My old problem was getting the better of me by then, if you know what I mean. I know Nell came back because, like I said, I remember we talked. But after that all I remember is I woke up one morning and she was gone. Her and her things. If you asked me what happened the day before that, though, I couldnae tell you, and if you asked me what happened the day after, I couldnae tell you that either. The next thing I remember, I was in hospital and those two biddies from down the road were asking where she was."

"And the next day you discharged yourself. Why?"

"I did?" She looks astonished. "Christ, that's news to me. Maybe that's where it all went wrong. If I'd had the sense to stay, who knows? I could be queen by now."

Again she gives the grating cackle. Her long fingers reach inside the packet for another cigarette. Allen stands and leaves.

19

Allen uses the number on the card to call for another taxi. As it makes its way to the station, she sits in the back, watching the Sunday walkers and the sun-dappled pavements and the trees just starting to bud. All of it is exactly the same as it was an hour ago, before she knew about Harry Speck.

Only once she's on the train does she give herself permission to think about what she's learned. Until McDowell said "Gucci," Allen had thought "Harry Speck" could be an alias. It even sounds like a false name. But hearing Tattie mention the party he'd taken Nell to, she'd remembered the watch Nell wore in the interrogation room. A round golden face banded by red and green stripes. The Gucci colors.

She types "Harry Speck" and "jeweler" into her phone. The very first hit is a page from a digital book of condolence. Harry Speck of Canterbury, Kent, beloved husband of Elizabeth, loving father of Henry and David, had died on April 17, 2017, after a long illness. Owner of Speck & Son, Jewellers, until his retirement in 2017, he was a keen golfer and a lifelong fan of Canterbury Rugby Football Club. Inside a misty oval is a photograph of a smiling man with thinning silver hair. His pink shirt is open at the collar, a tuft of white hair poking out. He does indeed have tiny eyes.

So this was the baby's father, this fat adulterer from Kent. Why this seems worse than a handsome adulterer from Somerset she can't say, but it does. Apparently, though, Speck's big belly and little eyes hadn't bothered Nell. But she'd thought she was getting something in return, and if McDowell is to be believed, that was enough for her.

Outside the window, the houses of outer London appear briefly before the Tube heads underground. Allen stares through her reflection into the tunnel's black void, thinking about McDowell's version of Nell. *That* Nell would never have fallen into a relationship with a freelance journalist or a low-level estate agent—nothing so minor for her. She wouldn't have felt the need to threaten a lover in order to get rid of her baby, and she wouldn't have given in to any demands he made. She would have done whatever she liked, and for her own reasons. In fact, if McDowell is to be believed, that's exactly what she did.

Everything Allen has believed is wrong.

The Tube stops at Colliers Wood, Balham, Kennington, Embankment. The farther it burrows into London, the more jumbled her thoughts become. She's understood the situation one way for so long that she has trouble seeing it any other. Now when she tries to put it together in a new way, she can only see details of it: the empty Moses basket, Tom Carpenter dry-eyed at the appeal, Nell's nonsensical story about finding the baby on a bench, the equally improbable tale of someone coming in through a window only open a few inches and taking Bella down the crumbling fire escape without waking her or either of the two adults in the room.

But finally she grasps one significant truth. The question of whether Tom Carpenter is a murderer has nothing to do with whether he fathered Nell Beatty's baby. Two separate witnesses had described his possessiveness toward his wife. That seems to go against the idea of involvement with another woman, not to suggest it. But it does suggest a man who had no interest in sharing his wife with a demanding interloper like a baby, or who would have had so little patience for any of the countless irritants a baby could produce that he killed his daughter in a moment's rage. She's still right about that, at least. She remembers Carpenter's shocked face at the sight of the baby in his wife's arms, and she's certain: What she saw was the disbelief of a guilty man surprised.

The problem is proving that. She can hardly just drive down to the big house in Wells and accuse him. Carpenter must have spent at least some of the past thirty years fearing that the scythe was coming, that the axe would fall one day. He would be prepared. She imagines him calling Beck while she stands on the doorstep, reporting her for harassment yet again. This time she'll look disobedient and mad, fixated on him and his supposed crime for virtually her whole career.

The easiest way to find the proof she needs would be to request a reexamination of the physical evidence from the Carpenter case. But thirty years after the case was closed, all the evidence will long since have been disposed of. The best way would be for Carpenter to confess of his own accord. Such things did happen. Criminals aged. They became ill. They found religion. Suddenly their crimes weighed on them.

Carpenter is only a few years older than she is, though. Still a bit too young for the kinds of diseases that prompt confession. And while she's not going to judge the reach and influence of a God she doesn't believe in, the Carpenter she remembers doesn't seem like much of a candidate for conversion. So barring a tragedy or a miracle, she'll need to wait another twenty or so years before circumstances might conspire to make him confess.

Still, there's something there—a toehold, a hint of possibility. It's scratching at the back of her mind. The Tube pulls into Charing Cross, but she's thinking too hard to notice. Like any senior police officer, she's intimately familiar with the Police and Criminal Evidence Act. She knows that under its rules officers can't lie to extract confessions from suspects. But PACE says nothing about how an officer might use the truth to move a suspect to make his own confession. There are excellent reasons why the woman who believes herself to be Bella Carpenter should know whose child she really is: Speck's "long illness" could mean cancer, could mean Parkinson's; Nell herself was an addict, and addiction seems to have a genetic component. Allen is beginning to see how the need to inform Bella of her true parentage might be used to get what she wants from Carpenter.

When the doors open, she stands up. She'd intended to go to Euston Station and head to the flat, but it's only ten minutes' walk to the Yard from here. Before she can get anything out of Tom Carpenter, she's got to find him, and for that she needs her computer's databases. Maybe Beck will be alerted about what she's searched for, maybe he won't. In this moment, she finds she doesn't care.

The big house in Wells is now owned by Peter Solomon and Maisy Ott. The last Wells telephone directory in which *Carpenter, T. S.* appears is from 1991. No Carpenters have been on the Wells electoral register since 1991. As the week progresses, she widens her search, but without success. She can find birth certificates for Thomas Spencer Carpenter, Vivien Diana Cook, and Annabella Evelyn Carpenter, and she can find the elder Carpenters' marriage certificate, but nothing else. Yet she can't find any death certificates for any of them either. There are no education or employment records for an Annabella Carpenter, an Annabella Evelyn Carpenter, an Annabella E. Carpenter, or a Bella Carpenter.

Next she tries to trace them through their connections of thirty years before. But Glaister Properties has become a pet groomer called Ears to Tail, and if Google Maps is to be trusted, the Brorsson Gallery is now a Sainsbury's. Typing Marjorie Wallingford's name into Google turns up a memorial website of the kind she found for Harry Speck. Marjorie died of breast cancer in October 2015.

She broadens the search even further. No passports have been issued to Thomas Spencer Carpenter or Vivien Diana Carpenter, or Cook, since their old ones expired in 1992. No passport was ever issued to Bella Carpenter in any possible permutation of her name. The FamilySearch website reveals no death certificates recorded in any foreign country in any of their names. In fact, once they disappear from the Wells electoral rolls, there's no official record that any of them existed after 1991.

The Carpenters have vanished off the face of the earth.

20

But no one really vanishes off the face of the earth. The obvious reason for the lack of official documentation is that the Carpenters changed their name. When she visits the National Archives in Kew in an effort to trace the change, though, an archivist explains to her that there's no legal requirement to announce name changes. Because people take new names simply by starting to use them, the change can leave no public trace. You could pay to have it recorded in the grandly titled Enrolment Books of the Supreme Court of Judicature, but you wouldn't do that if you'd changed your name in an effort to disappear. And by now Allen is certain the Carpenters were trying to disappear. Not that that stops her from spending a day searching through the Enrolment Book entries from 1990 onward. *That's why they call us the plod.* But all she discovers from that is that the chairs in the Archives' reading rooms are more comfortable than those in the College of Policing library.

The only other option, the archivist says, is to hire a solicitor. She's heard that a good solicitor can track a name change using government records. She doesn't know how they do it, but it could be worth approaching one if Allen is determined to find the people she's looking for.

No, Allen thinks. It's part of a police officer's job to know how to locate people who want to disappear, and she's a police officer.

Except, a voice in her head points out, she's exhausted all the ways she knows.

But there's still the difficulty of engaging the solicitor in the first place. She has no plausible or unsuspicious reason for wanting to track down the Carpenters. *The woman they think is their daughter isn't, and I need to find them and tell them; or, I think he killed his daughter thirty years ago, and I need to find him to make him confess:* Any solicitor who would take the job based on those explanations is not a solicitor she should get involved with.

"Can I help you with something else?" The archivist is frowning.

"No, no, thank you. I'm just thinking about solicitors." She takes a few steps to the side, smiling at the man queuing behind her. "Sorry."

What she's thinking is that she knows a solicitor. She knows Phil. It's true that they haven't been in touch for two years, but she's certain that if she calls and asks him to help he'll say yes. Not merely out of kindness or old loyalty, but because he's the one other person who can understand what laying this case to rest means to her. Even Desbury can't really grasp that.

But she won't call him. She can't call him. Not because he isn't part of her life any longer, as she told Kate, but because keeping him that way is a deliberate choice. The fact that she long ago stopped being angry means she could've been in contact with him. She could ring him up; they could meet for a drink every now and again. She knows former couples who do that. But what she doesn't tell anyone is that sometimes she worries she's only managed to build a life without him precisely because she hasn't done that. His absence from her life has been total, and as a result he's become almost unreal to her. She worries that if he becomes real again, her hard-won new existence will collapse. She'll see that really she's just another woman stranded alone in midlife.

But it could also give her the final piece she needs in order to set a thirty-year mystery to rest.

You're never too old to learn new things about yourself, Allen's mother used to say. Like most of her observations, it had turned out to be true. And what Allen learns standing next to an information desk at the National Archives is that her need to confront Tom Carpenter is stronger than her fear of emotional pain.

Still, if she's going to rip off the plaster, she wants to do it quickly. She takes her mobile out to the courtyard and dials Phil's number.

Kate's right: He is interested. In fact, she couldn't ask for a better audience. He's by turns surprised—"Really? After all these years? And it was Desbury who caught the case?"—disbelieving—"You're joking! No connection at all? She saw them in the paper and that was it?"—and eager.

"Of course I will," he says. "Send me what you've found so far and give me a few days."

Each day after that feels like a little eternity. Work, even with its long meetings and its seemingly endless processes that never lead to any resolution, isn't enough to fill the time. She tries to divert herself by going back to house hunting. She becomes familiar with the neighborhoods of outer London: Tooting, Hornsey, Haringey, and once an area of Wembley a short distance from George Macey's flat. That place she refuses outright, but a couple of others she sees are appealing. And yet, and yet . . . As she puts it to herself on the journeys back to the flat, they don't feel right. Nothing feels right.

At last Phil calls back. When she looks at her calendar, she sees it's been a week.

"I found them."

"How?" Her voice comes out high with disbelief.

"Through the Land Registry. I don't know why it took me almost a week to think of it. Every time a house is bought or sold in Britain, the transaction needs to be recorded with the Land Registry, and the record lists the names of both buyer and seller. The Carpenters obviously sold their house at some point, since now Mr. Solomon and Ms. Ott live in it. So I searched the register until I found the records for that house. It was bought in 1987 by Thomas and Vivien Carpenter, but it was sold in November of 1991 by Thomas and Vivien Ashford. At some point between the baby's reappearance and the end of 1991, the Carpenters changed their name. Because they didn't record the change publicly, when the Ashfords were born, the Carpenters just . . . disappeared."

"I can't believe it." What she means is that she can't believe she forgot about the Land Registry. What is this investigation doing to her?

But all she says aloud is, "I mean, I believed you could find them if it was possible, I just wasn't sure it was possible. This is terrific. I don't know how to thank you."

"Don't thank me yet. I have more." She can tell he's smiling. "I found their current address."

"You didn't."

"I did. Thomas and Vivien Ashford live at 6 Cherry Vale, in Nottingham. Google Maps tells me that's in an area called Mapperley. No Annabella or Bella lives with them, but since she'd be around thirty by now, that's hardly surprising. They don't have a landline, either, which is more surprising given that they're our age, but maybe they've moved with the times more than I have."

Allen no longer has a landline, but now doesn't seem like the time to tell him. Instead she says, "This is much more than I hoped for. I don't . . . 'Thank you' doesn't feel like enough. But thank you. Thank you."

"It was a pleasure. I know people are supposed to say that, but I mean it. I enjoyed . . . well . . . doing something for you." An awkward pause. Then he says, "And now that we're back in touch, we should meet up for a drink. You and I and Scarlett. A catch-up. I've told her all about the Carpenters; I'm sure she'll want to hear how it ends."

"Sounds great. Let's set it up when I have an ending to tell you about."

They say their goodbyes. Allen knows the three of them will never meet up. Not just because she can't imagine anything more unpleasant than sitting single across a table from her former long-term partner and his new girlfriend, but because amid her relief and internal celebration, she finds that whatever she felt for the Phil of the past, for the Phil of the present she feels nothing more than she might for any old friend she's lost touch with: a vague, benevolent interest.

Well, maybe just vague.

21

Four weeks ago, she called Desbury as soon as she read his email because dread had spurred her on. Now it's eagerness that makes her quick. She wants him to come with her to Nottingham. They have to end it together. She looks at the corner of her computer screen: 9:30 a.m. Even if she goes to Bristol first to pick him up, they can still be in Nottingham by late afternoon.

He picks up on the first ring. "We got Rainey! We just charged him for killing Nell Beatty!"

Investigations go like this sometimes, she knows. You think there's no hope, and then suddenly . . . "What happened?"

The flyer campaign had worked. A witness had come forward. She'd been walking her dog down by Stapleton Road on the night of February 5—well, really the early morning of February 6. She was a postgraduate student writing her PhD thesis on Restoration drama, she explained, and because of that she sometimes kept odd hours. It had been around one in the morning—she'd decided to take the dog out at one, anyway—and while she was walking back to her flat on Bannerman Road, she'd seen a man coming out of the park. She wouldn't normally have noticed, but Barnabas had just done his business, she'd stopped to tie a knot in the disposal bag, and anyway it seemed odd that someone would be visiting a public garden at one in the morning. She'd seen the man come out, not walking particularly fast but with his shoulders hunched. A couple of days later, on her way back from a meeting with her supervisor, she'd spotted the flyer at the bus stop and realized she'd seen him on the same night as the murder.

"Did she say why it took her so long to come in?"

"You'll never believe it. She keeps a few pots of *Cannabis sativa* in her place—it helps with her anxiety when the Restoration playwrights get to be too much, apparently. She was afraid we'd arrest her for possession. But she discussed it with her boyfriend, and he pointed out that cannabis is a Class B drug, while this is a murder. At which point she decided to pay us a visit and give a statement. When we showed her a photo array, she picked Rainey out as the man she'd seen. We asked her to come back the following day for a live lineup, and she picked him out there, too, so we kept him for an interview."

"And what did he have to say about all this?"

"Well, luckily for us, by the time we picked him up for the lineup, he'd already made a good start on his day's intake of Carlsberg. Once we had him in the room, he started off by insisting the witness must be wrong. Then he explained that he'd just been out for a stroll to clear his head. But it didn't take very long for him to see the extraordinary coincidence of that stroll taking him by the exact spot where his partner was being murdered around the same time. He waffled a bit, tried to stick to his story, but in the end he admitted it. Nell told him she was going to leave him. Told him she'd been to see the Cottington woman, and she'd found her a place in a shelter. According to him, he couldn't bear the idea of a life without her. He loved her so much that he couldn't see how he'd go on without her." His voice turns tight. "So naturally he killed her to make sure that didn't happen. When the witness saw him, he was on his way back from dumping her body. He took her to the park because he figured that'd make it look like a client had killed her. We wrote down what he said, waited until he'd sobered up all the way, and had him sign it. *Then* he asked for a solicitor."

"Thank God for the stupidity of villains."

She hears a door open on his end. Sounds of celebration grow louder in the background. "I got your email about Tattie McDowell. Did she tell you anything useful?"

She's not going to ask him to come to Nottingham. He deserves to bask in his success, undiluted and complete. She has her murderer; he should have his.

"Some things that could lead somewhere. I'll let you know later today."

22

She takes one of the Yard's company cars. On the journey to Nottingham, she listens to Radio 4, answering back to the announcers when they irritate her. As she pulls up in front of 6 Cherry Vale, the newsreader is telling her that the World Health Organization believes the new coronavirus is outstripping all efforts at control. It's proving to be highly contagious, he says; there are currently more than one hundred thousand cases worldwide. That's hard to grasp on a mild March day, parked on a street where new leaves are unfurling on the trees, but she scrabbles in her bag for the Purell she carries and applies it liberally.

Cherry Vale is a wide street with a Victorian church at the far end and humps down its length to slow down drivers. Number six has the standard attributes of a house built in the 1930s: a redbrick facade, a curved bay window on one side with a single peaked gable over it, and an integrated front porch in the shape of a wide arch. The front garden has been paved over to make a driveway, with a silver Hyundai coupe sitting on the biscuit-colored bricks. So the Carpenters traded in the BMW, anyway.

For a few seconds after the bell rings, there's silence. Then she hears the thud of footsteps and a quick scrape as the lock turns. The door opens. "Yes?"

Although Carpenter—Ashford—is a good fifteen years older than Peter Rainey, he looks at least ten years younger. In fact, he and Rainey could be a case study in the difference economic status makes to aging. Carpenter's hair is gray, and he's a little shorter than he was nearly three decades before, but his posture is upright and his figure is that of a man who goes to the gym on a regular basis.

"Can I help?" he says. It's clear he has no idea who she is.

"Thomas Ashford?" She holds up her warrant card. "Detective Superintendent Martha Allen, Metropolitan Police. We met many years ago, when I was a detective inspector."

"Detective Inspector Allen?" He looks mildly puzzled, but nothing more. "Yes, of course, I remember you. What brings you here? Come in."

Inside, the house has the same layout as Margaret Beatty's. The front room opens off a small hall and stretches the full length. At the rear on the left there's a doorway to what she presumes is the kitchen. Aside from the shape, though, the place couldn't be more different from Mrs. Beatty's blandly conventional lounge. The front room has a worn oriental rug covering its polished wooden floor, and terra-cotta-colored walls are crowded with art from a hodgepodge of periods and cultures. The space is messy, but it's the warm messiness of many interests and lives fully lived. There's a book face down on one of the arms of an easy chair. She cranes her neck in an effort to read the title but can't manage it.

"Is your wife at home?"

Carpenter stands next to the fireplace, where a copper fire screen takes the place of logs. "My wife is dead." He says this in the leaden tone of someone who's become used to saying it but not remembering it. In the same voice, he adds, "She died from a heart attack three years ago."

"I'm sorry to hear that." For the first time, she notices that the mantel behind him is crowded with photos. They're all of the Carpenters themselves, photographed in different places and at different times. There they are squashed together on a camel in front of the pyramids; here they're posing on what looks like the top of the Eiffel Tower; in another they're seated in a rickshaw pulled by a grinning man in shorts and sandals. In each of them, the adults have their arms around a little girl who grows from dark-eyed toddler to teen.

"We took her everywhere." Carpenter sounds at once proud and defensive. "We weren't going to let her out of our sight."

"Again" hangs unspoken in the air.

"She looks very happy."

"She is. We did everything we could to make sure she had a happy, normal childhood."

"Including changing your name."

He nods. "The media badgered us day and night for months after—and just when it seemed to be tailing off, the one-year anniversary came round and it started up again. Interviews, pictures, quotes . . . The phone never stopped ringing. We could see what the future was going to hold. So we decided to make ourselves unreachable while she was still too young to remember."

"You thought they wouldn't be able to locate you with a new name?"

"We left the country too. We taught English abroad for years."

"What made you come back?"

"Viv's parents were getting on. And to be honest, we missed England. After all, we hadn't really left by choice."

"So you came here?"

"We were in Birmingham first. We moved here when Bella got a place at the university." He stands a little straighter. "She's a lecturer now. In sociology at the University of Manchester."

It's like they're strangers at a party, Allen thinks, making small talk by the hearth. But they're not strangers, and this is anything but a party.

"Mr. Car—Mr. Ashford, could we sit down?"

He gestures at the sofa that's pushed against one wall, waiting until she's seated before he takes the chair. The coffee table between them is loaded with small exotic objects: a shallow brown stone dish holding a collection of multicolored polished stone eggs, a miniature brass gong with matching mallet, an oval soapstone box carved into the shape of a long-nosed, peaceful face.

"Mr. Ashford, I'm sure you remember the young woman who brought the baby into the station in 1990 and handed her over to you and your late wife." She's very careful not to use the words "your daughter" or "Bella."

"I'm hardly likely to forget that. But she left before we could thank her."

"That's correct. And at that time she gave us false contact information, so we were unable to locate her to pursue the matter further."

He lifts a hand to his forehead and rests the fingertips at his hairline. Then, as if exercising great control, he lowers it back to his lap. "But now you have."

"In a way. Unfortunately Nell Beatty was the victim in a recent murder."

"She's dead." He sits back in his chair. "You've come to tell me she's dead."

"That's part of why I'm here, yes. But I've also come because the investigation into Ms. Beatty's murder resulted in a significant discovery." She softens her voice. After all, it's still possible that this will be a horrible shock to him. "Mr. Carpenter—Mr. Ashford—I'm sorry to have to tell you that the baby Ms. Beatty brought to the station that day was not your daughter."

Carpenter looks at his hands. After a long moment, without raising his head, he says, "Yes, she was. I don't believe you. She's our daughter, Bella."

"Mr. Ashford, that's not the case. We have proof the biological parents of the baby were Nell Beatty herself and a man named Harry Speck."

He lifts his head. "That's nonsense. Don't you think a father knows his own child?" Springing out of the chair, he begins pacing back and forth. "Do you think I've forgotten that you came and harassed us after we got Bella back? Do you think I don't remember calling up that chief inspector and telling him he needed to get you to leave us alone? You've stayed fixated for thirty years! Thirty years! What is *wrong* with you? What's missing in your own life that you can't let go of this . . . this *delusion*? Why don't you worry about your own children, instead of obsessing over mine?"

For a second, Allen feels the familiar stab under her ribs, and she doubts herself. Could it be that he's right, that Bella Carpenter has taken the place of those children she never had, those lives she never had a chance to worry over?

But she's watched criminals cornered before. She's seen how the terrified bluster, how they attack in an effort to save themselves. In fact, so far this conversation has gone almost exactly as she'd hoped. He's given her what she needs.

She moves her lips into the shape of a smile. "I can understand why you'd want to believe that, Mr. Ashford, and I suppose there's a tiny possibility that you could be right. Fortunately it's easy enough for us to determine the truth. We'll contact your daughter and request a DNA sample." She stands up, settling the strap of her bag on her shoulder. "You just told me she works in the Department of Sociology at the University of Manchester. We can reach her there. I'm sure she'll be happy to give five minutes of her time and a few cheek cells to prove you're her father."

She turns toward the door, her hand out for the knob.

"No." Carpenter's voice is like a whip crack. When she turns around, though, he falls into the chair so heavily that the book slides off the arm and onto the floor. "Don't contact her." He looks up at her, a big man made into a child by their relative positions. He presses his lips together, then sighs. "She's not my daughter. I know it. I've known it since I saw Viv holding her in that lobby."

23

Once again Allen finds herself shaking, but this time it's her legs rather than her hands. She sits down so Carpenter can't see.

"Mr. Ashford, if I understand correctly, you're telling me that you've been aware that the, uh"—*baby? Child? Woman?*—"person known as Bella Ashford wasn't your daughter from the first time you saw her. Is that correct?"

He nods.

"Mr. Ashford, that admission implies that you had reason to know she wasn't your daughter. That you had reason to be certain of it."

He nods again.

"What was that reason?"

This is the moment that matters. If Carpenter has the presence of mind to say parents' intuition, or even to utter the suspect's favorite, *no comment*, it's all over. She needs to make him feel that there's no better option than the truth, that it offers him a relief other responses can't. *Nine times out of ten, people want to lay it down. Make it easy for them.*

"It's all right. I understand." Her voice is a stroke on a child's back, a cool hand smoothing the blankets on a sickbed. "I think the reason you knew the baby wasn't your daughter was because you knew that your daughter was already dead. Am I right? Did you know she was dead before you even asked Mr. Patel to call the police?"

His gaze meets hers. He looks exhausted. "Yes."

For a moment, she closes her eyes. Then she opens them. Once again she's Superintendent Allen, calm and prepared. She reaches into her bag for her phone, sets it to record, then clears her throat.

"Mr. Ashford, before we continue, I need to tell you that you do not have to say anything, but it may harm your defense if you fail to mention something you later rely on in court. Anything you do say . . ."

As she recites the caution, he stares over her shoulder. When she finishes, he nods. Then he says, "Would you like a cup of tea?"

She doubts that he's going to make a break for it, but nonetheless she stands up and listens while he's in the kitchen. If she hears a door latch click, she can catch him before he gets far. But all she hears is a cabinet opening and shutting, then another one, then the snap of the electric kettle shutting itself off and the suck of a refrigerator door being opened and shut.

When Carpenter appears a couple of minutes later, he holds a mug of tea in one hand, the neck of a whiskey bottle between the thumb and forefinger of the other. He grips the side of a tumbler between the index and ring fingers of the hand that holds the bottle. All of this he puts on the coffee table, pushing the mug toward her. Once he sits down, he pours a finger of whiskey into the glass. He takes a sip, lets it sit in his mouth for a moment, then swallows. Then he begins.

"My wife saved me. You need to understand that right at the start, because it's the beginning of everything. She saved me from a miserable, angry life. My father was a very angry man, and he made me into a very angry man. If I had other emotions, I wasn't supposed to know about them. So I fought against them. Literally. In my first year at university, I was nearly kicked out for going for another bloke with a broken pint glass. He'd mistaken my beer for his, and had taken a drink of it. They put me on probation.

"Then I met Viv. She was doing a completely different course; we had no friends in common. There was no reason why we should ever have encountered each other. But one day she asked if she could share my table in the student café, and we started talking. She was so calm. So . . . comfortable. Completely relaxed about showing her feelings. It sounds ridiculous, I know, but with her it was like . . ." He makes a fist with his free hand, then opens it slowly. "Like blossoming. It was wonderful. We moved in together, and a few years later, we married.

I made a living as a journalist—you could do that then—and Viv was a receptionist at a gallery. She painted on the weekends. She even sold a few things. We weren't rich by any means, but we were managing. Her parents loved me; I loved them. I was learning to be a person. A happy person."

He rolls the glass between his hands. Allen takes a sip from her mug. The tea is milky but good.

"Viv always wanted children," Carpenter continues. "And you know how it is. You hit your late twenties and suddenly it seems as if everyone you know is having babies. We thought it would be cheaper to have a family in the country, so we scraped together a deposit with her parents' help and bought a house. I had this crazy idea that I could write a weekly column about the comedy of it all. We waited for the kids to start coming." He pauses, then sighs. "But it didn't happen. It took longer, and longer, and even though Viv never said anything, I could feel her getting sadder. I used to go into London for assignments sometimes, and although I hated to leave her, at the same time I was so relieved. If an interview or something went late, I'd get blackout drunk and sleep in the car, just to get away from the feeling that we were failing, or maybe only I was failing. Failing to do what should've been easy."

Allen is too familiar with this story to want to hear it from someone else. She scrambles to figure out where Carpenter is heading. Is he going to suggest that the stress of trying for a baby made him revert to his early rage and kill the child he eventually had? In her experience, diminished-responsibility defenses almost never work.

Carpenter takes another sip. "Then finally Viv fell pregnant. And when Bella came, she was perfect." He smiles. "I used to tell Viv we'd got the best baby in the shop. She slept when you put her down, she smiled at you when she woke up, she never even cried when she was hungry. She just . . ." He imitates soft mews and coos, but then shakes his head. "But Viv couldn't enjoy it. She obsessed over everything to do with Bella. Was she warm enough? Was she too warm? Was she getting enough sleep? The baby coughed up a spot of blood once, and even though the doctor said it was nothing to worry about, after that Viv was always terrified that she was in pain but couldn't tell us. And she fixated on the idea that she was a bad mother. It didn't matter what the health visitor said, what the doctor said, how much I tried to reassure her and take some of the weight off her shoulders. She was convinced that she was somehow doing something wrong, or that she would do something wrong."

So Dr. Palmer and Naomi Frith had read the situation correctly, Allen thinks. Carpenter's presence at the GP appointments, his choice to be home when the health visitor came, even the protectiveness Alison Brorsson had described him showing when he came to pick up his wife, were all the actions of a husband trying to help the wife he adored, not an overbearing obsessive. She'd been wrong.

But she still doesn't understand where all this is going. Had Carpenter, faced with his wife's misery, murdered the baby who seemed to cause it? Or had Vivien Carpenter killed Bella under the influence of postpartum psychosis? Was she the one who'd lost control in the hotel room, and Carpenter had covered that up?

Carpenter lifts the glass to his lips and bolts the remaining whiskey, wincing as it goes down. He rolls his lips in and out between his teeth until they're dark red.

Finally he says, "Then Bella died."

Allen's vision turns hazy. For a moment, the room recedes. Tea slops out of her mug and onto her trouser leg, burning her thigh, but she doesn't cry out. She hardly notices. *So there it is*, she thinks. *There it is.* The thought seems too small for what she's just learned, but it's all her mind produces.

"It was cot death," Carpenter continues. "Fifth of June, 1990. We put her down for the night, and when Viv went to fetch her in the morning, she wasn't breathing. Her lips were white. She was cold."

"And the doctor said it was SIDS?" But she'd searched for a death certificate and hadn't found one!

"I didn't call the doctor. I didn't have time to call anyone. Viv went mad. Literally mad. She screamed and screamed. She pulled her hair so hard that bits of it came out. I'd never seen that happen before. I had to hold on to her to keep her from hurting herself. It went on for hours. And then she just . . . stopped. Everything, all of her. For the rest of the day, and the night, and all the next day, she was like that. She didn't move."

Shock, Allen thinks. *Or catatonia. The mind shutting down to protect itself.* If this story is true, Vivien Carpenter's mind had had plenty to protect itself from.

"I didn't know what to do. I was afraid to leave her. I put her in our bed and sat with her. But I'd been awake for a day and a half, and I was so tired." He closes his eyes. "I fell asleep. I don't know how long for. Well"—for a moment his voice is brisk, dismissive—"you never do, do you?" Then he retreats back into his memory. "When I woke up, Viv was sitting up in bed, and she was"—he swallows and looks at Allen—"holding Bella. Cuddling her." He makes his arms into a cradling shape, as if she might not know what he means. "She said, 'Bella was crying, but she settled once I picked her up.'

"She wouldn't let go. She wouldn't let me take the . . . take Bella away from her. Finally I told her it was time for Bella's bath, and because of what she could . . . she could smell, she believed me." Allen sees his Adam's apple jump. "She didn't come with me when I took her, and she didn't ask where Bella was when I came back. She got up, she made our tea, and while we were eating she said wasn't Bella good, to sleep so well even though we'd put her down early."

Allen thinks that she would very much like some whiskey. But she's afraid that if she reaches for the bottle she'll break Carpenter's reverie and he'll stop speaking. She takes another swallow from her mug instead.

Carpenter goes on. "What could I do? There's a name for it now. I saw on the Internet. Depressive psychosis. People become so depressed that they hallucinate. But at the time I didn't know that. I just thought she'd gone insane, and if anyone knew they'd take her away. And I couldn't survive that. So I didn't tell anyone."

He stops, reaching for the bottle. The monologue interrupted, Allen says, "But you must have known you couldn't manage that for very long." She remembers the doctor telling her he expected to see Bella soon for her six-month checkup, Evelyn Cook's wail that they had been going to visit Wells the next weekend.

"I wasn't thinking clearly. I didn't think clearly for a long while. I just . . . I focused on keeping everyone away from the house, on making them believe everything was normal." He shakes his head again. "Viv was actually a *help* with that. If anyone rang, she said Bella was having her nap or she couldn't talk for very long because she'd left her alone in the next room." He pours another finger of whiskey. "But, yes, after I came back to my senses, I saw we couldn't go on that way much longer." Again he downs the liquor in one gulp. He winces less this time. "And that's when I came up with my plan. My brilliant plan. I thought that if I could somehow work in Viv's world, I could make her accept what had happened. We'd planned a summer holiday in London, and I thought if I could do something while we were there . . ."

Allen is confused. There had been a baby at the Bellevue Hotel. Mr. Patel and his daughter had seen her in her basket; Patel had seen Carpenter carry her up and down the stairs. Where had he got this other baby? She wonders if Carpenter is the real kidnapper in the Carpenter case.

He's still talking. "The week before we left for London, I checked the forecast. It was when I saw how hot it was going to be that I had the idea. If there were other people who could confirm that Bella had vanished, other witnesses, Viv would have to accept that she was gone. And of course Bella wouldn't be found, or come back, and then Viv would have to come to terms with her death. At the time it seemed like a perfect solution."

Allen tries to imagine the mind that would see it that way. She can't.

Carpenter carries on. "On the day we went to London, I put the Moses basket on the back seat of the car like Viv asked. I put the books we were reading in it to give it weight. When Viv said Bella needed some cooler air, I stopped, and we took the basket into a rest stop. While she was in the toilet, I took a few nappies out of the bag and threw them in the bin so it would look as if we'd had a baby to change if anyone checked later.

"I knew the hotel didn't have air-conditioning, but it was a bit of luck that the room was so hot when we arrived. It made perfect sense to suggest we leave the window open a little overnight. I waited until after I was supposed to have done the 3 a.m. feed. I couldn't've done anything before then, anyway. There were two kids snogging in the yard until nearly three."

So much for Nisha Patel's assertion that she and Aanish Upreti had spent their time just talking! But Allen has no time to dwell on that. Carpenter keeps going.

"I waited until the boy left through the back gate, and until I saw the last light go out in the building that overlooked our room. Viv's sleeping tablet had started to work long before that." He gives a little bark that Allen thinks is supposed to be laughter. "She was still talking about Bella as if she were alive right up until she went to bed, telling me she'd gone right to sleep despite the heat. Once the last light was out, I took the pink sleep suit she'd packed and rubbed it along the fire-escape railing until a piece snagged. Then I sat up for the rest of the night. At six, I woke Viv and told her Bella was missing. I pretended to be frantic." A second bark. "Well, I didn't have to pretend very hard. I had three months of frantic waiting to come out. I made the man at reception phone the police. When I put my clothes on, I slipped the sleep suit into the waistband of my pants. I kept it there for the rest of the time we were in London, and all the way home. I finally burned it in the fireplace on the first cold night that autumn. And then . . ." He exhales, dropping his shoulders, and meets her eye. "You know the rest."

It's a plan of such cruelty and stupidity that Allen wants to lean across the table and slap his face. Instead she takes a drink of her now-ice-cold tea. Then another. Then she reaches for the whiskey bottle and fills the mug the rest of the way up. The mixture tastes disgusting, but she drinks it down.

She wants to tell Carpenter that he's perverted the course of justice. That he's committed police obstruction, that he's failed to report and register a death. She wants to tell him that these are all indictable offenses under the Criminal Law Act 1977. But when she finally opens her mouth, all she says is, "Mr. Carpenter, where is your daughter's body?"

"I buried her in the back garden of our old house, under a holly bush."

So she could have him for unregistered burial too.

But she doesn't. Instead she does something she hasn't done for years, not since she stopped being an investigating officer. She closes her eyes and imagines everything she now knows about the Carpenter case as a dot in the distance. She focuses on the facts, pushing her hopes, her anger and disbelief, all the moral questions, out of the way so that nothing clouds her sight.

Except that she can't. For the first time in her career, the facts fail her. Each one tells her something, but it also tells her its opposite, a correct legal response and a response that, although against the law, is also right. A fraud has been committed. A woman has gone to her grave without knowing that the most elemental belief of her life wasn't true. A child has grown into an adult while being fed a primal falsehood. But the fraud's perpetrator is beyond punishment, and the fraud itself removed an imbalance rather than caused one. A destroyed woman was rescued. A ruined man was saved. A child destined for a miserable life was given a happy one instead.

She looks across at Tom Carpenter, who loved his wife so much that he lied to her for the remainder of their marriage. He made her happy, but he also divided them. His wife never again saw him whole, or knew that he wasn't whole. He was never again able to confide in her fully, never had a place where he could . . . She sees his hand opening slowly again in her mind's eye.

She'll leave him to his knowledge of all this. She suspects that any sentence he'd receive for perverting the course of justice would be nothing by comparison.

She reaches for her mobile, taps the button to stop the recording, then, with a few more taps, deletes it. She slips the phone into her bag and stands up. "Mr. Carpenter, your daughter has a medical history she should know about. If I don't hear from you that you've told her, I'll do as I said and go to Manchester to tell her myself."

She sees that he's already poured himself another two fingers of whiskey. Now he looks up from the glass. Their eyes meet, his momentary confusion encountering her level gaze. Then he says, "Thank you."

She doesn't wait for him to see her out.

As she drives, she thinks of babies—lost babies, found babies, yearned-for babies, never-to-be-recovered babies buried under holly bushes or alive only in daydreams. Contemplating them makes her think of Nell Beatty, the one woman in this case whose loss was voluntary. Did she ever mourn for what was missing? When she looked back later, did she date the ruination of her life from the moment she'd given up her daughter? Handing over the baby must have meant something to her. She had kept the newspaper clipping, after all.

She comes to a roundabout, then another, then picks up the M1. A sign suspended overhead announces that the right two lanes are for London and Leicester, the left two for the exit to the southwest: Birmingham, Gloucester, and Bristol.

She slows down enough that the car behind her beeps its horn then changes into the right lane and zooms past her. She could follow its lead back to London, to the chilly flat and Beck's disapproval. She could keep silent about everything she's discovered, or, if she couldn't bear that, she could retire. No doubt in the speech at her leaving do they'd call her a pioneer, one of the first to break the glass ceiling that kept women from obtaining higher ranks in the Met. Then, as soon as the door shut behind her, they'd promote some younger, cheaper man.

Or she could go to Bristol and tell Desbury everything she's found out. It's Friday: She could stop by the nick to fill him in then spend the weekend in the hotel in the city center. She could have a look at some houses, maybe think a bit more about Elvina's observation that what Avon and Somerset constabulary really needed was more women. She might be an old dog, but she's pretty sure she has some new tricks in her.

She switches lanes and heads toward Bristol.

1990

Nell keeps her head down as she walks in the direction of Chelsea. She's managed to get round the corner onto Pimlico Road, and she can't hear any footsteps following after her, but she still can't be sure no one's coming. If she can get to Sloane Square, she can catch the Tube and be at the caff in twenty minutes. She didn't lie about that. She really is late for work.

It'd been much more complicated than she'd imagined. She'd thought she could come in, hand over the baby, and that would be that. All right, she'd figured they might ask her a few questions, but she hadn't expected to be kept for hours. Good job she'd prepared the name of that council block and been quick enough on her feet to remember the name of a pub Harry had taken her to and make up a phone number on the spot. If only the lady detective hadn't put her on the back foot by starting to question her when she wasn't quite ready, she would've been able to think up a fake name too. But it doesn't really matter. It isn't as if they can trace her to the squat.

Although, one way or another, it's probably time to start thinking about moving on from the squat. Put all this in the rearview mirror, as her father would have said.

Maybe what she's done will be front-page news, though. The kidnapping had been, so why not the return? Her first front page! WOMAN FINDS KIDNAPPED CARPENTER BABY. Or, even better, MYSTERY WOMAN RESCUES MISSING BABY. The only problem is, no one will know it was her. Still, if there is a story, she'll save it. She'll save it, and then years from now when she's rich and famous and the baby's all grown-up, she'll go and find it and show it the story and say, "I'm your mother!" The baby will be thrilled to have a famous model as a mother.

She'd been surprised when Tattie showed her the newspaper. She'd thought Tattie never left the house, just waited for Lucky to show up with her fix. That's why she was always around to watch the baby. But thinking about it, hadn't she said something once about liking to take the baby out in the sunshine? That's probably how she'd come across the paper.

The Carpenters, the article said. The Carpenters were desperate to find their abducted daughter, Bella. Once she'd read that, she'd come up with the plan. It hadn't been difficult. She had to work out the story she'd tell if anyone asked her, but once she'd done that there'd only be a little bit of nerves to overcome. Like when she left home, or the first time she'd done the glamour posing.

It had been a shock to see a photo of the drunk reporter from the party on the front page of a newspaper. She needed to read the story two or three times through to take it in that it was him in the photos. She thought she'd never see him again after that awful night. Harry showing his true colors. Promising her a glamorous event and then taking her to some party for a watch? No, thank you. She deserved better. And then he was too busy talking to his cronies to pay her any mind! That's how she ended up in the back with the drunk reporter. Not that she'd been completely sober herself—one rule broken. And he'd been so sad about the mess he'd made of his life—he'd worked at *The Times* once, he told her while they were sharing a cigarette, and now here he was covering this crummy party freelance for *WristWatch* magazine— and so sad about all the ways he was failing his wife. And he'd been so handsome! Second rule broken. She'd been right about those rules, because next thing she knew she was wiping the insides of her thighs off with her knickers and trying to catch her breath while he buckled his trousers and kept saying he was sorry, he was sorry, he was sorry. Had he told her his name was Tom Carpenter then? He could have and she'd forgotten it. It's almost as boring a name as Eleanor Beatty.

She hadn't told Harry what had happened, of course. No sense in causing problems when you didn't need to. And by the time she realized she was going to have a baby he was long gone, so there was no need to pretend he was the father.

The woman in the newspaper photos with the drunk reporter—with *Tom Carpenter,* she supposed she ought to say—hadn't looked anything like she'd expected his wife to look. Surely a fit bloke like him would want someone prettier. But it was obvious the woman loved their daughter, and missed her. It felt nice doing her a good turn. Although really, since this Tom Carpenter was the baby's father, he should take responsibility for it anyway. Still, it was nice to know she wasn't just getting it off her hands. She was giving it to someone who really wanted a baby.

She catches sight of herself in the window of Peter Jones. The eyelashes on her left eye are sticking together. That's what she gets for applying mascara in a hurry. She stops and uses the window as a mirror so she can separate them. She's meeting Charles after work, so she needs to look perfect. Charles has a lot of connections. When he'd first told her that, she didn't believe him. She'd learned from Harry, with his promises that never went anywhere and his contacts that never materialized. She wasn't falling for that again, no, thank you. She told Charles to show her some proof. And the next week he'd brought a photo of him and David Bailey together at a party. An actual photo! He's promised to introduce her. He says he's pretty sure he can persuade David to do some photos for her book. He calls him "David"!

She smiles at her reflection. The glass shows her a man over her shoulder, smiling back. He's wearing a good suit, and she can see he's holding one of those new phones, the kind you can carry around with you. She's seen one in a shop window. It costs eighteen hundred pounds.

She smiles again then turns to face him. Not even ten minutes since she left the police station, and already things are looking good. But that's the thing about life: If you have a plan and take the steps to make it happen, the only way is up.

ACKNOWLEDGMENTS

First and foremost, enormous thanks to my agent, Laura Macdougall, who has changed my life, and to Lochlann Binney at Faber & Faber and Lara Jones at Emily Bestler Books for making my dream come true, then guiding me to completion with gentleness and patience. I also want to thank Olivia Davies and Amy Mitchell for their belief in me, and Hayley Shepherd for her eagle eye.

This book would be riddled with inaccuracies without David McDonald, who advised me on police procedure, structure, and language. I have had to take a few small liberties, and I hope he'll accept my apologies. These mistakes are my own; everything that this book gets right is down to him.

I thank John Bolin, Karen Edwards, Lucie Elven, Kirsty Martin, Benedict Morrison, Sinéad Moynihan, Sam North, Vike Plock, Andrew Rudd, Richard Sha, and Suzanne Sanabria von Engelhardt for validation, patience, and camaraderie, and Ashley Bruce and Jennifer Piddington for unswerving support. The University of Exeter allowed me a term of unpaid leave in which to finish my manuscript, for which I'm grateful.

My greatest debt is to the authors of all the materials I read while writing this book. From forensics to the story of the squatting movement in England, from the history of female police officers to the experiences of women who wanted children but were unable to have them, hundreds of voices and writers supplied me with information. Once again, it goes without saying that any mistakes in here are my own, but all accuracy is the result of those sources I consulted.

I'm also grateful to *Law & Order: Criminal Intent,* an episode of which first gave me the idea for this story.

Although the book's geography is accurate, I have renamed some sites in Bristol and London. I also want to apologize to the people of Bishopsworth. I chose that part of town for its name rather than its condition. It's a lovely part of the city.